SINCE I DON'T HAVE YOU

At the birth of their daughters, best friends Rachel, Mariel and Jenny make a promise: to love and care for each other's girls exactly as they would their own.

Six years later, Rachel's daughter Emma is dead, killed in a road accident that the other two girls have survived. Within weeks, Rachel has packed up and left London for the beautiful, windswept island of Santorini. But, as she slowly rebuilds her world, she can't forget the vow she once made and with the help of investigator Johnny Palmer finds a way to watch over the families she has left behind.

SINCE I DON'T HAVE YOU

Louise Candlish

WINDSOR

PARAGON

First published 2007 by Sphere
This Large Print edition published 2008
by BBC Audiobooks Ltd by arrangement with
Little, Brown Book Group

Hardcover ISBN: 978 1 405 68586 3
Softcover   ISBN: 978 1 405 68587 0

British Library Cataloguing in Publication Data available

Printed and bound in Great Britain by
Antony Rowe Ltd., Chippenham, Wiltshire

For Miss Burton

Acknowledgements

A special thank you to my agent Claire Paterson for input on this one that went far beyond the call of duty—you are truly wonderful! Also to Jo Dickinson, Louise Davies and Sarah Rustin at Little, Brown for improving the book immeasurably and for championing it so passionately.

Thank you to Jenny McVeigh at Janklow & Nesbit (UK) for some very helpful insights, and to Rebecca Folland and Charlotte Bodman at J&N for working so hard to gain the book a wider readership. To Alex Richardson at Little, Brown for publicity and to all in the wonderful and committed sales and marketing teams there too.

In Santorini, thank you to Erika Moechel-Pitsikali and Triantaphyllos Pitsikali at Chelidonia Villas, Oia. An evening's conversation with you was worth a year's research on my own!

I am indebted to Christopher Johnston for legal expertise and Oliver Wilkins for private-eye know-how. Thank you also to Marion Gibbs and Janet Parkinson for allowing me a glimpse of the leavers' ceremony at JAGS, London, and to Dawn Terrey and Phil Carre for my lovely website.

Thank you to my sister Jane for early comments and unstinting support throughout; to Sharon and Nigel for the Monday afternoon breaks from writing; also Heather, June, Maureen, Joanna, Mikey B, Sue, Chalkie, Roni, Pat, Ricardo, Mats 'n' Jo, John, my parents and all others who have made life easier and more fun during this time.

And, not least on that score, Nips.

Finally, I found the guidebook *Oia in Santorini, A Journey in Space and Time* by Kadio Kolymva very useful when exploring the town.

Prologue

I don't remember exactly the day we made our pact, but it was Jenny, of course, who came up with the idea. Of the three of us, she was the one most likely to make a stand—or get carried away, depending on how you looked at it. Oliver called her our 'hothead'.

We were in our local café, the babies asleep in their pushchairs, when she suddenly looked about her at the neighbouring tables as though suspecting eavesdroppers and spoke with hushed urgency:

'We should make a promise that we'll look after each other's girls. You know . . . *if disaster strikes.*'

I looked up from my coffee, a little shocked. 'Disaster' struck only other people, didn't it? People you read about in the papers. Nothing was going to happen to *us*. Next to me, Mariel raised an eyebrow. I'd wait to see what she said, I decided, before replying myself. If Jenny was our demonstrator then Mariel was the cool one, the realist.

'The chances of both parents getting terminal cancer at the same time are very slim,' she said, reasonably. 'Or dying together in a plane crash without their child in the seat between them. Believe me, Jen, no one's going to be an orphan.'

Jenny pulled a face and began grabbing at a handful of her thick red-gold hair, a habit of hers. She'd plait it really tightly and then leave it to

1

unravel again over her shoulders. 'Even if it's just one parent who dies, then.' She met Mariel's eye with a determined look. 'Toby flies all over the place for work, doesn't he? Isn't he in the Far East right now?'

'Jen!' Now I was properly shocked, but Mariel just laughed. 'Well, thanks for that cheery thought. I'll let my husband know he needs to update his life insurance.'

'I'm serious, Mariel. These things happen!'

There was a pause as we all looked at each other. 'Well, I'm in,' I said, and they both looked at me, as surprised as I was by my sudden earnestness. Whichever 'one' of the three of us I was, a chord had been struck and I wasn't prepared to close my ears to it. With Oliver continuing to work silly hours—and drink frightening quantities—I didn't like the idea of something happening to me, and Emma having to be left in the care of a relay team of nannies co-ordinated by his mother or, worse, his PA.

'Mariel?' Jen asked.

Mariel nodded, the wings of her dark bob swinging forward over her cheeks. 'Of course I'm in. You know I'd do anything for the girls.'

'It's a deal, then,' Jen said, pleased. 'We'll wave them off to university together if it's the last thing we do. Oxford, I think. No, Harvard!'

Mariel chuckled at the thought, but I wasn't sure I was ready to lighten my own mood yet. 'And they'll always have each other too.'

'If it turns out they get on,' Mariel said, delicately.

'What are you talking about? They *will* be friends,' Jenny pronounced sternly, and now I *did* smile. I knew what they were both thinking, the same as I was: that if our daughters grew to be a fraction as close as we were then they would be lucky girls. They'd be three times as equipped for life, three times as protected.

Three times everything.

PART ONE

' . . . now I am six I am clever as clever
So I think I'll be six forever and ever.'

A. A. MILNE

Chapter 1

London, June 1994

As they came to collect their children from Emma's sixth birthday party, the mothers asked me where Oliver was. It was a Friday afternoon after all, the weekend, and everyone knew that fathers made their own children's birthday parties, in both senses of the word.

There was a certain amount of speaking in disbelieving italics to contend with:

'He's not here? Well, what a *shame*.'

Yes.

'He *must* be away for *work*, then? Some trip he couldn't get out of?'

No, just in his office in town.

'And he couldn't get away? Not even for a *couple of hours*?'

Apparently not.

'Well,' said Ruby Sherwood's mother Lesley, 'That's grounds for *divorce* if you ask me!' I noticed with relief that little Ruby was the last to leave.

'Rach, come and have a drink,' Mariel called from the living-room doorway. She'd been standing there for a while, I guessed, waiting for the right moment to step in and rescue me. 'The girls have flopped, look!'

'The girls'—we even used the term when Cat's baby brother Jake was present—were lounged across the sofa, party dresses puddled beneath them, legs stretched out, pale tights grubby at the soles. Little debutantes calmed at last by the breaking of day. Around them were scattered trails of ribbons and streamers, plates of cake crumbs and crumpled napkins. All eyes were on the TV screen, however, identically rapt. Disney. *Sleeping Beauty*, if I wasn't mistaken.

Catherine, Daisy and Emma: inseparable, just as we'd hoped. Cat was in the middle, resting her head on Daisy's shoulder. I thought, as I often had, how her face was a design of both her parents' in alternate horizontal bands, exactly like one of those children's drawing games in which one body part is sketched and the paper folded down and passed on to the next player, until the final figure is revealed in all its incongruity. The brush-thick brown hair was Toby's—fold—the wide-set hazel eyes and delicate nose Mariel's—fold—the strong mouth and jaw Toby's—fold—the slender neck and delicate collarbone Mariel's.

Daisy was a different kind of hybrid, with Jen's heart-shaped face and clear, trusting gaze and Bob's sharper profile. Only Emma appeared to be a perfect miniature of one parent, but I knew from photographs of myself at the same age that I had not been even half this winning: large blue eyes, the irises like blurred flower heads; cheekbones already defined enough to be remarked upon by strangers; her hair a buttery blonde no salon could replicate for adult heads. She's going to be a beauty, everyone said. Impossible to tell, I'd say, careful to hide my pride. In any case, they were all beauties, already; these three and every single one of the dancing imps who'd played here today.

I turned to follow Mariel into the kitchen where Jen was pouring the dregs of flat champagne into smeared flutes. 'Leave that, I'll get us something nice to drink.'

Past the pool of purple balloons and the leaning tower of unopened gifts, trailing a string of silver from my right ankle, I let myself into Oliver's wine cellar in the basement, the temperature and humidity of which was controlled by some incomprehensible device by the door, and picked pot-luck. Back upstairs I found some plain crystal glasses in a cupboard high above infant reach.

'Mmm, this wine is *really* nice,' Mariel said, settling on a kitchen stool.

Jen grinned. 'Hey, it's not something Oliver's *laid down* for Emma's twenty-first, is it?' She'd adopted a comically pompous baritone and Mariel and I giggled. Only my mother, busy at the dishwasher, remained silent and I gave her a look that I hoped communicated that this sort of talk was fun, just a little joke, certainly nothing to do with disloyalty.

'Are you sure you don't want to join us, Alysa?' Jen asked her. She hated anyone to be left out. Earlier, I'd heard her asking Mum how children's birthday parties were celebrated in Greece and I'd had to remind myself that at Emma's age Mum would still have been living in her native Santorini. No doubt Jen had hoped for details of feasting and plate-breaking and dancing in large circles. But Mum didn't like to talk about her homeland— unless to give warning of its being 'cursed'—and kind, caring Jen had been forced to give up trying.

'Mum, we're thirsty, we need some juice . . .'

'Ah, the birthday girl herself!' Emma came for a hug, her head nuzzling my ribs until I squatted to wrap my arms around her and bury my nose in that

9

lovely hair, with its scent somewhere between lemons and toffee. I wondered, as I often did, when the hugs would peter out and be replaced by sulks and demands for a TV in her bedroom and an ever-larger allowance for clothes.

Six. Was she still my little girl? Or was she now a big girl? It was she who had made a landmark of today. Ever since she could speak she'd been saying, 'When I'm six,' or 'I want to be six,' or 'Six is the best number.' It wasn't that she thought life began at six, as older girls might regard sixteen; she didn't yet think in that way. It was more that she thought six was all there was to reach. That A. A. Milne verse the girls loved to recite said it perfectly.

Now she squeezed away from me and moved towards my mother. 'Come and watch the film with us, Grandma.'

Mum took Emma's outstretched hand. 'All right, love.'

I felt pleasure, as I always did, at demonstrations of their closeness, and gratitude too that my own relationship with my mother had benefited from it. Extraordinary, now, to remember our near-silence of years ago when my father had died and we had almost allowed ourselves to give up on one another. (At least, I had almost allowed myself to give up on her. Now I had Emma I realised that Mum would never have thought to have given up on me.) A stalemate, that was all it had been, and if anyone was going to break a stalemate between two adults it was a child.

I went to sit for a few minutes too, because I knew Mum liked to have us both together, one on

10

either side of her, just as once she'd been flanked by husband and child. She'd had her own parents to herself for much of her childhood so she was happy in a three.

You two are all I have . . . She didn't say it aloud, but I knew it was what she was thinking.

Yes, happy in a three, but alert, too, to its risks.

*   *   *

In the kitchen, Mariel asked me, 'Where *is* Oliver? Seriously?'

'At work, of course. He has some Japanese clients in town. There was never any chance he would make it.'

'God, he really knows how to push it, doesn't he?'

I shrugged. 'It's not the end of the world.'

'Well, I think you're very understanding,' Jen said. She paused to glance at the open door before adding in a whisper, 'Especially after that business with Charlotte.'

That *business*. It was funny, in a way, to describe infidelity as business, especially in the case of Oliver for whom it must have been a rare incident of *non* business. Charlotte had been a graduate trainee, an evidently irresistible transfusion of new blood, and I remembered how I'd wept to Mariel and Jen about her, my body needing every morsel of the consolation they offered. But even as I cried I was already making my mind up to forgive him.

Jen's eyes glowed angrily. 'God, if I caught Bob with someone else I'd be like that woman in America, what was her name, something Rabbit?'

'Bobbit? The one who cut off her husband's

penis?' Mariel giggled. 'Well, you do have the scalpels to hand, I suppose, being a pedicurist. Or does Bob make you keep your tools in the car? I think that might be wise from now on. I don't want to be called as a character witness, thank you very much.'

I laughed, enjoying myself, but Jenny wasn't finished. 'I think infidelity is just, I don't know, *unforgivable*. If you don't want each other any more, why not just split up?'

There was a silence. I caught Mariel's eye and she bit her lip, a sure sign that she was thinking something of a restricted nature. I had an idea what that might be and knew I could count on her to change the subject on my behalf. We'd known each other for several years before we'd met Jenny and there were some things—well, one thing, specifically—that I'd told only her. Charlotte might have been for the three of us to discuss, that had felt right, but not what had come next.

'Do you think you and Bob will ever get married?' she asked Jen in that reasonable tone of hers, honed by years of working with NHS patients. What she half-meant, of course, was did Jen think they'd ever split up, and Jen understood this and after another cautious look towards the door answered accordingly.

'He annoys me sometimes, but he is Daisy's father.'

Mariel nodded. 'Yes, and if being annoying was a cause for break-up there'd be no couples left.' That was a typical Mariel remark. A by-product of her sureness in her own marriage to Toby was her tolerant line on other, less exemplary unions: infidelity, conflict, 'mini-rebellions', as she called

12

them, none was insurmountable. Imperfections were not only to be forgiven, but also forgotten. Personally, I was a little too inclined to remember.

'Jen! Hey, darling, what is it?' All of a sudden Mariel had her arm around Jenny who, to my great surprise, had started to cry. I leaned across and closed the kitchen door before moving to her other side. She was plucking furiously at her hair and blinking big swollen tears on to her cheeks.

'It's just, oh God, this is silly, but it's just the way he looks at me sometimes. The look on his face, it's *contempt*. He seems to find me so much more irritating than he used to. But I'm not doing anything different, I *know* I'm not.'

'It's all right,' I said, 'of course you're—'

'I'm just so sick of it all,' she cut in with a sniff. 'Sick of it!' She looked beyond me to the polished cabinets and high windows of my kitchen. 'I don't know, we just seem to work so bloody hard all the time and never get anything out of it.'

Gently, Mariel steadied the glass in her hand. 'You're exhausted, darling. Why don't Rachel and I take Daisy this weekend and you guys have a night away together?'

Jen shook her head. 'We're so broke at the moment, we couldn't afford it. Anyway, I'm honestly not sure I'd want to spend a whole weekend on my own with him.'

'Dinner then,' I said. 'Tomorrow night. Or just a drink. Some time on your own, away from the flat. That's all you need.'

'Thank you, that would be good.' Jen grabbed a pink party napkin from the worktop to wipe her eyes and nose. 'God, what am I doing? I don't want Daisy to see me like this.'

I glanced at the closed door. 'Don't worry, they can't hear a thing. Anyway, they're too busy being hypnotised by the handsome prince.'

Mariel looked from Jen to me and smiled. 'I wonder how long *that* will last.'

*　　　*　　　*

Oliver came home at ten, when Emma was asleep and I at least halfway there. Though his mouth spoke of traffic delays, the flickering figures of the computer monitor were still in his eyes. His once-fine bone structure was already blurred by a quilting of flesh. This, and the fact that his fair colouring seemed recently to have faded to grey, made him look older than he was; he could easily have passed for a man ten years older, one of those ageing City boys broken by their bank. As I finished unloading the dishwasher I listened to him pad up the stairs—he always did 'quiet' in so staged a fashion, like a burglar in his own home. Inexperience, you'd call it if you were feeling mean, for any parent involved in the bedtime process knew that their kid would sleep through Concorde taking off after a birthday party like today's.

On the counter the wine bottle was empty. Maybe it *had* been laid down for some other occasion. Poor Oliver. I didn't know precisely at what point I had begun to participate in— encourage, even—my friends' mockery of my husband, this idea that he could not be offended or, worse, had no right to be. I told myself that Jen and Mariel were practically sisters to me, as discreet as they were loyal, and that our remarks

14

were no different from those we made about Toby or Bob. But they were. Bob was far too complicated to dismiss so easily, with his impatient bursts of temper and passions that drew everyone into their heat: flying kites, drinking real ale, reviving classical learning (the last ignited a need so urgent he one day turned up at the children's school and tried to persuade the teacher to let him take them to see the Elgin Marbles, every last one of them, that very moment!). Yes, we despaired of Bob, but we never thought to mock him.

Toby, on the other hand, had been my friend first, before he or I had met Mariel, and so was exempt from the rule of secondary status by which he might otherwise have been judged. He was never going to be the kind of husband who remained two-dimensional in the minds of those who knew the wife better. Oliver, however, was. It wasn't so unfair a call for that matter, for what he chose to present to the other two couples, and these days to me too, *was* thin enough to be a stereotype, a wine-swilling, double-breasted banker stereotype. I knew what the others thought without them having to spell it out: he was one of those people who are likeable enough, you can't fault them as far as that goes, it's just that you can't imagine them ever engaged in anything real, like sex or excretion or putting the rubbish out, or, evidently, supervising a game of pass the parcel. I knew better, of course. Or at least I once had. And there it was, just as he reappeared at the kitchen door: that dangerous, instinctive shift in tense, the very thing I had been working so hard to deny.

'How is she?' I made an effort to smile properly.

'Out for the count.'

15

I suppressed irritation at the sports metaphor, his favourite form of communication. Stop it, I told myself, this is your husband, he has his own quirks and you have yours. Remember that! Did he conceal irritation at me too? Did he wish it didn't all have to be fairies and princesses and love hearts and glitter? Did he wonder if I'd created this pink and purple dominion specifically to exclude him? Then I thought, does he ever think like this, putting himself in my place as I do his, and, since he probably doesn't, should *I* continue to bother?

I found an open bottle of white in the fridge and poured him a glass. 'Well, she's had a great day. She loves being six.'

'Who wouldn't? She's not exactly worrying about her next tax bill, is she?' He dispatched half the wine in silent, open-throated gulps. 'Your mother's gone home, has she?'

'Yes, she was an amazing help, did almost everything in the end. All the clearing up. I must send some flowers tomorrow to say thanks.'

He was looking at me quizzically and I wondered what was wrong with the idea. Mum *had* been pretty wonderful. Then I realised he was puzzled by my friendliness; he'd been expecting hell and I should, by rights, now be giving it to him. I felt a bolt of pure guilt, followed by injustice at being associated with hell when all I'd been doing was trying to be a reasonable wife.

'Well, I've had a fucking appalling day,' he said and gave exactly the type of sigh I was expecting— long and heroic. I called it his Odysseus sigh, the one he used when he was the warrior returned, the provider in need of good food and a bed, not a

16

night of 'where the hell d'you think you've been?'s
from the wife. 'Look, I'm sorry I couldn't get back,
it's—'

'It's OK,' I said, noticing that his *it's* and mine
had synchronised precisely. Did he break off or did
I interrupt? It was a form of conversational
dovetailing so practised by now that it was
impossible to know. Marital communication on
autopilot: real, sentient people hardly need take
part. I thought about Jen, weeping in this very
room just hours earlier. Well, whatever her
troubles with Bob, I couldn't imagine them
speaking to each other like this. I put down the tea
towel I was holding. 'I'm going to have a bath, I'm
shattered.'

I had to remind myself to make contact with
him as I passed, lightly placing my hand on his
stomach and brushing my shoulder against his.
And he had to remind himself to acknowledge the
gesture, which he did by nodding, moving his lips
in my direction in a ghost of a blown kiss. That
done, we were free to go our separate ways.

Chapter 2

It was a clear, still day and the sounds of the traffic
from Pimlico Road seemed oddly magnified. Even
with the windows closed I couldn't seem to block
my ears to them.

'Rachel,' said my manager Simon in his best
office tones, 'have you got a second?'

I looked up dutifully from my files by the
window. Knowing Simon privately as I did, I had

come to find this professional persona of his comical. By his side stood an expressionless young girl in black trousers and a grey silk shirt.

'I want to introduce you to our new picture assistant, Harriet. Would you mind showing her the ropes?'

I did mind, as it happened. I only worked part time and had little to spare, especially if I wanted to pop out in my lunch hour to get any shopping I needed for the holidays. But Simon wasn't receptive to my signals and I was duly saddled. I would have to work late to catch up. Luckily it was Jen's turn to pick up the girls from school today, a task that included getting their tea and helping with homework.

It had happened quite naturally that she, Mariel and I had come to manage our affairs as one family, during the school week at least. Work schedules were complicated: I worked three days a week as a picture researcher for a small art publisher, an extra morning here and there if someone was on holiday; Jen, a freelance pedicurist, mobilised as and when her clients demanded; Mariel, coming to the end of her maternity leave with Jake, was a dispensing chemist in a local health centre, usually working Monday to Thursday.

At the thought of Cat's baby brother my mood lifted. Of course I would help the new girl. This was probably her first job; she would be feeling nervous.

I beamed. 'OK, Harriet, let's get some coffee and I'll show you where everything lives. After that, why don't you just shadow me and I'll explain what I'm doing as I go?'

18

I organised for her to be equipped with a phone and a Mac and some stationery and a coffee mug, showed her how to log in each transaction on the master file, locate and update agency contact details, label in-house transparencies and mark up copies of published books. Then I saw her notice the photograph on my desk.

'That's my daughter, Emma. On her sixth birthday a few weeks ago.'

Harriet's eyes glazed rather than rolled, but the message was the same: she hadn't asked, so why was I telling? I must be one of those obsessed mothers she'd heard about whose mission it was to work the subject of her child into any conversation, however unwelcome. I tried not to sigh. She was hard work, this Harriet. Damn Simon. Lately he always seemed to be singling me out for this sort of thing. I sometimes wondered if he was punishing me; other times I saw that what he was actually doing was keeping me in his sight—and himself in mine—and hoping the pendulum might swing once more in his favour. I pictured his face, just a few weeks earlier, when I had told him we had to end things. ('Things', so prosaic a euphemism!)

'Why?' he'd asked.

'You *know* why. I'm married. It should never have started.' Even as I spoke I felt I was demeaning him by trotting out such clichés, and demeaning myself for my reason for having started it in the first place. Oliver and Charlotte. A classic tit for tat, except I had succeeded in keeping mine secret.

I picked up a file marked Miscellaneous and handed it to the girl. 'Do you want to have a look through these transparencies and have a go at

19

identifying them?'

'Sure.'

How old was she? I wondered. Twenty-one or - two? Still a child. I found my thoughts wandering not to the memory of myself at her age but to my imaginings of Emma grown up. Would she have this same passive air of superiority? Would she be attracted to a quiet, bookish job like mine or would she be an adventurer, a risk taker? Whenever I started this sort of thinking, it rushed on and on until I was virtually in a daze, every inch the obsessed mother Harriet had been cautioned to avoid. Would Emma be as keen to reach twenty-six as she had been six? Who would she love? And hate? Would she know she could trust me for advice or would she do all she could to avoid telling me the smallest thing, as I had my mother, for fear of the killjoy sigh, the withdrawal of permission? What was going to happen to her? *Please, tell me!*

Simon sloped up, his eyes barely grazing Harriet as they sought mine: 'How's it going over here? I thought I might take you both out for lunch.'

'God, is it that time already?'

Harriet raised her chin with sudden enthusiasm. I hadn't noticed earlier, but Simon looked good today. He had dark hair curling long over his eyes, a smile that promised rather than reflected amusement, and a casual, thrown-together personal style that made him look a little rock-starish. I knew him to be the good boy, of course, the son of a schools inspector, never happier than with his head in a book, but here and now, to a twenty-one-year-old new girl, he was every inch the rogue.

20

'Thank you,' I said, 'but I've got so much to do. I haven't had a chance to prepare for our meeting at three o'clock . . .'

Harriet looked down, disappointed. Already with his back to her, Simon added to me in an undertone, 'You look stressed, Rach. How about a quick drink after work?'

'Thank you, but I need to get straight off. I've arranged to go out with Jen and Mariel . . .' I trailed off, not adding our partners' names and not quite knowing why. I wondered if it was ever going to be the same with Simon again.

'Fine.' He raised his eyebrows and turned away, running fingers through his curls.

Harriet followed his progress, her eyes returning to find mine with, it seemed to me, the first bud of interest in me detectable thus far.

'How long have *you* worked here, then?'

I smiled, ready to dismiss her earlier apathy as shyness. 'Almost ten years, but with a break in the middle . . .' It had been important to come back, or so I'd been told. It did all sorts of good: kept my brain ticking over, set an example to Emma that women were not subjugated stay-at-homes, earned me my own money. And it *was* my own, too, every penny, for one of the benefits of Oliver's super-earning was his lack of interest in the money *I* took home. He was perfectly happy for it to be kept in a separate account for a rainy day, while our joint account funded all conceivable expenses. I barely remembered it, dipped into it only for presents for him, surprises that I didn't want him to be able to price simply by looking at his own credit card statement.

Harriet was looking at me open-jawed. 'You've

21

been at Pendant *ten years*? So how old are you then, Rachel?'

'Thirty-two.'

She looked astounded, as if I'd said a hundred and thirty-two. 'God, you don't look that old, nothing like it!'

I laughed, genuinely amused. 'Oh, ten years goes by very quickly, Harriet, take my word for it.'

*   *   *

We arranged to meet at the pub on the corner of Hampstead Heath, the one with the vast park of a beer garden that was deserted in winter, crammed in summer. It was early June and the hum of traffic blotted but not quite obliterated the evening birdsong. The sky, deepening into indigo above, was still yellow at the horizon. It could have been dawn. I thought of something Oliver had said to me once on holiday somewhere, before Emma, as we lay by the ocean and let the breeze drift right through us like sleep. 'I like the sky when you can't tell if the sun is setting or rising,' he said. 'Like when you're little and you have to ask your parents if it's morning yet.'

I felt that now, not knowing whether the liquid feeling in my abdomen was nostalgia or anticipation: a city feeling. I'd grown up in London and, though considered by some to be a fastidious sort of person, in truth I'd never much minded the dirty hair and the black snot from travelling on the tube, the cigarette smoke in my clothes and the traffic that coughed exhaust fumes on to my bare legs. Walk on a little and there would always be tall trees swinging against the sky, and someone—Bob probably—would have heard an owl or spotted a pair of fox cubs.

That evening we were, as agreed, just the adults. Babysitters tended our lambs at a surprisingly diverse range of hourly rates and, once it had been established who was drinking, driving, smoking or phoning, Bob announced, 'OK, guys, no talking about the kids.' He had a tendency to dominate, and it wasn't because he was tall and powerfully built or, as psychologists found more interesting, short and easily overlooked, or in fact anything to do with his physical appearance, for he looked fairly ordinary. Medium height, stoutish, friendly faced. He was just that kind of man: eldest son, raised to lead. The stronger the personality encountered, the greater his need to bring its owner into line.

He and Jen must have been arguing because they had first pick of the seating and conspicuously took opposite ends of the long rectangular table. Mariel was opposite Jen, Toby and I faced one another in the middle, and Oliver, appearing now with a tray of drinks, took the last available seat opposite Bob.

'Here we go, who was the vodka and tonic?' He slapped the plastic tray on to the table, slopping beer and causing hands to shoot forward in assistance, and I couldn't help sighing with irritation. Oliver looked briefly at me, as if to say, 'Give me a break, won't you,' and I looked away. It was partly what events like this were for, these orchestrated get-togethers over dinner or drinks, the opportunity to assess each other in couple formation, to see if this week's sum was greater or lesser than its parts. Did the others drive back saying, 'I give them another year, tops,' or, 'It can't be good for Emma, all that repressed hostility'? But, spilled drinks notwithstanding, when I looked once more at my husband's face, with its gentle, careworn expression, I didn't think I felt hostility. In fact, seeing him set about engaging Bob in work talk (a known conversational black hole), I was grateful. He knew I didn't see enough of Toby and would want to focus on him; he *was* still thinking of me.

'How's your work, Tobe?'

Toby shrugged. 'The usual. I had a focus group cancelled this evening, thank God. Otherwise I'd be finding out at this very moment whether people will accept the same low-density offal chocolate product for a significantly higher price if it's been broken into bits and wrapped in cheap gold paper.'

I grinned. 'My guess is yes.'

'Mine too.'

'Surely that's good enough for the client?'

'Er, possibly not. I have a feeling they may be looking for a fuller debrief.'

He'd been going to 'get out', poach the best assistants from the slave owners he worked for and start his own consultancy, but since Jake came along the scheme hadn't been mentioned nearly as frequently. One child meant responsibility, plans on hold, two meant sacrifice, plans abandoned.

'What are *you* working on?' he asked me.

'A book about Florence. It's called *The Athens on the Arno.*'

'The title sounds a bit misleading, if you don't mind me saying.'

'I know, but Simon's determined to keep it.'

Toby grinned. 'How *is* Simon?'

24

'Fine, same as ever really.' I glanced quickly at Oliver, guzzling beer as he listened to Bob's harangue about something or other.

Toby straightened his face. 'So, the book, go on. Lots of pictures, obviously. Are you going out there to shoot?'

'No, not enough money in the budget, apparently. That seems to be the way it is now. A shame. I want to go anyway, though. Reading the manuscript made me realise I haven't been to Florence since college. Maybe Oliver and I can go on our own in the autumn.'

'Not that easy with kids,' Toby agreed. 'I can't see them wanting to traipse around the Uffizi for long.'

'It's the queuing that's the killer,' I said.

'Yeah, I'm afraid it's the Algarve for a good few years for us. Maybe with a break for Disneyworld some time. You'll like that, Rach, lots of nice high rollercoasters.'

'Don't, my hands are sweating just thinking about it.'

Mine weren't the only ones, apparently, for I could sense a rise in body temperature next to me and when I turned I saw that Bob was bucking with impatience. Oh dear, had Toby and I broken his rule? Then I gathered that Jen and Mariel had been discovered to be murmuring about children too, and not only those at home in bed but future ones. What heresy! The notion that family planning could be more interesting than the stories of work, work, work that consumed the rest of the table!

Seeing Jen's face, a marriage of frustration and guilt, I wondered how much Bob had overheard, for the question was sure to have come up, it always did when she talked to Mariel or me: a second baby. She and I had discussed this over and over, despairing at our separate, and oddly opposing, dilemmas. Financially, Oliver and I could have had more children, and Lord knew we had never intended Emma to be an only child. As one myself I'd had first-hand experience of the boredom that counteracted all that extra attention. But there had been two miscarriages, a false alarm or two and then tests revealed that I was unlikely to conceive again.

Jen and Bob, meanwhile, could do it biologically, but there was that question of money. I had always suspected their arrangements to be more hand to mouth than pride allowed them to let on. Rents were rising in our part of town, they'd never been able to raise the deposit to buy, nor had they been thrown a rope by parents or other relatives. Offers of a loan from us were dismissed out of hand. Money didn't matter, I knew that, but it was impossible for me to say that and unlikely that Jen would believe me anyway. I worried for her. She was only thirty years old, after all, why should someone else be allowed to tell her that her fertility ended here?

Noticing Bob's expression, Toby wagged his finger at Mariel and Jen, an indulgent teacher about to separate two schoolgirls caught giggling in assembly. 'Come on, ladies, there's more to life than babies.'

'Well, you'd *hope*,' Bob added. It was possible he'd meant it humorously but it came out with an unpleasant edge. I felt like kicking his shin under the table, an option all the more tempting when I noticed him look to Oliver for an ally in his ridiculous campaign. He respected and begrudged my husband's financial success—and therefore his opinion generally—in equal measure.

'Steady on, mate,' Toby was saying, his frown friendly, the practised moderator.

'Yeah,' Oliver spluttered. 'Come on, Bob, it's a bit late in the day to say we can't "bring up" the kids.'

'Oliver, that's the kind of pun I get from Toby,' Mariel said, 'I'd expect something a bit more sophisticated from you.' As she smirked at him he looked exactly like a schoolboy being scolded by a particularly sexy female teacher. Even Bob was distracted.

'More alcohol, vicar?' Toby said, standing.

'Same again,' Oliver said instantly. He'd brightened noticeably since the walk over here when he'd complained of tiredness. But that had been before he'd had his first drink. I'd been aware of whisky chasers with the last round of Guinness too, but that was usual on these evenings, with last orders and taxis home never far away. Just as you started to relax someone said it was ten to eleven and the night almost over. But the usualness of the evening was what I loved most. The usual conversation about how we women must take ourselves off for a night or two and pamper ourselves, *really* relax; they could cope, of course they could. The usual plan (and the one more likely to be realised) of a bachelor-style daytime drinking session, long overdue, got to be done.

'What about you, Ollie?' Bob said, raising his voice. 'Fancy the football next Saturday? The Half Moon's just got satellite, y'know.'

Oliver, in the habit of responding to invitations without checking with me first, said yes, that sounded like a fine idea. He would probably turn up too. He often took people up on social initiatives, though he never made them. This was better than complete withdrawal, it was true, but didn't it also mean that once your own enthusiasm had slackened the pair of you were doomed? I decided to bury the thought before it could grow. No one was *doomed*, least of all me. I looked at my empty glass and at the others still to be collected by the overworked staff. I must be drunk.

'Well,' Jen said, 'if you're doing that, we could take the kids to the city farm.' Her voice took on an edge of its own as she sought Bob's eye across the table. 'Is it OK to say their names now, Bob?' She enunciated them deliberately, one by one: 'Daisy, Cat, Emma, Jake . . .'

We all looked at Bob, faces betraying varying degrees of amusement.

'Of course it is,' he huffed. 'What are you on about?' and returned to his pint.

Chapter 3

Mariel always said that everything you needed to know about Oliver could be learned in a single five-minute conversation with his father Donald about his grandfather Frank. Frank Freeman had been a known bully who, when required by the dentist to have his decaying teeth replaced with false ones, had insisted his wife have her healthy set removed alongside him. He died of a stroke at fifty-five and the longsuffering Lynn scandalised their Hampshire village by throwing a rock at the coffin and yelling, 'I hope you rot in hell, you swine.' She then proceeded to drink herself into the grave next to him.

My father-in-law was Frank and Lynn's only child and had been raised in appropriately singular style. As a schoolboy he was given garden snails in his lunchbox and encouraged to sleep on school nights in his school uniform, knotted tie and all. Punishment was a beating with the buckle end of a belt, reward the dog-end of a cigarette to puff on. The subsequent relief of an escape to boarding school was marred somewhat by the discovery, on his first return, that Frank had eaten his pet rabbit.

Donald never recovered from his loveless beginnings, nor tired of recounting them. Emma would listen to his tales with exactly the same fascinated horror she did the stories of Hansel and Gretel or Rumpelstiltskin. Had he been a video, I would have turned him off and put him away until she was older. Meanwhile his wife Rosemary handled her husband's legacy of dysfunctions in the same way Lynn had the originals: I struggled to remember a time when her veins were not awash with London Gin. When not holding forth on her early career as a stage actress ('glory' days, she called them, 'salad' days, 'hey'-day—any day but the present), she would interrupt other people with observations about Oliver's childhood habits, observations that would be repeated dozens of times over the course of a weekend, inciting Donald to say with increasing impatience, 'Don't talk rubbish, woman!' We had a photograph of the two of them sitting together in our garden, large drinks on the table in front of them, both talking, neither listening.

With a new generation of Freeman children, the punishments and eccentric feeding styles were mercifully left behind, but the family weakness for hard liquor was not. Even before I met Oliver at university I knew of his reputation for drinking, or at least that of his set, the most glamorous on campus by some way. This was a group for whom off-site apartments were provided by parents and entry into societies noted for unspeakable debauchery a principal reason for their enrolling in the first place. Oliver was the blond, pale-eyed Sebastian Flyte of the group, glamorous and hard-living, and his following among the female student body was substantial enough for me to be discouraged from getting anywhere near him. But I was aware of his allure, everyone was.

Afterwards he moved straight into the City and surrendered himself unconditionally to the 1980s. By the time I bumped into him again he'd risen to Client Director level and already had the pink eyes and soft belly of the professionally blotto. It was a Thursday. We each had our sights on the last remaining table in my regular work bar just off Sloane Square.

'Hey, I remember you,' Oliver said, pleased with himself, and with that one line he resurrected all my old feelings of illicit admiration.

'I remember you too,' I said, raising an eyebrow, older now and more daring.

'Why don't we share,' he said, indicating the table, 'we've got enough seats for when the others arrive.'

And so it was that Oliver, as he crowed the

morning after we first made love, blew the 'others'—his on-off girlfriend Melissa and my new boss Simon—right out of the water. It had not taken long to win me with that blend of entitlement and vulnerability. The tribulations of his past, related with a wryness that could only mask genuine damage, only confirmed my notion that he was a different sort of creature from any I'd known before.

Stroking the socket of my left eye with his thumb, almost as though wiping away tears, Oliver said, 'I never noticed it at college but you look a bit like Faye Dunaway, don't you? A young her, I mean.'

'I think you might be getting carried away,' I said, embarrassed. 'I guess it's my wide face . . .'

'Great cheekbones,' he corrected. 'And the whole icy blonde look . . .'

'Highlights, you mean?' I'd never taken compliments well, knew I was being ungracious even as I rebuffed them. 'Anyway, my nose is longer than hers. I have Greek blood, diluted.'

He smiled. 'From what I know of the Greeks it's a hard blood to dilute.'

I would learn that Oliver tended to speak about other nationalities—particularly those he encountered in business—in curt, military terms: 'We're getting stick from the Japs' top brass'; 'Let's see what the Yanks have to say about that.' It was all just a shade away from *Dad's Army*. The sports references, his other tendency, were naturally complementary.

The 1980s was a vibrant time to be starting out in working life and Oliver was riding the kind of yuppie wave that was regarded with such

31

resentment by those still standing boardless on the shore. Money flowed in from the world's markets in great tides. To me, career success made perfect sense of my husband. In my romantic view, he'd been cast out by an uncaring family and found a new family in his colleagues. And in me, of course.

Friends thought of us as an odd couple; me cultured, him coarse, though that was simplifying things a bit. In reality there was a kind of symmetry in our coming together: I'd swapped the religious guidance of a father for the financial protection of a husband, while Oliver had left a godless home to make money his religion. We were not so dissimilar. And we were happy too, in those early days, as happy as any Freeman couple might have expected to be.

*   *   *

'Five more minutes, Mum, *please*!'

Emma was delaying lights-out as usual, hoping this would be one of those occasions, usually a work day, when I might be willing to play along. It was. I sat on the edge of her bed and traced my fingers over the letters of the alphabet embroidered on to her duvet cover—satin stitch— and she seized the opportunity to ask more questions about the school holidays. The end of term was only a week away. She was tired, though not as tired as she tended to be at the same stage of the autumn term, which seemed to hit the children harder. Then, two further terms loomed, but by the summer it was all over, what with the six weeks' holiday ahead, a long stretch indeed in short lives.

This year we were going to visit Donald and Rosemary, newly retired in France, overlapping for a weekend with Oliver's sister Gwen and her husband and their two boys, before driving on to a villa near Nice for ten days on our own. Clothes shopping, a Beatrix Potter exhibition and cinema outings were planned for the days between term breaking up and our departure for France. There'd be pizza and strawberry milk and games in the garden, a renewed closeness between us after the term-time separation.

I ran my right index finger over the raised stitching of the E. 'Don't forget, you've got your school trip to Kew Gardens tomorrow.'

'I know.'

'I've got you all your favourites for your packed lunch.'

'Thanks, Mum.'

It was Flower Week at school and the girls' class were going on a trip to see a big smelly flower at Kew. Miss Morrissey, their teacher, had even promised individual portraits with the gargantuan stamen (an ambitious pledge if ever I'd heard one).

'And you have to wear your uniform, do you, or is it own clothes?'

'Uniform, I *told* you.' She loved this pretence we'd developed that I was forgetful and in need of her reassurance in all kinds of practical matters. Girls did it naturally, bossing and fussing and shepherding; Cat, Daisy, Emma, all three of them loved to look after us, brush our hair, serve us snacks, correct our mistakes, demonstrate The Right Way.

'Are you looking forward to seeing the funny

33

flower?' I asked.

'It's not a funny flower, it's called a *titan arum*. That's Latin, you know. Miss Morrissey said.'

'Ah, is it?'

'Not Greek, like Grandma Alysa speaks.'

That was an interesting thing for her to say. I had spent almost two decades in the same house as my mother and had heard her speak Greek only a handful of times. 'Grandma Alysa doesn't speak Greek very often though, does she?' I asked casually, careful not to appear to interrogate. The girls were wise to that and would zip up straight away.

Emma considered. 'She taught us numbers, me and Cat.'

'Did she? I didn't know that.'

'Yes.' Pause. 'It was *really* hard. *Eno, thio, tria.* Harder than French. *Un, deux, trois . . .*'

'Well, what a grown-up girl you are these days, speaking *three* languages.'

'*And* the Latin words, remember. That's *four.*'

'Of course, clever you. Now, time to sleep. You can count your sheep in whichever language you like.'

It was a hot evening, the clouds had collected over the city in dense feather pillows, and I pulled down the top sash to let some air into the room. Then I picked up a few story books from the rug and returned them to their shelf, collected the stray hairbands and slides for the basket on top of the chest of drawers and adjusted the dimmer for the dusky light she liked for falling asleep.

'Is Daddy home yet?' Emma asked, already sleepier.

'No, not yet, and he'll be gone before you wake

up. He has to go to Paris tomorrow. But he'll be back for the weekend.'

'OK.'

'Night, pea.'

'Night, Mummy.'

I went back later, as I always did, to turn off the light and check she was asleep, staring into the gloom for a second or two before finding the shape of her face at the edge of the mattress. I marvelled at the sculptured beauty of her infant features, eyelashes still long over the cheek, mouth soft and unsuspecting, form and proportion designed by nature to inspire gentleness in those who were stronger. And that skin, so silken and pale, the most precious fabric on earth. And I thought, as all parents do, if not every day then certainly most, She is mine, this amazing little creature is mine.

I stood in the doorway, longer than usual, just watching.

Chapter 4

On Friday afternoons we always met the girls from school together and took them to the little Hungarian café for hot chocolate and cakes. The gate of Moss Hamlet School on a Friday was where the working week ended, it was our rule (though not one we thought necessary to share with the men, who we'd trained to imagine our every waking hour as some sort of Big Top juggling act). Friday afternoons were the ones you remembered when you grew up, Jen said; no one remembered who'd picked them up on a Tuesday.

Today the older classes were already out when we arrived, trooping by in a chest-high parade of royal blue and gold. Mariel wasn't keen on the blue, she said it reminded her of a Conservative Party conference, but I liked it because it brought out the colour of Emma's eyes. Navy at birth, they had been poised to turn brown, but instead faded slightly and settled. The process reminded me of oil paint drying a tone or two lighter than the colour squeezed fresh from the tube. For that pretty blue and her long flirtatious lashes she'd been nicknamed 'peacock', then after a while, when we were tired of the reminders that she was technically pea*hen*, we just called her 'pea'.

'Everything all right with Bob?' I asked Jen.

She nodded. 'Sorry about the other night. He was being a right idiot.'

'Don't be silly,' Mariel said. 'He was exactly the same as he always is.'

'He's always an idiot, then?' Jen laughed, merrily enough for Mariel and me to exchange a relieved look.

'Thank God it's almost the end of term,' Mariel said, adjusting the parasol over Jake, who sat propped forward in his pushchair, fascinated as usual by the sight of the older children. 'Where *are* they?'

'They're not back from Kew yet. Look, the minibus isn't in the car park. Must be stuck in traffic,' I sighed. 'You know what Fridays are like.'

'*Every* day,' said Jen. She was the nearest we had to an environmentalist and Mariel and I had been witness to much soul searching when she had finally bought herself a car for work. Before that she had hauled her equipment around from client to client on the bus. I watched with amusement now as she looked up at the sky as though confident of some ungodly smog, but it was clean and blue and fresh, perfect weather for a summer school trip. 'What's everyone doing this weekend?'

As Mariel began describing to us the mysterious structure Toby had promised to make using only tent pegs and bubble wrap, the word 'accident' registered on some faint, subterranean level. Distractedly, my mind sifted images of spilled drinks, wet beds, careless pushes, until I saw, with confusion, that the head teacher Mrs Wilkes was rushing down the school's main corridor towards the glass doors in front of us. In the two years Emma had attended Moss Hamlet I had never seen this woman rush; rushing was not permitted, though hurrying was (how a small child could make the distinction was anyone's guess). But here she was, tearing out as though chased by wolves and coming to a stop just short of Jake's pushchair. She opened her mouth and paused. I had a sudden sense that what she was going to say would change everything.

'Everyone, can you all hear me? I've just heard that the bus has been involved in an accident on its way back from Kew.'

'*What?*'

At once, twenty or more mothers gathered around, panic catching like a ball passed from one to the next. One voice raised itself above the others, 'Is anyone hurt?' and the collective sucking in of breath was audible.

Mrs Wilkes hesitated. 'We're not sure yet.'

That means yes, I thought, numbly, yes there are injured children, yes, Emma is one of them.

'Fucking hell!' Jenny cried and no one cared that there might still be infants within earshot. 'Where are they?'

With reluctance Mrs Wilkes named a junction about ten minutes' drive away and without staying to hear her out the parents, some carrying babies or toddlers, raced for their cars. I had come on foot, conscious of a few new pounds that needed to be lost before the summer holidays, and Mariel lived close enough to walk, so we automatically followed Jenny to her beat-up old Alfa parked in the next street. It took an age to get Jake out of his buggy and into the back of the car, where Mariel murmured to him and tried to coax him to sleep. I wish he were mine, I thought, irrationally, then I could concentrate all conscious thought on him and not let myself imagine what might happen in ten minutes' time, what might already have happened.

Jen turned the key in the ignition, ground the gears and stalled. Her knees were jerking and I could see the muscle in her throat convulse, as though keeping down bile.

'Let's stay calm, Jen, I'm sure they'll be all right. A big bus like that . . .'

'But it doesn't have seatbelts, does it?' Mariel said in a whisper from behind. So she was imagining too.

'They say you know,' said Jenny to the windscreen as we pulled off, 'in your bones, when something awful has happened. But I don't have that feeling, do you?'

I didn't answer straight away. What of that sense I'd had, some kind of whispered warning, before Mrs Wilkes had even registered in my eye line? Wasn't that *knowledge*? And what about this weird creeping numbness I was feeling in my upper body? Jenny's was responding with nervous spasms, but mine seemed to be shutting down. 'No,' I said, as firmly as I could. 'I don't either.'

'Then that's a good sign.'

She fumbled with the radio controls but got to the local station just too late. 'That's the traffic news at three forty-five, Friday the twelfth of July. Now back to you, Steve, for more feel-good favourites . . .'

I noticed the car phone between us. 'Can we ring anyone? How can we get more information?'

'I'll try Bob.' Bob had just started working as a graphics engineer for a local TV network near Euston, but when finally located, he knew less than we did. The fear in his voice echoed around the car. 'I'm leaving right now,' he shouted. 'Meet you there in ten minutes. Don't panic.'

'That's what Rachel says as well,' Jenny shouted back, braking abruptly. 'God, this traffic is horrendous.'

'Well, if they've hit another car they can't have been going very fast.' He hung up and the three of us sat at a red light for a moment listening to each other breathing.

'I'm scared,' Mariel said simply from the back seat.

At this, Jenny stiffened beside me. Mariel was the cool one, not just of the three of us, but of *all* womankind, that's what Jen was thinking. If *Mariel* used words like 'scared', what hope was there for the rest of us? And then the words of the pact came back to me from long ago: *We should make a promise . . . if disaster strikes. No one's going to be*

39

an orphan, that's what Mariel had said. But we'd never discussed what we'd do if it were not one of us, but one of them.

'I'll call Oliver.' I had to think for a moment to remember his office number. It had been a while since I'd phoned him at work and when I finally located his assistant Vanessa I found that I didn't know what to say, was absurdly self-conscious speaking in front of Jenny and Mariel. Why do I care what people think of our relationship when Emma could be lying injured in the road? Get on with it! My voice rose: 'Tell him he *must* come to the school, he must come to the school. It's an emergency.'

'I'll tell him just as soon as I can,' Vanessa said, in the bright, placatory tones of one who intends doing nothing of the sort. For as long as I could remember she had treated me as some sort of subversive influence, reminding me in all but words that on *her* watch, if not on my own, Oliver's word was law.

'Silly cow,' Mariel murmured. I felt her fingers brush my upper arm.

'He knows where the school is, right?' Jenny asked me. There was no teasing tone now, it was a serious question.

'Yes, he's been there before, d'you remember? On their first day.'

But Jenny didn't hear, just began intoning under her breath, 'They'll be fine, they'll be fine . . .' over and over, until she interrupted herself with a shout, 'Jesus, look at this!'

We'd reached the point of total deadlock. The road ahead was closed and a diversion in the process of being set up by traffic police,

40

overdressed for the season in thick black jackets, their fluorescent green panels flashing as they moved in the sun. Jen was right, we were as close as we were going to get from this approach. The crisp air of the playground had given way to a swirl of exhaust, car horns and music as drivers around us opened their windows and sun roofs and settled in for another Friday delay.

'Is this all because of the accident, d'you think?' Jenny asked. But I couldn't answer any more. One more reassuring remark and I knew I would surrender to the terror.

'Let's get out and walk,' Mariel said. 'I'm not waiting.'

Jenny revved the car on to the kerb and half into someone's driveway. As the cars behind us barped in objection, we got out and began running. Mariel carried Jake in her arms, ignoring his protests at the unusually violent rhythm. Jenny was in flip-flops and I could hear the smack of rubber against heel echoing against the walls of the high-rise to our left. I was worried she might stumble.

'Oh my God, look!'

We saw the bus before anything else: on its side, beached and lifeless, its nose squashed, comic-book style, the windscreen missing but for the teeth of crystallised glass around the edges. It had evidently collided with a car, now some distance away and lying on its roof, some sort of hatchback—red body, black undercarriage like an upended ladybird—and at least one of these two vehicles had also made contact with the central divider, judging by all the gashed metal and damaged stone. Beyond stood a bank of ambulances and police cars, uniformed figures scurrying from vehicle to vehicle.

Joining a small crowd at the nearest stretch of cordon, we craned to see the bus's interior: it was empty, there was no smoke, no evidence of fire damage and most of the seats looked untouched. They must all be safely out, then, but where? Jenny ducked under the barrier and grabbed at an approaching officer. 'Please, can you help us! What happened?'

'Would you mind stepping back behind the tape, madam.' His manner was cool, but his eyes looked unconvinced by his own voice.

'I will not!' Jen cried. 'Our daughters were in that bus. We need to get through and find them! Where are they? Tell us!'

He ushered us away from the tape and towards the pavement before saying, 'OK, I'll find someone to come and talk to you' and hurrying away, but the few steps we'd taken had brought us within range of voices, unmistakably infant voices, sweet and piping. We could even hear a cry or two of 'Mummy!' Now I saw the group of gingham-checked girls and short-trousered boys, further down the road beyond the ambulances, gathered on the only patch of green in sight. Jen and Mariel were already dashing towards them and I didn't know why I wasn't going too, why I was dipping instead under the tape and following that young, scared officer, the one who leaned now into the driver's seat of a police car and spoke into a radio transmitter:

'Yep, one, plus the driver of the car, nine injured. What? Nah, both on impact. Yep, closed now, northbound. It's still moving south, only just, mind. Yep, all right, will do . . .'

My body shuddered at that emotionless voice, that flat, matter-of-fact 'Yep', while my brain took the information and attacked it. 'One', one *dead*, that meant. The driver of the car, he had said. Thank God! My instinct had been wrong, she's fine, my darling is fine! But no, *plus* the driver of the car, he'd said, and *both* on impact. That meant *two* dead. So one must have been on the bus, otherwise he would have said two, both in the car; equally, it couldn't be the driver of the bus or he would have said both drivers, surely? That left a teacher or a child, then.

I looked up and saw Jen in the distance. She had found Daisy among the refugees and was squeezing her against her body. Not Daisy then, thank God. Mariel rushed up, still jiggling Jake against her, his cries rising into the hot air. 'There you are! Cat's been cut on her leg, it's pretty bad. I'm going in the ambulance to St Mary's. Have you found Em?'

Now I noticed the girls' teacher, Miss Morrissey. She was no longer the groomed official I was used to dealing with but a dishevelled urchin whose left arm had been folded into a sling and whose face was wet and stained. She was with another police officer, a woman. They were looking my way.

'Rachel?' It was Mariel's face, but now Jake's cry seemed to rise from her mouth and I no longer recognised her. 'I have to go, I'm so sorry, they're leaving now, oh God, but I'll get Jen. I'll come back and find you as soon as I can . . .'

I was on my own. It struck me all at once, that it was unnaturally silent.

'Are you Mrs Freeman?' It took me a long moment to register the speaker as the policewoman I'd just seen with Miss Morrissey. I couldn't place the giddiness between seeing them by the ambulance and finding them at my side, just heard that word again: yep, yep, yep.

'Yes, what? What? Is Emma all right? Where *is* she?'

Amid the crowd on the pavement it seemed to me that each of the royal-blue figures had now been matched with its adult protector. And I thought, very clearly, This is the end of the grace of not knowing. Now I am going to have to know.

'She was sitting at the front, in the jump seat next to the driver,' blurted Miss Morrissey, tears brimming. 'She felt sick . . .' She got carsick, Emma, always. We'd bought story tapes to entertain her on long journeys because looking at a book or a puzzle brought on the nausea within minutes.

I stared. My daughter's teacher's face was as unfamiliar as the policewoman's beside her, its eyes streaming and nose bubbling. One dead, I thought. My one, my little pea.

'Rachel . . . ?' Suddenly Jenny was behind them, filling the spot that Mariel had left, her hair backlit gold by the ambulance lights. Through the gap between the policewoman and Miss Morrissey I could see Daisy's head buried in her mother's clothes, Jen's hands clasped around it in a protective helmet. Then she took one of those hands away and reached through the gap towards me.

'I'm very sorry,' the policewoman said. 'I'm afraid your daughter suffered severe head injuries in the collision. There was nothing anyone could do to save her.'

It was Jen who made the animal sound they expected from me, but I still stared and stared until they braved a glance at one another. Throats gulped.

'Where is she?'

'She's been taken to the hospital. Would you like to travel there with us, Mrs Freeman?'

I tried to nod.

'I'll come with you,' Jenny said. 'Bob will take Daisy home, he'll be here any second.'

I thought of Oliver as I walked to the police car, still in his three o'clock with the Japanese, having warned Vanessa not to interrupt him under any circumstances. Even through acts of God, if the markets were open he worked.

I would never forget the blue of the sky that afternoon, above the stalled traffic and the overturned bus and all the blurred, wordless choreography of emergency. It might have been tinted with filters it was so unblemished, so lasting.

PART TWO

'Donmemeslik'

The name given by the Turks to Santorini in the
seventeenth century, meaning
'We'll never come back'

Chapter 5

Losing my only child when she was six and I thirty-two was not as I had imagined it would be. And I *had* imagined it, of course. All parents do it, persecute themselves with the thought of that loss commonly agreed to be life's cruellest, bring themselves to tears with notions of the hell they would inhabit for all of life to follow. They do it for the perverse pleasure of knowing that their little one is there, sitting on her beanbag and watching cartoons, safe as houses. And they stoop to kiss the top of her head, vow never to take her for granted or to let adult trials poison this one special, central love.

Only now did I discover what a poor game of pretend it had been. Never had I considered, for instance, the physical pain, and yet this was what dominated at first. It felt as though some unclean spirit had tried to pass through my upper body and had got itself stuck, choking my airways and twisting up my organs. At the same time my lower body ached with the contractions of a childbirth in which I knew already that the baby had been strangled with the umbilical cord.

'These are the throes of grief,' said the doctor, who came with sedatives and sad smiles, adding, 'Nothing will help, really, I'm afraid. Not yet. Nothing.' His were the only eyes I could bear to meet for longer than a second, for they at least seemed to absorb a little of what came from mine. The others'—Oliver's, my mother's, my friends'—theirs only reflected the horror, beamed it back to me, and I learned to evade them.

Chronology dictated there be a day after her death, a day after that, then another, and more days again. Too many, grumbled the voices around me, for police investigations had caused delays in laying her to rest. Then, finally, there had been the day of the funeral service: the palms cupping my elbows, the murmurs in my ears, and the eyes, more eyes, *so many eyes*, all morning long, impossible to avoid in such searching numbers . . . And the days that followed, no more distinct, no more bearable, just a timeless, oxygen-scarce abyss.

It surprised me, then, when the medication ran out, that I knew quite quickly what I was going to do next.

*   *   *

Two weeks after burying our daughter, I went into the study, up on the sunny middle floor of the house where Oliver had been sitting pretty much continuously since her death, and told him I was leaving.

'Where are you going?'

'I'm not sure yet,' I lied, automatically searching for a truth to add in consolation. 'Just somewhere . . . somewhere where nobody knows.'

'A change of scene, yes, of course . . .' He nodded, letting his eyelids close for a moment. His skin was slack and shadowy at the jowls, his well-built form clothed in shapeless dark-grey garments I didn't recognise. 'When will you be back?'

I swallowed. 'I don't know if I will be, I'm afraid.'

50

'Oh.' The eyelids drifted open again. Through the tall windows behind him our garden shone in the sun, moved in a dance, almost. His eyes, colourless from this distance, squinted back at me as though it were he who faced the sun's glare. 'Is it because . . . ?'

He faltered at once and I heard my voice fill the void, flat and emotionless, as if it didn't belong to me. 'Because what, Oliver?'

'It doesn't matter, I didn't mean . . .'

It had been some time since he'd completed a sentence and I knew not to linger for the second half of this one. But, all the same, I couldn't end eight years of marriage without some last stab at fair play.

'We've both been at fault,' I said, gently. 'Not just you, you mustn't think that. But now Emma is gone . . . Oh, Oliver, you know I have to go, don't you?'

I took a step forward, the breath twisting in my lungs. His upper body strained a fraction towards me, but he couldn't find the strength to stand. Before I could change my mind I turned and walked downstairs. Earlier I had placed a leather holdall, a hatbox and a pile of letters in the hallway and I now picked them up and opened the front door. Not once, as I walked down the street towards Swiss Cottage, did I turn for a final look at the house, the street, the trees that had been my daughter's and mine. Not once did I wonder if Oliver would conquer that paralysis and come after me. I posted the letters in the box by the café and waited on the kerb for a taxi. When one swung into view, a bent right arm tanning out of the rolled-down window, I spoke to the elbow in my new hollow voice—'Heathrow Airport'—and heard the driver's response ring around my new hollow ears—'You realise that'll be at least forty quid, love?'

I ignored the question. 'Can we make a stop in Ealing? I'll only be a few minutes.'

He all but rolled his eyes. 'I'll have to keep the meter running.'

'Of course.'

'Your money.'

I sat in the back not moving, except for when the momentum of the taxi caused me to lean this way and that in my seat. Being in motion helped, I'd found; riding with the tidal wave delayed the inevitable crushing. It wasn't quite respite, but it was suspension, at least.

When I next checked my watch I saw that it was the first full waking hour I had survived without crying.

*   *   *

My mother was expecting a farewell and already teetered on the brink of hysteria when she opened the front door and led me to her sofa. She took the side nearest the door and sat forward in her seat as though guarding against my flight.

'I'm leaving,' I said. 'My bag's in the taxi.'

Her eyelids swept down and she took a big mouthful of air, in that way of hers, as though bracing herself for bodily harm. When she spoke she was unable to keep the accusation out of her tone. 'I know where you're going.'

I didn't reply but waited for her to pour tea from the glazed brown pot she'd used since I was a child. The skin on her hands gloved the bones more loosely now, and was spotted a little with red and brown. Though she was in her fifties, hers looked like an old person's hands.

I drank. Already I was used to not tasting, not registering temperature. The sofa was under the window at the front of the room, just a pane of glass away from the waiting taxi, and I could see through the lace curtain that my driver had flipped open the *Sun*, every so often glancing up to eye his meter with disbelief. Oliver had told me a while ago that there was a new climate of distaste for extravagant spending ('It's not the eighties any more, you know'), but I could hardly believe that this would extend to London cabbies. No, my misery had offended this man, somehow, or perhaps he had miseries of his own. A bad day, he would complain to his wife later. A *nightmare* of a day.

Mum said, 'You know *I* can never go back there?' Though the hurt was gone from her voice it remained in her eyes and I looked quickly away. I knew she wished she'd never filled my head with the place all those years ago, that I still might not be lured, even in these circumstances, by the one place she considered the most terrible.

'I know, but it feels right. I can't think of anywhere else that does.'

Here, she was thinking, what about here, your childhood home, the safest of all places. 'What about Oliver? He shouldn't be alone at a time like this.'

'Mum, he's *always* been alone.'

'What do you mean?' she asked, taken aback.

'Oh, I really don't want to explain, not now.'

She paused again and I watched her rewind her thoughts ten seconds. 'Stay with me. This isn't such a bad place. Or we'll spend some time in that cottage we used to go to with Grandma . . .'

. . . after Dad died. I finished the sentence for her in my head. I didn't say what I thought next, which was that if I did as she bade and stayed with her we'd never get through it, we'd see Emma's face in one another's every waking moment, scratch away at the 'If only' game until we were red raw.

'I don't want to be anywhere I know, *with* anyone . . . I can't explain, I'm sorry.' For the first time I noticed that the room was filled with flowers, most past their freshest, the petals crisping at the edges and the stems greying under the water line. Vases bought new in my childhood and long retired from service had apparently been recalled to accommodate the surfeit. Blooms to soothe her mourning. Crazy, really, watching a flower die—how could that possibly console? My own deliveries I had redirected to the hospice on the Finchley Road, keeping only Cat and Daisy's shared basket of sweet peas.

'I should make a move. The taxi . . .' I was starting to mention the ticking meter when Mum cried out in violent interruption.

'You've lost your daughter, Rachel! Please don't make me lose mine. *Please*. I beg you!'

She'd jolted even further forward, distraught by her own outburst, and even through its swollen mass my heart responded with a series of horrible clenches. For a moment vision blurred and I was relieved that my mouth seemed to know which shapes to make to produce the right words. 'Oh,

Mum, you haven't lost me, I promise. It's not for ever. I'll send you my address as soon as I can. And if you could only change your mind, you could visit me there as often as you wanted.'

It was the word 'visit' that made her finally heave and cry. I was going to be gone long enough to be receiving visitors—and on a repeat basis to boot! Whimpering, I put my hand on hers, but she took hers back at once and sat with her knees and wrists together as though cuffed, her face in profile. Her hair was greying, her eyes veined and watery. She looked so weakened, so wobbly, like the old woman in that painting by Hockney, *his* mother, I remembered. But that was a double portrait, there was another to balance that frailty, a father, a co-parent to submit jointly to the child's desires. Mum, she was alone.

'If I hadn't been in this morning I'd have missed you, wouldn't I?' She spoke into the space in front of her.

'I knew you'd be in. Anyway, I would have waited, don't worry. I wouldn't have gone without saying goodbye.'

I knew she'd be safe in her little house near the green where the neighbours had been her friends for thirty years. Nothing could happen to her here. Safe as houses.

'What about your work? Have you left?'

I nodded numbly, banishing Simon's face, Simon's voice from my thoughts.

'And Mariel and Jenny? Do *they* know what you're doing?'

I considered lying, but couldn't summon the imagination. 'No, not yet, but I've written to them—'

'*Written* to them?' Mum cried and swung around, eyes freshly accusing. 'They're your *friends*, Rachel, they want to *be* with you, to talk to you, *help* you!'

I shook my head helplessly. I couldn't think about Mariel and Jen now and I certainly couldn't begin to explain to my mother that they were part of the reason I needed to go.

We had met, of course, since Emma's death, they'd visited me frequently, the two of them (*the two of them*: how seamlessly that phrase had replaced 'the three of us' of the previous six years. Unavoidable, of course, but still so cruelly defining). It was hard to recall much of my part in any conversation, but what I did remember was that every glistening look sent my way, every caring syllable uttered, had been underpinned by the terror of their near miss. Thank God, that's what they thought when they looked at me, Thank God it wasn't . . .

They had left Cat and Daisy at home when they came.

Outside, there was the sound of the cab driver starting up his engine and I stood, stooping to kiss the top of Mum's head. 'I'm sorry. I have to go.'

*   *   *

Somewhere on the M40 the cabbie remembered his manners and sought my eye in the overhead mirror. 'Off somewhere nice, are you?'

I tried to smile, to repay the effort. 'Santorini.'

'Santorini, I've heard of it. Italy, is it?'

'No, Greece.'

'Greece, yeah, that's right. I prefer Spain.' He

told me of his last holiday, a trip to Fuerteventura where he'd discovered a passion for surfing. As he spoke, I marvelled at the existence of a mind that didn't contain my pain. I knew that it would be impossible for me ever to know that lightness again. Then, the airport closer now and the traffic braking, he resumed his personal attentions. 'Just you, is it? Going away on your own?'

'Yes.'

'Good for you. Nice, now and again, I suppose.'

He pulled up at the departures bay and our eyes met once more. 'I couldn't do it myself, mind you. I'd miss the kids too much.'

I looked away.

Chapter 6

When people learned of my Greek heritage, they naturally assumed I'd been immersed in the culture from the get-go, raised to respect the Greek faith, Greek tradition, Greek family culture. They imagined a riot of song and celebration, children by the dozen, the strong-jawed matriarchs of the movies. *Zito i Ellada!* (Long live Greece!) In fact, we were an insular nuclear family, friends and relatives invited only occasionally, and it was my father's, not my mother's religion that formed our scaffolding. The Church of England, so constant and unshakeable; all that was asked was that promises be kept, good turns done, praises sung.

I knew of Santorini only as a place of doom. My mother's older sister Phoena had died in an earthquake there in 1956 and Mum had moved away with her parents, first to Athens and then to London. The experience had instilled in her a terrible fear of her birthplace, one that she duly sought to transfer to me: the earth wasn't safe beneath your feet there, she said, how did I think the island had come about in the first place? It had come out of a volcano, a big one, and then part of it was reclaimed by the sea in another eruption. I could still recite the statistics she'd taught: fourteen volcanic eruptions since 198 BC—the period of the 1650 eruption was known to the Greeks as 'the time of evil'—a column of limestone 1,900 feet high reported in 1870 (I was shown a copy of a cutting from the *Illustrated London News* as evidence) and then, of course, the earthquake of '56, fifty-three dead, my own aunt among them, almost two-and-a-half thousand homes destroyed, including my own grandparents'. Mum would return, she vowed, 'over my dead body'.

'You wouldn't like Santorini, anyway,' my father told me. 'Where your mother is from is a little village called Oia—'

'*Ear?*'

'No, Oia, *o-i-a*, you say it like "ee-a". It's right up on the clifftop, high above the sea. The last place *you*'d want to go.'

'Oh, OK.' My problem with heights was already well established, having been first noted on a trip to Bournemouth. Positioning me up on the wall of the pier for a photograph, my father had relaxed his grip for an instant and I'd glanced behind me, rocking slightly backwards as I gazed at the bubbly grey water below. I'd heard a horrible banging noise, then, coming from inside my own body, and terrified to realise it was the sound of my own heartbeat had shrieked at the top of my voice. Mum dashed forward to grab my legs, and very quickly both of us were hysterical.

I asked to see a photograph of my dead aunt, but my father shook his head. 'I don't think there are any, darling, not any more. Mum threw away all the old photos your grandmother left her when she died, everything. Best we all just forget about it now.'

Naturally, I didn't. I became fascinated by this dangerous and magical place and determined to see it for myself. But a family holiday was out of the question, and somehow I never did get there as an adult, either. Then, a few years ago when we were moving house, I came across a scrapbook labelled 'Santorini', a school project of mine, evidently. It was full of newspaper cuttings, including an article about how the island had transformed itself and was now at the heart of a tourist boom. I'll take Emma there, I thought; we may no longer have family there but it is part of our heritage, whatever Mum says. But at the sight of the next photograph, a white village spread low across the top of a dark cliff like icing on a Christmas cake, my breath quickened. It was just as Dad had said: I couldn't possibly spend a night in such a place, not with my fear of heights. In any case, its precipitous position did not look suitable for a child. I decided I would take Emma when she was old enough to appreciate it and when I had confronted my own neuroses.

*   *   *

59

Later, I would not remember that second taxi journey of the day, the one that took me from the airport to the northern tip of the island. The transfer was short, no more than thirty minutes, and then I was there, in Oia, standing with my holdall and my hatbox at the end of a pathway paved with white marble. Along its length, tourists gathered as far as the eye could see, leaning over walls to see the little whitewashed houses dug out of the rock face, hair pulled by the breeze, eyes transfixed by the distance of the drop down to the sea.

I had not made a hotel reservation so decided simply to follow the marble path deeper into the village. As I walked, the dazzle of the light felt otherworldly, dissolving everything around me until I seemed to lose my senses in the whiteness— exactly the numbness I had craved those past weeks in London. A tiny flare of hope—this was going to work, I might never feel pain again! But oblivion lasted just long enough for me to find myself a hotel room, unpack my bag, place the hatbox under a chair and generally absorb the unfamiliarity of it all for the few moments that it remained so. Then, no sooner had I locked the door and closed the shutters on the intense August heat than *they* returned. Thoughts, a horrible bleeding mass of them: 'There's been an accident'; 'I'm so sorry, Mrs Freeman'; that grotesque 'Yep, yep, yep', like the sound of a barfly's chuckle; a houseful of wet, appalled eyes; children at the door with flowers . . . And all memory dominated by the heaviness of my daughter's body in my arms, a sensation inseparable from that of carrying her sleeping form up the stairs to her room after a long car journey. I had always thought of that limp surrender as the most tender of all maternal experience; now it was the most ghastly. My father used to say that dying was God's embrace and there, in a hotel room in Oia, I wished with all my heart that I'd been submitted to Him with her.

*   *   *

In the first week I went out into the street only twice. The first time was to find a shop for bottled water. I only needed to walk a few steps, but as I groped my way through the brightness I was quickly in disarray: so many people, hundreds, maybe thousands, and always I seemed to be moving against the swarm.

'The sunset,' said the woman at the hotel reception desk, watching me scuttle back within minutes of setting out. I looked at her, seeing her for the first time, though it was possible that this was the same person who had checked me in and served me every one of the cups of coffee I'd been surviving on these last few days. She was about forty, short and slender, with dark, chin-length curly hair, a lemon-shaped face and the heavy-lidded, close-set eyes of a Modigliani. Lithe shoulders shrugged under a knitted green vest.

'I'm sorry . . . ?'

'The sunset,' she repeated.

'Sunset?' I was aware that I was speaking and listening as though in an unfamiliar tongue; no wonder she stared at me with open disbelief.

'Yes, they come in the buses from Fira.' I had a vague memory that Fira was Santorini's capital, not far from the airport. 'They go to the old castle above Ammoudi, we call it the Goulas. It is famous in Oia, you don't know this?' And she gestured to one of the postcards on sale on her counter, to the picture of a hilltop ruin silhouetted against an orange sky.

'Oh,' I said. 'I see. Yes, it's very pretty.' I paused, remembering now that I had a question of my own.

'I was wondering about . . .'

'Yes?' Her eyes widened in encouragement.

'Well, it's just that I'd like to find somewhere to stay, I mean longer term.'

'Here? In Oia?'

I nodded. 'I wondered if you knew of anywhere. Anything will do, it doesn't have to be . . .' Again I trailed off.

She looked back at me curiously, before saying, 'Perhaps later, in September, when it is quiet. I will ask in the village for you.'

'Thank you.' As I turned to leave through the arch that led to the staircase up to the bedrooms, I heard the phone ring at reception and the woman exclaim, 'Yes, of course, please wait . . .' and she scurried from behind the desk, calling to me, 'Mrs Freeman, it is your husband!'

I froze. My mother was the only one who knew where I was. How easily she had disclosed my location. I could hardly blame her, however, for Oliver was her son-in-law, her grieving son-in-law. I marvelled at his industry—or hers—for there had to be a hundred hotels in Oia, most of them full if the throngs outside were anything to go by. The two of them must have worked through a list. I sensed the impatient breathing of the receptionist just a few feet behind me, before the hiss of her voice made me start. 'Mrs Freeman, *please*! Your husband, we are receiving telephone every day. Over and over. Is there some message I can say, perhaps . . .?' Then her footsteps retreated and her voice changed. 'Hello? Mr Freeman? You have missed her this time, I am sorry about that. I will pass on your message. Of course, of course. Goodbye.'

I turned and peered back through the arch. She was staring straight back at me. 'Thank you, I really appreciate your doing that.' My voice was a whisper, lost in the empty reception space.

'You have not answered your phone so many times.' There was concern in her voice and I struggled to answer. It was true, the phone next to my bed rang most mornings, and assuming it to be the maid I had got into the habit of vacating and sitting in the café downstairs until the maid reappeared.

'Anyhows, he say he will write instead.'

I nodded. 'Fine.'

Upstairs, I considered the implications of this incident. No matter how incoherent my feelings, I knew that I did not want to see Oliver. Someone had said to me, or perhaps I'd read somewhere, that dreadful though my loss was, I at least had someone to share the pain with, as though pain shared was pain halved. But how could I find consolation in knowing there was another who felt as inconsolable? In any case, it could never apply to us, this platitude, for I had been the one to handle the emotions in our marriage, just as he had handled the finances, and we'd learned not to bother the other with anything outside our respective remits. Now that the worst had happened, I found it impossible to process his agony as well as my own, for mine was already too vast to comprehend. I *had* to leave to survive. Had it been financial ruin we'd faced, he would probably have done the same.

One of the worst moments between Emma's death and my departure had been the morning I woke to find Oliver's face just an inch or two from mine, his eyes staring into my face. Those milky eyes I'd once found so beautiful, incongruously dreamy in one so materially focused, now the colour might have been designed specifically for mourning. 'You gave me a shock,' I was about to say, for by morning we'd usually drifted to the outer reaches of the mattress, he towards the window, I towards the door, the better to hear Emma's nocturnal calls. Why was he here and not at work? Was it the weekend? Was Emma awake yet?

'I was thinking,' Oliver whispered, 'would she have still looked like you when she . . .' He couldn't finish and I couldn't listen. The unbearable tenderness, the unspeakable null.

*   *   *

The proportion of Emma's sleeping hours to waking ones had decreased incrementally with every year of her life, from the early luxury of twelve-hour nights to those skilled prevarications of the schoolgirl who longs for nothing more than to stay up late—'I'm not sleepy yet', 'I'm thirsty', 'I need the loo', 'Just one more story, please.' She didn't like going to sleep at the best of times, especially in summer when the evenings were light and it was obvious it wasn't 'proper' bed time yet. And those precious few nights after her sixth birthday she'd campaigned harder than ever:

'Mum, *please*, I'm *six* now. I don't need as much sleep.'

'Who told you that?' I laughed.

'No one told me, it's *totally* obvious!'

Now my own hours of rest increased heavily, sometimes to twelve, sixteen, eighteen hours a day, though my day and night no longer corresponded with the twenty-four-hour cycle followed by the world outside. I thought of a submariner I'd met once for a marine photography book who'd told me of the eighteen-hour day of his military training: six for work, six for leisure, six for sleep. It seemed I'd taken this condensed programme and adapted it for the bereaved: six for sleep, six for crying, six for more sleep, though it was often impossible to know where one shift ended and the next began. I would fall asleep mid-sob and then wake up hours later to find myself still in tears. My throat was raw, my face bloated, my eyelids translucent. I wanted to be what I had started to resemble, a corpse washed up on the shore, waterlogged, unrecognisable.

Sometimes, before sleep, I tried a technique of delusion. I imagined that that Friday in July had never happened, that it was the next day, a Saturday, a day of ballet and piggy-in-the-middle in the garden and omelettes together at the kitchen table, and I was in the house, on the stairs, and she was in her bedroom, behind the door with the painted letters that spelled her name. I was calling for her to hurry, we needed to leave for ballet, for her end-of-year show. 'Coming,

65

Mummy.' And she looked so pretty in the gauze dress we'd made together, with its green skirt cut like tulip petals. She was a sprite, a fairy, a creature of the Faraway Tree.

'Are you sure you don't need your hair in a ponytail, darling?'

'Yes, Mum.'

'Got your shoes and tights?'

'Yes, Mum, in my bag. Come on, let's go!'

'OK, don't forget we're picking Daisy up on the way.'

'I know.'

And we'd walk together in the sunshine, my heart full of pride as neighbours cast glances at this beautiful girl in her green dress.

The problem was that I didn't fall asleep in time for the trick to work but, remembering, felt the pain reconquer me, every atom of me, every atom of the world around me. I'd go to the window and lean right out, swallowing mouthfuls of the cooler night air. You couldn't see the water from here but I knew it was there, hundreds of feet below, a shivering skin waiting for the heat of the sun.

Chapter 7

'Mrs Freeman! Do you have one minute for me?'

As I sat in the hotel lounge waiting for the maid to finish in my room, the manager beckoned me to the desk and told me she had found a *skapho* in the village that was available for off-season rental. '*Hyposkapho*,' she explained, 'the cave house inside the white earth where the sailors lived. Now, mostly tourists.' I had gathered from a guidebook in the café that the place I'd been staying, Hotel Ilias, occupied one of the grander of the town's residences, the *kapetanospita*, which meant 'captain's houses'. These were the mansions that lined the central street and those of the hilltop neighbourhood to the east of it, positioned so as to give their original occupants first sightings of the ships rolling in from the east.

'Cave house,' I repeated, still a foreign student of my own language. 'Ah, good.'

She looked at me uncertainly and sighed. 'I will take you myself. In one hour, OK? This landlord, he stay always in Thessaloniki.' The house was in the nearby Monastiri neighbourhood, she added. It was in need of work and the owner would see to repairs before the spring, at which time he would probably want to let the property by the week once more, as he did the other couple of *skapha* he owned in the village. In his absence, I would pay my monthly rent to the Ilias. I nodded at the amount required in drachmas, still unfamiliar with the fabulous figures quoted for the smallest item.

'That sounds fine. Thank you very much for arranging it.'

As I settled my hotel bill, surprised to see that I'd been in residence for almost three weeks, she said how sorry she was to see me go, but I didn't believe her. Quite reasonably, she considered grief bad for business.

*   *   *

The first house Oliver and I owned was a larger-than-average north London terrace, arguably a bit dark, certainly a little damp, definitely the wrong side of the Finchley Road, but for me it was a residence beyond my aspirations. It seemed impossible that in such an inflated market we'd got it, as Oliver trumpeted, for a song, but it certainly made *me* want to sing. Such high ceilings, so much space! Not only a bedroom but a master bedroom, which by definition meant there were other less commanding ones besides. I'd grown up in a house where the bathroom was reached through the kitchen and remained several degrees cooler than the rest of the house at all times but high summer; now I had a luxuriously warm en suite just steps from my bed.

Oliver, less impressed with the contrast between this and the accommodation *he*'d enjoyed at home and college, complained frequently: the electrics were temperamental, there were no right angles or flat floors, which made the laying of tiles an ordeal for all who tried, and any attempts at renovation seemed only to reveal unknown layers of missing this and rotting that. Later, after Emma was born, we moved somewhere less crooked, over the Finchley Road and into Belsize Park, where the floors were bump-free and the postcode digit-perfect. Not that she would have known the difference; she cared only about the colour of the front door.

'I live in the black house,' she used to say, for she identified all houses this way. Brick was colourless in those eyes alert only to primaries and any shade of pink. As soon as she could speak I would repeat to her our street name and number in the hope that she'd remember it if ever lost. I imagined her in the back of a police car riding around the area, the officer looking for a house painted entirely black.

*   *   *

My *skapho*, House Callidora, was a blue house, the classic Greek-island blue of the postcards. The terrace was large, draped on one side with bougainvillea still in flower, and a table and two deckchairs had been set out at the spot with the best view of the sea.

'You like the Caldera, no?' my guide asked.

'The Caldera?'

'This is what we call the sea, of course. Your word in English is "cauldron", like the witches have.'

'Of course.' I remembered from the guidebook that it was not simply the ocean here but a bowl of sea created by the volcano. In the distance a pair of charred islands rose up from its depths, small volcanoes sheltered by the crescent of the main island.

'Some people think Atlantis is under there, but I do not believe this fantasy.' With a dismissive turn on her heels she led me inside. But for a fanlight above the central doors it was quite dark. There was a bed—a mattress on a stone platform—with fresh linen and pillows stacked on top, a small sofa, a chest of drawers and a dark-wood table with a starched tablecloth and two chairs tucked symmetrically beneath. I had no idea whether this was typical of modern style or designed to evoke bygone living for the benefit of the tourists, but the plainness was comforting. Two smaller rooms led from this main space, one in the deeper recesses was a bathroom with a shower, the other a very basic kitchen with its own window overlooking the sea.

'Here is your coffee maker,' my companion pointed out, and began detailing the proportions of water, ground beans and sugar required for a Greek coffee. She tutted at the quality of bean preferred by the previous occupants.

'Please,' I said, exhausted by carrying my luggage downhill and unable to keep up pleasantries any longer, 'I don't think I ever asked your name.'

'Eleni.' She produced a business card from inside her sleeve and handed it to me. The surname was long and unpronounceable.

'Thank you, Eleni, you've been very kind. This place is just right for me. If you don't mind, I think I need to rest now.' I fumbled in my pockets, remembering a tip, but she shook her head, surprised.

'Of course, of course.' She slotted my key into the inside lock of the door and pulled it shut behind her.

I was too tired to unpack, but sat for a while on the terrace in my new deckchair, to all outward appearances the satisfied holidaymaker with the plum rental. The air smelled of grilled meat and oregano and the sun shone lemon-yellow in the sky. For the first time, I tried to examine the reasons for my blind insistence on coming here. To walk into rooms guaranteed never to display mementoes of my daughter? Yes. To separate myself from the suffering of those who loved her as completely as I did? Yes to that too. But why Santorini of all places? The very place my mother had suffered such trauma as a child that she would now consider revisiting only in a coffin. It looked suddenly like a perverse act of defiance on my part after years of peace between us, some sort of delayed reaction to all those dark pronouncements she'd made about the place when I was growing up. I remembered how details of earthquakes and volcanoes had merged grotesquely in my infant mind: seas glowing fluorescent green, sailors incinerated, tidal waves washing away whole towns, animals choking in clouds of red dust, everything silver turning to blackest black. Once I'd resented Mum for making me into 'the nervous type', for using my childhood to incubate fear. But now? Oh innocent days, when my nightmares contained such images as green seas!

Oh my God . . . I sat forward suddenly in my deckchair, thinking. Getting up, I walked slowly to the edge of the terrace and just stood for a moment, looking all about me. Behind, below, to either side, the houses of Oia emerged from the cliff in an Escher puzzle of steps and pathways and rooftops and doorways. It was impossible to see quite how each connected with the next. Leaving my own door unlocked, I stepped over the low terrace wall and down the first path I came to. Further and further down the cliffside I moved, changing direction with every bolted gate or padlocked church, every door that opened on to thin air or passageway that gave way directly to the sea. At every turn there was the illusion of the drop, before steep steps or a flat roof pressed into view like a safety net.

Then, at last, my brain registered what my eyes had merely scanned: this place was the most precipitous perch I'd ever set foot on. *You wouldn't like it*, that's what Dad had said, and he was right, I *shouldn't* have liked it, not for half a minute. It was hundreds of feet above the sea, with low-walled terraces giving way to near-vertical cliffs. Truly vertiginous! Terrifying!

And yet I was not terrified. My heart rate remained exactly the same, my palms dry. No snatched breath, no sense of growing panic, nothing. How could it be? And now I came to think of it, that route from the airport, those roads cut into the rock hundreds of feet above sea level, weren't they just the sort of hairpin turns that set whole lives flashing before your eyes . . . ?

I faltered, sank on to a nearby wall, realising. *Before the eyes of those who still valued their lives*, that was what I meant, wasn't it? I was cured of my long-time fear of heights because I no longer cared to live. To use Emma's phrase, it was totally obvious.

*   *   *

At first I didn't notice the children. The school building on the far side of the main square was empty when I arrived, the pupils presumably with their families at home or down at the local beach, and though I had spotted the playground, with its bank of swings and a court for ball games, I had never seen it in use.

Then I began to hear the voices, raised as one in that unmistakable song of high spirits that signals a release of infants from indoors to out: school playtime. A short time later, just as abruptly, the air would be reclaimed by the adult hum of coffee time. No doubt the grief counsellors would have forbidden it but I allowed myself to be drawn to the school gate at noon, the time when the smaller ones were collected by their mothers. The teacher would count them out, one by one, each new set of eyes searching the waiting group for its matching pair. Some parents would stand and talk as they waited, or pet one another's babies, others zoomed off at once with their little ones tucked behind them on a scooter or bicycle. I watched as one boy emerged with a huge paper bouquet, a cone made of sugar paper, decorated with a clown face and stuffed with pink tissue. He presented it to his mother as though to a visiting queen.

'Ah, beautiful,' she breathed, and kissed him with a joyful smack. '*Very* beautiful.'

It was a rhythm so familiar to my body that I strained to be a part of it, yearning for the little girl who now emerged, still unclaimed, to be my own. But, of course, someone always stepped forward to take her hand.

Chapter 8

Identifying the moment of falling out of love is considerably tougher than identifying that of falling into it—and there is no satisfaction in the accomplishment. For one thing you don't declare it, not even to yourself, not for a long time. But it seemed to me that there *had* come a time when I had acknowledged to myself that if Oliver and I did not have Emma to bind us I would no longer wish to be bound.

My realisation was nothing monumental, just a thought, struck at random one day. Not on a sunny day, as we drank a glass of wine in the sun and surveyed our kingdom together, but on a dull day, a day when the boiler was on the blink and the car playing up, when everything around me seemed to be falling apart. Then, when the physical world was repaired and humming happily once more, I'd simply noticed that the love was not.

Mariel used to say to Jen and me that you only knew how you felt about your partner if you looked at him when he didn't know you were looking. 'Because you're not reacting to anything. When you see them off their guard, vulnerable, that's the test. That's when you know you still love them.'

How many times had I caught Oliver unawares in exactly this way and, far from being touched by his vulnerability, wondered how on earth I could ever have mistaken selfishness for vulnerability in the first place? But I hadn't been mistaken, surely. There *had* been vulnerability once, which meant that it had faded over time or—a rather more frightening idea—I had lost my ability to recognise it. Either way, I had come to develop a test of my own: photographs. I would look at a picture of us together, perhaps from our wedding day or from a holiday, and then I'd wait for the stirrings. They were hard to define, these stirrings, like glimpses during the day of a dream you'd had the night before, but as long as they were there I knew something was right, I knew I didn't need to act. Until one day I'd simply stopped looking at the photos, I'd stopped testing myself, just in case.

Later, when Emma was buried and my bag

74

packed and ready in the wardrobe upstairs, I tried to express some of this to Mariel. It was the first real conversation I'd managed with anyone since the accident.

'I think I didn't admit it to myself before because I didn't want it to be really happening, for Emma's sake. Don't you see? I don't need to lie any more.'

She looked at me with those hazel eyes, mediator's eyes that even in catastrophe searched for ways to repair. 'But you haven't been lying, Rach, you've just been in a normal marriage.'

'How can you say that? What about Oliver and Charlotte? What about—'

'What about *everyone*?' She interrupted me, emphatic now. 'Just look at Toby and me, look at Jen and Bob, they argue all the time!'

'Because they care,' I cried, frustrated. 'They argue because they still *get* to each other. I'm talking about . . . oh, I don't know . . .'

She hushed me. 'Darling, you're in shock. You mustn't think of this now. You and Oliver need each other more than ever, you must hold on to that. Give yourself time.'

I shook my head. 'I don't need time. Emma was our time, Emma was *our* reason.' Mariel just nodded, saying she understood, of course she did, we would talk about it again next time. But she still doubted me, or doubted perhaps her own interpretation of what I was saying, too shocked herself by tragedy to see beyond it.

I said nothing to my mother, of course. My father, who'd died just months before my engagement to Oliver, had viewed marriage as sacrosanct. He of all people had believed in till

75

death us do part. In the end, I supposed, for Oliver and me, that was what it really had been.

FAO Mrs R. Freeman, c/o Hotel Ilias, Oia, Santorini . . .

I recognised Oliver's handwriting straight away and fingered the slim white envelope unhappily. It had been pushed under my door with a note from Eleni, who'd guessed, correctly, that I wouldn't have known that mail arrangements here were poste restante. I sincerely wished she hadn't taken the trouble.

I could bring myself neither to open the letter nor to destroy it, but left it on the table face-down, consoling myself that its very arrival meant there was to be no visit in person, not immediately, at least. I was reminded of the only other time Oliver had written formally to me, before our marriage, a missive sent with roses to apologise for his failure to appear at a dinner for my mother's birthday. My father had been unwell by then, and it had been quite a feat for him to wash and dress and travel to the restaurant, only to have to postpone eating for an hour and a half while we awaited our missing fourth. We'd eaten, in the end, in near silence. I'd decided on that occasion that Oliver's behaviour was callous and humiliating. How I had wanted his letter then, had torn it open the second it arrived, indignant, triumphant, indulging in the drama of the moment with real appetite. Now I saw his no-show for the unfortunate office delay it had been and wished I had been more gracious about it at the time, for my father's sake if not my own.

It was to avoid the letter that I began my ritual

of climbing down the cliff steps from the Goulas side of the village to the old fishing quarter of Ammoudi, once a day at first, with a break for water or coffee for I was weak from weeks of little food or activity, then twice, sometimes three times. The path was roughly cobbled and soon my soles blistered and my calves ached. I counted the steps—two hundred and fourteen down, two hundred and fourteen up, over and over and over, like a penance.

About a week after the letter arrived I decided to open it. I had spent the morning down at sea level, sitting on the rocks by a little bathing area I'd discovered close to Ammoudi. I would watch as others swam to a tiny islet across the water and took it in turns to dive off a platform that had been cut out of the rock. A guidebook on the shelf in House Callidora revealed this to be the island of Aghios Nikolaos o Peramataris—St Nicholas the Channel Keeper—and mentioned a *skapho* chapel that was dedicated to him there. I liked the idea of a hidden room, where a single flame kept alight the belief that one man might guard the islanders from all that the elements held in store.

'Coming in, huh?' The voice that carried up to me from the water was American, male, young and shot through with exhilaration. Above a bobbing sunburned forehead his cropped fair hair was glossy as fur.

'Maybe. Yes, why not?' I'd never so much as dipped a toe into the Caldera before, but now felt myself unzip my dress, slip off my shoes and drop straight in in my underwear. It was deep, up to my neck, and my whole body was assaulted by the coldness, causing me to gasp and twist from side to

77

side. The American, repelled perhaps by my failure to change into swimwear, had already moved off towards St Nicholas; I could see the angles of his elbows and ankles breaking through the surface and catching the light. I began to swim too, but about halfway across stopped and trod water for a minute or two before changing my mind and turning back through the swell. I struggled out, frustrated by the lack of strength in my arms as my feet hunted underwater for a rock edge to use as a step. Then, pausing only to pull clothes over wet skin and strap on my sandals, I hurried, dripping, past the Ammoudi diners, up the endless steps and back to my house.

I went straight to the letter and opened it. Inside were two one-page notes, one from Oliver and one from Mariel. Just seeing the curled letters of Mariel's signature made me remember our last conversation and dread her pleas for my return. Before I could change my mind I tore her note into pieces and went outside to throw them into the breeze. Oliver's, I read:

Dear Rachel,
I am getting a little concerned that I haven't been able to speak to you directly. I understand your walking out like that and you must of course take all the time you need. It goes without saying that I am here for you. You do know that you can draw whatever funds you need from the bank in Fira?
All I ask is that you let me know you are safe.
With love, Oliver

It was an odd note in a way, with more of those first halves of sentences I knew of old, each with its 'but . . .' erased. I checked the postmark: just a fortnight or so after my arrival here over a month ago. How long had it been sitting in the post office before Eleni had found it? And had the absence of a reply caused him to grow worried and set out to find me? Panicking, I rushed to the nearest shop and bought a postcard and pen:

> *Letter received. Yes, I am safe. I have no phone line, but I am in a house called Callidora if you need to know for emergencies.*

What emergencies those might be, I didn't know. The word no longer had any meaning for me and didn't, I imagined, for him either. After a moment's thought I added a P.S.—*Please do not pass on my address to anyone else*—and underlined 'anyone' with a heavy stroke.

*   *   *

Someone was visiting Callidora. Several times I'd returned from my treks to find flowers on my terrace table or by my door, roses and carnations tied with white ribbon or loosely bunched with sprigs of basil. Recently, I'd also found deliveries of bread, honey and orange juice too. Once there was grilled lamb and potatoes in a takeaway carton, another time brown paper bags of apples and tomatoes. When I tried to enquire at the nearest grocery stores, the owner claimed to know nothing about the arrangement and, embarrassed by my non-existent Greek, I didn't press the issue. I decided it was time to drop by the Ilias to find Eleni.

'Thank you for bringing my letter,' I said, 'a little while ago. I wouldn't have known to go to the post office.'

She nodded. 'I am there for my other guests and I see your name.' She added that the local postal workers found it hard to decipher the handwriting on overseas mail and so simply abandoned the normal alphabetical system and placed it in one big pile for the foreigners to sort through themselves. She apologised for their lack of skill. '"Idiot", you say in England, I think. This is a Greek word, you know?'

I smiled at that. I liked the way her cynicism didn't quite mask her good-heartedness. 'It's not a problem,' I said. 'In fact, there were hardly any letters when I called in this morning.'

'Everyone leaves now,' she nodded. 'The season is over. After October it is very lonely in Oia.'

This was a sentiment repeated soon after by the village doctor, who visited me, unbidden, at my house one morning in early November. He happened to be passing, he said, and I allowed him to prod and squeeze, to search my eyes with his, for he meant well and this was another act of kindness on the part of the community I'd entered. Afterwards he packed away his equipment at the table, stooping to pick up a couple of bougainvillea petals that had blown into the room. They were brown and curled now, like paper snails.

'It's colder, yes?'

'Yes,' I agreed. For some time now I'd needed to wear my only sweater every time I went out.

'You are not returning home for winter, Mrs Freeman?'

I frowned. 'This *is* home, Doctor.'

'You have some work, perhaps?'

'Not exactly. But I keep myself busy. I go for walks every day . . .'

'Yes,' he nodded, 'to Ammoudi, I have seen. Up and down, up and down.'

'It raises the heart rate,' I said, feebly.

'You remember, of course, to eat? Every day?'

I thought of the bread and the orange juice by my door. 'Yes, of course. Maybe not huge amounts, but something.' I pulled my sleeves down over my scrawny forearms and wrists as he cast discreet glances around the room. The bed was unmade, the cups unwashed, an apple shrivelled in the bowl, its leaf black. What he wanted to know was whether I was capable of looking after myself for the winter. I felt defensive, like an elderly parent objecting to suggestions of removal to a nursing home.

'You have met the other English people here in Santorini?'

I just shook my head discouragingly. I was not here to *play* at being a hermit, as I imagined these others might be, and I certainly didn't want a schedule full of expats and gin-and-tonics. I had left my friends in London. What could I possibly have to offer new ones?

Chapter 9

Don't tell *anyone* where I am, that's what I'd written to Oliver, my only message to the world I'd left behind. And he would have known at once what I meant by that vehement underscoring of the 'anyone'. Even my closest friends, even Mariel and Jen.

Jen. She was hardest of the two to think of now, for we'd come together through motherhood and motherhood alone—we'd entered the order together, shared its code; how, then, could she not have been as revolted as I was by my sudden defrocking? Mariel, though, I could picture still as the woman I'd known before we had jobs, husbands and children. Her I remembered as something more than a version of my maternal self.

I'd met Toby first. Toby Challoner. He and I were neighbours in our first-year university hall of residence and ate our first catered meal together—shepherd's pie, chips and sweetcorn. We bonded over starch, he'd later joke, and so did our intestines. Toby was wiry and quick, with a sense of humour to match. He began every observation with the phrase 'Let's put it this way . . .' 'Let's put it this way,' he told me of one nocturnally active neighbour of ours, 'if they buried her tomorrow she'd need a Y-shaped coffin.' He'd then insert the tell-tale pause of the amateur stand-up waiting for his laugh and I was happy to oblige. As far as I could see, he always put things most amusingly and we became friends.

'I want you to meet this girl,' he said at the beginning of the third year. I'd spent the summer travelling, he doing work experience in a market research agency in London. We were sophisticates then, finalists, confident of our right to the booth to the far left of the union bar, the one by the window.

I grinned. 'Sure, whenever.' His last girlfriend had been a Goth who'd come out for my birthday meal in a wedding dress dyed black and a waist-length train of purple rags woven into her hair. One had come to rest like a dead snake in the pizza pan in front of her alongside her discarded pineapple pieces.

Mariel was a different matter. She was self-confident, charismatic. She had mystique.

'You're doing History of Art, right?' she asked me, hazel eyes the same tone as her tanned face. 'My friend Liz says she knows you.'

'Mariel is a pharmacist,' Toby put in.

I laughed. 'You make it sound like she's selling packets of Tunes or something.'

'I probably will be, one day,' she shrugged, and just as I was struck by her lack of vanity, I also noticed how her hair swept across her shoulders like two perfect strokes of black ink. The necklace she was wearing was made of silver and shell and I knew, without needing to ask, that she'd spent the summer somewhere glamorous.

It was hard at first to see any difference between Toby's treatment of her and that of her predecessors, for it was his style to maintain an eager-to-please manner with girls even when he was known to be deep in consultation about breaking up with them. But as graduation approached and Mariel was a firm fixture in our booth by the window it was clear she was for keeps.

I wasn't sure about her for a while. I suspected her of being too needy of male attention. There was also the matter of her devotion to aerobics. What was a student in the early 1980s doing jumping up and down in organised formation? 'Let's put it this way,' Toby said of his girlfriend's commitment to keep fit, 'if she needs to open a beer she doesn't use her teeth.' What was wrong with a bottle opener, I wanted to know?

Soon I saw that she suffered male attention rather more than she sought it. And she had something more useful than mere mystique too, she had staying power, which meant that anyone not immediately intrigued would, sooner or later, be charmed into surrender. I was no exception.

*   *   *

I couldn't say exactly how long passed between the doctor's visit and the arrival on my terrace of Ingrid Sullivan, but I'd had another letter from Oliver and was aware of Christmas decorations starting to appear about the place, so it must have been several weeks. She was about five-foot-five or -six, of meaty build—'athletic' was probably the better word—and had warm brown eyes with short, fine lashes. Her freckles were almost, but not quite, indistinguishable from her tan and her long blonde hair was pulled back tightly in a ponytail. Her fingernails were painted the burnt orange colour of the rock at Ammoudi.

'Hi, I'm Ingrid. I live over in Perivolos.' As she

gestured along the cliff towards the far end of town, I registered the optimistic lilt of Australia in her voice. So, one of the good doctor's expats come to seek me out. Perhaps he had even sent her specifically, to check if that apple had ever been eaten.

'Hello. I'm Rachel.'

'Really?' she exclaimed, 'with an "a"? I mean, before the "e"?'

'No, just an "e" on its own.'

'Oh, good.' She sounded genuinely relieved. 'My mother's name is Rachael with an "a" and it's no recommendation, I can tell you.'

She settled her bottom on the wall behind her, not my terrace wall but the one on the farther side of the pathway, as though keeping her distance from an untried household pet.

'How long have you been out here?' she asked.

'I don't know, a few months. I came in August and decided to stay.'

'Surprised I didn't see you in the bar. I worked at the Greco over the summer, the place next to the Delfini.'

'I haven't been in any bars.'

'Ah, you've been lying low, have you? If you can say that here.' She glanced over her shoulder at the cliff edge beyond. 'Lying high, I suppose it is. Yes, well, I have to admit I'm not passing accidentally. I heard from Alexandros there was another long-termer.'

I didn't know who Alexandros was. Perhaps the butcher. 'You make us sound like prisoners.'

She laughed. 'You mean we're free to leave?'

But I was reeling by then; I'd used the word 'us' and I'd made a stab at a humorous observation. I was half smiling! Evidence of life, indeed!

'You should meet him,' she said. 'He's really nice. They all are, the locals.' She paused, considering me. 'They're very curious about you, you know.'

'Oh?'

'Yeah. They call you, let me get this right, my Greek is pathetic: "*I orea me ta mavra*".'

'What does that mean?'

' "The beautiful in black", something like that.'

I blinked. 'In London everyone wears black.'

'That's exactly what I told them. It doesn't have to mean you're a widow.'

'I'm not.'

Ingrid nodded. 'So, you must be a writer or something?' Her eyes moved to the pen and paper in front of me on the table; I was composing a letter to my mother but had so far managed just a couple of flat sentences. Though I'd sent her a postcard when I arrived, promising more communication when I was settled, subsequent attempts had been abandoned—I'd never quite got the phrasing right.

'No,' I said. 'I'm . . . well, nothing really.'

She raised her eyebrows. 'Nothing?'

'I used to be a picture researcher, back in England.'

This seemed to satisfy her. 'That'd be right. We get a lot of photographers here. It's a bit of an artists' colony, you know. Everyone here does *something* cool, even if it's just . . . well, *thinking* about doing it.'

'What do you do?' I asked. I had no intention of explaining that thinking made me press my head into a pillow until I began inhaling my own tears.

'Sorry, you said already, bar work . . .'

'Oh, that was just to pay my rent. I'm painting at the moment, but my pictures are pretty useless. I showed Manfred, you know, one of the German artists, you've probably met him?'

'No, sorry.'

'Anyway, I could tell he thought they were awful even though he pretended they were "promising". He had to look up the word in his dictionary. He's so sweet. The paints cost me a bloody fortune as well—what a waste of money!' She sighed. 'It's funny, I thought I'd just be able to copy what I saw, all of this . . .' she gestured to Callidora and the other houses in view, to the sea below us, 'but it turns out I can't.'

I nodded, struck by her honesty. From years of assessing photographers' work I was familiar with the delusions that set in whenever there was a shortfall between talent and ambition. And the Greek islands in particular tended to have this effect on people, turning civil servants into watercolourists, insurance salesmen into poets. An artists' colony? I doubted that.

'I'm starting to think I might make jewellery instead,' Ingrid said. 'There are so many stores here, if I can just get my act together over the winter then I'd be ready for when they start buying stock in the spring. I could use shells or something, those little shimmery ones, you know?'

'That sounds more promising—sorry, your friend's word again . . .'

She laughed at my doubtful expression. 'It's all right, I'm a walking cliché, I know. No doubt I'll probably be hopeless at that as well. But hey, what's wrong with a vanity project or two? I'm not

Shirley Valentine. It's not like I walked out on a family or anything. There's only me, so why not please myself for a while?'

'Walk out', the same phrase Oliver had used, the language of industrial action. If only this *were* a strike and I might be invited to return to my previous conditions, slate wiped clean, no hard feelings. Emma would be getting excited about Christmas by now, we'd be choosing a tree. Letters to Father Christmas would be being revised hourly.

My face must have expressed some of the pain that passed behind it for my new friend added quickly, 'Don't get the wrong idea, Rachel.'

'Sorry?'

'I'm not looking for a bloke. I mean it, I'm not.'

'Of course not.'

I was surprised by the turn her thoughts had taken, and she looked suspicious that this was all it was going to take to put my mind at ease on the matter.

'Not that you'd find any this time of year,' she added. 'It's a case of feast or famine here, I'm afraid.' She squinted up into the floodlit blue dome that encircled us. 'This is great, though, isn't it? Now the hordes have gone. So *remote*. What do they call it? Splendid isolation?'

I appreciated the crack of uncertainty in her voice, wondered for a moment who, for her, 'they' might be. She struck me as someone who spoke as much—if not more—to convince herself as her listener. She was younger than me, in her twenties, and I couldn't for the life of me think how she came to be here in this small community as it bedded down for winter.

'It's isolation,' I agreed.

She was already standing up and smoothing the back of her skirt with her hand. As she turned, her hair fanned from its band like a bride's veil lifted from her face after the exchange of vows. 'Well, Rachel, give me a shout if you ever fancy a coffee, or something a bit stronger.'

Unexpectedly, I found myself agreeing to do so.

Chapter 10

Cat was already crawling and Emma almost sitting up by the time they were introduced to Daisy. She slotted neatly between the two of them both in age and alphabetical order. As for her mother, Mariel and I liked Jen from the moment we met her. It was at our regular Young Mums group and we had arrived late one week to find a newcomer in our midst, not only one who wore lipstick (a rare mark of inspiration among the rest of us sleep-deprived lot) but also one who requested a glass of wine instead of the standard black coffee. She was hands down the most relaxed of the three of us, taking the terrors of motherhood in her stride and rarely allowing herself to miss the freedoms of old. I remembered our gasps of admiration when she reported that she and Bob had had a drink in a pub garden when Daisy was only days old. And they'd even taken the baby along to a wedding without bothering to check with the bride if that was all right! ('Who cares what she thinks! Is she going to pay for a wet nurse or something?') What was more, they weren't married themselves, which shocked and impressed us more than we were willing to admit.

Though Jen hadn't been to university, it was apparent from the outset that wherever she had learned her optimism and big-heartedness it had provided her with an education far superior to ours. Before Bob and the baby, she had been a committed Friend of the Earth and her past was full of episodes involving demonstrations and blockades and banners flown off motorway overpasses. 'I've done a lot of outdoor shouting in my time,' was how she put it. She still made efforts where she could, using environmentally friendly products on her clients' feet and insisting on unleaded petrol for the car she resented having to drive.

Jen had short, shapely dimensions that drew male eyes from less-than-discreet angles, but her defining physical characteristic was her streaked red-blonde hair, teased ever outward in the manner of a Rod Stewart consort. The girls loved winding bands into it and pinning it up with their glittery slides, while Jen pulled silly faces to make them giggle.

She was the most empathetic human being I had ever met. If Cat or Emma were in the smallest distress she would dash forward, eyes focused, exactly as if it were Daisy who was in harm's way. Mariel and I would do the same, of course, but only after an infinitesimal delay. With Jen there was never any delay.

*   *   *

'Ah, Mrs Freeman, you are here, thanks God!'

'Eleni, hello again. Call me Rachel, please.'

Though I had yet to leave the house that day, I was lethargic as I greeted Eleni on the terrace, ready to sink back into my bed. 'What is it? Is anything wrong?'

She flung her arms out wide, palms to the sky, as if to say, 'It's too late for that now,' and then announced, dramatically, 'He has come. He is here, in Oia.'

'You mean . . .'

'Yes. Your husband.'

My face flushed and the sudden heat made the tear stains around my eyes sting under my sunglasses. My first thought was to wonder if I could summon up the energy to run.

'Where is he?'

'He is waiting at the Ilias. He wanted to come here, to Callidora, but I told him he must wait . . .' Behind the flurried arm gestures I saw an intentness in her expression that wasn't quite right. She had drawn her own conclusions about my reasons for fleeing home, clearly; she thought I was in danger.

'It's OK, Eleni,' I said, calmly. 'He's not here to hurt anyone, I promise. Let's walk back up together and I'll introduce you.'

'If you are sure.'

I had expected this, of course, from the moment I'd arrived here myself, but now it had happened I felt utterly unprepared. I pressed my sunglasses tighter against my face, as though they might act as a shield against his words. Poor Oliver. Whatever he hoped to achieve by confronting me, this could only be a wasted journey for him.

He had already had suspicions of his own about our go-between, it seemed, because he had left the

Ilias and begun walking up Marmara when Eleni and I emerged at the top of my lane, intending, no doubt, to find some local official who might direct him more willingly. He was dressed in heavy London clothes, the skin on his face already singed pink by the winter sun. At the sight of him Eleni recoiled, gasping: 'There he is!'

'Oliver!'

'Rachel, thank God!' He reached out to clasp me. His shoulders and chest felt thin beneath the clothes. Seeing us hug, Eleni withdrew, though not before adding, 'Remember our arrangement for later,' as though she still believed there was an abduction to be foiled.

'What on earth have you been saying?' Oliver asked in an undertone. 'That woman was jumpy as hell.'

'Nothing, I'm sorry. The locals are just a bit protective. We don't get too many visitors out of season.'

He looked at me oddly. 'I see. Well, which way are you? Down this passage here, is it?'

'No. I mean yes, that's where I live, but let's carry on along here and sit in the square.'

'If you like.'

'You should have warned me you were coming,' I said as we walked, but half-heartedly. We both knew I hardly had the right to say it.

'You don't have a phone.'

I nodded. All I could think was that it was wrong for him to be here. And it was wrong for me to have drawn him here by my silence.

In the square I indicated the stone seats on either side of the main church, which stood guard on the inland side. The blue line of the sea completed the square. The sunshine was warm and clear, but we both moved instinctively to the side in the shade. I noticed that we had automatically seated ourselves a child's width apart from one another, an Emma width, and I felt that heat behind my eyes that usually signalled immediate wetness.

'So this is where Alysa grew up?' Oliver said. 'It's a lovely place, isn't it? We should have come before.' He looked at me. 'Sorry, but would you mind taking those off . . .'

My sunglasses. I slipped them off and looked back at him, at his gentle, tired, bewildered face. He needed me to slide across that space between us and take his head in my hands, whisper words of comfort and apology. I wished there were another ending to this meeting, but I knew there could not be.

'You've been crying,' he said, softly.

I blinked, remembering the photograph I'd been looking at when Eleni had called. I'd left it on the dining table indoors before going out to greet her. It was of the two of us, Emma and me, on a train in France about a year and a half ago, looking out of the window together on to the platform where Oliver had stood with the camera. (He'd been making a special effort to take part, I recalled, to contribute to family joy, soon as it was after the crisis concerning Charlotte.) She was five, slender-boned, her blonde hair following the curve of her neck and shoulders in a smooth outline. Her cheeks were flushed from the afternoon heat, and as I looked I could remember *just* how she felt moments later when the train began to move and she snuggled against my side on that long journey south, her head burrowing restlessly into me, hunting for a softer part of my body to make its pillow. Then her sudden excitement the instant we saw the sea. 'Mummy! Mummy! We're here! This is going to be so much fun, isn't it?'

I'd caught Oliver's eye then, and for a moment the skies between us had brightened at the sight and sound of her energy. Whatever had become of the two of us recently, we always shared her. Nothing could ever replace her unifying power.

'How's the house?' I asked, breaking the silence.

'The same, well, except for . . .'

I supplied the words for him. 'You've packed away her things, I suppose?'

He nodded, dully. 'I gave most of them away, the toys and books. The school took some of them. They've got a corner in the library now, the kids made a sign: Emma's Story Corner. They asked if we wanted to go and see it . . .' He broke off, his voice cracking.

I closed my eyes, unable to watch his anguish, but my mind's lens focused at once on an image of him kneeling on the striped rug in her bedroom, staring helplessly at the shelves of story books, fingering her lifeless clothes, opening and closing her music box. As I panned towards the mantelpiece, stacked with rows of her drawings ('my gallery'), I turned off the switch. I wasn't ready for this, I wasn't ready for him.

But he was already continuing his story, his composure regained. 'I was in a bit of a mess, but Toby hired a van; he and Mariel helped sort everything out. Jen suggested I give the furniture to a children's charity. She knew one in Kilburn near the High Road.'

'Right.' That was a shock: her furniture, too! I wondered who slept in the white-painted bed now, with the love heart carved out of the headboard ('heart love' she'd called it, when she was very little). When she'd first moved into it from her cot she'd been suspicious of all that unfamiliar stretched-out whiteness and I'd lain next to her, helping her fill it. I'd closed my eyes to encourage her to do the same, and then, just as I was on the verge of dropping off myself, I'd opened them a fraction, only to find two huge dark-blue circles an inch from mine and a delighted giggle in my ear. She'd taken it for a game: pretend sleep. Then she'd announced, 'My eyes are blue.'

'Like Mummy's,' I agreed.

'Like Mummy's,' she repeated and looked at me, so pleased to be mine, so pleased . . .

'Oliver—' I began, but he was speaking at the same time, turning to me as though choking with the agony of his own words.

'Rachel, I know I haven't been a great husband. The last few years . . . If I could change what happened with Charlotte . . .'

'Don't say it,' I said, blinking furiously, 'please! This isn't about her or any of that, it's about Emma.' Glaring at him, it was then that I saw it: beneath the agony, beneath the slack skin and the dead eyes of the bereaved, the flat black of guilt. He couldn't forgive himself. He even believed that Emma's death was his punishment.

'I told you before, we were both . . .' I paused, instinct telling me to leave it there. A confession of my own transgressions was not what was needed here. Somehow I had to try to ease this guilt of his without destroying what little was left of him in the process. 'We both forgot about us, it wasn't just you. I was always wrapped up in Emma.' And I was lost for a moment in the image, her arms around me, her cheek pressed against mine, enveloped in her presence, her voice, her smell, her breath.

He changed approach. 'Alysa's worried sick. She says you've hardly been in touch.'

'I know. I'm sorry.' It was all I could think to say.

'Don't you care?' he asked, suddenly turning to face me square, absolutely square, and I jumped a little in surprise. I felt a shiver of familiarity and it took a moment for the memory to come into focus. Our wedding vows, that formal face-to-face choreography, his face engaged wholly in the moment, in me. His voice rose, 'Don't you care about the rest of them? Your friends? Mariel and Jen have been torn apart by all of this. I've had Jen fucking breaking down on the phone, and Mariel, Toby, with the kids—they're desperate to see you . . .' He reached suddenly for the flight bag at his feet and fumbled with the straps. I watched with dread as he extracted a package and thrust it towards me. I could see my name in blue ink, Mariel's handwriting. 'Here, open this.'

Reluctantly I took it from him and placed it on the seat between us. 'I'll open it later.'

'No!' He picked it up again and pressed it into my hands. 'Open it now! Please! I want to be able to tell them I've done this, at least!'

'Fine, there's no need to be so—' I pulled at the flap and shook the contents on to my lap. Two handmade Christmas cards, both decorated with snowmen cut out of polystyrene and coated in glitter. Particles fell on to my trousers, picked up

the sunlight in little stars. 'It's Christmas already?'
My voice sounded dreary, pathetic, and this
seemed to provoke Oliver further. He gestured
impatiently to the note clipped to one of the cards,
dusted with glitter from where the surfaces had
been knocked together in transit.

Another letter from Mariel.

With Oliver about to snatch it from me and read
it aloud I had no choice but to look at the words
myself.

Dear Rachel,
We wanted to come and find you but
Oliver has been very clear about you
needing to be alone, and we respect
that, of course. But we are thinking of
you always. We love you, Rachel. Please
get in touch whenever you want to. We
can come to you at the drop of a hat.
All our love, Mariel & Jen

'See?' Oliver demanded. 'They care, they miss
you.'

'They understand,' I corrected him, as firmly as
I could.

'Understand what?' His eyes moved wildly
about the square as though unable to make sense
of the blocks of white and blue that surrounded us.
'This can't go on indefinitely, can it? You don't
really intend to *live* here? Think what it's doing to
Alysa, to all of us!'

I watched, horrified, as his upper body suddenly
furled like the dying stem of a flower, his head
dropping into his hands. He was sobbing.

'Oliver! Oliver, please . . .' The terrible thought

struck me that this might be the first time since I'd left that he had allowed himself to break down in front of someone else. He was, I knew, the sort to cry in the shower, with water coursing over his face, a guilty man obliterating the evidence, telling himself afterwards that it hadn't happened.

'I'm sorry,' I said, 'I'm so sorry. But I just don't think I can handle anyone else's . . .' I struggled for the word, before adding, 'fallout. Anyone else's fallout. I have to deal with my own first.'

He looked at me with appalling wet pale eyes. 'Look at the cards, Rachel. What about the girls, Cat and Daisy? Don't you care—'

'Oliver,' I turned angrily to interrupt him, 'please stop asking me if I care! What do you think? That's why I'm here. *Please* try to understand. I've lost everything . . . *We*'ve lost everything. We can never go back to normal, never!' And it came to me, as it did every so often, the succession of ghastly hits that this separation was real, it was permanent, I would live the rest of my life and never see her again.

My chest was rising and falling, rising and falling; I was close to hysteria. I wanted to scream and flail and curl into a ball. 'Oliver, you're the only person I can hope might understand this.'

He closed his eyes and when they reopened I saw that the guilt had returned, blacker even than before. He nodded. 'You're right. You need more time. It doesn't matter how long. I'll wait.'

'Please, Oliver, don't ask me this . . .'

'I'm not asking anything,' he said, shortly. 'I'm just saying, just so you know, that I'm going to wait.'

The square was empty. After dark it filled with

local children, playing tag, skipping rope, fighting over a mechanised car. The bigger kids ruled while the toddlers watched from the sidelines, inching ever closer to the action. I couldn't always tell who was supervised and who was not and sometimes I'd wait for every last one to be called home before allowing myself to return to my own bed.

I turned to him. 'I can't stop you waiting if that's what you want to do. But you need to go back, back to London.'

Again he nodded. He reached for his bag, secured the straps, stared ahead at the sun-baked wall across the square.

It was easier to walk away from him a second time than I could ever have imagined.

*   *   *

It was only when I was back at the house that I looked properly at the Christmas cards from Cat and Daisy.

Dear Auntie Rachel, have a Very Merry Christmas and a Happy New Year.

Daisy had signed her name in purple felt-tip, careful to remember the flower she used to dot the 'i'. I'd practised writing with them when they were first learning and we'd devised special signatures for each of them. Cat's was incorporated into a pussy-cat's face, the whiskers painstakingly symmetrical; Emma made a smiley face out of her 'a'. She alone had stopped the practice, just before her sixth birthday, dismissing it as babyish.

Turning them over in my hands, noticing details,

99

something inside me buckled. I missed them, Cat and Daisy, I really, really missed them. Hadn't I always loved them as dearly as Emma herself? I wished I could be with them that second, watch for a moment their joy and energy, their *growing*.

But I couldn't see them, not yet. Mariel and Jen were right to stay away and to keep the girls from me too. It would be too painful; it might always be too painful and who was to say it would do them any good either? But that didn't mean I had to be absent.

I locked up Callidora and walked up to the Ilias. Eleni rushed out from behind the reception desk and hurtled into my arms. 'I am so glad to see you! Your husband, he is still here?'

'No,' I said, withdrawing from her grasp as discreetly as I could. 'He's gone back.'

She nodded. 'That is good, I think. I will get us some wine. Wait here.'

'Eleni, while you're doing that, could I possibly borrow your phone?'

She gestured to the desk. 'Of course. It is here.'

'And do you have a number for the airline? I need to book a flight.'

Chapter 11

That promise the three of us made when the girls were babies, we decided to make it official. Though Mariel was already Emma's godmother and I Cat's, Daisy had never been christened and Jenny asked us to be her legal guardians. We happily agreed; it was only right that the pact be formalised.

'In a way, they've all got three mothers now,' I told Oliver. 'We'll be understudies, sort of shadow mothers.'

'How is this different from being a godmother?' he asked, reasonably.

'It's something stronger. More of a pledge.'

He chuckled. 'Stronger than the Christian Church? What would your father say?'

And I'd taken his comment seriously and gone away to think about it. What *would* Dad have made of it? To him, there existed no more important a role in society than godparent, after that of the parent itself. How proud he would have been to know I'd come to hold that responsibility with Cat. And this new arrangement with Daisy, just as heartfelt, just as permanent, he'd be proud of that too.

I told Mum about it and she nodded, pleased. 'This closeness you have with Mariel and Jenny, it's a wonderful thing. You mustn't let it slip away, not ever.'

*   *   *

It was a lunatic idea, an impulse that should have been overcome and forgotten, but I chose to follow it. That was the only way I knew how to conduct myself now, by instinct. And my instinct was to avoid the natural sources of information— to ignore the years of closeness with the people who loved me best and get what I needed from a stranger.

Having chosen at random from a list offered at Heathrow arrivals hall, I checked into the

Gloriana, a B&B near Gloucester Road underground station. The bed was lumpy and the breakfast swimming in grease, but I supposed I ought to be grateful it wasn't the other way around. In truth the battered kitchenette and frayed upholstery were merely a variation on my own long-stay facilities in Oia, but here they unsettled me. That someone should *live* here, even temporarily, with this view of damp-ridden brick, not a single slant of sunlight from one day to the next. And that low double mattress with its bunions and bumps—love had doubtless been made on it, but had it ever been felt?

It did cross my mind once or twice during that sojourn chez Gloriana that guests at my house over the years had had it easy, what with the freshly pressed Egyptian cotton and the lavender bags under the pillows. How house-proud I'd been; and how redundant that instinct had now become. Beyond this, however, I didn't allow myself to think of my old home, of the little girl's bedroom at the top, dark now, like a disused theatre. And Oliver, only a thirty-minute taxi ride away in the City: all I had to do was walk into his office, brush Vanessa aside and . . . and what? Tell him I was back, after all? That his words in Oia had brought me to my senses, that there was no return part to the airline ticket in my bag? No, nothing had changed. If his visit had convinced me of anything at all it was that seeing him again wasn't going to help either of us. I was back in London for Cat and Daisy; and for Emma.

First thing in the morning I asked the receptionist for a copy of the Yellow Pages and, once supplied, found the section I wanted and

102

began dialling. Of the five private investigators I spoke to, three were not available for an immediate appointment. I arranged for the remaining two to come to my B&B after lunch, an hour apart. Anthony Ditroia was the name of the first.

I disliked him straight away. He had the elongated face of a fox and an oily, insinuating voice, some kind of approximation of a doctor's bedside manner.

'What can I do for you, Mrs Freeman?'

I cleared my throat. 'I've just moved abroad, Mr Ditroia, but there are some people here in London who I want to keep up with.'

'I see.'

'It's mainly two children I'm interested in, two—'

'So not . . . ?' He caught himself at once, shifted in his seat, as though dislodged by his own curiosity, then laughed. 'Excuse me.'

'Not what?' I asked, frowning. An ex-husband? A new wife who'd taken my place? 'Go on, please . . .' I could feel myself bristling, daring this horrible fox-like person to presume he knew for a second what was taking place inside my head. But I remembered enough of my old world to know that the fallen contours of a female face would always be seen as those of the broken-hearted. Well, he didn't need to know how mine had come to be broken.

He seemed to be searching for the appropriate recovery and, to my horror, settled on a leer. 'I have to tell you that most female clients *are* wanting information about a spouse. It's a sad fact that husbands *will* stray.'

As he smirked to himself, I imagined a dozen

women lining up to entrust their privacy to him, each wishing with all her heart that it had not come to this. 'You're probably not supposed to tell me about "most" clients. You wouldn't tell other clients about me, I assume?'

'Certainly not.' Now he looked irritated to have been tricked into something close to a professional apology. He was not handling this interview well and nor was I. We were bickering, not doing business. Already I felt exhausted.

He shrugged. 'All right then, tell me more about these girls.'

My eyes drifted over his shoulder to a family just arriving, pulling backpacks and jackets from their shoulders, sighing and grinning at each other. A journey ended, a holiday about to begin, a little boy of about Emma's age.

I found myself standing up. How could I even begin to think of sending this man anywhere near Cat and Daisy? 'I'm sorry, Mr Ditroia, but I don't think this is going to work out.'

'What . . .?' He glowered, but irritation turned quickly to false sympathy as his voice took on a new smoothness. 'Look, perhaps we got off on the wrong foot. Shall we start again from the beginning, Mrs Freeman?'

Now I wished I hadn't given my real name, but had made one up. 'No, it's not that. Please, can I at least pay you for your time?'

'That won't be necessary.' He made a great show of unbuckling his briefcase and slotting his notepad into its depths at precisely the required angle. As he left, he looked over his shoulder at me with a deliberate sigh, as if to say, I had a feeling she might turn out to be one of those.

Left alone, I wanted to cry. A flush had spread all over my face and down my neck. This was madness. I tried not to watch as the mother drew the boy close to her, reading from a story book while the father checked in. Just be good for five more minutes, darling, and then we'll go out and get you an ice cream, a pizza, a Beefeater hat. We're in London!

I looked at my watch. Almost an hour before my second man was due to arrive. Johnny Palmer of JMP Investigation, Victoria. I tried to replay the sound of his voice in my head, for it had definitely been him I had spoken to on the phone that morning and not an assistant, but found I couldn't summon it at all.

Well, if I wasn't to fail the girls, I could only pray that he would turn out to be better than the first.

*   *   *

He was so unobtrusive that I didn't actually notice him arrive. Who knew how long he'd been standing there waiting for me to look up, whether he'd needed to be directed by the receptionist or had located me himself by process of elimination. After all, this wasn't the crowded lobby of a large hotel; I was alone and dejected, easy enough to single out.

'Pleased to meet you, Mrs Freeman. I'm Palmer.' He was quietly spoken and had a courteous, old-fashioned air that took the edge off my anxiety straight away. He was in his late thirties or early forties and had the face of a character actor—his features might have been modelled in

105

clay by an apprentice rather than in marble by the master sculptor—with a deep furrow between his eyebrows, a mark of perpetual questioning, that seemed absolutely right for a detective. As I rose to shake his hand, I found that he was only a little taller than I. He engaged me directly with very clear grey eyes.

'Mr Palmer, sit down. Would you like some tea? I can order some from reception.'

'Please. White, no sugar.'

By the time I returned he had settled on the sofa opposite and, having acquired an ashtray from somewhere, was rapping out a rhythm with the filter of an unlit cigarette on the pack. 'You don't mind if I . . .?' He let the question trail off, as smokers always did, their signal that even if you did object they'd go ahead and do it anyway. I had once shared cigarettes with Oliver, with Simon, and the smoke that drifted into my hair recalled intimacies that seemed ancient now, impossible to revisit. I considered asking Palmer to stop, but thought it best not to disturb his working processes. Smokers must be better observers, I thought; Eleni smoked and she had the eyes of a jackdaw.

'Our tea will be here soon,' I said.

'Thank you.'

He lit his cigarette and waited. Now the time had come to explain myself my disquiet returned. 'The reason I've asked you here is that I'm looking for someone to keep an eye on two girls for me, two little girls. They live here in London.'

'Relatives of yours?'

'No.'

'Do you have any formal relationship with

them?'

'Yes, I'm godmother to one and the named legal guardian of the other.'

His grey eyes widened a fraction. 'But you're no longer in touch with their parents?'

'I'm not in touch with anyone here any more.' A trace of something passed across his face, then—curiosity perhaps, or compassion, but I knew instinctively that it was a curiosity that wouldn't be indulged, a compassion that wouldn't be expressed. 'I live in Greece now. What I suppose I need is for you to be my representative here.'

He nodded. 'I understand. Tell me a bit more about the subjects.'

'Well, they're both six, almost seven, and live with their parents very near each other in South Hampstead. They're best friends, always together . . .' As I continued he remained quite still, only the occasional flicked glance in my direction with those clear eyes.

'How often would you like reports from us, Mrs Freeman?'

'I don't know, maybe every month. Does that sound usual?'

'Yes, that shouldn't present any difficulties. And when do you see this culminating?'

I paused. 'In about eleven years.'

'*Eleven years?*' Now he allowed himself to react, letting out a well-I'll-be-damned whistle, a sweet, drawn-out sound that made me smile in spite of myself. Then he reached for his notepad, as though something as extraordinary as this was not to be trusted to memory.

'I know it sounds crazy,' I said, leaning forward, 'but I'm worried that if anything happened to them

I'd never know, never be able to help.'

Palmer looked up. 'You think they're in danger, do you?'

'No,' I exclaimed, 'of course not! They both have excellent homes.'

'OK. Perhaps you could help me out . . .' He watched my face, eyes obliging again as I struggled to explain myself.

'I mean I want them to reach the age of eighteen happy and healthy. If there's anything I can do, you know, if they're being bullied or they're neglected at school, that kind of thing, something their parents might not be able to deal with . . .' I petered out, aware how clichéd my notions must sound to his ears (not to mention skewed to my own: what could I 'deal with' that Mariel or Jen couldn't?). 'The thing is, I haven't thought this through, not the details. I'm not looking to interfere or create any kind of problem, I just want someone here to let me know they're all right.'

He nodded. The trace had returned to his eyes, the trace, I now saw, less specific than curiosity or compassion, but rather a general tenderness. I stared, unblinking.

'And it goes without saying that I don't want anyone to know I'm doing this. They might not understand. I wouldn't blame them, either.'

'They won't know, you can rest assured.'

'Oh, and one other thing, do you have a female colleague? It's just that I wouldn't want the girls to be scared if they saw you. No offence, but . . .'

Again he waited until he was quite sure I'd finished speaking before he replied. 'There's no question of the subjects seeing us, please don't worry about that. But yes, I can assign this to a female colleague if you'd feel better.'

'I would, yes.' I watched him make a note at the top of the page and underline it twice. 'Does any of this make sense?' I blurted. 'I mean, do you think we'll be able to look after them, if they need anything?'

'It depends what comes up, exactly. We'll know in due course.'

And that phrase, for some reason it comforted me, it sealed my trust, and I smiled at him with real gratitude, grateful that he was treating me with courtesy, grateful that he wasn't the other man.

'Why don't you tell me their full details,' he said. 'The children, the parents, and anyone else in the picture.'

I dictated the names and addresses of the two families and a rough outline of their schedules, then wrote down my own address in Santorini.

'I'll need your phone number as well, if you don't mind.'

'I don't have a phone,' I said.

He looked up. 'What if I come across sensitive information?'

'You could leave a message at Hotel Ilias in Oia. They know me there.'

We discussed fees, agreeing that he would devote one week a month to surveillance, with any necessary administrative checks to be done at additional cost. I could see that he didn't expect the relationship to last eleven years or anywhere close, and furthermore, eleven years at his monthly rate would be enough to buy him a house in a decent part of London and lose me mine. This reminded me that I needed to consider the financial aspect of my new existence. Oliver had said I should take as much money as I needed from our joint account and requests from my new bank in Fira had been duly honoured. But that wouldn't be the case for ever—and nor should it be. When the numbing eased and the guilt faded, when he no longer wished to 'wait', resentment towards me would start to seep through, it was sure to.

I had my own money, of course. There'd been a small sum from my father, as well as several years of untouched salary payments from Pendant. I would pay Palmer from that, and my rent in Oia too. For the first time since my wedding day I would be self-sufficient.

*   *   *

My mother wasn't at home and, unsure what to do next, I lingered on the pavement outside her door for a few minutes, shivering in my summer-weight jacket and struggling in the wind to control the umbrella I'd bought from a street vendor outside the Gloriana. I had my own door key, but didn't want to use it without her knowing I was even in the country. She was not one for surprises. I considered knocking on the neighbour's door—Marion she was called, her daughter and I had been at primary school together—but exhausted by my interviews with Ditroia and Palmer I couldn't bear the idea of explaining myself to someone else.

I would have to make the visit alone, a prospect that both relieved and terrified me. I walked to the high street and searched the flower stall by the tube station. No sweet peas—it wasn't the season—so I chose pink roses, hardly English at this time of year, artificially grown God only knew where. Then I found a mini-cab firm and ordered a car to the cemetery in north-west London, the one that for so long, back in blissful days, I'd been unaware had even existed.

The traffic was relentless and dirty, the trees that lined the approach road sawed back into stark black forks. The cab dropped me at the gate. It was raining hard now and as I crunched between the graves, looking for that small headstone with the least-weathered surface, I gave up on the brolly and gave up on my own self-control, sobbing by the time I reached her and sinking straight away on to the wet ground. 1988–1994. Six years, that was all I'd had, six precious years of growing and learning and getting closer to what she would become. And the longer she didn't exist, the shorter the period she *had* existed. It was almost six months since she'd been gone, a twelfth of her life.

There were already two bunches of fresh flowers laid out for her. Oliver, I thought, and Mum. I must have missed her by a matter of minutes. I laid my roses at Emma's feet and caught sight of a corner of white under one of the other bouquets. It was paper, a note placed flat on the earth beneath the flowers, and I pushed the stems aside to read the single line:

We miss you, Emma, every day. Love from your best friends, Cat and Daisy xxx

There was something stapled to the corner, and lifting the paper I saw it was a photograph of a group of children. I huddled forward, sheltering it under my jacket as the rain dripped off my chin. Emma. She was in a greenhouse looking up at a large potted flower exhibited on some sort of podium. The school trip to Kew. She'd been lifted up by Miss Morrissey, the royal-blue gingham of her summer pinafore gathered at the waist, and she was reaching for the plant, lips pouted in concentration. In the row below were her classmates, Cat and Daisy standing together in the centre, watching their friend with matching expressions of wonder.

The last photo of my daughter, taken just hours before she died; the last photo of her with her two best friends. I agonised over whether to take it, then, making my mind up, stood to leave.

'I wish . . .' I whispered to the ground, losing the words to the wind, 'I wish you could come back with me, back to Oia . . .' Then I ran, hardly seeing through the rain and my tears, until I reached the gate again, each breath burning in my ribcage.

Looking into the traffic for the yellow light of a taxi, I thought I saw the rear of an old Alfa, stationary for a moment or two at the lights before it accelerated south.

Chapter 12

Oia was a 'traditional settlement', according to the authorities, and that meant mules for the tourists and, for the locals, greetings by name, whether one sought them or not. Even for a recluse like me it was impossible not to know those members of the tourist trade community who remained in the village in winter, so thoroughly had its ranks been depleted. Most of the businesspeople had shut up shop and returned to Athens or to other cities where work was available. Only a few hotels stayed open, the Ilias and two others, and all had dismissed their maids for the low season. In the central area there remained a café and a taverna, a couple of bars and one grocery store, while on the traffic side of the village only the supermarket, the butcher's and the baker's stayed open. Also out and about I recognised the icon painter who worked from a studio on the main street, some German students who lived near the windmill at Ammoudi and the staff of a couple of the bigger jewellery shops. I now knew the doctor as well, of course, and Eleni's husband Anatole, whose business commitments in Fira had also wound down for the winter months.

Perhaps I had made the assertion 'I live here' enough times—to Oliver, Palmer, the doctor—to feel the urge to justify it by making friends, or perhaps I was missing Mariel and Jen more than I was willing to admit, but it wasn't long before I asked Eleni for Ingrid's address and walked along to Perivolos to look her up. Perivolos was the part of Oia farthest from Ammoudi, which meant it was the least developed and the best endowed with views.

Ingrid was already leaning out of the window when I arrived, which made me suspect a phone call from Eleni. 'Hi there! What are you doing all the way up here?'

I tipped my head up, surprised by how pleased I was to see her. 'I wondered if you wanted to go for a drink?'

'Sure, let's go to Damiri's, if it's open.'

Damiri's was a bakery-cum-souvenir shop in a row of odd barrel-shaped buildings along the clifftop stretch between Perivolos and Oia proper. A couple of tables and chairs outside in the sunshine served as the café. 'You know these little buildings were put up after the earthquake,' Ingrid said. 'They were supposed to be temporary accommodation. The villagers call them *tholia*. I looked it up, it means "vaults". Cute, aren't they? I wouldn't mind living in one myself.'

I considered mentioning my family's own experience of rehousing after the earthquake, but decided against it, at least for now. Whatever I thought I was doing in Oia, I could hardly kid myself that I was here on family business, knocking on doors and asking if anyone remembered my aunt and the falling stone that killed her, hoping to discover that House Callidora was my ancestral home, dug from the rubble by heroes. No, my coming here was not 'meant to be', it was simply all that was left, and I wasn't about to explain that to Ingrid, however instinctive my liking for her.

She ordered the sweet local wine, visanto, in a tumbler with lots of ice ('They think I'm mad, but that's how I like it') and I did the same. With my back to the sun, I took off my sunglasses and could see at once her sorry glances at my bloodshot eyes. I realised I would need to get this out of the way right at the beginning.

'Eleni might have told you my husband came out here recently. I left London after we split up.'

'She did say. Sounds pretty tough.'

'He wants me to go back, but I've decided to stay.'

She nodded. 'At least there weren't any kids.'

I did not correct her.

'You know what?' she said. 'You need to read. A book a day. When I split up with my boyfriend back home all I did was read.'

I *had* been reading, as it happened, it was one of my primary daytime pursuits. I could never have emptied my mind of Emma without force-feeding it with something else. There was no bookshop in Oia—'Santorinians do not read,' Eleni had told me, eyes rolling, as they often did when she commented on her compatriots—but Rena, the maid who serviced my landlord's other tourist villas, let me take my pick of their shelves and I was in no danger of running low. I took care to choose impersonal stuff, thrillers and history books, the donations, I imagined, of the male halves of holidaying couples.

'Music too,' Ingrid advised. 'I had a whole tape of those old singer songwriters. Janis Joplin, Patti Smith. I knew all the words.'

No music, I thought, not yet, and perhaps never. Where crime novels gripped, music stirred. And it was not only the fault of the lyrics; classical music also encouraged me to make pictures, to fantasise, to *feel*. Music was dangerous.

'It's just a matter of killing time,' Ingrid went on, 'until you start to feel human again. My friend Susan, back in Melbourne, she used to say it takes a month of healing for every year you were together.'

'Really?'

'Everything has a formula, Susan says.'

What was Susan's formula for a dead daughter, I wondered, imagining Ingrid's horror if I were to speak the words aloud. I didn't know why I was so certain I should keep Emma from her, just as I had from Eleni, but presumably it was part of the reason I had come to Oia in the first place. It was not the sympathy of strangers that I needed, evidently, but the guaranteed absence of it. In any case, Ingrid had her own troubles to reflect on and, unlike me, relished their recounting.

Before leaving Melbourne she had discovered her boyfriend Patrick in bed with another girl. Well, not bed, in fact, but the fully reclined passenger seat of his car. She had thumped on the window and watched him surface, mouth gaping for oxygen and the words to explain. Then she had said to him, 'I wouldn't worry about it, mate. You know, strictly speaking you're not a cheating arsehole, anyway'—pause, to direct a significant look at her wristwatch—'because we are now officially over.' Though she was pleased to have thought of something clever to say then and there and not ten minutes after the event, she didn't expect him to take her at her word and resume his humping. But this he did, leaving her to slink away, humiliated.

'Who was the girl?' I asked. I was starting to relax; conversation was much more manageable than I had expected, once the spotlight was removed from me.

Ingrid drained her visanto and scooped an ice cube into her mouth. 'Oh, you know what? The sitter.' She crunched hard. 'What a fucking cliché.'

The *baby*sitter? I had gone cold, all at once my

116

thoughts leaping ahead of the conversation: *Ingrid had a child*. Who had she left it with while she loafed in the Cyclades? This lowlife character Patrick? No, I thought, please tell me life couldn't be this cruel. As I struggled to live without my daughter, surely my only companion hadn't willingly abandoned hers?

'You mean you and Patrick had a baby?' I realised I was whispering and she looked puzzled, before bursting into laughter.

'No, of course not! Don't be mad! She was babysitting Pat's sister, well, half-sister, his mother's youngest. He used to give her a ride home when he came back from his shift. Yeah, he gave her a ride all right.'

As I tried to conceal my guilt and relief, she told me that she'd spent a year in London, post-Patrick, doing bar and office work before drifting with the spring tide to the holiday resorts of the Greek Islands. She heard about the job in Oia at a bar in Fira and when she saw the place she knew straight away it was for her. 'I thought I was such a city girl, but this is better for me. Barefoot, leading a goat, that kind of thing.' She paused. 'OK, I haven't actually seen any goats yet and I always wear shoes, obviously, I'm not stupid, but the light here, the sweet little houses—oh, it just makes me so happy! To have all the complications taken away, you know?'

I nodded, understanding, if not able to share, her enthusiasm. Though by no means immune to Oia's appeal—the brilliant southern light, the grilled fish and thyme smells of a late lunch, the clatter of the mules, natural relaxants for any normal person—what Ingrid experienced was pleasure far beyond my reach.

'Anyway,' she said, 'I *told* you I've got no family.'

'None at all? What about Rachael, your mother?'

'Well, if you can call her that.' She was twenty-four but she spoke in the jaded tones of one whose troubles had begun well before adulthood. Now I learned that the errant Patrick was the least of her former troubles. The mother, it seemed, had neglected Ingrid and, on rare occasions of attention, been violent towards her. She drank, she lost jobs, she went missing. Once she threatened her daughter with a knife, before slicing at her own wrist and spending a month under observation in hospital. Eventually, the parents of a school friend took Ingrid in and she went from one week to the next without setting eyes on her parent.

'I used to come out of school dreading she'd be there. I mean, that's the opposite of how you're supposed to feel, isn't it?'

Horrified, I tried to banish memories of the Moss Hamlet playground, the girls flying through the doors and into our waiting arms. The smiles, the news, the Friday hot chocolates.

'You've had a terrible time,' I said, gently.

'I was fine once I got away from her.'

'Thank God you did.'

'Just don't tell me she loves me really. Everyone says that.'

I shook my head. 'Actually, I was thinking she sounds as though she doesn't deserve you.'

'That'd be right,' Ingrid nodded. 'Anyway, that's another thing I like about being here. No one knows me, no one feels sorry for me. I don't want to be a charity case, you know?'

'Yes.'

'I can meet someone here and, I don't know, it's not like I'm making up a different version of my past, I don't mean that, but more like I have no past at all. That sounds dumb, I suppose?'

'No,' I said. 'I know exactly what you mean.'

*   *   *

Palmer's first report came a little over a month later. It was in letter form, headed, I guessed without any intended humour, Project Godmother. The phrasing reminded me of insurance claims, or, perhaps more appropriately, a police statement. A key showed that Daisy Barnes was to be known 'hereafter' as Subject A and Catherine Challoner Subject B:

- Carrying out observations in the Swiss Cottage/South Hampstead neighbourhood, we noted Subject A and her mother meeting with an unknown person . . .
- Subject B was collected from school by her father and accompanied to her home in Goldhurst Terrace, NW6 . . .
- Subjects A and B were driven by the mother of Subject B to the Fairhazel Dance Centre for their ballet class . . .
- Subject A arrived at school for morning break after a doctor's appointment . . .

Stilted the syntax may have been, but the information it contained was as familiar to me as drawing breath. Offices and schools, supermarkets and swimming pools, parks and children's parties—how easy it was for me to put names to Palmer's 'unknown persons', to follow his route around my old neighbourhood! There was a new arena too, for Jen was taking Daisy to church every other Sunday (though not, apparently, with Bob). This struck me as wholly fitting: of all of us, she was the one who needed to *believe*. All that environmental campaigning in her past: saving the trees, saving the countryside, saving the animals, so much *saving*. She had a big heart, Jenny.

Along with his log Palmer enclosed photographs, not the oversized black-and-white prints I'd seen in detective series on TV, but ordinary colour shots developed at one of those one-hour places you saw on every high street back home. One showed Cat cuddling Emma's doll Lucy; in another, Daisy, who had always been the slightest of the three, wore a pair of Emma's jeans that I'd passed on to Jen last winter. Another pictured the girls together, in school uniform, coming through the gate with Mariel amid a crowd of departing pupils and parents.

I'd vowed I wouldn't crumble, that I'd stay strong, but tears flowed for the rest of the day as I imagined again and again those other parents, not only Mariel and Jen but all of the others from that terrible day, all of those who had somehow been granted a reprieve and allowed to slot themselves back into the bones of family life. Yet, thanks to some cruel singling out by the gods, here was I, childless, boneless. It had, until now, felt quite right that I should be in a cave in a cliffside far away, staring at the domes, mesmerised by the sea, but it had never felt real, not real in the way of the events described here in black type and snapped for me in full colour.

And all the while Jenny took Daisy for her Saturday swimming lessons and Mariel strapped the kids into the back of the car for the supermarket runs. They'd be clamouring for sweets, as Emma invariably had—'I *need* a treat, Mummy. I'm *still* hungry!' 'Just wait,' Mariel would be saying over her shoulder, exasperated to have to queue so long for the car park. 'Just wait!'

The contrast made me feel primeval.

Chapter 13

One by one, the hotels in Oia reopened for the new season. Ingrid, after a winter of sporadic cleaning work, secured daily shifts in a café by the main square, serving spinach pie and walnut cake to the coachloads of day-trippers who returned to clog the narrow streets and fill the ruined watchtower at sunset. I could no longer deny that I might have to prepare myself for a move from House Callidora. Judging by the local hotel tariffs on display about the place my house could be let weekly for more than I was paying monthly. Though I had few other expenses in Oia, with Palmer's retainer to consider it wouldn't be wise to stay at an increased rate.

Thinking Eleni might have ideas for a cheap alternative, I set off up the steps, only to be caught in a downpour of rain that drenched me in seconds. I didn't like Oia in the rain, at least not for long, for the picturesque tumble of houses was fast transformed into a mass of soggy shanties. And I always seemed to be somewhere inconvenient when it happened: down by the shore, out on the most exposed stretch of the walk to Ammoudi, outside a strip of cafés with CLOSED signs in their windows. This time I was caught on the slippery marble, struggling to keep a foothold. With the nearest open café no closer than my own house, I decided to turn back. Even out of season Eleni's tables filled in a flash when it rained, so she wouldn't be free to chat anyway.

It was teeming down so ferociously that I didn't notice the white-haired man beside me until he'd taken my arm and pulled me out of a puddle and under his umbrella. 'This is better, yes?' Then, satisfied I was sheltered, he turned automatically for the main street.

'Thank you,' I yelled, pulling back, 'but I'm heading back down this way!'

'No problem, I will come!' He insisted on escorting me, careful to keep the brolly directly over my head even as we lurched and dashed, but by the time we reached my terrace the water was less forceful and I was relieved to be able to step away from him.

'Thank you,' I said again, hoping not to have to invite him in, though all too aware that this was the exact opposite of the Oian way. Already I should have been pouring us large drinks and bringing out warm towels. To make matters worse, he now closed the umbrella and tried to press it upon me to keep. 'Please, you'll need it later. Today, the weather is not to be trusted, I think.'

'No, I'm sure you'll need it, too,' I said, handing it back.

'I insist.'

Still he didn't give up, so I took the umbrella and placed it against the wall before busying myself with getting the key in the lock.

'You are Mrs Freeman, I think?'

I turned in surprise, blinking through wet eyelashes.

'I am Christos Kafieris.'

This meant nothing to me and he saw this and laughed. 'From Thessaloniki.'

Ah, the man himself, my landlord. 'Well,' I said, 'Nice to meet you. Would you like to come in, Mr Kafieris?'

'Christos, please.'

It was dark inside and I moved around in the blackness switching on the lamps before I could turn back and look properly at my visitor. Out in the rain, thanks to that white hair of his, I'd taken him for an old man—an unusually spry one, admittedly, for he'd matched my frantic bid for shelter step for step—but now I saw that the frown lines were only moderately deep and he was, in fact, an unusually grey middle-aged man.

'You have made this very nice,' he said, looking around the room. That was kind, for Callidora remained, at best, exactly as I had found it.

'Would you like some coffee?' I asked.

'Yes, please.' He followed me into the kitchen and made a comment about the fridge being noisy. I didn't mention that at first this had been the cause of some distress in keeping me awake, that I'd often lain in bed and stared down the night to its soundtrack, watching the shifts in light from black to blue as the morning seeped through the fanlight. Lately, though, I'd found the sound comforting, like the hum of a car engine as you snuggle under blankets, half-asleep, in the corner of the back seat.

'You know how to make Greek coffee?' he asked me, just as Eleni had the day I'd moved in. The locals were particular about coffee, it appeared. Before I could protest he had manoeuvred me aside and begun heating a pan of water on the hob, measuring out the sugar in quick, precise heaps, turning to me to demonstrate each new step. Though his English was immaculate, his body language was unmistakably Greek, and even the smallest movement contained pure drama: the pouring of the sugar high above the coffee jug, the swirling of the water, even the wiping of the lip of the cup. Watching him, I felt both fascinated and embarrassed.

'Good, it is ready.'

We sat opposite each other at the table. I still drank my coffee the British way and tried not to wince at the sweetness of the first sip. 'I know you need the house back,' I said, not wanting to make this awkward for him. 'You've been very kind to let me have it for so long, and at such a fair price. I'm sure Eleni has told you how grateful I am. It's been a life saver.'

'A life saver,' he repeated, his tongue testing each syllable.

'So, please, just give me a date and I'll be gone.'

He looked at me with very black eyes—I realised I couldn't tell the irises from the pupils—and leaned forward towards me until I felt I was inhaling breath still warm from his airways. It was humid inside and I wished I'd left one of the doors open for air.

124

'Tell me your story,' he said.

I blinked. 'What?'

'Tell me your story. The story of why you are here. Please, I am a good listener.'

I frowned, looked away. 'I don't know what you mean, Mr Kafieris. There is no "story".'

'This bad, eh?'

I didn't reply. He drank the rest of his coffee in a couple of gulps and leaped up. I watched, confused, as he toured the room, inspecting sockets and taps and heaters. Finally he came back to the kitchen for a second look at the troublesome fridge. I felt both helpless and indignant. Whatever subjects we'd each tried to open back then, they were for now, evidently, closed.

After he left I wondered if it were not, after all, *I* who had offended *him*. This was my landlord, not some local busybody nosing about. He had been trying to be kind. I would need to find him and apologise, try to re-open negotiations.

In fact he found me first, returning later in the afternoon when the sun was flickering back to life. He told me that I could stay on at Callidora at the current rate. He was not interested in making money, he said; this was not what life was for.

'Thank you,' I said, bracing myself for his theory of what life *was* for. It was the least I could do to listen and nod as though I too believed in some higher purpose. But he didn't elaborate, just buttoned up his jacket to leave.

'Mr Kafieris? When do you think you *will* want the place back?' I called after him.

He held up his hands as though to dismiss the detail of time altogether, before turning to cut diagonally up the hillside. It was a moment before I made out a flight of steps, partially overgrown, the stones still streaked dark with rain; I'd never noticed it before.

When I reported my good fortune to Eleni she just nodded—'Of course, this is how Oia used to be'—and asked me if I knew how the village had come about its main street. I didn't. Many years ago, she said, a ship had arrived in the Caldera with a large order of marble bound for Russia, but word came through that the order had been cancelled and the ship owner decreed that the cargo be donated to the village. It was used to pave a road—*Marmara*, which meant 'marble'.

'It was his gift to us.'

'What a generous thing to do.'

'This is how Oia used to be,' she said again. 'Of course, when they pull up the stones for to lay the electricity, they put them back so messy. Fools! They are not craftsman now. You have seen how this makes the big puddles, no?'

A few weeks later, a new fridge was delivered to my house and the noisy one removed.

Chapter 14

In Oia there was never a moment when someone was not gazing out to the water. The sight of a huge passenger liner cruising by, or even the more modest inter-island ferry working its timetabled way around the Cyclades, automatically drew a crowd to the walls. Our elevated viewpoint made it natural to keep an eye on the comings and goings

126

below, but it seemed to me that there was something more arcane than that about this collective vigil. It was as though the people had a need to confer romance on every passage, however routine it might be in reality. This part of the world was defined by seafaring, after all, its history stuffed full of pirates and adventurers. Once, women had spent nine months of the year up here, protected only by their clifftop position, waiting for their sailors to return to them. For those who waited now, wasn't there the possibility that the next boat might be returning someone to us too?

This, for me, was precisely the problem. The sight of a boat ploughing past in the direction of Athinios signalled the same threat as that of a plane approaching overhead: Oliver had arrived without warning—who was next? And how long did I have before I was found?

It was a morning when I'd been busy with laundry and had paid little attention to the criss-crossing of the ferries that a visitor for me actually *did* arrive on one. Approaching my terrace with that same silent tread I'd failed to notice when we'd first met, he appeared at my gate quite suddenly, without so much as a wave from the steps above to warn me. Initial confusion gave way almost at once to a horrible choking panic as I pictured police cordons and ambulances and emergency lights blinking death-blue in the sunshine. Cat? Daisy? Something must have happened, something must be wrong.

'Mr Palmer! What are you doing here?'

'Mrs Freeman, hello.'

'What is it? Please, just tell me straight away . . .'

'No need to worry,' he said, 'Please carry on

with what you're doing . . . I just wanted to show you some photographs.' With his left hand he indicated a large envelope tucked under his right arm. It looked exactly the same size and weight as the one that arrived from him each month.

My pulse eased a little. I looked back to his kind, expectant face and wondered for a flustered moment if I had not made this appointment myself and simply forgotten it. 'Well, you could have posted them, as usual.'

'It's a little more sensitive than usual. But nothing too serious, really. I apologise for giving you a fright.'

'What do you mean, more sensitive?'

'I'll show you. I just thought it made sense for me to give you an update in person once a year or so.'

As it happened, it didn't make sense to me on at least two counts: it was only a few months since we'd met in London and set up our arrangement, so hardly time for any 'annual' update; nor, by his own admission, was there any crisis to report. What was more, I disliked the idea that unnecessary expense claims might be coming my way. Some of this must have struck him, too, for he added quickly, 'I've got a friend based in Naxos, so it was easy enough to get the ferry over here. I wasn't sure when I'd next be coming to this part of the world.'

I took in his bland lightweight clothing, the polished brown lace-ups, and marvelled at the easy way he slotted into the backdrop, as though it were perfectly natural that he should have arrived there. He'd done the same in that B&B in London, I remembered. He was like some sort of cartoon chameleon travelling through time, he'd probably not been noticed by a soul. If I asked around later, I'd be told I'd made him up. And yet it was quite real, this mysterious arrival of his, and oddly meaningful too. What it meant, I guessed, was that this thing I had entered into with him, it was real now, too inescapable, something larger than a letter sealed to all eyes except my own.

I looked around me, willing Ingrid or Eleni to materialise, finding instead only the distant stooped figure of Rena at work in the sun several terraces below, far too busy to look up and think to rescue me.

He took a step towards the terrace table, apparently all set to take over and start spreading out his documents. 'Is now a convenient time? I could come back . . . ?'

'No, of course, it's fine,' I said, and as my hostly instincts of old returned I finally smiled in welcome. 'Sorry, you just took me by surprise. I can't believe you've come all this way. Why don't we go and have some lunch and you can bring me up to date while we eat?'

'Sounds good.'

I wanted to get him away from Callidora, I realised, just as I had kept Oliver from it before him, and I wasn't sure why. He waited in silence for me to finish with the washing, close the interior shutters and lock up. Then he gestured for me to walk out ahead and let him take care of the bolt on the gate, but the fixtures weren't properly aligned and he fumbled for a few seconds before managing to secure it.

'Thank you,' I said, 'I don't usually bother.'

'Better safe than sorry . . .'

'Of course.'

Usually I set out for a walk at this time, ate something down at Ammoudi, but I could hardly subject Palmer to one of my silent breakneck treks. Instead, we strolled in the sunshine to a taverna visible from my house, a spot popular for its excellent local specialities and views of the famous blue domes of Monastiri, and of the sea, of course.

'Is that the famous Caldera?' he asked, squinting down. 'It's funny, you can sort of sense trouble brewing, can't you? How deep is it, d'you think?'

'Two hundred metres at some points, apparently.'

'Jeez, I wonder what's down there.'

The water, it seemed, could be counted on to take care of any conversational gaps that weren't filled by speculation about the vessels gliding over it. Well, I was happy enough with that. I pointed out Palaia and Nea Kameni, the two volcanoes, and Thirasia, the separate island that formed a municipality with Oia. 'The view is even better from further south. Did you see it on your way over?'

'Yes, it must be quite a bit higher down by Fira.'

'A few hundred feet higher, I think. Imerovigli is the highest point.' I'd learned the names of the villages, too, by now: Finikia, Imerovigli, Firostefani. I pointed out, too, the odd rock that fitted into the cylindrical earth beneath it like a cork stopper in a jar: 'That's Skaros, the old medieval capital. Princes and bishops used to live there, I'm told.'

We discussed his journey from Athinios. The taxi driver, it seemed, had perpetrated the classic

130

local trick of tripling his revenue by taking three separate customers at once and charging each full fare. 'I didn't bother taking his details,' he said. 'You win some you lose some.'

As he studied the menu I studied his face, the bump at the bridge of his nose, thick mid-brown hair, greying at the ears, swept an inch off his forehead and flopping forward over the edges of his eyebrows. He was unmistakably English, good looking in a rough-hewn way, and he had that self-contained, enigmatic quality that reminded me a little of Mariel. He lit a cigarette with deft fingers, face and hands motionless between puffs. All his movements were economical, I noticed, so controlled and abbreviated that they made me want to fidget. And the growing silence, with which he was evidently quite comfortable, it was the sort that invited others to gush foolishly. I wondered if it might be some sort of investigator's technique.

After we'd ordered, I took a breath. 'Do you want to show me those photos you mentioned?'

He settled the burning cigarette in the ashtray and slid his fingers into the envelope. 'It's Daisy Barnes. She's not doing quite so well as her friend.'

'Is she ill?'

'No, nothing like that. But she's been bullying some of the other kids at school.'

'Bullying?' I struggled for a moment to comprehend the photo placed in front of me. A small girl, her shoulders hunched and eyes downcast. Poor darling Daisy. I couldn't think of a friendlier girl and yet here she was, looking angry and excluded. Bullying? It was *she* who was the victim, surely. I wanted her in my arms that very instant. I wondered at the resolve of the photographer, Palmer's associate, how she could have resisted throwing down the camera and comforting the broken creature herself. Irrational, I told myself, she didn't know Daisy—nor Daisy her—of course she couldn't approach the child. That would be disastrous.

'What do you mean, "bullying"? She's a bit young for that, isn't she?'

'Well, as bullying goes at that age. Slammed the school gate on someone's leg, swear words, that kind of thing. Anti-social tendencies, they call it. We've seen the school psychologist's report.'

'How did you get hold of that?'

He just raised his eyebrows as if to say, Let me worry about that. Though I wasn't sure I had the right, I felt suddenly let down by him. I'd thought he'd understood, that he'd got my measure in some unspoken, instinctive way, but I now saw myself as he very well might, as some eccentric recluse with a whim to be serviced. Money for old rope. It struck me that he must have run a check on me (whatever that meant) right at the beginning, to reassure himself that I could afford his rates and wasn't some sort of bounder. Standard practice, no doubt, with a client living overseas. Presumably he had access to police files, credit profiles and so on. He probably knew my place of birth, my current bank balance, the number of fillings I had in my mouth.

'Anyway, forget the psychologist's drivel,' Palmer went on. 'It's fairly obvious to me that the kid is having a tough time at home and that's why she's acting up at school. Her parents aren't getting on, lots of rows, I hear.'

Bloody Bob and his short fuse. We'd seen time and again how exchanges between Jen and him could escalate into the sort of arguments that cleared rooms, before evaporating as suddenly as they'd materialised. Daisy was copying hostilities at home, she had to be. I remembered Jen in my kitchen the day of Emma's party, she'd been upset by Bob's attitude towards her, by his contempt. 'But I'm not doing anything different,' that's what she'd said.

'Her teachers report that she talks about Emma more than usual as well. She's become almost like an imaginary friend.'

I looked at him, shocked. *An imaginary friend*, my beautiful, blue-eyed, hot-cheeked pea. His eyes were unblinking as they met mine and I saw at once that I'd been wrong to feel let down; he *did* understand. 'I know about your daughter's accident, Mrs Freeman,' he said, quietly. 'I'm very sorry.'

Of course he knew, he'd reported visits to her grave and only last month there'd been a letter from Mrs Wilkes to the parents that referred to the accident and mentioned Emma's name. This psychologist who'd been observing Daisy, he or she was probably on call every time anyone so much as whispered the dead girl's name.

'Mrs Freeman? Are you all right? I'm sorry to have brought up her name . . .'

'No,' I interrupted, 'it's all right, really.' I met his eye. 'And since you're getting to know so much about me, you might as well call me Rachel.'

'Thank you,' he said, rather formally, adding, 'I would say the same, but people just call me Palmer.'

'What, even your wife? Assuming you have one
... you know, I don't think I've ever asked you ...'
I broke off with a laugh that sounded false even to
me. If not quite impertinent, the remark was
unnatural—for how could the occasion have
arisen, our previous contact having consisted of a
single business meeting? But I was off balance
now, rocked by that reference to Emma, desperate
to escape this situation and be on my own again. A
napkin was being patted over my knees, however,
keeping me in place, and a selection of starters
placed in the space between us.

'Your *fava*, please. Tomato *keftades* ...'

Though we'd ordered separately the dishes
were, it seemed, designed to be shared. Of course
they were, this was Oia, the favourite of
honeymooners. Waiters here were probably
surprised if couples *didn't* want to hand-feed one
another across the table like babies.

Palmer tore at a piece of bread and dipped it
into the *fava* purée. 'To answer your question, no,
not any more. We got divorced two years ago.'

'Children?'

'Two, both at secondary school now.'

'You're close to them?'

'I like to think so.' He shrugged and I searched
for a new question, anything to stop the
conversation working its way back to Emma. 'And
your friend in Naxos ...?' I meant a woman, of
course, but then remembered that Ingrid had
talked about one of the other islands as a magnet
for European gays, a 'hotbed', she called it. Was
that Naxos, or had she said Mykonos? I felt my
cheeks redden.

Suddenly his face split with laughter and

134

surprised me with its attractiveness. 'Bloody hell, you think I'm gay, don't you?'

'Not at all,' I said, stiffly, irritated at my own awkwardness. What on earth was I doing speculating as to his sexual preferences? It was beside the point to say the least. 'And if you were, that would be your business, not mine.'

He gave me the 'Well, you asked' look that I deserved and then returned to the photographs on the table between us. The next showed Jen escorting Daisy across the empty schoolyard, an unwitting pastiche of prisoner and jailer. Both looked thoroughly miserable.

'What are Bob and Jen arguing about, do you know?'

'Money, from what I can ascertain.' 'Ascertain' was one of Palmer's private-eye words; it cropped up several times in each of his reports.

'Bob's freelancing isn't working out, then?'

'Nope, work's dried right up. He'd been on contract to ITV, I understand, but they didn't renew. He's got virtually nothing on at the moment and the agency he uses says business has slowed across the industry. Something starting next month, possibly. But our checks have shown a substantial credit card deficit. Their rent has just been put up as well. They'll be in real trouble if they don't watch it.'

'Really?' Worse, then, than I'd imagined. I looked towards the terraces of a hotel that had just opened nearby, reportedly booked up for months in advance. I had never seen a guest emerge from its doors looking anything but serene ('lobotomised', Ingrid said). An idea occurred. 'How about if Bob were to get a new client to tide

135

him over? Someone who's willing to pay over the odds. Maybe someone who works in the tourist industry, who can get them a discount on a holiday while they're at it?'

'Go on.'

As we ate, the plan took shape and I was surprised by how enthusiastic my tone now sounded. Palmer set down his knife and fork to make notes, interjecting only to clarify some logistical issue or other. After a while, something in his face made me put down my own fork and ask, 'What?'

'Nothing.'

'Come on, Palmer, you've come all this way, you might as well give me your opinion. This is my first attempt at intervention, after all.'

There was a flicker of resistance in those eyes now, though his voice remained even and pleasant. 'If you insist. I was just thinking it takes more than a nice holiday to mend a marriage.'

I thought of the trips Oliver and I had taken in recent years, the villas with sea views, the chocolate-box chalets in the Alps where you could ski right to your door, the city hotels with Michelin-starred restaurants. Just months before Emma had died we'd spent a long weekend on our own in Paris. I'd watched him in the armchair by the window, face distracted, entirely unenticed by the view, by me, by any of the charade.

I looked at Palmer. He'd been considering his failed marriage too, I supposed. What oddities we were in a place like Oia, and yet here we were plotting to revive someone else's relationship, a relationship that had been well beyond my influence even when Jenny and I had known each

136

other inside out. It was absurd. Shouldn't I just stop now before I did any damage?

'You're right,' I said, finally. 'We can't make them love each other. But it might repair things a bit. I can't remember the last time Bob and Jen had a holiday, and Daisy obviously needs one. She's my number one concern. I can't bear her to be unhappy.'

He nodded. 'It's certainly worth a try.'

'And somewhere safe, Palmer, not like here. Somewhere suitable for children, with no cliffs or rocks.'

'Rocks?'

I was aware that I was starting to sound like my mother, just a fraction away from producing statistics about drowning. 'You know, just nowhere dangerous.'

He lowered his eyes. 'Of course.'

'I'll transfer funds to you tomorrow. The usual Bank of Greece account. It will take a few days but you can make the call as soon as you get back to London.'

'Consider it done.'

Over coffee he announced his intention to go straight from the restaurant to the port, and I was surprised by how the news lifted my mood. I walked him to the square where the taxis made their drop-offs, pointing out buildings of note along the way. He seemed about to say something else, so I lingered, wanting to be helpful, but I was hardly able to guess what it might be.

'You're looking better,' he said, finally. 'I mean, you know, better than last time.'

I didn't know what to say, so I just patted the envelope of photographs, now in my possession, and said goodbye.

*   *   *

Just days after Palmer's visit to Santorini a Mark
Houghton of Inspired Travel rang Bob at his office
desk at home in Fairhazel Gardens. He said he
wanted some material produced quickly for a
conference in the Far East, a dummy travel
brochure and media pack and some other bits and
pieces. He'd seen Bob's work for ITV and other
clients and wondered if he was available?

When the work was done he paid in full
immediately and declared himself so pleased that,
though he didn't normally do it, he would be
happy to arrange a substantial discount for Bob at
any of the hotels in his portfolio. He didn't know if
Bob had children, but some places in the chain had
excellent kids' clubs, which gave parents the whole
day to relax by themselves. Flights would be
thrown in free of charge for he'd had a
cancellation on a competition prize and could
transfer the seats for a nominal fee. When Bob
accepted his offer, all paperwork was handled
personally by Mr Houghton, right down to the pre-
paid taxi transfers to and from the airport. He
asked Bob to be discreet about the special offer
once at their destination in case other guests got
wind of it and made a fuss.

The hotel in Majorca was one selected by
Palmer from a brochure called Luxury Family
Escapes, picked up from a travel agent near the
JMP office. In the picture he sent me, it sat above
a gently shelving cove, the water smooth and glossy
as polished glass. 'This award-winning resort is

perfect for young children,' the caption read. It made quite a dent in my account, but photos of the family's arrival back in London showed it to be money well spent. For now, Bob, Jen and Daisy were all cuddles and sun-kissed smiles.

Chapter 15

A further term at Moss Hamlet came and went. There were no school outings this summer and, as the first anniversary of Emma's death approached, Palmer forwarded me a copy of a letter sent to parents, encouraging them to visit her grave. 'Make time to talk to your son and daughter about the occasion in a meaningful but unpressured way.' Palmer noted trips to her grave by both the Barneses and the Challoners, and on one occasion Oliver was present too.

- Subject A spent the morning in the library with her father.
- Subjects A and B were walked to school by the father of Subject B . . .
- Subject A was taken by her father to Swiss Cottage pool for her weekly swimming lesson . . .

It was odd, but I'd never thought the contrast quite so marked between the extent of Toby and Bob's involvement in their daughters' day-to-day lives and that of Oliver's in Emma's. I couldn't remember a time when he had ever taken her to the local library or dropped her off at school. The idea that he, and not I, might strip naked in a public changing room and take her swimming was absurd.

Throughout Emma's life I had simply accepted that Cat and Daisy were daddy's girls and she not. Even before she could articulate 'I want my mummy', she made her preference clear in other ways, raising her whimper to a wail when Oliver tried to comfort her, wriggling in his lap when he read her a story, her eyes moving over the top of the book to watch for me. When she took her first steps, it was from him to me that she tottered.

Oliver seemed not to be hurt by any of this; he loved his daughter, of course, but he was content to restrict his contact with her to the occasional weekend exchange over the top of *The Times*. He would draw together the two halves of the broadsheet, an act of exaggerated care that reminded me of folding bed sheets, and find her little face waiting behind to surprise him.

'Daddy!'

'Hello, pea, what are you up to?'

'Making ginger men with Mummy.'

'Ginger*bread* men, you mean?'

'Yes, I *said* ginger men. And hot cross bums.'

'Hot cross whats?'

'Hot cross *buns*, Daddy, that's what I said.'

'Well, make sure you save one for me.' He didn't need to add, 'Run along, then,' for she usually already had, and his thoughts were back to the business pages, scarcely having broken their thread.

When I went back to work at Pendant, I thought I might understand the distance (or rather 'balance') that fathers like Oliver enjoyed in their

140

family arrangements. But, concentrate on work though I tried, I thought of Emma constantly. I would write my faxes to the museum curators of Buenos Aires and Geneva and Tokyo, process my cheque requisitions, hunt through the catalogue cards at the reference libraries, all the while enjoying the gathering excitement of knowing I'd soon be travelling home to see her again. Ours was a proper, heart-popping love affair: sessions apart only heightened the pleasures of those together.

'My mummy', 'Silly Mummy', 'Nice Mummy', 'I need a cuddle, Mummy', 'My knee hurts, Mummy' . . . It was the only relationship I'd experienced in which my position was reiterated at the end of every sentence. Was there any wonder it superseded all others?

*   *   *

Oliver's next letter felt heavier than usual and I found he'd enclosed a second piece of mail with his own. A stiff, formal-looking envelope of powder blue, it had already been opened, the flap tucked neatly back inside. Both our names were written in black ink in handwriting I suspected to be habitually scruffy but smartened up for the occasion. The lines of the address were neatly spaced too, reminding me of a schoolchild tracing over lined paper fixed beneath.

Dear Mr & Mrs Freeman,
I am writing in the hope that you will read my words and not throw this away—as you have every right to do. I know you must despise me.

141

I stopped, startled. Then I turned the page over to see who the sender was. Ah.

> I want to say I am sorry, truly sorry. I know that cannot mean anything, but I need to say it anyway. I did not know your daughter and I am not a parent myself so I can't say I know what you are feeling now or anything like that. I know you won't ever forgive me. My parents haven't forgiven me, whatever they say, and I don't even forgive myself to be honest. I just wanted you to know I am sorry. If I could change what happened last July I would, please believe me.
>   Yours sincerely,
>   Andrew Lockley

Andrew Lockley, the surviving teenager, the one who had been in the passenger seat when his friend Darren Morris veered into the minibus and forced it into the central divider. Attention had focused on Morris then (his body had been taken to the same hospital as Emma's, and Jenny and I had narrowly missed the arrival of his mother at the morgue), and the illegal substances found in his bloodstream that day, but I remembered a little of Lockley's story too. Unlike his less fortunate cohort, he came from a wealthy north London family. It was he, I recalled, who had regularly supplied marijuana and cocaine to the driver. Oliver and my mother had agreed that it had been an odd reversal of social type, in that respect, for one would have expected it to have been the more socially deprived of the two who was supplying the moneyed one. ('Fucking wastrel', Oliver called him and Mum had nodded, despite the profanity.) It had made more sense, however, that it was Lockley alone who, perhaps conditioned by years of school runs in his mother's BMW, had remembered to fasten his seatbelt for that fateful journey. Well, he was right: his communication couldn't mean anything. It was as impossible for me to put myself in his shoes, or even those of his parents, whose suffering I did not question. I wasn't sure if it would ever be possible.

Just stay away now, I whispered into the air with real urgency, as though it might travel the full distance between us and reach his ears. Stay away from Cat and Daisy. Please don't reappear further down the line, in some other context, as a colleague or a neighbour, or a stranger on the tube who picks up the scarf one of them drops and starts chatting about the weather.

You've done your worst, you've said you're sorry. Now leave us to survive on our own.

*   *   *

July the twelfth, three-thirty in the afternoon. Fingers numb and swollen with the heat, skin, where it was bare and exposed to the sun, stung red in nasty little lashes. Exactly a year to the hour of Emma's death, I drank on my own in a tourist bar overlooking Ammoudi.

I had in front of me on the table the photograph I had taken from her grave. Every so often I looked from Emma's face to the broken ramparts

143

of the castle, the old Venetian Goulas. The sunset ritual. Even now, with hours to spare, tourists scouted for a special spot to experience the magic. I caught the waitress's eye and gestured for a refill. Ouzo on an empty stomach—I couldn't help thinking of Lynn and Rosemary. I was the third generation of women who'd married a Freeman and been broken by it. I remembered a joke in the best man's speech at our wedding, something about the groom being a Freeman all right, but his lovely new wife no longer being a free woman. Our guests had lifted their glasses and laughed in delight.

The first anniversary. As soulless an occasion as a first birthday was joyful. A year was a long time, but I knew time had not healed, nor ever would. I understood that. I no longer sweated and wept the days away in bed—grief of that intensity couldn't last for ever, not for anyone; if it didn't kill, it passed, and it had passed me—but still I thought of her always. Not having Emma defined me as exactly as having her had: it was everything.

Still I tormented myself with memories of my own imperfections as a mother. My impatience when she dallied over dressing in the morning, my meanness over a television programme she wanted to watch but I thought too old for her, the time, when she was a baby, that I'd burst into tears and slumped on to the bed, done in with exhaustion and frustration. She'd lain there beside me, quite quiet, listening to the unfamiliar sound of her mother sobbing. Then, as soon as I stopped, she revived and resumed *her* cries, confident again of the natural order of things.

And that day, that last day, while the Morris and

144

Lockley boys still lazed in bed, did my goodbye hug at the school gates lack its usual conviction? Did I think only of the chores to be ticked off before I returned later to collect her? Had I slept badly in the heat and squashed her enthusiasm for the trip with my morning grumpiness? Had there been a sign, a snivel, a cough, something I missed that might have made me keep her home that day, keep her *alive*?

In better moments there was comfort in the knowledge that I had never taken her for granted, never, not even before the discovery that she was to be my only child. From early on, when she wrapped her arms around my neck, the full length of her body pressed into mine, legs tucked around my waist, I would try to steal the moment with all my senses, preserve it just as it was, so that when she was older and the cuddles weren't so easily granted I'd be able to draw over and over on that precious, sensuous cache. And I drew on it now, almost every waking moment.

My secret trips to the school gates continued, but there was little talk of children in my small circle. Eleni's two were in their late teens and studying in mainland Greece, and Ingrid was barely grown up herself. Relatively few children were brought in by the holidaymakers either. (I must have intuited this, of course, in those jumbled thought processes that occurred between Emma's death and my departure from home. If I'd once considered the combination of eight-hundred-foot cliffs and knee-high walls inappropriate for my child's holiday, then other parents were sure to have too.) If I was lucky, I didn't see children from one week to the next. Only when I closed my eyes;

then they were all I could see.

'Rachel, I've been looking for you!'

Looking up, I saw that the tables around me were now crowded with tourists. Ingrid stood among those queuing at the café gate, tanned and flip-flopped like the others, but with concern in her eyes.

'Do you mind if I join you?'

'Of course not. Here, let's get you a glass.'

As she settled herself opposite me and helped herself to the liquor, I slipped the photograph into my bag. 'Looks like you've been having quite a session. Who are we toasting?'

'Actually, I was thinking about two women back in England. They're called Lynn and Rosemary.'

She looked at me quizzically, and when I didn't elaborate she picked up her glass and clinked it against mine. 'OK, to Lynn and Rosemary! And perfect timing, the sun is setting exactly . . . now!' She rolled her eyes as applause broke out around us. 'Did you know they do this?' she said in an undertone. 'Crazy, like they expected anything different to happen!'

'Just look at that!' exclaimed a woman nearby to her companion. 'The best one this week by far. You're lucky to have picked tonight to come!'

'Well, I sure am.'

Ingrid and I were the only people there not to lift our eyes in worship, but I could still see the orange and pink reflected in the flesh tones of her face, and in the skin of my own hands on the table in front of me.

I'd been in Santorini almost a year. The cliff hadn't sacrificed me, the sea hadn't swallowed me. I walked, I breathed, I lived.

146

PART THREE

'Wherever I turned I saw a picture before me.'
Elli Souyioultzoglou-Seraidari (known as Nelly's),
photographer, on Santorini, 1920s

Chapter 16

1996, one year later

Oia was changing. I could see it happening before my eyes as disused caves and ruined mansions were restored and polished to a shine for the tourists—the numbers of whom had increased startlingly since the summer of my arrival. Armies of workmen criss-crossed the cliffs on those crumbling short cuts no holidaymaker dared use, women with their buckets and mops following closely behind. The hallmarks of transformation rarely differed: smooth external walls rollered some sun-washed pastel or spotted with stones; the treads of the steps painted smooth matt grey, which made so striking a visual effect against the white but turned treacherous with the first splash of rain; sometimes a pool too, carved ingeniously into the rock so that the water and horizon line were one. Infinity pools, they were called, though one enjoyed the effect only if actually submerged. From above they were more like tinted puddles, little cakes of watercolour set in the rock.

My own terrace, a little rough around the edges and, in any case, a tier or two too far down the hill, was spared the tour leaders' beat, but the chatter would often drift my way: Italian, French, German, and the various accents of the English speakers, their bon mots destined ever to be appreciated out of context: 'Move your head, will you, Nick? Wow, that's awesome!' or 'Urgh! There's sumink on me arm!' and 'Bugger, Barbara, the sun's in the wrong

149

place.'

Eleni complained that some of the renovation projects were no better than cellars, humid, uninhabitable units bought sight-unseen by greedy developers who expected to rent them out for more than could be fetched for an apartment in New York. Others, still filled with rubble from the earthquake forty years ago, simply became dumping grounds for broken furniture and empty paint pots.

'What happened to the people who lived there?' I asked her. 'Did they die in the earthquake?'

She shook her head. 'But no, in Oia only these people in the *kapetanospita* or down at the water were injured. The *hyposkapho* is the safest place to be when there is a shaking. Look . . .' She sketched a quick diagram on her desk pad to show how the vaulted shape and local plaster (made from, among other things, vine twigs) acted together like an elastic cage that protected everything held within. Then she pulled out a book from the shelf behind her reception desk and found a photograph of Oia just after the earthquake. There were fallen stones everywhere, the streets were impassable. Half the façade of a building had peeled away like a mask and you could see right inside, the chandelier still hanging from the ceiling. I thought of my Aunt Phoena; for all I knew she could have been killed in that very building. For all my mother's warnings of boiling seas and runaway boulders, she had never described to me the sequence of events, the immediate circumstances of Phoena's death. The earthquake had started in the early morning, that was all I had gleaned. Mum had still been asleep in her bed, and the rest of the family had managed to escape without injury.

'So different in these days,' Eleni said, and turned the page to a picture of Armeni, the old Oia post where the passengers used to disembark. I had lost count of the number of times she had told me how the blare of the ship's horn transformed the atmosphere of the community in an instant. What excitement, what anticipation as the villagers gathered at the top of the steps while the tenders brought ashore their loved ones below! The mules would appear first, straining with the weight of the luggage, then the passengers, crumpled and breathless from their journey, pulled into the arms of family and friends. The romance of real travel, Eleni called it, the way of 'old Oia'.

'So different in these days. Such a secret place, then, a special place. Not artificial like now.' And it was true that the houses in the pictures were camouflaged by the earth, built for invisibility, not pleasingly contrasted in colour schemes designed with travel brochures in mind.

'Did I tell you there is a shop now that sells pictures of Oia made in China or somewhere for only a few cents? And they sell them for so many thousands of drachmas! These factory workers, they only copy a photograph. I will show you, Rachel, and you will see the flowers in the pictures are orchids, not geraniums!'

'That's terrible!' I said. I knew what was coming next: the reprehensible decision to rename the local beach Paradise. What was wrong with the original? Where was the Greek left in Oia?

She had a point. In high summer during daylight you'd struggle to find a local face among the throng, and when you did—the cleric waiting for the bus, an old woman in her headscarf on the bench outside the church—you'd be forgiven for thinking it had been planted there by the mayor to create a photo opportunity for the tourists. In a way, even the holidaymakers were artificial versions of themselves: women with their hair in girlish pigtails that would be laughable in their home lives, men in holiday prints chosen for them by someone else, shirt sleeves still creased from the packet they came in. Eleni called it an invasion, lucrative for her and her family, she was the first to admit, but an invasion nonetheless.

'These couple I have this week, they ask me if the dogs have the fleas!'

'What did you say?'

'*They* are the fleas! I did not say this, of course, only to my husband. Thanks God they leave tomorrow. Only complaining, night after day.'

'They sound awful,' I agreed, half-heartedly. But despite their complaints, recently I'd sometimes been finding the tourists rather wonderful, the way they strode towards Ammoudi with such purpose, such determination to get what they'd come for. And each time one of them made me smile I'd experience a second lift at evidence of my own enthusiasm. Oia was changing, and so was I.

*　　　*　　　*

There'd been a moment when it had started to happen. Recovery, acceptance, whatever the word was they used to express when loss stops being unbearable and starts simply to be. I'd been walking along the clifftop, past Perivolos—I'd dropped by Ingrid's lodgings but she had not been home—and something made me continue up to the church on the hill beyond. Aghios Vasileios, it was called, St Basil's. It was a perfect spot. From here you could look back down across Oia and far beyond; beyond the volcano, beyond Santorini altogether, towards the distant islands whose bodies broke the endlessness of the sea.

It was afternoon and the sky was quite beautiful, the cloud drawn fat-over-lean in long textured streaks. It was not the sky I stared at, however, but the sea; here, it was always the sea. And the longer I looked at its billions of droplets of light, the clearer it was to me that these islands were nothing but accidental miracles, clinging on against death—death from the sea or from somewhere deep inside themselves. And when I understood that, I also understood that Emma had gone, that she and I and Oliver, all of us, had never stood a chance in the first place. We were defenceless, lucky to tip this side of the abyss for as long as we did.

*   *   *

Ingrid, like Eleni, owed her livelihood to the tourists while at the same time being perpetually maddened by them. She was particularly scornful of her customers at the café, the way they always wanted Greek salad without the olives or the capers or the Feta. 'Greek salad, hold the Greek! Why don't they just stay home in Minnesota?' Invariably she was asked to take pictures of happy couples in front of the view when she was

153

supposed to be inside frothing milk or settling bills. There were always new cameras involved, which caused delays, and once, when one failed to wind on properly, its owner even implied that Ingrid had broken the thing. 'The photos, all they care about is the fucking photos! How about enjoying the view without having a plastic box stuck to your face!'

Again, I thought I understood differently. For most of these crazed snappers Oia was just another pretty place to pass through and try not to mispronounce. The photograph was the only thing that ensured it would never quite be forgotten. Ten years from now it might spark a sensation, a flicker from the dark, and for a tiny moment its owner could feel exactly as he had when he had been there. I'd forgotten all about that, people would say. It takes me right back. Photographs were a kind of wonder drug for the memory. I thought of my pictures of Emma, so precious, more precious still for the scores of other images they pulled from my memory, each a different shape, like charms on a chain.

But Ingrid, like Eleni, needed appeasing. 'I know what you mean,' I told her, visiting her at work just after the lunchtime rush. 'Imagine all those photographs stuffed full of other people pointing cameras. It's very post-modern when you think about it. I prefer the old pictures, from before all this, the black-and-white ones.' I thought of the images in the book Eleni had shown me, before the earthquake had reduced the village to rubble.

'We should get hold of some of those old photographs and sell them,' Ingrid said. 'Then at least we know the poor sods are taking home something real. *You* know about photos, don't you, Rach, from your other life?'

My other life. This was how she'd come to refer to my past, the details of which I continued to guard. 'Other' life, a subtle variation of the 'old' she used when describing her own history, and an astute one too, for London *did* live on for me in a parallel way, in a way that Melbourne did not for her. Sometimes I envied her the simplicity of her clean break.

'But we'll need money, I suppose,' she murmured, half to herself.

'I have a bit of money,' I said, and she looked up, serious-eyed.

'But I don't.' She dipped into her pocket and displayed her morning's tips in a smeared palm, Oia's own Oliver Twist.

I grinned at her. 'It doesn't matter. You know what? I think it's a really good idea. As you say, no one else is selling old photos, so why not us? How about we own the business fifty-fifty and if we ever sell it, I'll get my investment back. Easier than trying to apply for a local bank loan.'

Oliver would have had a coronary to hear so casual an offer ('An Aussie, Rachel? No better than a tinker!'). Indeed, more caution might have been exercised by kids swapping marbles in the playground. But it felt right, it felt like the way business had always been done here, at least before the cruise ships and the tarting up of houses by out-of-town investors who'd never bothered to step inside. Eleni would approve, I was certain, and so would Mr Thessaloniki.

'You really mean it, don't you?' Ingrid cried.

'This is amazing! Our own shop!'

'Yes, it could be sort of a gallery too.' To my surprise, a picture of the interior was already fully formed in my mind: a clean airy space with black-and-white pictures displayed on easels, the only colours the changing shades of the sea through a wall of glass.

Ingrid looked down at her apron and picked at a fibre of green glued to the fabric. 'Oh my God, I can't believe I might not have to smell of spinach any more!'

I smiled. 'I think we'd better see if there's anything out there to sell before we go quite that far.'

Chapter 17

We were undeniably 'separated' now, Oliver and I, but divorce was still not mentioned in his letters, nor any deadline or ultimatum that might bring to an end his period of 'waiting' for me. Instead, his news was of his family, his work and of the house, as though I were away on an extended business trip and he thought I might be homesick for the detail of everyday life:

> The burglar alarm went off again and the police took over an hour to contact me . . .
> I attended the annual Stiles-Gray charity dinner, but did not bid . . .
> Gwen and family plan a sailing holiday in Turkey this summer . . .

I was reminded of a pen-pal craze in my childhood, which to my mother's bemusement brought letters to me almost daily from Delhi and Mexico City and Hong Kong, strange, dry little commentaries filled with non sequiturs, written as though part of an English language assignment or at the behest of a third party: 'Today my guinea pig demised. Moreover, I have seen an excellent film.' These clipped little snippets, they hardly sounded like Oliver's voice at all. But I couldn't be sure I even remembered it properly, lost as it had so often been in messages passed on by Vanessa, or silenced by the atmosphere we'd allowed to sink into the space between us.

I missed him, sometimes, in a way. In the early days, before Emma, we'd travelled well together. I wondered what he would make of this place, where in different circumstances we might just as easily have come together on holiday, choosing one of those costly hotels with the Caldera view. Not that he was one to enthuse over views; pretty, he might say, a decent enough day trip. He'd soon twig that most of the food here was a rung or two below that served in the better tavernas of Charlotte Street or that place on Regent's Park Road we used to like. And the wine? Improved, yes, he might allow that. Plentiful, at least.

*   *   *

Eleni loved books. She had brought boxes of them with her when, after falling in love with Anatole, she moved from the mainland to join him in Santorini in the late 1970s. Following two decades of neglect, the island was just starting to get back

157

on its feet, thanks to a state sponsorship programme. Over two thousand homes had been razed in the earthquake or earmarked for demolition and the couple settled in one of the few *kapetanospita* that had survived relatively intact. They lived in chaos, with two young sons to raise, a huge building to renovate and an improvised business that incorporated B&B, a bar run from the kitchen and even, for a while, a disco. In their small community skills were exchanged as readily as currency, and Anatole, a trained stonemason, was often busy with other properties in exchange for the furniture and other essentials needed for his own guest rooms. Consequently, the family's own sleeping quarters—three rooms on the upper floor—were the last to be renovated and this became the subject of much argument. Anatole complained that Eleni's piles of books were getting in the way and he would move them into storage in one of the outhouses, only to find them returned, dustier than ever, to their original spot. And so it went on until, finally, they'd fallen out properly over it and Eleni packed up and took the children to visit friends in Crete and cool off. When she came back she found her husband had swapped two weeks of his own labour for a beautiful dark-wood cabinet to store the books in, with glass doors to keep the dust off them. That was the beginning of the Ilias library and, since then, no publication about the Cyclades had been issued without Eleni ordering a copy for her collection.

Now, as Ingrid continued to serve her coffees and take her customers' effing holiday snaps for them, I was granted access to Eleni's beloved hoard. I spent several long days poring over the illustrations until I had a reasonable idea of what imagery was known to exist. First, there were the celebrated shots by well-known photographers such as Nelly's (Elli Souyioultzoglou-Seraidari), who had first visited the island in the 1920s. The originals were held in archives in Athens or cities in Germany or France. At the other end of the spectrum were those handful of shots I recognised from the stacks of reproductions available in every shop in Oia, even at the supermarket checkouts: the Goulas when it had still stood intact, solid and square, with the church of the Virgin Platsani behind; views of Ammoudi from the water; the volcano with its thick plume rising into the sky. These, typically, had been taken by sailors and travellers and any copyright information invariably included a mainland or foreign address.

I made pages and pages of notes. My plan was to contact all of the archives and copyright holders listed in the books and ask if they might be willing to let us produce and sell prints. The Ilias had a computer and fax machine in the office and again Eleni offered her facilities to me to use as my own. As the responses trickled in, with details of fees (prohibitive) and time frames (slow, even for someone who hardly knew which month she was in), I became increasingly convinced that the only way this venture was going to work was with local help, the old Oian way, without the involvement of Athens and the smart photography institutes beyond. Agreeing, Eleni translated notices to put up around the village asking locals for information of photography pre-1950s and to submit any unwanted pictures of their own for valuation. We'd either offer purchase fees outright or act as a

159

gallery, taking a percentage of the profit made from sales.

Meanwhile, Ingrid and I searched the local shops and markets. One of the antiques places on the main street had a couple of portraits of women and families in traditional dress, but, not knowing our mission, the assistant confessed they'd been sourced in Athens. Further trawls of Fira and the other tourist hotspots of Perissa, Kamari and Pyrgos turned up local finds, though barely enough to stock a starter portfolio, much less a shop.

'Y'know, I wonder if Nikos could help,' Ingrid said one evening when I reported my day's progress. We'd got into the habit of a daily debrief over coffee and visanto.

'Who's Nikos?'

'Oh, a guy I knew last summer in Fira. I went to his family's house once and they had these great black-and-white photos on the wall, loads of them. They were definitely old, you could tell by the funny clothes.'

'Can you call him?'

'Sure. I'm just trying to remember if he was the one who was getting married . . .'

I rolled my eyes. 'Yes, we don't want to find ourselves selling your ex-lover's wedding photos, do we?'

'Ha, ha.' Ingrid rolled her eyes. 'Y'know, Rachel, I can't wait for *you* to get back in the saddle . . .'

'Ingrid, please, I hate that phrase. It makes me think of the mules.'

'Well, we'll just have to work on that.'

Avoiding her grin, I gathered up our postcards into a neat pile, head low, dumbstruck with sadness. Behind me, oblivious to my altered mood, Ingrid added, 'You can't be alone for ever, you know.'

*   *   *

Though I had withdrawn from the notion of a private life and had found in Oia the perfect couples' paradise in which to pursue my abstinence, Ingrid had enthusiasm for two. Typically, by early summer she had sifted through most of the more attractive waiters in range, matching, or simply sitting out, their long shifts in the restaurants before joining them at the Epik, a noisy bar in the Lotza neighbourhood that was the established meeting point for staff and locals after the tourists had gone to bed.

This being Greece, there were few contenders without a wife or girlfriend 'back home', in Athens perhaps, or, more riskily, Fira. Lone male holidaymakers, meanwhile, were a rarity in a resort full of honeymooners, but Ingrid knew where to find them too, when they did slip the net: in the cheaper hotels on the other side of town, located just minutes by foot from the five-star villas but, without the view, available for a tenth of the price. These anomalies might be German, British, Dutch, American; students with a gap year to fill; backpackers with islands to tick off their list; office workers here for their week in the sun; drifters with no job to take them home. Every so often, beguiled by Ingrid, one would extend his stay in Oia by a week or so, moving out of his tourist accommodation and into her rooms up at Perivolos, and she'd enjoy the temporary illusion of a shared life.

During such interludes she would drop by my house on her lunch break to tell me about her man of the moment. Delivering me a portion of something she'd pilfered from work, she'd watch me eat while she talked.

'I keep telling you I'm a cliché,' she said on one occasion. 'Obviously I'm searching for love, thanks to my history of parental neglect, and I mistake sex for love.'

I smiled, wondering what she'd been reading this week. 'It's an easy mistake to make,' I agreed. 'Remember the American?'

'Oh, don't remind me, please!'

'And the Dutch guy . . .'

Ian, the American, had pronounced his name 'Eye-un', and wore an expression of such pinched fluster that I suspected him of not being quite truthful about his past (it took one to know one, perhaps), while Karel, the Dutch guy, who had fair hair cut full over his ears like headphones, had been remarkable for responding, 'Ya, for sure' to any query set before him. After about five minutes I learned to avoid putting questions that required a yes or no answer, but even one such as 'How long are you staying in Greece?' would bring the answer, 'Ya, I'll stay for the summer, for sure,' as Ingrid chortled openly beside him.

I decided not to mention Phil. He was a Brit, a south Londoner, travelling around the islands using redundancy money from his last sales job. Before introducing us, Ingrid had mentioned only his good looks and deep tan, undeniable on both counts, though for me the sight of glowing blue eyes in a skin of chestnut leather was oddly

162

disarming. As pleasantries progressed, it became clear that she had failed to mention his most marked characteristic: a verbal tic that involved the placement of the word 'fucking' between components of any phrase or compound noun (Santa-fucking-rini, about-fucking-time, and so on).

'Rachel's from London too,' Ingrid told him.

'Oh yeah, where yuh from?'

'I used to live in Swiss Cottage, Belsize Park way.'

'North-fucking-London, never go up there m'self.'

'Nor do I, any more.'

'Pretty fuckin' pricey up there.'

Such coarseness bothered me little per se (I couldn't think of any better f-words—forsaken, perhaps), but nor did his attitude spell 'life partner', and this, I sensed, was what Ingrid was actually seeking and was never going to find among this tourist flotsam. I could only hope that our new business might be enough of a distraction for her to forget these characters altogether.

Just once, when it emerged that she had become involved with a man on his honeymoon, did I allow disapproval to surface. 'Oh, Ingrid! How could you?'

'What? If he's willing to sleep with someone else so soon then he's not good enough for her.'

'Doesn't that make him not good enough for *you*, either?'

'I'm not the one daft enough to marry the guy, am I? Anyway, it was just a one-off, she only had the one afternoon of beauty treatments booked. They'll be all loved up for the rest of the trip, don't

163

worry.'

I gave up. The crime was essentially the man's, not hers, and I was in no position to judge. It wasn't as if in that 'other' life of mine I hadn't fallen short too.

*   *   *

The morning Palmer appeared for his second update in person, I had woken with my heart racing and innards flipping. I'd been dreaming of Cat, Daisy and Emma. They were swimming in the big pool in Swiss Cottage, where the water had taken on the charcoal-dark depths of the Caldera, and I had watched helplessly from the diving board as each struggled in agonising turn to stay afloat. 'Get off,' Emma shouted, 'get off!', over and over, and no one seemed to hear her cries except me, and all I could do was produce screams of my own, 'But I can't swim . . .'

In fact, Palmer's news *was* of a physical accident, though nothing to do with swimming: Cat had broken her wrist. She had fallen off some kind of swing contraption in the local park, one that, frankly, I'd always thought unsuitable for a children's playground and rather something you'd find on an outward-bound or army training course.

'Which arm was it?' I asked.

'Her right arm.'

She was left-handed, Cat; she and Emma had bumped elbows sometimes when sitting together to do their colouring in.

'She'll have to wear a cast for a few weeks, but she's absolutely fine. Looks as happy as Larry in the pictures. I've got them here for you.'

164

The photos showed a beaming Cat with a pink plaster cast covered in scribbles. 'Her schoolwork shouldn't suffer. A bit of home tutoring over the summer should get her back up to speed.' Palmer's voice, low and a little gravelly, had a soothing quality that seemed to work directly on my nerves.

'I'm glad she didn't feel too much pain.'

'Yes, as I said, they got her to A&E straight away and gave her painkillers. They usually make X-ray fun for kids, give them soft toys to cuddle and that sort of thing.'

I took the opportunity to ask about his investigation methods and he told me that in his 'game' surveillance was often nothing more sophisticated than parking his car (a 'blend-in' model, as he described it) on the street across the road from the property in question, facing the other way so that observation could be done in the rear-view. 'Much more discreet, and it eliminates any possibility of eye contact.'

'You are using a woman, as I asked?'

'Yes, of course.' A female associate had befriended a teacher at Moss Hamlet and it was she, therefore, and not he who lurked by school gates and back doors. 'They'll be applying to secondary schools before we know it, so we'll need to set about infiltrating that next.' He laughed. 'I'm making myself sound like an FBI agent or something, aren't I? It's honestly nothing like it, much more mundane.'

I smiled, surprised by how pleased I was to see him again. 'I may be opening a shop here soon,' I said. 'With my friend Ingrid. So next time you come there might even be something to sell you.' *Next time.* Nothing more than a figure of speech, but he didn't deny that there would be one.

'I've got to hand it to you, y'know,' he said, looking at the potted flowers and rainbow-coloured rugs on my terrace, 'this is a bloody good place to hide.'

I looked at him, surprised. 'I'm not *hiding*, Palmer. I came here because I couldn't stay where I was.' I paused. 'After Emma.'

He nodded.

'I'm based here now, I'm planning to work here, as I've just said. I've got no reason to *hide*.'

'OK,' he said, quickly. 'Perhaps that's just the way my mind works. I expect people to have more secrets than they do. Occupational hazard, I suppose.'

But he'd been taken aback by my vehemence, I could tell, and I hastened to make amends. 'Tell me then,' I said, smiling, 'why's it such a good place to hide?'

His eyes moved to the Caldera. 'I don't know, it's an unusual spot here, that's all I mean. Kind of untouched. It doesn't get better than this.'

'I don't know about untouched. Some people think it's completely overrun.' On cue, a procession of mules clattered by for the path to Armeni, just across the bay from my house, the muleteer riding side-saddle as he guided their tightly zigzagged progress downward.

Palmer grinned. 'Compared to London, though, it's pretty sleepy.'

'That's true. No mules there.'

He fell silent, evidently reluctant to argue. He was an odd fish, the type I'd paid little attention to in my previous life, but there was also something instantly familiar about him; even as we fumbled

166

our way around each other's conversation, we had an affinity of some sort. I wondered if it was to do with Emma, to do with his knowing. 'I couldn't stay where I was . . . after Emma.' Well, that was more than I'd ever been able to confess to Ingrid or Eleni. Perhaps he was right about secrets, after all.

'How are your children?' I asked him. 'Did you say you had a boy and a girl?'

He nodded. 'Matt and Zoë.'

'How old are they?'

'Matt will be fifteen in September. Zoë's about to turn thirteen.'

'You started a family young, then?'

'Yes, fairly. Makes you grow up in a bit of a hurry. They wouldn't consider having kids at the age their mother and I did, not if you paid them.'

'I was twenty-six,' I said. 'It seemed right to me, but I know some people thought I was a bit young. My mother-in-law said we were crazy to give up our lives. That was the phrase she used.'

'Funny way to think,' he said. He told me he didn't see as much of the children as he would have liked for they lived with their mother an hour away from his own home in east London.

'What's her name, your ex-wife?'

'Tracey.'

And he said it so factually, so emotionlessly, his face perfectly impassive, that I was overcome with dejection. In the past I'd been so good at picturing lives for people I hardly knew, even passers-by, concocting elaborate histories for them and imagining the objects and furnishings in their homes. But hard as I tried, I couldn't place him, not in a family, a house, a context. All I could imagine was him sitting in his car, parked the wrong way round in a stranger's street.

'Which area do you live in?' I asked.

'Wanstead.'

'And you live alone? Do you have a garden?'

He gave a short laugh of surprise. 'Er, yes, I do. I've become quite green-fingered, as it happens.'

'That's good.' Not his marital home, I thought, with the swing in the garden, a sandpit from when the kids were young; she'd got that, as it usually went in family separations.

He watched me with amusement. 'Anything else you'd like to know about me while you're at it?' And he readjusted his posture with some care, as though about to submit himself to the scrutiny of a body-language specialist. He was humouring me.

'What do you do, when you're not working?' I asked, seriously. 'You seem so . . . dedicated.'

'I don't know, what everyone else does, I suppose.' He caught himself, remembering, I sensed, that I could no longer be counted among 'everyone', I no longer had the same references. But it had taken a moment, I saw, which meant that my tragedy must no longer be so visible in my face. 'I see the kids, of course, I watch TV. In the summer I might go to the cricket. I go for a drink with mates . . .'

'And is there anyone new on the scene?'

He shrugged. 'Off and on.'

I was getting close to prying now. It crossed my mind that I might be sizing him up for Ingrid, but that was crazy; I'd never before linked the two of them in my thoughts. In any case, the last thing she needed was a man for whom subterfuge was a profession.

168

I asked after the friend in Naxos, but didn't press when he gave me his 'you don't want to know' look. Of my personal situation, my separation from Oliver, my plans, he asked me nothing. It hardly mattered, I supposed. What I was was what he saw in front of him. And besides, if he had any more questions, he of all people would know where to look for the answers.

*   *   *

Later, I looked at the picture of Cat with her bandaged wrist—a symbol, somehow, of innocence and vulnerability—and realised that she would be, at this very moment, as pampered as any patient could hope to be. Propped in front of the TV, demanding fizzy drinks and furry blankets from her armchair HQ. Mariel had probably taken time off work—her practice manager was more understanding about such things than most—or, if not, would have recruited her mother to mind her daughter and supply her with a steady stream of treats.

I wished with all there was of my heart that I could do something to comfort her too, but there was little practical use I could be here in Oia. What would I do if I were still there, I wondered; her godmother, her parents' friend, the mother of the girl who'd once been her best friend? I'd read stories aloud and take her to the cinema, careful to protect her arm from the jogs of other people as they squeezed in and out of their rows. I'd ruffle her hair and feed her cocoa with whipped cream and marshmallows. Tell her she would heal, she just needed to be patient, to imagine how

169

wonderful it was going to feel to swim and swing and climb again, having for so long had activities restricted. It would be like the first time, except she'd know just how to do it. I longed to do and say those things, and Palmer was hardly going to be able to do and say them for me. I hoped, instead, that Oliver might mention the news in his next letter, or better still include a note from Mariel, which would at least allow me to send a card and gift to the patient. All I could do in the meantime was instruct Palmer to send letters of complaint to the local council about that dangerous playground equipment, as many as his office could produce.

Mariel must wonder what was next, I thought. Did she and Toby look at each other and say, 'First the crash, the leg injury, and now this!' And after all those babyhood ailments too. Then they'd remember and, feeling guilty, say, 'But she's alive, that's the important thing. What Rachel wouldn't give for a child with a fractured wrist.'

Chapter 18

As a girl dressed in sequined mini-skirt and an England football shirt leaned over a wall and vomited right in front of me, I decided that there was nothing like a trip to Fira to make one see how authentic Oia had remained, whatever Eleni's laments. I'd been to the capital a handful of times on errands, only once lingering long enough to explore the old clifftop quarter of shops and bars. Then, I'd made a slow circuit of the main street, clotted almost to a standstill with tourists and the shop staff who competed for their cash, and headed straight for the taxi rank.

This morning, Ingrid needed to stop by the bank, so I set off into the hub on my own. Jostled in the narrow street by clubbers, including the girl still divesting herself of a night's worth of cocktails, I felt scarcely kindlier towards the place than that first time. It was nine o'clock in the morning, for God's sake. Who *were* these people?

Nikos's family business was easy enough to find, at least, a typically garish emporium in the passages behind the cable-car station. The elderly man behind the counter was clearly not Nikos—Ingrid's taste, while reasonably inclusive, did not, I felt sure, run to seventy-year-olds with hairy ears and jaundice-yellow fingernails—so I wandered around the shop as a regular tourist, prodding the dolls and the pumice stones and the unidentifiable musical instruments, an oddball assortment of objects, linked only by the possibility that some last-minute shopper might pick one up as an afterthought for the colleague or friend they'd left behind at home. There were the usual carousels of postcards, but the only photographs on display were those in a brown grocery box half hidden in the corner between the pistachios and the bars of olive-oil soap. Some were encased in plastic, snagged and dusty, others mounted on scuffed yellowing cardboard. The foremost picture was instantly familiar: Fira from the water, before the cable car linked the town to the bay below—this was a stock image sold all over the island, available as a print just as cheaply in Oia and popular as a postcard too.

171

I nodded towards the man behind the counter before squatting in front of the box and idly flicking through. 'Arrival at Ammoudi, 1950s', 'Goulas, 1951', 'Nea Kameni, 1929'—again, the same images we'd seen in a dozen supermarts. What a shame. The ones Ingrid had seen must have been family portraits, perhaps shot recently in a sentimental sepia style. There was a studio in Fira that specialised in just that sort of thing. I would need to be careful to hide my disappointment when she arrived; she was full of enthusiasm for our new venture.

And then I caught my breath. Just five pictures in was one I knew I'd never seen before, a simple view of a *kapetanospito* in Oia, with its elegant row of tall windows and wrought-iron railings. Even the paper was unfamiliar, with a fibrous, matt consistency that recalled much earlier tastes than the glossy standards I was used to handling. Exhaling, I flipped to the next: a stark, Cubist composition of steps and roofs, deep angles of shadow against white stretches of sunlight; and the next: children playing ball in a narrow passageway, unaware, or perhaps forgetful, of the camera's presence. And they only got better: a wonderful tableau of an outdoor meal at the water's edge, it looked like it might be Armeni; schooners stacked several deep in the harbour, figures crowding the shore, preparing perhaps to load the season's wine; a dark gorge, the patterning of the rockface picked out so baldly in monochrome; the empty coastline at Kamari, long before it featured on the reps' itineraries; the labyrinth of Pyrgos's passageways below a sky of swirling cloud . . .

Over the last weeks I'd examined hundreds of

images, yet I'd seen none of these before. In each, Santorini was a different place from the one that lay outside the shop's door. How on earth did they come to be here, buried beneath the cookery books and the weird puppets in shiny clothes that crackled when you touched them? Not one was signed and, where marked, the prices varied randomly from one to the next.

'Rach!' Ingrid was by my side. 'Sorry to take so long, there was a terrible queue. You know what they're like. *So* slow. How are you getting on? Anything decent?'

I wondered if she could hear the roar in my ears. 'Look at these, Ingrid, they're amazing! I think they must have been taken with a thirty-five millimetre camera, a Leica.'

'Is that good?'

'It means the photographer must have been fairly progressive. And talented too, I'd say.'

'What, you mean they're all by the same guy?'

'I think so. They have the same sort of feel.'

She picked one up at random, a street scene; the caption said simply 'Oia'. 'I don't recognise that church, do you?'

'It's St George's. Destroyed in the earthquake. Quite a few were.' I was surprised how much I'd absorbed in my reading, how familiar to me this earlier Santorini was from the books I'd studied in Eleni's library.

I caught the old man's eye. 'Who took these pictures, do you know?'

A shrug, a cigarette lit and drawn on between dry lips. I tried not to think about the effects of years of tobacco smoke on unprotected photographic paper.

'Where are the negatives?'

Shrug, suck, stare. Infinitesimal narrowing of the eyes.

'I don't think he speaks English,' Ingrid said, amused.

'We'd like to buy them all,' I announced boldly.

Now her smile was less indulgent. 'Hey, slow down. I think I'd better ask for Nikos and get him to translate.' She spoke to the man in Greek and he replied in such curt, reluctant mumbles I wouldn't have been able to identify the language, much less the meaning. Finally, Ingrid understood enough to learn that Nikos was picking up stock from the other side of town and wouldn't be back for an hour or so.

'Let's get a drink while we wait.' She motioned to a coffee bar across the street. 'Come on.'

'Do we have to? Can't we wait here?' But Ingrid took my arm, called *adio* to the old man, and a minute later I was stirring a cappuccino in perfect rhythm with the beat of my nerves. 'Ingrid, what if someone slips in and buys them under our noses?'

'They're not going to,' she said. 'If they were worth anything they'd be long gone, wouldn't they?'

'It's not what they're worth that matters, it's just that they're so beautiful. We *have* to get them!'

'OK,' she said, patiently, 'but we are hoping to run a profitable business, aren't we, so we need to buy cheap. When we go back in, try not to show how much you want them.'

'But who knows how many more there've been, just stuffed in a drawer or left in someone's suitcase? Thank God you remembered seeing them!'

174

She grinned. 'I've never seen you this jumpy. Of course we'll get them, don't worry. I just think we'll get a better price if Nikos is involved. And we've still got other places to try here before we go back home.'

Ingrid was the only other expat I'd met who by 'home' meant Oia. And with her dark island tan, vivid cotton dresses bought from local markets and a natural grasp of the language, she *was* at home here. I, on the other hand, the one with native blood, had the facial bone structure but little else. Extraordinary that there were any Greek genes in my body at all, so wholly deaf was I to the language. I would try to make sense of tone and gesture instead, only to be amazed later when the actual subject was revealed.

At the sound of a deep voice singing what sounded like 'Ingrate! Ingrate!', all at once Ingrid was flying to her feet and I noticed the blush across her cheekbones as she embraced a tall, attractive man in his early twenties, broad shouldered and light footed, skin surprisingly pale. I realised this was, in fact, the mating call of a former love. *Ingrid*, that was what he was cooing, *Ingrid*.

'Rachel, this is Nikos. Nikos, meet Rachel, the one I told you about on the phone.'

'Nice to meet you.'

He looked me over, in that way some of the young locals had of assessing foreign women. Sex, money, or both? I could barely hide my impatience as they chatted about the work rotas of mutual acquaintances, before agreeing at last to be led the few steps back to the shop.

This time, a pair of squat wooden stools were

produced, then cigarettes. Ingrid took one, guiding Nikos's hand with hers as he offered her a light, and then the negotiations began. I listened dumbly. The English translation, when it came, was bewildering enough. The old man, it transpired, was Nikos's great-uncle Dimitris, while the photographer was his grandfather's cousin, also named Nikos. 'He took classes in Athens and apparently he had some kind of friendship with a photographer who came here in the thirties or forties. The guy emigrated to the United States and Nikos Senior lost interest and had no use for the pictures.'

I nodded. 'If we can find out who this teacher was, it could make them more valuable . . . ?'

Ingrid gave me a stern look. 'Hardly likely to be anyone well known if the family's flogging them off like this.'

'I don't know,' I said. 'I don't want to cheat anyone.'

Ingrid ignored this. 'Nikos, are these all you have? What about the ones I saw on the walls in your house?'

I gathered from Nikos's explanation in broken English that his family had held on to their favourites in their house. 'The portraits and stuff,' Ingrid said. 'I guess our man was pretty busy.'

I tried my best to look unbothered either way.

'Dimitris says they've been sitting in that box for years. The tourists only buy the volcano postcards and the cheap jewellery.'

I looked around. A group of young British girls were discussing their hangovers with the kind of pride one might expect to see in Olympic medallists:

176

'I know, it was so cool! Did you see her peeing on that roof?'

'Urgh, rancid. S'prob'ly still there.'

'D'you think the dogs would drink it?'

'Shut up, that's gross!'

'OK,' I said to Ingrid. 'I think they'd be more appreciated by the kind of people who'll buy from our shop.' *Our shop*, as though it already existed. We had yet to view a single premises.

She took over, hardly budging from an opening price well below what we'd agreed to spend per photograph, and, soon after, a bottle of whisky materialised and there came the clinking of glasses.

Afterwards, I waited outside in the shade, clutching the box to my body and trying to avoid the overtures of the sales assistants, first in Greek, then in German—Hey, lady, was I in need of something to make me even more *schön* than I already was? Some 'real' Minoan bangles, perhaps?

When Ingrid appeared she was breathless. 'Sorry, Rach, just catching up with Nikos. I'd forgotten how sexy he is. And he *isn't* married, just engaged! Isn't that great news? I've invited him to that music festival at the weekend. Hope he can come . . .'

But I couldn't think about Nikos's marital status or how he might be shoehorned into Ingrid's sexual calendar. 'You were amazing in there, Ingrid. Well done!'

'Better than you,' she agreed. 'You're way too nice. In future I'll just send you ahead to pick out the good stuff and I'll go on my own afterwards to do the actual buying.'

'I just want this business to be, well, ethical, I suppose.'

'What does that mean when it's at home?'

She dismissed my explanations with a snort. 'Of course it's ethical. Selling ignorant buffoons nice things when we could just as easily palm them off with junk?'

'Well, I think that takes care of our slogan,' I said, laughing.

As we sat side by side in the back of the taxi we lapsed into our own thoughts, Ingrid's of Nikos, perhaps, or the triumph of her first negotiation. Myself, I was content to feel some facsimile of excitement, of pleasure. I remembered the first time I'd travelled this Fira-Oia route, not long after my arrival in Santorini, when I could no longer put off a trip to the main bank. There'd been no exhilaration then. As the taxi had accelerated out of a corner, just feet from the cliff edge, I'd wondered if we might simply lose contact with the ground, sail forward, weightless for a second or two, before the nose of the vehicle dipped and plunged us into freefall. I'd felt nothing at all, nothing. How different from my instinct when Emma was alive: then, any journey taken without her, every small risk made me nervous. Seatbelts were secured, eyes and feet dutiful to the speedometer, safety demonstrations properly observed. I would have fought fire, breathed underwater, sprouted wings; I would have endured anything to return home to her.

*   *   *

Back at Callidora, we laid out Nikos's photographs

178

on the dining table and set about checking each one against the lists I had prepared from Eleni's books, a process that took several hours. Not one appeared. They were, as Nikos had said, originals, and without negatives this made them, to my mind, priceless. Though he'd been perfectly happy with the sum paid, I wrote to him confirming that we would credit the photographer and keep a record of each buyer. Eleni agreed to go through the pictures with us and help identify the streets and views we couldn't, so each could be given a caption. I wanted to show customers how the buildings pictured were used today, match up these simple grey houses with the holiday villas or cafés they'd become, make it more personal for the whistle-stop admirers with little time to do their own investigations.

Soon after our visit to Fira we heard from an elderly Santorinian, now living in Crete, who told us he had recently offered first pick of his modest photograph collection to the naval museum. Those that remained, mostly portraits, were for sale— and he had the negatives for at least half of them. We would be free to make multiple copies and sell these more cheaply, mounted and framed or print-only.

One picture was of a young woman with a deep hairline, strong nose and broad mouth. She was one of the few for whom our source couldn't give provenance; he couldn't be sure the woman was even Greek. She reminded me a little of my mother, and watching Eleni and Ingrid examine it together I sensed my game might be up. My father's fair colouring and blue eyes had thus far been a useful red herring in Santorini, but this

179

woman's dark hair was covered with a pale scarf, the shadows of her face slightly bleached from over-lighting. She looked like my mother, yes, but she also looked like me and, sure enough, the resemblance was quickly spotted.

'I haven't told you before,' I said, casually, 'but my mother's family are from Santorini, actually.'

'What?' Ingrid said, amazed. She put down the book she was holding and stepped towards me, eyes moving across my bare arms as though expecting to find a stamp on my skin to authenticate the claim. 'I thought you said she was from London.'

'She grew up there, but she was born here and lived here until she was about ten. They left after the earthquake.'

'How come you don't speak Greek?'

'I wasn't taught it. Mum was in a kind of denial, I think. I never went to Greek church or anything like that and we never came here, only once to Athens, before I was old enough to remember. My father was Church of England, and quite devout in his way. Maybe that was partly what attracted my mother to him. She was trying to get away from her own culture, I suppose, avoid any reminders. Her sister was killed in the earthquake, you see.'

'Killed in the earthquake? Here? That's terrible!' Ingrid cried and Eleni exclaimed in agreement. 'I don't get it, Rach. All this time! Why didn't you say anything before?'

I bit my lip until I felt pain. 'I don't know. Sometimes I forget all about it myself. I guess it just hasn't been the first thing on my mind.' How callous I sounded, how unnaturally lacking in curiosity about my own family. And how could that last remark possibly mean anything to them when I'd given no inkling as to what *was* foremost on my mind: Emma. Still I kept her from them. As far as I knew, they continued to believe I had left London to escape my unhappy marriage, and any attempts to extract details from me had been met with shrugs or remarks of the 'I'd rather just forget about it' variety. It occurred to me that the less I had offered the two of them the more generous they had been to me. Eleni had found me a home, fed me, made me a part of the community, and now she was putting all her office equipment and local contacts at my disposal too. As for Ingrid, how many times had she come to find me at Callidora with a carafe of wine, a slice of warm pie wrapped in a napkin, a dog-eared thriller she hoped I hadn't already read? She would have done anything for me, and yet I hadn't even let her know who I really was.

'I'm sorry, I've been foolish, I know . . .' I began, but to my surprise Ingrid just nodded and went back to her task, apparently willing to withdraw and say no more about it. She was reminding herself, perhaps, of the dangers of stirring up family history. There were plenty of memories of her own, I suspected, that she thought best kept tucked away.

Eleni looked again from the photograph to me and said, 'I have known this.'

'You mean you recognise this woman? You know of my family from the old days?' The thought frightened me; I wasn't ready for this.

'No,' Eleni said, 'I do not know this person. I came to Oia only when I have married Anatole. His family is in Fira.'

181

'You know the name, then? My mother's maiden name was Vlachos?'

'No.'

'I don't understand, then.'

She shrugged. 'A swallow can tell another swallow.'

I stared. 'Is that some kind of Greek proverb?'

Ingrid raised an eyebrow. 'I think it might be some kind of Eleni proverb.'

Grateful of the light relief, she and I laughed together.

'One of the villagers might know this woman,' Eleni said, still serious. 'When the shop is open perhaps we will see.'

I nodded, ashamed to have to leave the two of them with so poor an explanation, and to have lied too, for my mother *had* been on my mind. Of course she had, and would have been even if the local faces hadn't reminded me sometimes of hers. More unexpectedly still, for I had never realised she had much of an accent, I'd begun to recognise the inflections of Mum's speech in Eleni's and in some of the other women's. She'd been young when the earthquake had struck and the village evacuated, but she'd retained the local rhythms into adulthood. And the memories, she'd retained those too, surely: the boats, the mules and their bells, the games in the main square, all the things I'd come to discover for myself.

I thought now of what she had said to me that last day in London: 'You've lost your daughter, don't make me lose mine.' To the outward observer it might have the flavour of manipulation, melodrama, but to me it was a rare expression of feeling, real feeling, from a mother I'd only

182

engaged with properly since I'd become one myself. And now that I no longer was, was I trying to disengage?

Don't make me lose mine.

It was almost two years since I'd been in London and stood at the door of her house. I'd never even told her I'd been there: in our relationship, a knock on the door counted only if it were answered. If she really couldn't come to Oia, I knew I would need to go to her.

Chapter 19

Dear Rachel,

I hope you are well and enjoying better weather than we are getting here. Every day is grey. Even the indomitable Vanessa claims she suffers from Seasonal Affective Disorder and I know better than to dispute anything she says!

I will be spending Christmas with Gwen and family. I understand the boys are getting excited about the go-kart they are to be given . . .

Still Oliver's letters came, with their drip feed of inconsequential snippets. The thread between us was as slight as spider's silk, but it was a thread I was not yet ready to break.

I wrote back promptly, told him a little about the new business. Like him, I did not mention Emma or the fact that this would be our third Christmas without her. I did not mention that for me, too, every day was grey.

*   *   *

My father died at Christmas time and his passing discoloured the season for my mother for ever. The cards, the tinsel, the presents under the tree, all came with black edges from that year on. One could arrive at her house buoyed with seasonal goodwill and leave, an hour later, drained of all hope.

It was not until the third anniversary that I allowed myself to be persuaded to escape the seasonal mourning. Oliver's sister Gwen and her husband were renting a chalet in Zermatt with friends of theirs and she invited us to join them. My mother was frostier than the Matterhorn the next time we met. For all it had been my father who'd striven to teach me religious faith, she was hands down the more pious. Suddenly I couldn't ring her to say hello without being made to feel like Judas. But guilty though I was of neglecting our shared remembrance, I was liberated too, especially when I saw the holiday snaps of myself beaming on chairlifts and laughing into my fondue. I'd forgotten I could look so alive. I thought Dad would have preferred us to remember him with joy, and I told Mum so.

She pressed her lips into a thin, bloodless line. 'There are different kinds of joy.'

As far as she was concerned, none quite as attractive as misery, it seemed to me. I didn't like the sense, every time I broke into a smile, that I was being judged and found wanting by the one person whose approval should surely have been my right. She'd never been a demonstrative mother, the kisses-and-cuddles kind I'd seen at my friends' front doors, but now that I was an adult and planning a family of my own I found her coldness, her pessimism less forgivable. Why dwell so determinedly on disaster? Yes, her sister had died in frightening circumstances, but Mum had been young enough to pick herself up and rediscover happiness, surely? And Dad, well, we'd been prepared for that, we'd had so much time to say goodbye, our mourning had been half done by the time he died.

The truth was that with him gone our common purpose had collapsed. Though there was no specific incident to divide us, no landmark row, there was ongoing hostility. Distance was the better word. And the way I saw it, it was *she* who had created this distance between us. I found myself visiting her less and inviting her more, knowing how probable it was that she would decline, which would make it her fault, technically, and not mine when months rolled by and we still hadn't managed to meet. I told myself it wasn't deliberate—I was busy with my new marriage, my new house—and in any case, any willingness of mine to join in such a cold, wordless battle could only be the result of her conditioning of me. *She* had taught *me* about human relationships, not the other way around.

Emma was our saviour. Everything shifted with her arrival. She adored my mother as I should have done, as I must once have, and, in her turn, my mother offered her granddaughter all the unconditional generosity I felt had been kept from me. While Rosemary was the more glamorous of

Emma's grandmothers, she was also the natural dragon, with her sudden bursts of laughter and hot, gin-vapour breath. My mother was the easy, comfortable one, the one with the milky drinks and colouring books, the smiley one. In the full eighteen-year term of my own childhood I had never seen my mother smile so much as she did in a few hours with Emma.

Now there was no question of lesser contact. We met regularly, went on holidays together and my new insights into how she had once cared for me made me appreciate her in an entirely different way. Only one time, later, did she refer to the earlier period of difficulty.

'I know you were always closer to your father. You must miss him.'

'We both do,' I said. I flushed with shame that I had ever sought to marginalise her. She was only in her fifties but she was both an orphan and a widow. I was her only child, her only anyone, and yet how easily, without Emma, I'd been willing to disown her.

She never once mentioned earthquakes to Emma.

*   *   *

London, December twenty-third. The reflections of Christmas lights dissolved into the puddles like dabs of cadmium yellow into a wash of brown. The smell alone stirred something in me: a complicated, big-city smell of traffic fumes trapped in winter clothing, of a thousand restaurant doorways gushing savoury heat into the air, and traces, barely there, of party fragrances on showered skin. It was familiar in the same way the smell of a roast lamb used to be on a Sunday. It made me happy to be there at that moment, at that time, no matter what had come before. Even so, I couldn't make up my mind whether I'd done the right thing coming back.

My mother had made efforts to welcome me, that was evident from the moment I stepped through the door and saw the bowls of clementines and dishes of nuts, the proper tree and the cards arranged on the mantelpiece.

'Mum, you've made it lovely in here!'

'Yes, it is nice. Festive.' She looked as if she might have been crying. I had known that it would be hardest at this time of year. Christmas, anniversary of my father's death but also Emma's favourite time, every child's favourite. Now I glimpsed the agony behind each small decision: the pink and silver baubles Emma had chosen for her three years ago or the new ones with no memories attached beyond those of the length of the queue in the shop where she'd bought them two Saturdays ago? Or maybe the new ones now reminded her of the sad thoughts she'd had as she stood in that queue and wondered if she could survive all of this.

'I'm sorry it's taken me so long to come back and visit, Mum. I needed to focus on something new, I suppose.'

She nodded. 'You'll want to catch up on sleep after that long journey.' She spoke as though I'd flown non-stop from Australia. Perhaps that was how she had been justifying my absence for me all this time, by telling herself it was simply too complicated a journey for me to manage.

'I feel fine, actually.'

'Shall I make us some tea?'

'Yes, please. It doesn't taste the same in . . . away, does it? Look, I've brought some . . . walnut cake . . .' I broke off doubtfully. I'd been going to use the Greek word, *karithopita*, having begun to train myself to include Greek vocabulary where I could, but, as Mum regarded the cake with horror, I saw that I was going to have to forget all that for the moment. Was this how it was going to be, then? Was it going to be possible for me to stay for the whole week that I'd planned without crunching the eggshells underfoot?

But after the initial hiccup it was clear that the practicalities of the reunion were going to be abundant enough to distract us. Would the single bed in my old room be comfortable enough? The timer on the boiler had been reset to give more hot water, so I should feel free to have a bath whenever I liked. She didn't have a whole bird for Christmas Day, what with it being just the two of us, but a joint, ready stuffed, and she'd got all the trimmings. There were chocolate-covered almonds too, though she could never remember whether I liked them or not. And so on. I added my own few presents to the small pile under the tree, going through the motions of squeezing those with my name on the tag. One, I noticed, had no tag at all. For Emma maybe, a way of including our absent angel.

Soon I felt confident enough to broach a subject I'd been fretting about since boarding my flight that morning. 'Mum, I hope you don't mind, but I just want to get one thing straight from the start.'

She looked surprised. 'Yes, all right.'

'I don't want you to tell Oliver I'm back.'

'Oliver? You mean he doesn't know?'

'No,' I said firmly, 'I've come to spend time with *you*, not him.'

She hesitated. 'Yes, of course.'

I saw my mistake at once, as I so often had when warning Emma of some hazard or other. All I'd succeeded in doing was giving her the idea in the first place.

I would need to be on my guard for the remainder of my time here.

*   *   *

Christmas 1993, ten years after Dad's death. We'd had no conception—how could we?—that it would be Emma's last. Oliver and I had established the custom of giving her a Big Present, with an eye to its being passed down through the generations (for we imagined, of course, that we'd be grandparents one day): a rocking horse, a doll's house, a special jewellery box. That time I wanted to get her a painting. I searched the little galleries in the streets around the British Museum, deliberated over the subject (something that would please her now or something she could enjoy as an adult?) and the frame (painted milky pink or classic polished wood?). I settled on a Cornish boat scene, the style direct and naïve, appealing both to children and adults. Emma loved the water, was a good swimmer, and had been sailing with her cousins a few times.

Oliver said the picture was lovely but we should get her a new bike as well, since that topped the list of requests in her letter to Father Christmas.

We both knew she would receive everything on her list, and then some. I asked her what she liked about Christmas Day, besides the presents, of course. Breakfast in bed, she said, when Daddy makes bacon sandwiches for all of us. 'Not just you and me, Mum, *Daddy* as well.' I'd felt guilty, then, she was talking like the child of separated parents, as though we didn't all live under the same roof. I persuaded Oliver that we should postpone the grandparents' arrival until Boxing Day, and for a whole day it was just the three of us. We set the timer on the camera and took a picture of ourselves, Emma in her fur-trimmed elf's costume, Oliver and I in finery chosen for each other and unwrapped that very morning. She kept the picture on the mantelpiece in her bedroom, next to the new painting and a wooden jigsaw that spelled her name.

*   *   *

I hadn't spent so much time alone with my mother since I was a child and, Oliver besides, there were difficult subjects to curdle every conversation. Thinking it silly to avoid the subject of Oia altogether, I showed her maps, pointing out the routes I walked to Ammoudi, to Armeni, down the coastal path past Perivolos towards Imerovigli.

'Where did the family live?' I asked, deliberately avoiding Phoena's name. 'I might have seen the house without realising?'

Her glance, when it came, was stony. 'Our house was abandoned. We never went back.'

'But there's been so much renovation, Mum. Look, where I am, all across here they're opening

190

up the *skapha* again . . .'

But her disquiet at seeing the familiar place names was palpable—she seemed almost to be holding her breath until the torture ended—and I had no choice but to put the maps away and give up. I barely mentioned my plans for the shop (the last thing she wanted was fresh evidence of my putting down proper roots there) and we talked instead about her neighbours, their families, current affairs. We watched television, mostly, hours and hours of it.

Many times during those few days in London I felt myself comforting her as I might have expected to be comforted myself. After all, only the bitterest of fortunes could have brought a woman in her thirties, a wife and a mother, back alone to her childhood home for Christmas. I didn't want to compete with Mum, however; I understood her grief for Emma better than anyone. Rosemary had told me, in a rare insight that stayed with me, that one fell in love with a new grandchild with exactly the same intensity and permanence as with one's own child. My mother's ache for Emma was as primal as mine.

There was something else too, something that had not occurred to me before. My bone structure may have been hers, but my spirit was entirely my father's and I brought him to mind for her every waking hour with the smallest of gestures or comments. On this reluctant mercy mission of mine, I'd brought with me not one ghost but two.

*   *   *

On the evening of the 30th there seemed to me to

be something unusual in the air—or was it simply the way Mum was moving through it, more self-conscious somehow, as though she were trying to make herself lighter, less visible. It was the too-discreet tidying up that finally tipped me off.

I sighed, put on my coat and picked up my bag. 'I'm just popping out.'

She looked up. 'Popping out?'

'Yes. Is there anything we need from down the road? Milk, maybe?'

'Oh, no, we've got plenty, no need to go out. Nowhere will be open anyway . . .' She followed me to the front door, watching in panic as I pulled gloves from my pockets and slipped them on.

'I'll come back when he's gone, shall I?'

'What? Rachel . . . !'

'See you later, Mum.' I chose a pub with a view of the lights that held traffic from the north before releasing it into my mother's road, and waited in the bar until I saw his car. At the wheel, his profile was dark grey, almost a silhouette. It was a cold night and I guessed he'd be wearing his overcoat, the navy woollen one I'd chosen for him the winter before Emma died. The bar was empty and well-lit enough for him to have made out my figure in the corner, though the distance too great for him possibly to have recognised me. I kept my head low, just in case. I felt ridiculous running away and hiding like this, but my instinct to evade him was, if anything, stronger now than it had been in Oia. And still I wasn't ready to confront the reasons why. All I could do was acknowledge to myself that they were dark and complicated reasons, intertwined so tightly with the events of Emma's death that I would not be able to deal with one without dealing with the other. No, best I stayed away.

'Did I miss him?' I asked, closing the door behind me. The television was on but there were two wine glasses on the coffee table.

Mum swung around to face me, furious now. 'What on earth do you think you are doing? You are not a teenager any more! This is not adult behaviour!'

I felt my face curl into an adolescent scowl. 'Mum, I asked you, I *specifically* asked you! Why couldn't you just respect my wishes?' I stopped, not having expected my voice to sound quite so shrill. 'Look, please accept that I need to make my own decisions about Oliver. We've been separated a long time now, and we've seen each other, anyway, you know that, out in Oia, and it didn't make any difference.'

'But that was so long ago now,' she protested, 'so soon after it all happened. The worst is over now, you're ready to—'

'We're not going to be getting back together,' I interrupted, exasperated. 'We're not!' I felt defeated then, allowing myself to glimpse for a second how it had been before, before Emma, when the relationship with my mother had seemed just too hard for me to continue to pursue. The relentless consolations, that was one thing, but I needed to know that underneath it all she was on my side and not speaking always for Oliver. I was *Emma's* mother, I wanted to cry out, not *his*!

'I just wish there was a way.' She turned away and covered her mouth with her hands, not daring to voice the pipe dreams that played inside her head. Dreams that I'd get back together with

Oliver, that we'd confound those pesky fertility consultants and produce another Emma, several of her, so many more of her that the joy of them all couldn't fail to eclipse the pain of losing the original. Desperate and hollow, they were little more than variations on the platitudes offered after a miscarriage: 'You can always have another one', more often than not teamed with, 'You're still young'. As though the fruit grabbed from the bowl has been found to be bad: well, no matter, there are others, just choose another one!

I wondered if she knew I could have recited those fantasies of hers back to her, word for word, note for note.

*　　　*　　　*

Later I asked, 'So how did he react, anyway? You might as well tell me.'

I saw from her expression that she had not warned Oliver in advance, either, fearing that he would be as reluctant to see me as I was him, or wanting to be careful not to give him false hope. He'd been through enough, let's not forget. Perhaps they still met every so often for a drink and he'd been oblivious to anything untoward about this one. Once entrapped, however, he must have seen evidence of me, mustn't he? My cardigan, for instance, left in the armchair, the one he had bought me for my last birthday in London, baby-soft wine-coloured cashmere, though I'd never got to the bottom of whether he had been the one to pick it out or Vanessa. Or had Mum had time to clear away my belongings, close the door to my bedroom and remove any of my toiletries from the bathroom? I imagined him sharing a glass of sherry, accepting a nut, exchanging niceties with the woman who used to be his daughter's grandmother, then standing, apologising, saying he needed to get on his way. He had some work to catch up on.

Mum sat down and indicated with her eyes that I should do the same. 'Rachel, I have to talk to you. I can't understand this. If this separation is to be permanent then you should tell him.'

'I can't face it,' I said, simply. 'I'm not ready.'

'But it's been over two years now, love.'

The way she said 'love' made me remember the way she used to speak to Emma. 'Come on, love, let's see what treats I can find in the kitchen . . .'

'Listen, Rachel, whether you stay married or not, there are things you two *should* share.'

'There's nothing, honestly.' My eyes pleaded with her to understand.

She sighed. 'He hasn't told you about this lawsuit, has he, in his letters? He only told me about it just now.'

I turned back sharply. 'What lawsuit?'

She sighed. 'I've *told* him you should know this sort of thing. It concerns both of you.'

'Who's he suing?' I asked.

'The killer, of course.' I'd forgotten how they'd called Morris 'the killer', Mum and Rosemary. The killer from Stonebridge Park, that was the full version (Lockley was referred to only as 'the killer's friend'). Accidental death had not been punishment enough for him; they would have rather seen him hanged.

Mum dabbed at her eyes with her middle fingers, pulled back her shoulders, determined, evidently, to stay strong. 'Well, not him personally, of course. The insurance people. They are investigating it all at the moment.'

'Ah.' Now I understood. For money-minded men like Oliver, someone always had to be made to pay, someone had to be held accountable; it might just as easily have been the local education authority or the driver of the bus. He'd been thinking about this lawsuit of his, no doubt, as he waited at the lights, unaware of me watching from across the road. And it broke my heart to think of him venting his grief in this way, in this bid to redress a balance that could never be.

'I wish he wouldn't,' I said finally. 'I'm sure Morris's mother is miserable enough, don't you think, without having it dragged out? Do you remember her letter?'

It had come just before the funeral, misspelled fragments of sentences written in a state of shock. Oliver and Rosemary had passed it between the two of them; they'd found it inadequate, I recalled, adamant that this woman's claims to grief were less than our own. But I'd never imagined for a moment that she felt anything but the same as I did, that she had lost the centre of her world and it would never be returned to her. I remembered one phrase in particular: *Whatever he has done, I will always be his mother.*

Mum nodded, on my side finally.

I saw the boxed pair of crystal brandy glasses on the counter in the kitchen, a scrap of Christmas paper still attached to the side, before I noticed that the gift without the tag was now gone from under the tree.

'Rachel? Rachel! Over here!'

It was a strange moment when I recognised Toby Challoner at Heathrow Airport. I did the dance for a moment, toyed with the idea of slipping away and pretending I hadn't heard his voice, hadn't seen him seeing me. I'd already checked-in my luggage, I could whizz straight through to Departures and forget all about him.

He did no such dance. Slipping his boarding pass into his breast pocket, he called out again, louder this time, more forceful, so that people around us looked to me as if to say, Why aren't you answering? Are you deaf or something?

'Rachel? I don't believe it! You're back? Well, leaving again, obviously.'

I smiled and stepped forward. 'Yes, I've been visiting Mum for Christmas.'

'Oh, you should have let us know! We've been at home the whole time.'

'I thought you might be skiing,' I said, lying.

'No, not till half-term this year. Oh, come here, sweetheart . . .' He strode forward and pulled me into his arms so decisively that I had no time to react. I managed to stay limp until he withdrew a little, kissing my forehead through my hair, as one might a child who'd been temporarily lost and returned, a little dishevelled but otherwise unharmed.

'Anyway,' he said, releasing me and grinning broadly, 'we just gave the kids a puppy for Christmas, so we can't leave him just yet. That might be considered cruelty and you just know Jen would shop us to the RSPCA.'

Already I could feel my spirits rising in some primitive response to goodness. I forgot for a moment that I'd be finding out this information in Palmer's next report, in a way that invaded this old friend's privacy. 'A puppy? How exciting! What kind is he?'

'A black lab. They've called him Bertie, of all things. God knows where they got that from, not P. G. Wodehouse, that's for sure.'

'It's a sweet name. It must be some character in a cartoon or something.'

'All I know is things were pretty much at fever pitch in the house when I left and it wasn't even light yet. But I'm sure things'll calm down eventually.'

I admired his willingness to make all of this sound perfectly natural, as though this were a routine catching up; we might just have mislaid one another's number or been too busy at work to remember to call. It was his way of saying that no offence had been taken by my long neglect, that anything I chose to do now was forgivable, anything.

He glanced at the check-in desk behind us. 'You're going back to Santorini? Oliver told us you were there. I remember you used to talk about it at college.'

I hesitated before nodding. Of course Oliver would have shared the information with our friends by now, if not right from the beginning. In any case, I was hardly on a witness protection programme. I was a registered resident in Santorini, my location a matter of public record. 'Yes, that's where I've been living. It's a bit of a pain getting there at this time of year, actually.

198

You have to go via Athens.'

He nodded. 'Must be chilly even down there?'

'It's not too bad. I'm sheltered where I am, and it's still sunny most days. It gets cold at night, of course, but I have a heater. Anyway, the houses are dug right into the rock so they stay nice and warm in winter.' This, it struck me, was more information about my accommodation than my mother had allowed me to give during our whole week together. 'Where are you off to?'

'Prague. Just a quick overnighter.'

'It'll be cold there!'

'Yes,' he agreed. 'It's a booze client, though, some kind of eighty-per-cent-proof poison they're flogging, so that'll warm the cockles. Listen, have you got time for a coffee once we've gone through?'

I couldn't refuse; the briefest glance at the departures monitor would reveal how prompt we both were for our check-in times, not to mention the DELAYED sign already pulsing for Athens. I didn't want to refuse, either. It was good to see him.

We queued together for coffee and pastries and sat on immovable plastic seats to drink the scalding liquid. Maybe it was the low-grade instant coffee or maybe it was his humour, irrepressible even at this hour, but for a few minutes with Toby I allowed myself to go right back, to before Emma and the girls, before Mariel and Oliver too, back to those first terms of university when the things that passed for cares were nothing of the sort, and we were growing up just quickly enough to suspect that, underneath it all, that might be the case.

He showed me a photograph of Cat and Jake surrounded by a mountain of torn wrapping paper. At first glance it looked as though the two of *them* were the present that had just been unwrapped.

'Oliver encloses notes from Mariel sometimes. I feel bad for not replying, but I still like hearing from her. Does that sound awful . . . ?'

'Hey,' he said, frowning gently, 'don't be silly. No one expects anything from you, honestly.' His face brightened. 'Cat likes getting your birthday cards, though, and Daisy, as well. It's the foreign stamps, makes them feel grown up. They cut them out and keep them in some secret trove. You know what they're like—' He tried to swallow it back, that last remark, but I smiled to show him it was all right, I didn't want him to censor himself. And I *did* know what they were like.

'I think about them a lot, the girls.' Think about them, look at their pictures and trace the side of my thumb over their little faces, follow their lives. I looked at Toby's face, tender with compassion; would he feel the same sympathy for me if he knew about Palmer? I couldn't possibly tell him, or even hint at my activities, every bone in my body warned against it. Did that mean, therefore, that it was wrong?

'Are you OK, Rachel? You've gone a bit . . .'

'I'm fine,' I said, hurriedly. 'Please tell Mariel, well, just tell her that I hope she's OK.'

'I will.'

'Thank you.'

It was time to go to our gates.

'They miss you, you know,' he said, kissing me goodbye.

It was only after we'd parted that I wondered whether he'd been talking about the adults or the children.

Chapter 20

The early travel photographer Maxime du Camp defined the camera as an 'instrument of precision', and it was this very preciseness that led me to dismiss photography so easily when I studied History of Art at university. As far as I could see, painting was the truer act of imagination, on the part of both artist and viewer. When you looked at a photograph, you merely saw the same thing someone else had seen before you. He or she might have taken the time to record it, but that was all. No, photography was the product of science, not art.

When I started working as a researcher at Pendant I changed my mind almost overnight. It was a daily surprise to me what photographs could do, how they could restore the past and promise a future at the same time. Images would stay with me in a way that paintings never did, wrapping me unexpectedly in moods that proved hard to shed. Now I saw that the effects of paintings were often more passive, appreciated for the way they soothed and consoled, for what they subdued. But photographs often inspired people to act, to cross the globe, to explore.

I was delighted when, at about the age of three or four, Emma and the girls began to enjoy looking at photos. It was about the same time that they became fascinated by the idea of themselves as babies; they loved to guess who was who in the baby pictures and screw up their faces to recreate newborn wails. Whenever I appeared with my own camera, Emma would pose with her toys, arranging them just so and signalling her own readiness with the stillness of a Velázquez *infanta*. Then, when the prints came back, she would bring the toys to see themselves immortalised, exclaiming for each in turn as they were identified. 'Show me again, Mum, again!' That was when I recognised the difference: painting was an obvious pleasure for Emma and her friends, an everyday activity. But photography, that was like magic.

*   *   *

Not long after my return to Oia, Eleni came to find Ingrid and me at Damiri's. She must have been sprinting flat out for she was panting by the time she reached us, arms outstretched and frantic as if to warn us of quicksand ahead, her dark curls falling across her eyes.

'Ladies, you must come now!'

Ingrid and I, sitting with our faces raised to the warm winter sun, exchanged a look of amusement. 'What? What is it? Have you run all this way?'

'A shop! I have found your shop!'

'What? *Where*?'

Not bothering even to finish our coffees or duck inside to pay, we left money on a saucer and ran up at full pelt after Eleni, who was attracting smiles from the handful of tourists out walking. Soon Ingrid and I were panting, but Eleni just kept running, on to Marmara, past the square, past the turning for Callidora.

'Eleni!' I was baffled. We were entering the most expensive stretch of retail in Oia, the one that led tourists from car park to sunset and back again. Ingrid and I had long dismissed it as beyond our reach, expecting instead to find our premises at the quieter end of town or back on the traffic road. But since Eleni's own hotel stood on this strip, we could hardly doubt she knew where she was going—and at speed! Past the old town hall and the weavers' shop, the small marbled square that in summer was host to impromptu open-air markets, and into Lotza, Oia's tourist heartland where some of the oldest cafés and bars pulled in the customers day and night. And then . . . she stopped, turned, and threw out her arms once more: 'Here!'

We stumbled to a halt and followed her gaze—downward. The unit was below street level and there was only one small window, barely noticeable from the path. Above the door, painted in a shaky hand, were the words 'Gift, Souvenir, Kamera Film'.

'Come in,' said Eleni, 'I have a key, I can show you.'

Ingrid and I exchanged another look—this one of scepticism—before following her down the steps. It was obviously out of the question that customers would have to climb down such steep steps to get inside. And that one small square window was all there was to let in natural light, display goods and attract custom in the first place. Most importantly, it looked too small, and once through the door, secured on the outside with a rusting padlock, I saw just how tiny it was. There certainly wasn't the space to set up the easels I'd envisaged, and the walls were bumpy and crumbling in places, which would make conventional hanging difficult. But, as I knew from Callidora, flat surfaces were hard to find in Oia's *hyposkapha*; for most people the irregularities were a big part of the charm.

I looked again. If we fixed sturdy shelves on the left and used console tables and lamp stands below them it could work, in a thrown-together higgledy-piggledy sort of way. Decent lighting, some new tiles for the floor, a little desk on the right, and that alcove behind it would be perfect for storing packaging materials. There was even enough room for a couple of stools (presumably there'd be hours of inactivity—I really had no idea at all). There was also, directly under the street, a surprisingly sizeable storage vault, almost the same square footage as the shop itself, where we'd be able to keep our stocks and framing equipment, a computer and a safe, perhaps . . . if we ever took any cash.

'Can you imagine your shop here?' Eleni asked me, by my side, exultant.

I nodded, realised my eyes were glazing a little and was glad of the dimness. I felt again the adrenalin of that day in Fira when I'd seen our photographs for the first time, and I thought too of that liquid feeling of coming home I'd experienced in the rain in London. So this was how it was, now, these tiny sweet punctures of pleasure in the blackness. How small and tender they felt compared to the grander, almost traumatising jolts of old: Oliver telling me he loved me; my wedding day; the first time I'd walked into our house in

Compagne Gardens; and the first time I'd felt Emma move inside me . . .

I blinked, shook the memories away. 'Who was in here before?' I asked Eleni, noticing a half-empty water bottle on the floor. 'They must only just have left.'

'I've walked past here a thousand times on my way to the Epik,' Ingrid said, frowning, 'but I don't remember anything here at all. Some sort of gift shop, obviously.'

Eleni ran her fingers over the only remaining piece of furniture in the room, a shelving unit under the window on which two yellow sponges, a pumice stone and a toppled tower of soaps gathered dust. 'This tenant, he is not coming back from Athens in the spring. Their son, he owes money, and his wife . . .' She stopped there, shrugged the expansive, all-encompassing shrug the Santorinians use to say, just life, life's dramas, nothing special.

'How do you know?' Ingrid asked. 'Who's the landlord?'

Eleni blinked those heavy lids and flashed us her broadest smile. 'This is the best part. It's Yannis.'

'Who?'

'Yannis Frangidis. He is the cousin of Anatole.'

'Something tells me you've already negotiated our rent for us,' I laughed.

'I have spoken about this, yes.'

'Eleni, you're amazing!'

The figure was lower than the hundreds of thousands of drachmas I'd been warned to expect for so central a site, a reflection, Eleni said, of the modest size of the unit and the lateness of the availability—the new season was just weeks away.

'What d'you think, Ingrid?' Operating as I did now entirely on instinct, I was certain this was the place for us, a view only improved when I followed Eleni upstairs and saw the roof terrace, which was large and surprisingly private. Reached only by external steps at the front, it seemed to float above the Caldera, as flooded with sunlight as the deck of a cruise ship. I imagined outdoor exhibitions, evening drinks. Now I really could have my ocean backdrop.

'Ingrid?'

She was still frowning. 'Well, I think the older tourists won't want to go down those steps, but we can think of something to solve that, a rail definitely, or maybe some kind of ramp if we're allowed. We'll need to use the shopfront to make it absolutely clear what we're selling. You can't really tell through that tiny window and I don't think people will just wander in. We'll have to spell it out, maybe hang a picture outside, display it in some kind of cabinet. Actually, the wall to the street is wide enough to display some of our stuff, isn't it? That's if there aren't any restrictions and we can make it shoplifter-proof somehow, and that storage space is pretty good for Oia . . . We'll need to do something with the lighting, of course . . .'

'We'll take it, then?'

'Yep, I think we should. Definitely.'

'Yes!' Eleni cried and the three of us hugged, up on the roof, sidestepping a little with the excitement until the momentum took us in circles and we were dancing our own ring-o-roses.

*　　　*　　　*

It wasn't long, of course, before such eureka moments were buried by bureaucracy. Eleni acted as interpreter at various meetings until we found an English-speaking lawyer to handle our contract with the landlord and our application for the licence granted to product traders by the local guild. I ignored the spectres of Oliver and my mother as I signed my name on page after page of documentation. In the end, mine was the only one to appear since Ingrid was Australian and subject to sterner visa requirements. It wasn't entirely clear whether she was legally entitled to work in Greece at all, but I told her it didn't matter, the shop was still jointly ours, and I meant it.

Other shopkeepers, friends of Eleni and Anatole, briefed us on social security requirements, on the current arrangements for tax-free shopping for tourists and on the strict laws about bookkeeping. This, we were told, would have to be available for checking by inspectors even before the shop opened and, once it had, as often as weekly. Not that we had a cash register yet—we intended to use a padlocked vanity case until ours arrived from Athens.

Until now our precious stock had been kept, uninsured and barely concealed, in an alcove next to my bed. Now these piles of prints needed to be mounted and framed. With Anatole's help, Ingrid negotiated a good price with a glazier in Fira and, having consulted some of her artist friends in the village, was referred to an outlet that could supply the stiff, cream-coloured mount board we wanted to use. We were teaching ourselves how to cut the internal windows with a small craft knife (Ingrid proved the better at this precision work). We'd chosen small five-by-seven formats for the bulk of the stock, small enough to fit in hand luggage. Larger pieces, like the Nikos originals, we would frame with dramatically generous mount sizes and ship at Greek postal prices.

I was in charge of finding materials for the frames. I knew I wanted wood, but this threatened to become more costly an element of the enterprise than the photographs themselves, for Santorini didn't produce its own timber and supplies had to be imported from Ios, Crete or Russia. Again Eleni came to our rescue; she knew the late master's apprentice down at Armeni, a young man called Dymas, who still used the boatshed to work on repair jobs and on what were now only occasional commissions for new boats. Who knew what other stocks lay forgotten in those long narrow buildings by the water. She would introduce us.

Though the path down began close to my house, I had been only a handful of times to Armeni, the old Oian harbour where the boats had once docked. As we made the hike Eleni repeatedly held me at bay and urged me to listen to the thud of the hammer from below and imagine a time when such sounds filled the air from every direction, 'When Oia was alive.' Then, the rhythm was set, year on year: repair in winter, sail in spring. Everyone knew what was coming next, as much as they could know anything.

And did I know that *armena* meant mast and rigging? 'Now Armeni makes none of its own. This is a terrible thing.'

'It is sort of eerie how deserted it is now,' I said.

208

'But that's what I like, in a way.'

Dymas was a young man of few words and none of the manner developed by his fellow villagers for dealing with tourists and foreigners. Unlike most other people, he had no tickets to sell. The upturned boat on the trestle in front of him was probably his last job, he confessed, he might soon find himself working on a construction site. (This elicited much pah-ing from Eleni: Nonsense, she would order a fishing boat herself if it came to that.) Of course we could have the old offcuts, Dymas said, shrugging, no one had any need for them and the museum had acquired the charts and other documents of any interest.

As he and Eleni chatted in Greek, I followed a couple of tourists to the far side of the shore, where they were looking at the bits of driftwood washed up on the pebbles. Each piece, the man told the woman in English, was uniquely coloured with paint and water and salt and air, a survivor of the bashing and baking it had received in its working life.

'It's incredible, when you think about it. I mean, how many years has this stuff spent in the ocean?' His voice became louder with enthusiasm as he spoke and I thought for a moment of Bob, a smile tugging at the corners of my lips.

'Can we use this too, d'you think?' I asked Dymas and I watched, fascinated, as he took the piece from me, running his thumbs over the grain as though reading those layers of paint and salt like a kind of Braille.

'This, I think, will work very well,' Eleni agreed. 'This wood is beautiful for itself. You hardly need the picture at all.'

When I went back the next day with my list of dimensions Dymas had already mocked up a sample for me using the driftwood. I promised there and then to send all future work his way for as long as he cared to take it. I was absurdly pleased when he cracked a smile, and the thought of it sustained me for the climb back up.

> Dear Rachel,
> I am writing with some news that may surprise you . . .

I wasn't sure if I'd hear from Oliver again after my foolishness at my mother's, limited though his grasp of it may have been, but his letters had continued to arrive, and now, evidently, he was ready to share with me the news Mum had already broken for him.

>> I decided not to mention it before because I didn't want to burden you with distressing detail, but I have been involved in suing Darren Morris's estate for damages—a time-consuming process that is now at an end. Actually, it has been relatively straightforward (liability has never been the issue, of course), simply a matter of negotiating a settlement with the insurance company.
>> I know you'll think this ill gotten . . .

Not ill gotten, Oliver, just never should have been gotten in the first place, *mis*gotten. Reading on, I saw that he proposed to turn over the damages—a sum that made me draw breath—to me. There was to be no argument about it, he wrote, and I made none. I was in no position to be proud: there were Palmer's payments to make, and now, of course, there was the shop.

*   *   *

'Come on,' said Ingrid, 'we *have* to make a decision about this.'

'I know.'

We sat side by side on the low wall opposite our shopfront, a scrubbed, whitewashed new version of the one Eleni had shown us several weeks earlier. At Ingrid's feet was the pot of paint we'd bought to paint the name of our shop on the exterior—a kingfisher blue, richer than the classic island mid-blue. The problem was we still didn't have a name.

'We probably can't say Oia Gallery or Archive or anything official like that.'

'I think that's a bit serious, anyway,' Ingrid said. 'It might put people off. We need something kind of romantic sounding, a Greek word, maybe.'

'Not the name of a goddess, please.'

She pulled a face. 'Agreed. What was that old name for Oia we saw on the maps in the museum?'

I thought. 'Pano Meria?'

'But the way they spelled it, all one word and with an "e" . . . Panomeréa?' She scribbled it out on an envelope and showed me.

'That's nice.'

We painted the letters above the arched door and on the upper wall. Ingrid designed a stamp and spent long hours writing up my captions in a lovely stylised italic. Having seen her talent with

211

both paintbrush and blade, I shouldn't have been at all surprised by such accomplished penmanship, but I was. Somehow I'd always imagined her previous artistic ambitions to be nothing more than that.

'I won the fountain pen in a calligraphy competition at school. I used to practise in my room. It's one of the only things I've still got from Australia. That and my passport.'

I watched her finger the pen, tapping it to get the ink flowing. 'Do you ever want to go back?'

'No,' she said, firmly. 'No way. Especially not now.' She was flourishing in Oia, anyone could see that. Her fresh start was the making of her. I, on the other hand, was what? Getting on, filling my days, manufacturing purpose wherever I could. That was what Panomeréa was, wasn't it? Something to fill my days, to fill my heart, my equivalent of Oliver's lawsuit. A time-consuming process.

Probably. But, still, it was beyond the point that I'd ever expected to reach.

Chapter 21

I made no protest when Palmer's next visit brought with it little in the way of official news. Nor did I voice concern when he proposed to extend his usual day trip and stay a night or two at the Ilias. Rather, I found myself looking forward to our meeting and saving up new places to show him, places I'd discovered on my walks or that Eleni or the other locals had told me about.

212

I took him to Finikia, the neighbouring village a few minutes' stroll inland, where the main street, called *potamos*—'river'—sloped into narrow alleys and the church had weathered to a lovely salmon pink. Then I showed him a new beach I'd found beyond Ammoudi at Kantharos, site of a former leper colony. The *louviarika* were empty now, standing hollow and wind-whipped above the water.

'*Louva* means leprosy,' I said. I persevered with my little bits of Greek, constantly ashamed of my ignorance in business dealings and of the fact that of the two of us Ingrid alone could get by quite competently, even though we'd lived in Santorini for the same length of time. 'And *katharos* means clean. They were brought here to be cleansed.'

'Poor sods,' Palmer said. He stood, one hand in his pocket and the other shielding his eyes from the sun, and looked about the place. He'd lost weight around the middle, I noticed as he turned. The slightness made him seem defter, stronger.

I led the way down to the beach, a beautiful glittering curve of volcanic stones backed by pumice cliffs that had been whipped by the wind into thousands of tiny peaks. You could hear the crunch of the rocks as the water pressed into them, then, as it was sucked back out, see how steeply the ground shelved, far more steeply than you would expect. Though it was not yet Easter, it was warm enough to sunbathe and we dropped our belongings close to the water's edge, watching as a group of others picked their way to a remoter spot before spreading out their towels. They felt intrepid, you could tell, thrilled by their edge-of-the-world adventure.

213

'You know,' Palmer said, 'if we're just below the *louviarika* then what we're looking at now must have been exactly what the lepers saw.'

'They often got the best views,' I said, drily. 'That way they didn't have to look at themselves.'

He grinned. 'Tough, though, facing out to sea like this. I'm guessing they must have been mostly sailors.'

'Yes. I hadn't thought of that. How cruel.' I fell silent.

'What is it?'

'Nothing really, I was just thinking, if you count up all the people here who've died young over the centuries . . . the sailors, the lepers, the earthquake victims, it must be way out of proportion to the size of the population. I mean, what kind of a place *is* this?'

He nodded.

'My aunt died here, you know. In the big earthquake in 1956.'

'She did?' There was something about the way he said it that made me wonder if he had already known, if I'd told him before.

'I don't know anything about it really, I mean, how she was actually killed. Hit by falling rocks, I suppose. I've seen all the books from that time, but there don't seem to be many eyewitness accounts, not in English, anyway.'

'There must still be people alive from then, though, it wasn't that long ago. Couldn't you ask your friend to help you find out? The lady at my hotel?'

'Eleni? Yes, I suppose so. I don't like to delve, though. I'd feel as if I were going behind my mother's back.' I grinned at him. 'I suppose that

214

sounds a bit hypocritical when you think what I'm doing to Mariel and Jen.'

His eyes narrowed a little. 'Family is different.'

'But we *were* family, the three of us.' I was surprised by the passion in my own voice. 'Well, that's how it felt, anyway. I was closer to them than anyone.'

'You still haven't been in touch, then?'

'Mariel has written to me, but I haven't replied. I wouldn't blame them if they'd just given up on me. When I was in London, that time I came to hire you, I thought I saw Jen's car at the cemetery where Emma is buried. And I know they know I was there last time because I ran into Mariel's husband at the airport as I was leaving, but I just couldn't bear to see them, with the girls, in all our old places . . .' I broke off this odd little stream of confessions, my breath coming in thin, shallow gulps.

'You've been back to London?' Palmer asked, surprised. 'I mean, a second time?'

'Yes, to see my mother. She won't come here.'

'Why not?'

And, though I hadn't expected to, I told him, starting with Mum's move to London after that first family loss, and then my father's cancer and her premature widowhood. It was so miserable, it gave the impression there'd been no room for joy. 'It all sounds so tragic, doesn't it. But there've been lots of happy times over the years, with Dad, and then with Emma, of course. It was tough for Mum to lose her husband and then her granddaughter.'

'Tough for you to lose your father and your daughter.'

215

I looked down. 'Yes.'

Long after we'd finished speaking and had lapsed into silence I sensed him still looking at me, as intent as if there were still words to follow. He was utterly motionless; if you couldn't see his eyes you might wonder if he'd nodded off to sleep. It seemed to me that his work had required such anonymity on his part, such an ordinariness, that he'd purged himself of every gesture, every exclamation, until he'd reached the point of expressing himself only through his eyes. At this moment they appeared to contain something between compassion and yearning and it was an intimate blend. Something had shifted between us, it was obvious; I was talking so freely to him. And it was a relief, a relief to share some of my secrets. I rolled my hips slightly towards him. Our clothes were fluttering in the breeze and I had an impulse to touch him, to thank him for believing in me, maybe even to kiss him. A laughable, girlish impulse. I noticed bits of rope amid the pebbles and, picking at a couple, saw that they were just the knots, the ends cut or worn away.

'Anyway,' I said, looking back to the water, 'it doesn't matter, does it, how you go, or how young you are when it happens? If it's disease, or drowning or just old age . . . it's all meaningless whoever you are, wherever you are.' I laughed, embarrassed by myself. 'Sorry, I sound like some kind of existentialist teenager, don't I?'

'It's not meaningless,' he said, seriously. 'I was just thinking the exact opposite, actually. Down here, especially, it all feels so *loaded*.'

I nodded. 'I think that's probably what I mean. All of this, it's all about something so much bigger than us. You know, I get the same feeling when I walk up past Perivolos. You can see everything stretched out before you, the volcanoes and Thirasia, there's so little land compared with the sea. It's like we're clinging on for dear life.'

'Dear life, yes.' He followed my gaze, nodding, as though agreement lay in what we saw rather than in any words that came from our mouths. The sunlight was hazier than usual, making the metallic colours in the water more dominant. I was right, I thought, there *was* consolation here, in the sea and the sky and the way they merged into one vast, smooth organ. As close to consolation as I was going to find.

'I still think we're all pretty important, in our own way,' he said, turning back to me.

The sun was hurting my head, making my eyes sleepy. I closed them, lost track of where I was for a moment.

'You're doing great, you know,' I heard him say. 'You're in the right place.'

I squinted up at him. 'Among the lepers and the dead sailors, you mean?'

'Among the Ingrids and the Elenis,' he said.

*   *   *

Noticing was Palmer's job and I couldn't help wondering what he noticed about me during that afternoon at Kantharos. In the time I'd lived here I had glanced at myself in the mirror only occasionally and with little interest beyond checking I hadn't contracted scurvy. There was no full-length mirror in House Callidora in any case, just a small one in the bathroom, but they were

217

sometimes inescapable in bars and shops and I knew my body had become thin and my hair unkempt. I hadn't cared a bit; just as I had relinquished all pride in my social skills so I had worried little what people thought of the way I looked.

Now I leaned forward and looked at myself properly. On my face, new lines abounded, and not the lines of laughter that bring a person's spirit immediately to the surface, but the downcast ones of sobbing that bury it. It's a person's pattern, my father once told me when I asked why my grandparents had 'scratches' on their faces. 'As you live longer, your pattern gets deeper because you've learned more.' Well, my pattern was irreversible now.

I combed my fingers through my hairline and pressed the waves down in an approximation of my former bobbed style. Now I noticed the grey hairs sprouting all along the parting. The highlights had long since grown out and my hair was fair enough to mask the grey, but without its pigmentation the texture was coarse. Funny, the natural disgust at one's own greying, like discovering soil riddled with worms. One drew instinctively back before plunging in further and searching for worse.

Next I examined my eyebrows. Once neat little curves, they were heavier now and what Jen would call unruly. That made me think of the time she and Bob and I were sitting in their living room and she'd taken a pair of tweezers from her bag and picked off a hair from the end of his nose, so quick and precise I doubted for a moment the evidence of my own eyes. I'd waited for a fit of anger from him but he'd gone the other way and crowed with laughter. 'No room for vanity in this house,' he'd said, and the remark had stayed with me for the rest of the day.

I thought again about how comfortable I had felt with Palmer, how it had been something more than familiarity or even attraction, a sense of kinship. Adolescent as it felt to try to articulate it, he just seemed to *know* me.

I followed the course of a ferry through the channel between Santorini and Thirasia, the stretch so sacred the islanders had given it its own patron saint, and I wondered if it was the one that took him away.

∗   ∗   ∗

Ingrid had seen me 'in cahoots', as she put it, with a man she didn't recognise and asked straight out if he was my husband.

'No, no, that wasn't Oliver.'

'That other bloke you've mentioned before, then, Simon?'

I glanced up. 'Simon? Have I? No, not him. Palmer's nothing to do with either of them, actually.'

'Palmer? That's a strange name.'

'It's his surname.'

'Why do you call your friend by his last name?' she asked.

'I don't know. People just do. Anyway, he's not a friend, exactly.'

She raised an eyebrow, clearly intrigued. 'Oh yeah? What is he then, *exactly*?'

I could see she wasn't going to give up and I felt a catch release inside me; I'd just bared my soul to

Palmer, perhaps it was time to open up to Ingrid too. Lord knew, she'd waited long enough. 'The thing is, Ingrid, well, Palmer and I have a business arrangement.'

'You do?' She suppressed a cackle. 'That sounds fun. What kind of "business" arrangement?'

'It's a long story.'

'I'm not going anywhere,' she said, adding wryly, 'as you've probably guessed by now.'

'OK.' We'd been cleaning the unit downstairs and were now resting with cold drinks up on our roof, sitting on the chairs with fraying rush seats that had been abandoned there by the previous occupants. The late-afternoon light glowed, the sky pure cerulean blue. My final privacy was about to be lost and it struck me as both farcical and shameful that I had managed to keep for so long from my friend the true reason for my being here.

I took a very deep breath. 'Palmer is a private investigator.'

'Shit, are you in some kind of trouble?'

'No, no. He's just keeping an eye on two children in London who I used to know.'

Ingrid frowned. 'I don't get it.'

'One is my god-daughter, I'm the legal guardian of the other. I used to be very good friends with their mothers.'

'Used to be? Why aren't you now?'

'Oh, Ingrid, it's complicated. I don't know if you want to know, it's a lot to take in . . .'

'Try me,' she said, gently.

I paused. 'I had a little daughter myself, in London. The same age as the girls.' I looked away but I could sense her holding her breath and praying I wasn't going to say what I was going to

220

say. 'She was killed in a road accident just before I came here. That's *why* I came here . . . I couldn't stay at home. I couldn't live there without her.'

'No!' She grasped my hand with both of hers. The skin on her fingers was dry and warm, I could feel the sun in it. 'Oh, Rachel, I knew there had to be something.'

'You mean no one's this depressed by nature?'

'I *knew* it. I thought it was something to do with your husband. But this . . . Oh my God, all this time you haven't said a thing . . .'

'I know.' I tried to joke. 'First I'm half-Greek, now I'm a secret mother . . . You must be wondering what else I've got up my sleeve.' But neither of us could summon a smile.

'Oh Jesus, all this time. Is it, like they say, like losing a limb?'

So they did, but a child is no appendage. She had been the whole of me, in fact she had made me more than I was, more than I had a right to be. Parents spend so much energy trying to shape their children into the people they wish them to be, it comes as a surprise to discover it is the children who are the making of them. 'It's more like, I don't know, being hollow. That's why I don't get excited about things in the normal way. There's nothing left inside me, nothing at all. That's the only way I can describe it.'

She pulled up her chair close to mine and we sat, shoulder to shoulder, like lovers in the sunset photographs. 'There is, Rachel, there is something inside you, of course there is. You still care about people, it's obvious you do.'

I just shook my head, sucked my lips together to try to stop the tears. She followed my wet gaze

221

across to the island of Thirasia, to the clifftop village we'd neither of us thought to visit, as though Oia was as far as either of us needed ever go.

'What was her name?'

'Emma,' I whispered. 'Emma Jane.' I'd wanted Emma Laura but Oliver had laughed, 'E.L.F., her initials will spell Elf.' Michelle, then? 'Nope. European Monetary Fund.' We'd talked about her grandmothers' names too, but been mutually resolved to let our daughter start her life with a clean slate; neither Rosemary nor Alysa had been the luckiest of souls.

'Could I see a photo, maybe?' Ingrid asked. 'I mean, you don't have to, if . . .'

'No, it's fine. Here.' I took it from my bag and handed it over without daring to look myself. I knew it, anyway, dot for dot: Emma on the swing in Mariel's garden, arms straight, body arched right back and feet kicked forward as though aiming for the camera. Squeezed between her hip and the chain was her doll Lucy, and the thrust of the swinging motion had dislodged her, she was almost falling, another frame and Lucy would be gone.

Ingrid held it up to the light as though it were a transparency.

'Oh, she's beautiful, she looks just like you, doesn't she?' Where once that present tense would have caused in me a gush of senseless hope, now it was a tiny shoot of colour, one of those flowers in the parched black sand, 'sea daffodils' the locals called them.

Ingrid was shaking her head, angry with herself. 'Shit, I'm sorry for all those things I've said about my mother. I can't believe I've been so insensitive, you must have thought, God, I don't know what . . .'

I looked at her, concerned. 'You've done nothing wrong, Ingrid. You're right to criticise her. It's *her* love that should be unconditional, not yours. Take it from me.'

'Unconditional love,' Ingrid said, still staring at Emma's face. 'I've heard the phrase. But I guess I never really knew what it meant.'

We sat in silence for many minutes. Ingrid pressed the photograph against her stomach, as though she might absorb more of Emma that way. And then the shuffle began behind us, the clucks and the murmurs, as tourists began moving along Marmara towards the Goulas, the sunset ritual underway once more. An hour from now the sky would be washed through with pink and orange as couples contemplated one another in dreamy silhouette. They would notice us sitting, already in place, envy us our private balcony seats for the big show.

'I'm sorry I couldn't tell you sooner,' I said. 'I feel awful about it. The longer I left it the more impossible it became. But it's helped me, I think, people here not knowing. It's made it more bearable. But now I want you to know.' I knew she would intuit from this that I hoped she would tell Eleni for me. I wondered what our friend would say, whether she would say it again: 'I have known this.'

Chapter 22

Dear Rachel,

I hope you are well. Oliver tells us you are opening some kind of photography gallery in Santorini, which is fantastic news. It's not something you've ever mentioned wanting to do, but it makes perfect sense now that you have. Congratulations!

You'll be pleased to know that Cat and Daisy are getting really interested in art. They have a new after-school club that organises trips to the National and the Tate, and they may go on a school trip to Paris, as well.

Jen sends her love. Things are not great between her and Bob at the moment. Some things never change, I'm afraid.

Thinking of you, as always,

Love, Mariel

On the surface, there was nothing different about this note from the handful of others Oliver had forwarded over the years. The tone was warm, but not sentimental; news of the girls consisted of brief, upbeat details, not landmark events, and Emma's presence suffused every sentence, though she was never directly mentioned.

But the note was not where the message lay, not this time. The message lay with the envelope. For Mariel had written independently of Oliver, which meant that she was in possession of my address— or, to be more accurate, she was demonstrating to me that she was in possession of my address. Her letter was as good as official notification of a visit.

*   *   *

As we prepared Panoméréa for opening, word reached those locals previously unaware that a new business was setting up and every day someone new would come in with photographs, landscapes they couldn't remember taking, portraits no one in the family could identify. My efforts to authenticate were amateurish, little more than instinct, but it felt natural to operate in this way.

Ingrid arranged for the German artist, Manfred, who sold his paintings in a boutique near the main square, to come in and show us some of his photographs. He'd never offered them for sale before but had kept them until now as a private project. They were black-and-white vignettes that could have been from any time and were without any sense of having been set up or styled: grape pickers bent over their panniers; lines of fishermen with their spines curved towards the water; details of the unrenovated houses in the village, a window frame, weathered and grey; steps, rough and scuffed; a bell, pale and oxidised against the deeper tone of the sky. Worried I'd be breaking our rule of stocking photographs only of 'old' Santorini, I called in Eleni to make the final decision. She complimented Manfred on his eye for the traditional image, and we put in an order straight away.

Dymas's wooden frames were as beautiful as I'd hoped and no two pieces were the same. Some of the painted timber had been sanded and smoothed, some left flaking still, with layers of paint—orange and blue—flecking the greyed grain. I loved that this was the colour of the water and the sea air, the real colours of Santorini before the pinks and pastels appeared. We arranged to have the stock brought up by mule and fit the mounting and final fixings on site. The tourists took photos as the mules clattered down Marmara, and Eleni stood outside the Ilias with a satisfied smile.

Inside, across the wall we painted a quote from Nelly's, from a visit she'd made to the island seventy years earlier: 'Wherever I turned I saw a picture before me.' In more ambitious moments I liked to think that Panomeréa would become the link between pioneers like Nelly's and the snappers on the hilltop whose sun was in the wrong place.

Dymas donated a large piece of reclaimed wood the size of half a door and Ingrid painted information on it about the materials and the photographs' origins and hung it on the wall outside.

'It'll probably be nicked,' she said, adjusting its height so it could be read plainly from street level. Her friend, the icon painter with a studio near the Goulas, had put up a sign when he was painting: DO NOT DISTURB THE ARTIST. The sign disappeared and he'd put up a second: DO NOT STEAL THE SIGN. That had gone too, and he'd resorted to locking his door.

*   *   *

We opened for business in May 1997, just as the

charter flights began shuttling in the Northern Europeans for high season and the cruise ships began delivering the Americans. I bought the first piece myself to hang above my dining table and make a focal point of it (focal points; I'd been obsessed with them once. Oliver had said that they should put a box on his tax return for focal points). Although I had the advantage of having been free to borrow and rotate a selection of my favourites in that spot, I still hadn't made up my mind when the time came for us to pull back the door and hang the OPEN sign. I walked slowly around the shop, considering each picture in turn. How solid they stood on the marble table tops in their ocean-soaked wooden frames and tough glass windows, yet how fragile; it wouldn't take much to destroy them.

'This would be the perfect time for an earthquake,' I said to Ingrid. 'Just look at all this marble and glass!'

'Hey! Don't tempt fate.'

In the end I chose a view of the beach at Kamari, all creamy sky and iron-grey ocean. I'd visited Kamari once since I'd lived here and it looked nothing like this now, with its rows and rows of sun loungers. The place in the picture had a sense of desolation that was immense for such a small image; it was as if it had been scaled down in all but atmosphere. I watched as Ingrid wrapped it, stamped the receipt, and entered the details into our sales book. It felt like playing shops with Emma, her miniature cash register, the plastic shopping basket for toy vegetables. ('That will be two thousand pounds and thirty-six pence.' 'That much? For a few carrots?' 'Yes. This is a very

227

special shop, you know.')

'How do you feel?' Ingrid asked. 'And don't say you've changed your mind and want a refund.'

Though she joked, I could see she was expecting a proper answer.

'I feel proud,' I said. 'Very proud, of both of us. And Eleni as well. I think we've done a fantastic job.'

'Me too.' She looked no different from usual in her hand-dyed shift dress, winter tan, woven sandals and those perfectly coloured toenails, but to me she seemed transformed, every inch the artistic expat she'd dreamed of being when I'd first met her. She leaned back against the desk. 'You know what? I feel like we need to make a *proper* sale before I really believe it, to a *real* tourist.'

'Like the ones that always drove you mad at the café?'

'Exactly. Someone in a T-shirt that says I Love Santorini, with an exclamation mark. Someone who'd rather jump off a cliff than eat an olive.'

I laughed. 'Oh, I think you can allow yourself to believe it before that happens.'

Anatole bought next, a picture of an Oian bell tower with the silhouette of Thirasia melting into the distance; then Ingrid's friend Alexandros chose a view of Ammoudi for his grandparents, who still lived down by the water there. Manfred bought a Nikos he'd had his eye on and Ingrid joked that she'd get Nikos Junior to buy one of *his*. Then a woman we didn't know came in, browsed, lifted up a small picture by Manfred of women working the vines and brought it over to the desk. She fished in her bag for her purse and handed us her credit card. Schlier, that was her name. When she signed our customer's book we saw she lived in Frankfurt.

'*Adio!*'

'*Adio!*' we sang in unison.

'Now it's real?' I asked Ingrid.

'Yes. Thanks to Frau Schlier from Frankfurt, it's real.'

*   *   *

On the first Saturday of business we had a drinks party up on the terrace—Ingrid's idea (already I was starting to notice that the good ones generally were). Our neighbours left their shops and hotel desks to come and celebrate, expats known or not came to introduce themselves and chatter all night in English, and Eleni joined us when her evening arrivals were all present and correct. She told us the picture Anatole had chosen was now above her reception desk and already two of her guests had commented on it. Ingrid suggested a discount for all Ilias guests.

'Eleni,' I said, warm with wine and sun, 'we want you to know that we consider you a third founder of Panoméréa.'

'Absolutely,' Ingrid agreed. 'It would have been impossible without you, you know. We'd still just be hoarding a bunch of nice pictures in Rachel's bedroom!'

'And if it ever takes off, well . . .'

Eleni shrugged all of this off, but she was pleased, we could tell. As Ingrid was claimed by a clutch of new arrivals—her former colleagues from the café—I watched Eleni straighten the sign that we'd brought upstairs from by the front door, before stepping back and reading it, as though for the first time: ALL THE PHOTOGRAPHS IN THIS SHOP ARE ORIGINAL WORKS OR LIMITED-EDITION PRINTS. This morning, she'd sent us the most wonderful bouquet of flowers. There was no florist in Oia—here people gave flowers picked from their gardens—so she must have gone out of her way to order them from Fira.

'Eleni?'

'Yes?'

'I was just thinking. When I first came here, when I moved into House Callidora, people kept leaving flowers on my terrace.'

She looked surprised by the change of subject and glanced quickly towards Ingrid, still busy with her friends. 'Perhaps to welcome you, I think?'

'Maybe. I thought it was strange to just put them there, that's all. Not to knock on the door or leave a note or anything. And I never understood why there was always basil in there too. Is that a Santorini thing?'

'Ah.' She lowered her eyes, sadly. 'In Greece, basil is very important in our religion. You will see it in the decorations for the icons in the churches. We believe that it grew from the first drops of Christ's blood.'

'Oh?'

'We give it for condolence. *Zoi se sas.*'

'*Zoi se sas?* What does that mean?'

'Life for you. Life for your family. We say it when you have lost someone you love.' She slipped her arm around my waist and squeezed. 'Perhaps they could see you had lost someone. In a place like Oia, in the whole of this island, there is not a person who does not know how this feels.'

I thought of the favours done, the kindnesses given but never announced. I thought of the lowered rent I paid Christos and the surprisingly reasonable rates agreed with Anatole's cousin, and of those first groceries on my doorstep when I'd hardly left my terrace from one week to the next. Below our feet, on the desk in the storeroom, sat my latest report from Palmer. Still he headed it each month Project Godmother, as though it were something so kindly and benign, my position just a notch away from the fairytale figure with her magic wand and a pumpkin for a carriage.

No, if anyone had acquired a fairy godmother, it was me.

'Thank you, Eleni,' I said, and pulled her arm tighter around me.

Chapter 23

Two years later

- The eleventh birthday of Subject B
  was celebrated with friends, including
  Subject A, at the local cinema and pizza
  restaurant. Subject A stayed overnight
  and was collected in the morning by her
  mother.
- Secondary school applications have now
  been filed with the local education authority
  by both subjects' families. Notification of
  results is expected in early April.

Parents often say that the growing of their children seems to accelerate their own ageing, meaning, simply, that it multiplies the number of milestones that mark the way. Easy enough to let your own birthday pass without remark, but you know you've aged precisely five, six—*ten!*—years when you're holding aloft a cake with candles to be counted, one for every year burned through since the creature now standing at your shoulder lay in his hospital crib, since you signed away for ever whatever semblance of peace of mind you once had.

Now, rather than any calendar of my own, Cat and Daisy's milestones marked my time, both reported and imagined: not only birthdays, but also Christmases and Easters, school plays and sports days, new passions (pop music) and forgotten favourites (ballet), fallings out and special friendships—some of them with boys!— inconceivable landmarks all.

It was, however, the physical changes that transfixed me. By now, puberty had taken hold. Cat was growing taller than Daisy, coltish and pale, as though she were outgrowing her Moss Hamlet uniform in style and colour as well as size. The juxtaposition of the raw and the refined in her features was more pronounced than ever: that unruly thicket of hair like her father's, the eyebrows his too, strong, asymmetrical lines that gave her the air of perpetual impertinence (an irritant, surely, to any teacher); it was her mother's hazel eyes and delicate nose that separated those fierce brows and that broad, full-lipped mouth, the teeth slightly larger than you'd expect, making the smile huge and dominating.

Daisy, less spectacular in the photographs, was, I didn't doubt, the more alluring of the two to their peers. Her face was framed by soft falls of blonde hair and her shorter body was already beginning to curve into a woman's. Palmer reported that she was popular and clever, too; likely to leave Moss Hamlet top of her year. There was no sign of a sibling, however. Bob, it appeared, had continued to overrule on that one.

It was impossible to look at the pictures without instinctively searching their corners for Emma. Hers was the face erased from the official portrait, the unperson, the girl-no-more. How might *she* have grown and changed? Might more of Oliver have emerged in her appearance by now? What would she have wanted to be when she grew up? As her old friends' limbs lengthened and their hair darkened, as those adult features lurked ever closer to the surface like second teeth poised to break through the gum, hers remained always the same. Looking at those pictures, I would have exchanged my own life in a heartbeat for a glimpse of her as she would be now, and the grief came, as it often did, viciously, like a smack to hot skin.

*　　　*　　　*

As Panomeréa began to attract customers from around the world, England included, I resolved to redouble my secrecy over my arrangement with Palmer, particularly where Ingrid was concerned. We met too many Brits for comfort and a great asset of Ingrid's was her recall of details from casual conversation long forgotten by me: 'Where did that lovely couple from London say they lived,

Rachel? Was it Richmond?' or 'Do you remember the woman who said she'd had to move house to get her son into that really good school?' It would be easier than you'd imagine for her to tell someone who happened to be Jen's neighbour news of Daisy's exam results, or a new colleague of Toby's about Cat's visit to the optician's. No, it wouldn't do to lose sight of the fact that I had hired a stranger to spy on my friends. However convinced I was that I was acting for the right reasons, I was also sensible enough to recognise that my conduct was hard to explain to the outside world. It could look weird, sleazy even. Palmer was the only person I could count on to understand.

Most of the time, of course, the subject didn't come up. I picked up the packages myself, studied and stored them at Callidora. The danger lay in the periods just after Palmer himself had made a visit, for that was when Ingrid became most persistently curious about the situation. And I could hardly blame her: though jittery before he arrived, often I was visibly elated after he'd left. It was a contradictory kind of elation, however, born partly of his reassurance that the girls thrived and partly of my relief that his visit was over and my obligations done with once more. But there was a third part too, the curious pleasure our time together had given me, and Ingrid being Ingrid, she couldn't help but be drawn towards conspiracies of this more personal nature.

'I know you said he was an investigator, but why does he need to come all the way out here? He wants to keep an eye on *you*, I reckon.'

I raised an eyebrow. 'Don't be silly. He's only been here a handful of times. He's got a friend in

Naxos and it's convenient, I suppose.'

'Yeah, right! What "friend"? Why do you encourage it, that's what I want to know?' Her eyes widened with sudden inspiration. 'Oh my God, of course, he must be some sort of father figure! You've always said you were really close with your dad.'

I protested, only half amused. 'They're nothing alike, Ingrid. Dad was very enthusiastic, very earnest about things; Palmer is completely dispassionate.' This sounded a little too pat, as well as being unfair to Palmer. 'Besides, he's probably not even ten years older than me. He couldn't possibly be a father figure.'

'You mean you don't know his age?'

'No, of course I don't. It's none of my business.'

She pulled a face. 'What do you talk about, then, you two?'

'I told you, he's updating me on the girls.'

'He doesn't need to come here to do that. Don't get me wrong, I think it's great that you're so close—'

'We're not "close", Ingrid, not like that.'

But she just looked entertained by my protests. 'Well, tell me one thing: does he know you're still married?'

I shrugged. 'I'm not really, am I?'

'Aren't you?'

'It's nothing to do with him whether I am or not.'

'OK, I know what you're saying.' With that sudden change of gear that I was becoming used to in her, she looked suddenly thoughtful. 'Oh, Rachel, do you think you'll *ever* be ready?'

'Ready?'

'You know, to have a new relationship?'

How to respond to a question like that? For so long, it had not occurred to me that my marriage might end, not even when it had become entangled in infidelities. For so long my love for Oliver had been eclipsed by that of a greater force, for Emma. It seemed almost quaint now to remember a time when my husband was still the desirable, leading actor of my stage. It had happened overnight that he'd been sidelined—and Toby too, even Bob to a degree—recast as some sort of older child whose schedule had to be integrated with that of the younger one. I'd always assumed that Mariel and Jen shared this perception, but I now wondered if it hadn't been mine alone. Mine was the only marriage that had collapsed, after all.

My thoughts returned to Palmer, to Ingrid's question. Even now I found it easier to change the subject than to answer personal questions honestly. 'Talking of father figures, you never say much about *your* father, Ingrid. Is he still in Australia?'

Now it was her turn to shrug. 'Oh, I expect so. He left when I was little, but I've never tried to track him down. Another waster. He only married my mother because she was pregnant. Don't know why they bothered. You know, I probably wouldn't recognise him if he walked in here right this minute—mad, isn't it?' She paused. 'No, he's probably not in Melbourne any more. He was from a place up near Darwin originally. Could be anywhere now, I guess.'

'Maybe one day he'll track *you* down?' I regretted saying it just as soon as I had, ashamed that I of all people would dangle the fairytale

236

ending as though it were mine to give, as though Ingrid needed only to unravel that golden hair of hers over the cliff edge and up would climb the father, the handsome prince, the saviour.

*   *   *

As it turned out, he arrived in an air-conditioned Mercedes—much more practical. Not Ingrid's father, of course, but a man certainly old enough to be taken for such. My first thought when I looked up and saw him, paused in our doorway with palms pressed flat on either side of the frame—about as close to making a dramatic entrance as was possible at Panomeréa—was that he'd come to throw me out of my house. In the few seconds it took to exchange our greetings I'd already pictured myself homeless, on a mattress in the storeroom while Callidora was refilled with weekly changing sets of canoodling honeymooners. And I could hardly object, either, since I was practically in a grace-and-favour situation. But did it have to be just as the shop was taking up every spare second of every day?

'Well, Mrs Freeman, I see things have moved on here in Oia. A *gallery*, very nice . . .'

'Hello, Mr Kafieris. It's just a shop really . . .'

'Call me Christos, please. And you are being modest. This is more than a shop, I think.'

As he glanced around, I succumbed to a desire to stare, for this was a different Christos from the rain-sodden philosopher I'd met before. This man looked glossy and expensive and immaculately groomed; above a dark tailored business suit the abundant white hair and brown skin were dazzling,

237

glamorous. He looked like some veteran Mediterranean tennis player modelling for a Milanese fashion house. He was arrogant, too, that was clear from his manner, but, still, he couldn't quite hide the smile of a boy who was back in his home town and knew there may be treats ahead.

'How long have you been open?'

'Over two years now. It was slow at first, but the location helps, of course.' To his right, I watched Ingrid emerge from the storeroom, where she'd been reorganising framing equipment. Her hair was a little disarranged and a flake of dried paint hung over one ear. 'Please, let me introduce my business partner, Ingrid Sullivan.'

'Business partner . . . a pleasure . . .'

'Ingrid, this is my landlord Christos Kafieris.'

Christos looked her over extremely thoroughly, returning his hands to his thighs after the handshake as though he couldn't trust himself not to carry on touching her. Then, losing the battle, he reached out and picked the paint out of her hair, placed it in the palm of her hand and closed her fingers over it. She, in turn, smoothed her sun-bleached mane with her free hand and all but licked her lips. Their attraction to one another was instant and undeniable, and it felt a little false of me simply to ignore it and continue with the niceties.

'All is well with your business, Christos?'

'I will soon find out,' he said, with an exaggerated mime of weighing up two equal loads. 'I meet with the mayor here in Oia this afternoon. I have my life in his hands.'

'That sounds rather high risk,' Ingrid said, head cocked, tongue slightly visible between her teeth, and I watched, amused. I'd seen her flirt a thousand times, but never with quite this precision.

'High risk? Of course it is high risk, this is Oia.' As Ingrid's laugh tinkled around the room he promised to return later in his visit for a closer look at our collection and, in the meantime, proposed he take the two of us for dinner the following night. I felt certain this had not been his original intention when dropping by and was taken aback when he suggested the Black Pearl, Oia's smartest restaurant by some way.

'That's very kind of you,' I said.

'Not at all. I'm very interested in hearing how this enterprise has come about.'

Interested in hearing how Ingrid had come about, I thought, trying not to smile.

*   *   *

The Black Pearl was housed in a *kapetanospito* on the main street, not far from the Ilias. Though I'd passed by its gates a thousand times or more and seen the honeymooners waiting to be seated, faces as patient as mules', it was only now, as a bona fide customer, that I fully appreciated its allure. Intimate corner banquettes with sequinned cushions, waitresses in kitten heels, food flavours fused so mysteriously one could scarcely tell what the original ingredients had been—it was perfect for that idyllic last holiday supper. And, of course, it had a sunset view: the sky was hot and flame-streaked this evening, a piece of Turner, and the ocean seemed empty without the battleships.

'Champagne, I think,' Christos said, closing the wine list and beaming at us. Behind him, the shadow of the wrought-iron railing patterned the plasterwork like wallpaper.

'You're celebrating?' I asked. I was glad I'd worn the only smart dress in my wardrobe, a black shift that hung off me in a way that I hoped disguised how unfashionable the style must have become so many years after purchase.

'*We*'re celebrating,' he said.

'Ooh,' said Ingrid. 'I can't remember the last time I had champagne. Your meeting with the mayor was obviously a success then, Christos?'

'Yes indeed!' His proposal, he told us, was to build a hotel complex of luxury suites in Perivolos, converted from some of the very ruins Manfred had photographed for us for Panoméréa. It had taken him years to bring the bureaucrats around, but he had finally done it and his plans had just that morning been stamped. He intended to divide his time equally between Thessaloniki, where his business was based and his family lived, and Santorini, where he'd been born. The facilities in his house in the Sideras district would do perfectly well until an on-site office could be constructed. Had we seen his house, by any chance? It was the pale green one with the white shutters, just a few streets behind the Ilias. We had. It was a lovely neo-classical villa, one of the grandest residences in the village, with exterior plasterwork as smooth as a freshly iced cake and a veranda tiled in a gleaming marble chequerboard. The effect was all the more striking for its being flanked by two *kapetanospita* that had been reduced in the earthquake to single storey ruins and marked unsafe to reconstruct.

'I can't believe that place is yours,' Ingrid said.

240

'That's got to be my favourite house in Oia.'

I nodded, though I couldn't agree. As beautiful as Christos's house was, it was as empty of soul as its neighbouring ruins; whenever I'd walked past the shutters were closed and the gate locked shut. It looked lonely and disregarded. I'd always assumed it to be the rarely used holiday home of some Greek dignitary or celebrity.

'My house is called The Swallows. The hotel, I will call the Swallow Suites.' Christos snapped a breadstick in two as if to underline the concept.

'Very nice,' Ingrid said. 'How many suites will there be?'

'Twenty, perhaps. Very exclusive, very private. It will be a real hideaway.' For some reason, he looked at me when he said this and I held his glance as firmly as I could. What had he said that day, when he'd first come to find me: 'Tell me your story.' Well, if he was planning a return to Oia he would hear it soon enough, I expected.

Ingrid allowed him to light her cigarette with a little silver lighter that made a satisfying clunk when the lid was closed. 'And have you always been in the hotel business, Christos?'

He shrugged modestly. 'Since I was twenty-five or something around that. First I worked for a businessman in Athens, very famous in Greece, he was one of the first to have a chain of hotels here. Then I decided to try for myself. It was always my dream to open a hotel here in Oia.'

He told us he'd studied at the LSE, which explained the good English. How he'd got there from Oia he didn't explain, but I was beginning to see for myself how pleased the students of London might have been that he had. Charisma pulled bystanders to him like so many iron objects to a magnet. Heads turned every time he lifted his chin and laughed, eyes swivelled whenever he exclaimed one of his greetings or leaped up to thump the back of someone he recognised at another table or even in the street beyond. I was starting to flow with the current myself, finding my eyes drawn to him even as he excused himself from us at one point and spoke privately to a third party. Ingrid, meanwhile, appeared cool, but was obviously hooked. She'd hardly eaten a thing all evening and was sending me regular questioning glances, as if to say, 'Can you believe how great he is? *Can* you?'

'I wonder why it's taken you so long to do this?' I said. 'If having a hotel here has been your dream for a while.'

His eyes darkened. 'Enemies.'

'Enemies?' Ingrid cried, dramatically. 'Surely you don't have any, Christos? Look how pleased everyone is to see you!'

But he was not to be drawn on the subject, continuing instead with his family history. 'My father, he worked in the factory here making socks, eight in the morning till ten at night, even as a boy.'

'Didn't he go to school?'

'Not high school—this is a two-hour ride on the mules to Fira. Imagine that! Even on the days when it rains barrels from the sky!'

'I just love the way he speaks,' Ingrid whispered to me when he had slipped away after the main course to catch up with yet another well wisher. 'Perfect British accent but these little mistakes and funny sayings. He's like a poet.'

242

'Yes.' I wondered if he were a married poet.

Typically, Ingrid didn't wait long to find out. 'So, Christos, is your wife here with you on this trip? Will she be helping you build the Swallow Suites?'

He pulled a pained expression and gave a little boyish shrug. 'I had a wife once,' he said, 'but I gave her back to her mother some time ago.'

They both laughed delightedly, then Christos apologised for all the interruptions to our meal. 'My socialising is done, I promise. I am all yours, ladies, for the rest of the evening.'

'Don't we count as socialising, then?' Ingrid asked, pouting.

'Well, I'm thinking you probably do,' he answered, duly admiring her lips. They leaned in a little closer to one another and I resisted the urge to push their heads the final couple of inches and be done with it. Deciding they'd do better without me, I turned down the waiter's offer of coffee and, pleading exhaustion, left the two of them alone together. I could only marvel at Ingrid's stamina, for she worked sock-factory hours herself; constantly on the move, she had a waitress's conditioning to remain on her feet at all times, filling every lull in the shop with tasks that might benefit us when the rush came. She put in twice the physical effort I did. But she was young, I reminded myself, still in her twenties. Life was all ahead of her.

*   *   *

Christos surprised me by keeping his word and returning a few days later to look at our collection

243

more closely. He all but ignored the remains of our Nikos collection, still our star exhibits, preferring a range of Manfred's work that we'd only just bought, idiosyncratic shots of details that had caught the artist's eye: a triangular danger sign for falling rocks; a notice in crooked English, BOAT TRIPS TO VOLCANO; the outline of an open gate—black and white, of course, and all containing those abstract stripes of sea and land and sky in the background. Christos was right, these were just right for upscale hotel rooms, exactly the kind of quirky details that would appeal to the type of discerning (and wealthy) traveller he expected to attract.

He proposed an arrangement for Panomeréa to supply the new villas exclusively, and phoned his interior design consultant on the spot to report his decision. This was generous of him, and honourable too, for the 'exclusive' contract Ingrid and I had negotiated with Manfred applied only to other shops, not to hotels—Christos could have discovered this quite easily and done business with the artist directly. Besides, he hadn't even begun digging yet, he hardly needed to be worrying about finishing touches at this stage. But his vision, it seemed, was already complete to the smallest detail. He even talked about choosing a collection for his reception and for the poolside restaurant, about the idea of offering the works for sale, perhaps, with the commission split between us.

All he said about House Callidora was, 'Maybe I should put up your rent now I am helping improve your profits. To think of this, an Oian paying the British and Australians for photos of his own land!'

'Hey,' Ingrid protested, all pink cheeked and

flirtatious eyed, 'Rachel has native blood too, you know!' And before I could stop her she'd unhooked from the wall the picture of the woman in the pale headscarf and thrust it into his hands. 'Look, don't they look alike? We think this may be an ancestor of hers. Her aunt, possibly.'

'Ingrid! We know it's not.' I tried to take it back from Christos—the last thing I needed was to have to explain my family tree to him—but he held firm.

'Yes,' he said, studying me, 'there is a resemblance, I agree.'

'I bet *you* know who it is,' Ingrid said to him, persisting. 'I got the impression the other night that you know *everyone* in this place.'

'It is important to keep up with the new arrivals,' he agreed, and I thought I might have caught a wink.

'Anyway, we're doing Oia good,' I told him, determined not to be distracted by the picture or their flirting. 'The more beautiful photos there are out there the more new visitors will come here and see for themselves. Maybe they'll stay in *your* new villas.'

'I am teasing,' he smiled, and I was embarrassed by my earnestness. 'This is the right kind of business for Oia. You ladies have my congratulations.'

'Thank you.' I couldn't help being pleased that he approved.

He wiped a trail of dust from the glass before looking closely once more. 'Do you know why I think this lady is familiar to us?'

'Why?'

'It is obvious, no? She looks to me like Santa Irini in the icon paintings.'

I smiled. 'Your lovely patron saint? Well, possibly, but I'm not sure they had the benefit of photography in the third century.'

Ingrid snorted. He seemed pleased by my attempt at humour and keen to play along. 'But you must be mistaken, of course. We are the Greeks, we do everything first!' As he replaced the picture on its hook by the door his eye fell on a nearby Nikos of the monastery at Pyrgos. 'You know, of course, the story of Profitis Ilias?'

We shook our heads, both a little shamefaced.

'But it is such a charming story to tell your customers! Surely you have asked Eleni. Her hotel is named after him, is it not?'

'Just tell us,' Ingrid said, impatient.

He smirked at her, playfully. Already I was getting used to this dynamic between them. 'Well, Ilias came from a little fishing village, but he travelled all over the island in search of somewhere so removed from his own life that the people would not even recognise the oar he carried over his shoulder.'

'A full-sized oar? He must have been bonkers,' Ingrid grinned.

'Well, that's exactly what they thought, I suppose. Everywhere he went he asked the villagers if they knew what it was, and of course they answered, "It's an oar, stupid!" Then he came to the mountains, to this very spot in the photo, Pyrgos, and the people didn't know what the oar was. So this is where he founded his church.'

'I find that very hard to believe,' Ingrid said. 'There's nowhere on this island where you can't see the sea, or at least walk to a spot where you can.'

'I think the point is that he was searching for people who knew nothing of that kind of life.'

I sensed Christos glance beyond her to where I stood listening, but he didn't try to catch my eye. I knew that he would gather by my silence that he had successfully made his point. He had heard about Emma, that was what he was saying; he had heard that when I had come here I had not spoken about her and he wanted me to know that he understood why, that I would never have to explain myself to him.

When he'd gone, Ingrid said, quite matter-of-fact, 'Well, I'm glad I didn't sleep with him the other night. It might have felt like he was paying me. You know, now he's put in this order.'

I laughed, in spite of myself. I couldn't deny that I was as lifted as she was by his arrival in our lives. It was that same sensation of a shot in the arm that I remembered from the early days with Oliver. 'It would have been an excellent fee if you had. Did you see how much it's all going to come to?'

Ingrid winked. 'Just entering the figures now.'

From that time on we fell into the habit of referring to our mystery lady as Santa Irini.

Chapter 24

'Mummy?'
    'Yes, pea?'
    'Sometimes I don't like you.'
    'Oh? Why not, darling?'
    'When I'm crying.'
    'You mean when I tell you off?'

'Yes. You're nasty to me.'

That candour in her voice, those mournful eyes, still a little pink from crying over some admonishment or other. Crayoning on the wallpaper, or was it pulling the shutters off her doll's house? Breaking the stems of tulips in the vase on the hallway table? She was three. The crimes occurred so frequently I'd learned to act only on the serious ones. Pick your battles, Mariel said often. She was our advance party: Cat's adventures were always a few months ahead of the others', and at least twice as daring.

I laced my big fingers through her little ones. 'Well, that's fair enough, my love. It's not nice to be told off. But it's part of my job. In a family you have to have rules, you know.'

She sniffed. '*Whose* rules?'

'My rules. And Daddy's.'

Suspicious pause. 'But *I* want to be the one who says the rules.'

'I know, but we're older than you. We're grown-ups.'

'When I'm grown up,' she said, 'I'll say the rules. When I'm six.'

'When you're six. All right, it's a deal.'

Later, when she was six, I remembered the exchange and told her she was allowed to introduce a new rule of her own. She thought for ages, before saying, 'Well, it's not allowed to eat leaves.'

I tried not to laugh. 'That's true. That's a very good rule. Anything else? Is there nothing for us, for Daddy and me, at home?'

She thought again, not for nearly so long this time. 'I know! It's not allowed to love anyone else.

Only us.'

It seemed to me that our children are born with the knowledge of how to break our hearts.

- Subject A confirmed to attend Greencroft School for Girls: September 2000.
- Subject B confirmed to attend St Jude's Secondary School (Co-ed): September 2000.

As my eye surveyed Palmer's report the abrupt banging of my heart told me something was wrong. I read the lines a second time, just to make sure, and felt a switch of panic snap on inside me. Separate schools for Cat and Daisy after Moss Hamlet? What was going on? They *couldn't* be parted, this had to be a mistake!

For the first time I called Palmer in his London office.

'I'm worried about this. Something must have happened.'

'OK,' he said, patiently, 'let's go through all the possibilities. Could it be the girls' own choice?'

'Of course not, it's obvious from the photos they're still best friends. Anyway, Mariel and Jen wouldn't let them choose, not at this age.'

'Then perhaps it's them who want it this way?'

'No, definitely not.' Apart from anything else, Greencroft was much the better school of the two, as well as being the natural destination of Moss Hamlet girls. No, Mariel would never have chosen St Jude's over it.

'Well, there's been no entrance exam, either,' Palmer said. 'Different catchment areas, perhaps? I remember some sort of trouble when my boy was that age.'

'Palmer, you know where they live! They're only a couple of streets apart, they're virtually neighbours. That's how we met Jen in the first place.'

I heard the creak of a Zippo lid swinging open, then breath drawn and expelled. 'OK, I'll look into it.'

He called me back the next day. 'Catherine's parents *did* apply to Greencroft, but she didn't get in. Quite a bit further from the school gate, apparently. They do it according to walkable road routes, I'm told, not as the crow flies. Cat is nineteenth on the waiting list.'

'Nineteenth? That's crazy!'

'It was way oversubscribed. Five applicants for every place.'

There could only be a street or two in it, but this was the state system; worse, it was the state system in London. Now I remembered reading of children living on the fourth floor of a building who were judged outside a certain catchment area, while those who lived feet below qualified without question. I couldn't help reflecting that my own house—my old house—was even further from the school gates. Emma wouldn't have got in either. So much for all those jokes of ours about the three of them graduating from Oxford side by side before flying off together for Harvard Law School. To think I'd wasted time planning strategies to persuade Oliver to let Emma move up with her two friends in preference to her entering the private-school system; there'd been years to go, what had I been worrying about? I should have been enjoying the time with her then and there, as she was, while I still had her!

'Palmer, what can we do?'

My voice was shrill with anxiety and I could hear him making murmuring noises of the sort one might hear at the vet's. 'It's all right, don't panic now, it's fixable.'

'How?'

'We just need to get to someone in the system. Don't suppose you ever came across the headteacher at Greencroft? Jackie Ratcliffe, she's called.'

'No, I'm afraid not.'

'That's a shame.' He paused, sucked on a cigarette. 'There's always a donation—if she's open to that kind of thing. Schools often are.'

'You mean offer them money? They couldn't go for that, could they?'

'I've learned not to discount any possibility.'

'Let me think about this,' I said. 'There must be some other way, someone who can help.'

The sense of threat continued to make itself evident in my nervous system throughout the day. I could hardly eat or sleep or think about anything else—and quite irrationally, for neither girl was in any bodily danger over this. How Ingrid would laugh if I told her: schools, such a parochial concern! If only *her* mother had had such cares. But it felt imperative to me that Cat and Daisy should continue their childhood journeys together, whatever the destination. I imagined I would feel exactly the same about news of one family moving to the other side of the world. No, whatever delusions I had about this guardianship of mine, this was at the core of it: I *had* to keep Cat and Daisy together.

But how? It was safe to assume that whichever

normal channels of appeal existed, they would by now have been investigated by Mariel. She would have called this Ratcliffe woman herself, tried her best to charm her. If she couldn't do it, then I certainly couldn't.

What then?

It occurred to me in the middle of the night. Simon. More specifically, Simon's father. He was retired now, but he had been, I remembered, a senior civil servant, a schools inspector. If anyone I knew could pull strings, he could. The thought startled me. *Anyone I knew*—well, I hardly knew anyone in London now. Not even my picture research or business for the shop had led me back there, not even by fax or email.

I pulled myself up on to my elbows and exclaimed into the darkness. Email. Of course! I would send Simon an email. In an email I could say everything I needed to without bottling out or breaking down or being asked to explain how so many years could have been allowed to pass without so much as a word. It was a length of time meaningless to me, but surely hurtful to him. Would he understand? Would he even respond?

*   *   *

I remembered very clearly the moment I decided to let Simon's ten-year infatuation with me take us into the wrong. We were having a drink after work—that in itself was a concession for I usually rushed home to be with Emma—and it seemed to me that every direction I looked there were women who reminded me of how I used to be: carefree, desired, desiring. Women like Charlotte.

252

I was suddenly scared that I had been written off or, worse, had written myself off. Simon, conversely, was the picture of unshackled sexuality, hair grown long at the neck, skin tanned from a holiday unimpeded by the need to keep small children in the shade, the corners of his mouth curled roguishly upwards at the merest flirtatious encouragement; there'd been a promotion too, an extra gloss of power that had turned out to rather suit him.

He took me to his tiny flat in Warwick Avenue, the kind of peeling, book-lined place I might have rented myself if I hadn't married Oliver, and we had sex on the sofa. I was drunk and encouraging, he was for the most part silent, as though he feared the sound of his voice might risk bringing to my attention some terrible case of mistaken identity. For me, the contact with unfamiliar skin after several years of marital fidelity brought both shock and pleasure. Since I'd made this decision to transgress, I was determined to enjoy it. Afterwards, he appeared traumatised by the breakthrough and not a little guilty, and I kissed his forehead with real love.

Oddly, I felt I had betrayed not Oliver—he had got there first, if we were being petty—but Emma. Though I'd still be home to relieve the babysitter hours before her father returned, I had surely set in motion real jeopardy, and everyone knew that children suffered the most from parental conflict. No, I told myself, with confidence, Charlotte hadn't broken our family, and nor would Simon. All I'd done was level the playing field (to use an Oliverism). It was strange, though, to feel my moral high ground yielding underfoot. More unexpectedly, there was a scrap of relief involved too, if I was honest, relief that I could finally stop passing myself off as a perfect wife, a *blameless* wife.

Soon after I had admitted to myself that these lapses with Simon had become an affair I said to him, 'You mustn't let this stop you looking for someone else, you know, a proper relationship.'

He turned his face towards me, careful to keep it impassive. 'You'll never leave Oliver, will you?'

I made an effort to meet his eye. It was awkward, but in a way I appreciated his coming to the point sooner rather than later. 'I could never take Emma away from her father. She sees so little of him as it is.'

He thought a while, then said, 'That's fair enough.'

I was lucky to have this fair man in my life, even if it was not especially fair of me to have complicated his with this mid-term reshuffle of roles. I knew that there was no way, were the tables to be turned, that he would have betrayed a wife in this way. Simon had had many girlfriends since we'd begun working together, but none who had been allowed to stick; I prayed I wouldn't become the one he couldn't get over. I excused myself with the idea that he was less likely to idealise me now that he had first-hand experience of my true, flawed nature.

He was the last person I made love with and the only person I forewarned of my departure from London. We spoke on the phone, my own voice sounding as thin and mechanical as the one coming through the receiver from his desk high above Pimlico Road.

'You'll have to get someone else, Simon.'

'What . . . ?'

'For my job. I don't know if I'll be back.'

For a moment I thought he was going to say it, exactly what I didn't want him to say, 'I'll come with you, let me come too, this is our chance,' something terrifying and impossible like that.

'I'm always here.' That was what he said. *I'm always here*. I remembered those words now.

*　　*　　*

In the morning I caught the early bus to Fira. We were not entirely reclaimed from civilisation here—Santorini was not the moon even if the tourist office liked to play up the lunar qualities of its landscapes—and the World Wide Web had reached us in the form of a single 'cybercafé' in the capital. Ingrid and I had set up accounts for ourselves for business, though it was still more practical to use faxes as Oia had yet to be connected. (It was just a matter of time, Eleni said, the only problem being that this was *Greek* time.)

Simon's address was simple enough to deduce from the contact given on the Pendant web page. If I followed the standard formula, with a succession of clicks I could be waiting for him in his inbox when he turned on his computer that morning—assuming he still worked there.

It took over an hour to formulate the short message:

Dear Simon,
I know it has been a very long time and this must seem a little out of the blue. I am living in Santorini now and am doing well, better than I ever thought I could. I've been thinking of you and hoping you are well too.
  Simon, I hope you don't mind me getting in touch like this, but I have a favour to ask. I wondered if your father might be able to put in a word for my god-daughter at her local school . . .

How civilised I'd made my tone, how very polite. Adding Cat's details, I tried to picture his face as he read my message. Would he go white and reach for his cigarettes or, remembering us alone together, blush (he always used to blush a little, which I'd thought sweet). Might he cast his mind back to how it felt in the office, remembering not to touch each other in that proprietorial way lovers automatically did? Or would he think, Rachel, which Rachel? Oh, *that* Rachel.

Let me know if you are ever in this part of the world.

I deleted that last line; too flippant, he didn't deserve that.

I really hope we can meet again in the future. I would like that.
  With love, Rachel

Three days later a response arrived:

Dear Rachel,
Dad may not be able to pull strings these days (you do know we have a Labour government now, don't you?), but I'll certainly pass on the details and ask him to try.
   All is well here at Pendant.
   I would like to see you too.
   Love, Simon

How many lines did *he* delete before he pressed 'send'?

I didn't hear from him again on the subject, but Palmer reported soon after that Catherine's name had been moved to the top of the waiting list for Greencroft. School applications were processed several months in advance and, typically, the parents of at least five children of the ninety in each year's new intake changed their minds or moved out of the area before the following September came around.

'She's as good as in,' Palmer said, pleased.

'I hope so.' I wasn't quite so ready to declare victory. 'I can't bear them to be separated.'

'They won't be. And there's nothing more you can do.'

'But I—'

'I mean it, nothing. Promise me you'll stop worrying.'

I closed my eyes, silenced by his uncharacteristic interruption. 'OK. I promise.'

'Good. Now just forget about it.'

What was odd was that the voice I heard was Palmer's, but the face I saw was Simon's.

Chapter 25

Though my mother had always refused to speak about the events of that day in 1956 that killed her sister and caused her family to flee Oia, she did talk a little about the year that followed, when she'd been taken to live in Athens with relatives on her mother's side. There was one conversation I remembered in particular, from when I was about ten. I was sitting in the kitchen one weekend, fiddling with the radio—a yellow transistor kept on the counter by the breadbin—and she started to tell me about the time she'd first heard the radio, in Athens, not long after the earthquake.

'We hadn't had the wireless in Santorini. I thought there was a man inside, a little man. We all thought this. Then I heard a woman's voice and I thought she was in there as well!'

'That's silly,' I said, scornfully.

'Well, you know, there were so many of us living together then, Yiayia and Papu, my uncle and aunt and my cousins, all of us refugees from Santorini. We were squashed all the time into small rooms, and it seemed quite possible to me that you could fit inside a radio!'

'Did you have to go to a new school?' I asked, imagining being taken from my own and put somewhere strange where nobody knew me.

'Well, of course. I couldn't go to my old one, could I? Everyone knew my sister had died and was nervous about upsetting me. I was very lonely. Yiayia and Papu were worried about me, I think.'

She took the radio from me and tried the knob

herself, turning it back and forth, hardly noticing which channels she was passing. 'I remember when my mother took me to the cinema in Athens too. I'd never been before, of course. I kept asking questions, how could this be, how were they doing it?'

'Like the radio,' I said, laughing. 'You thought there were people behind the screen.'

'Just like the radio. But my mother, she just said "Shh!" all the time, "Sshh, Alysa! Don't ask so many questions, people will think that we're uncultured."'

'What does "uncultured" mean?'

'It means ignorant, not knowing anything. But we *were* ignorant, we *didn't* know anything. There were so many fruits and vegetables I'd never seen before! In Santorini, we had only oranges from Naxos, or our own tomatoes. We were very isolated, you know. Then we came to London and I was sad here too, for a long time.'

I was fidgeting by then, unused to this sort of confidence from her and ready to fast-forward to the happy ending. 'And then you met Dad.'

She smiled. 'Yes, I met Dad, and I had you.'

'So now you're happy.'

I said it as an observation, even a dismissal, but she replied as if it were a question with more than one possible answer. 'Yes,' she said at last. 'Now I am happy.'

*　　　*　　　*

'Please, Madam, it is not right that you are here.'

I looked up at the face above me: young, local, no older than fourteen, anxious-eyed, quite

259

beautiful. 'I'm sorry,' I smiled, 'I was just . . .' I pulled myself upright from the squatting position in which she'd found me. We were in the village cemetery, a pleasant walled space full of fresh flowers, even in winter. I'd walked past the site numerous times but this was the first time I'd actually come in and walked up and down, methodically checking every grave. Behind the girl a group had assembled, a burial service evidently about to take place. There was quite a crowd, not surprising, perhaps, since so many of those buried here appeared to have been local dignitaries. Some of the graves were quite grand and housed the remains of whole families. There were photographs, as well as flowers; framed in gold or marble, they showed ladies in lace and pearls, captains uniformed and moustachioed, their smiles expectant and jolly, as though about to set out for a dinner dance. Silly that it struck me as so incongruous, as though one would prefer to see pictures taken on deathbeds.

'Please,' the girl urged once more. 'It is my grandmother, she asks that you leave us.'

A little startled, I pulled the strap of my bag over my shoulder and looked about me. Other than the members of the girl's party, I was the only person here. 'Of course, I didn't mean to intrude. I'm just going.'

As I passed them, their black clothes fluttering in the breeze—it was an unusually gusty day, even for winter—I couldn't help thinking of a gathering of crows. Conscious now of the cheerful colours of my own clothes, I wasn't at all surprised when a couple of heads turned to look with disapproval. One woman, next to whom the young girl was slipping into place, appeared particularly insulted. She must be the grandmother, I thought, or great-grandmother. An elderly, veiled figure, she was rasping out complaints of some sort to the man on her other side and I caught her eye to try to communicate my apologies. Her expression changed in an instant, not, as I'd expected, in acknowledgement or even reproach, but to that of someone who had—there was really no better image—just seen a ghost. I wondered who she was here to bury; her husband or brother, perhaps. The dates carved on the headstones told of long lives—many inhabitants had lived into their nineties or even to over a hundred.

Phoena did not appear to be among them, however. Though the names were in Greek capitals, which I couldn't read, I had been quite thorough in checking each of the dates alongside them and not one was from any earlier than ten years ago. Where was Phoena now, then? It was unthinkable that Yiayia and Papu would have left the island without laying their daughter to rest. I was struck for the first time by the possibility that her body might never have been recovered, but had remained forever sunken into the rock until its accidental excavation some day by a developer like Christos.

As I walked back, I thought of the ways over the centuries in which children of this community had been taken from their parents. Disease had claimed its slice, as had, of course, those many acts of God; pirates snatched girls for the harems of Muslim leaders; and then there was the *devshirme*, which I'd read about in one of Eleni's history books, a tax imposed by the Turks on their Greek subjects whereby Christian children were taken off to be converted to Islam and serve in the sultan's corps. My Aunt Phoena had been barely eighteen when she died, when life changed for ever for *her* mother. Yiayia still had her younger daughter, of course, my mother Alysa, but according to Mum Phoena had been her favourite. My mother, I realised, must have lived in her sister's shadow both during Phoena's life and after her death. Perhaps that was why my father and she had chosen to have just one child themselves.

Growing up, I'd never thought to ask, only to complain.

*   *   *

It was ridiculous to attempt further investigation of the whereabouts of my aunt's remains without even rudimentary Greek. I decided to recruit Eleni. I dropped by the Ilias most days and it wasn't long before I was able to raise the subject. 'Why are the burials in the cemetery all so recent? Where is everyone who died before buried?'

She looked up from her guest roster, evidently trying to judge my mood. 'Oh, this system in Oia, it is strange! You are allowed only three years or so, then the bones are taken out and washed. They go in a wooden box in the cemetery chapel, all on top of each other, boxes and boxes, so many.'

That must be where Phoena was, then.

She watched me, eyes softening. 'There are lists in the Town Hall if you want me to look up your family's number for you?'

'Well, if you're ever there for some other reason . . .'

262

She tapped her pen on the pad in front of her. 'You have to pay every year, you know, like rent. Anatole and I call it the bone bill.' She chuckled to herself.

'Someone must be paying for my aunt's then. My mother, I suppose, or a relative in Athens.'

'Of course, otherwise they would not keep them. Our neighbour, one year, he hadn't paid for his mother's bones, and they were going to throw them out. And he had washed these bones himself, with his own hands!'

'Really?' I shuddered, thinking of the body I'd seen laid to rest so recently. How grisly to imagine the tomb being opened and the skeleton removed; some ancient ritual down at the shore, I supposed. 'What do they use? Sea water?'

'Wine,' Eleni corrected me. 'You have noticed, of course, in Santorini everything is done with wine.' She lowered her voice and glanced towards the guests' lounge. 'We have a guest with us now, so demanding, I would like to wash her head with wine! That would be a fine use for it!'

'Eleni, you can't say things like that!' I worried that one day she might carry out one of those threats of hers. 'There's a funeral going on this afternoon,' I added. 'Quite a big one, by the looks of it.'

'Yes. Mr Gaitis. I saw the procession.'

The name meant nothing to me and I nodded, about to turn to go, when she surprised me by adding, 'He was a bad man.'

'A bad man? Well, he seemed to have a lot of friends there today.'

Eleni shook her head. 'Tonight they will celebrate, this is my opinion.'

263

Christos's business was hotels, but his passion was wine. Noticing Ingrid and me drinking visanto he laughed when he discovered we didn't even know that the name was a corruption of *vin santo*—'wine of Santorini'—and insisted on taking us to its source, to the local vineyards we'd seen from the roads but never got around to visiting. The vines, fed only by dew in the rainless summer climate, grew in dry, coiled nests, the new branches plaited with the old to create a protective structure for the grapes within. Picking took place in late August, the grapes collected in the wide baskets called *kofinia* that we recognised from Manfred's pictures.

'*Vendema*, you know the word? In Italian it means abundance. We Therans use it to mean vintage.' Christos always used the native word 'Thera' rather than the foreign 'Santorini' and we found ourselves adopting it too.

He pointed out the caper plants and thyme bushes and made us raise our noses to the breeze and identify the other herbs we could smell there. Ingrid was right first time about sage and I guessed oregano, not because I could actually identify it but because it featured in so much local cooking it had to be grown on our doorstep. He took us into the fields to demonstrate the islanders' tradition of bird catching—fishing, they called it, for the poor things were trapped in nets at the end of long upright rods. I was glad Manfred had overlooked them when out with his camera.

Appalled by our ignorance of the Santorini

beyond Oia (my own forays with Palmer had all been well within walking range of the village, and Ingrid and I visited Fira only when business demanded), Christos insisted we accompany him to the archaeological sites at Akrotiri and ancient Thera, to the Profitis Ilias monastery and the small inland villages we lived alongside every day in our own photographs but had never actually visited.

We had gathered from that first dinner date that he was a well-regarded local figure, but now that it was known he was bringing considerable new employment to the community he was quite the local hero too. Everywhere we went doors opened, standard tourist hours no longer applied and wine was offered in place of coffee.

Only now, under Christos's tutelage, did I understand properly the rhythm of life here. As summer gave way to autumn, he drew our attention to the seasonal details we'd only ever half noticed: the flocks passing over southward as the temperature cooled; the cats, well-fed by the tourists in summer, becoming hunters again in winter; the increased barking as the strays that looked so photogenic in summer on their borrowed sun-warmed roofs were now left to fend for themselves. Attacks by packs of wild dogs on mules or pigs were not uncommon.

'We solved the problem once, you know,' Christos said, and Ingrid and I settled down to enjoy another of his stories. 'Years ago. To stop them breeding a vet came and, what's the word in English . . . ?'

'Neutered,' Ingrid said, with satisfaction.

'Yes, neutered the male animals. Food was put out for them too, so they wouldn't need to steal.'

'What happened?' I asked.

'It was all fine until some hikers came from Fira and the dogs followed them to Oia. A whole line of them.' He used his fingers to demonstrate a line of dogs walking the cliff path. 'When the hikers went back the dogs stayed, and it all started again.'

He told us that there was a lava tunnel under the skinniest part of the island, just beyond Finikia. It was possible in the event of another earthquake that the tunnel would collapse and Oia might break off and become an island of its own, like Thirasia.

'No more dogs,' Ingrid said.

'No more coaches full of Americans,' Christos said.

I laughed. 'No more customers for any of us, so let's keep our fingers crossed it doesn't happen.'

'Indeed. Now, who is for a drink in the oldest bar in Oia? Where all the famous captains used to get drunk?'

'Me, definitely!' Ingrid cried.

I had to remind myself to decline his invitations occasionally, to leave Ingrid and him to each other and let their relationship develop, for a relationship was what it was turning out to be. At least that was what I took from her uncharacteristically tight-lipped response to Eleni's and my teasing. Definitive proof came when Eleni and Anatole's younger son Andreas was home for a few months, dividing his time between his parents' base and the house of a friend down by the Goulas. He was handsome and athletic, charming too, precisely the type for whom Ingrid would once have made a beeline. But no longer. Whenever Christos was back in

Thessaloniki or in Athens or one of the other European cities that claimed his time and attention, she was scrupulously faithful. She didn't say as much, and I didn't press her on the subject, but it was clear that she had fallen in love.

Chapter 26

- The mother of Subject B was observed in Drabble's bookshop on West End Lane, NW6, and we were able to ascertain the title of the item purchased: *Lonely Planet: Greek Islands*
- The mother of Subject A visited the home of Subject B and remained for three hours before returning home . . .

First thoughts: they know about Palmer. They must have found out I've been having the girls watched and they've come to confront me. Was it the schools situation? Had Mariel tracked down the source of that convenient reversal? She and Simon had met a couple of times in the past, but I couldn't remember if we'd ever spoken about his father in her presence. Do I have any contingency plans for this? Honesty, only honesty. Maybe they'll understand; I'll bring up the pledge . . .

Then I dismissed all of this. No, this is a planned trip, not an emotional spur-of-the-moment dash, otherwise they wouldn't be browsing bookshops for tourist guides. They're here because they've respected Oliver's wishes long enough, they've waited for me to come back of my own accord and I haven't, and so they're here to persuade me, to reclaim me. A few years is nothing when you're *true* friends.

*   *   *

I saw them before they saw me. It was a Friday in November, late afternoon and out of season, so they must have arrived in Santorini on the two o'clock flight from Athens. They were standing outside the Ilias with overnight bags, presumably having been directed by the taxi driver to the nearest central hotel still open. They would have walked exactly the route I had that first day, five years ago, from the car park behind the school, along the marbled path past the succession of blue-domed churches and the shop windows crammed with trinkets, until the green and terracotta façade of the hotel came into view on the right, the VACANCIES sign—in English—in the window.

I watched them go inside, one head ink-dark, the other that burnished red-gold. As they stood together by the reception desk, looking about for a bell to ring, a pair of hands drifted up to the red-gold and began braiding.

I waited five minutes and then strolled into the hotel after them. The reception area was empty again so Eleni must have been showing them their room—they were probably her only guests. How long did I have, then, before they'd unpacked, remarked on the decor and set out on their search? It hardly mattered, I didn't need to be anywhere else any time soon. Though the shop was open and would be until after sunset, it was quiet in the off season and didn't need both of us on

268

duty; Ingrid and I had therefore established a system of alternate shifts, each taking time off to get some air and run errands. I often took my walks at this time of day.

'Rachel, hello!' It was Eleni, a little hot-cheeked from the efforts of an unexpected check-in. 'I have new guests, just arrived! English, you know. I will send them to Panoreméa, yes? After the sunset, perhaps.'

As she drifted off to tidy up for the new arrivals I tried to concentrate on the music piping from the room corners, local music, instrumental; I could make out the violin and the lute, and then, far sooner than I expected, English voices. They were just feet away now, at the foot of the stairs, shuffling into the sunken lounge area where Eleni arranged magazines into an orderly pile. Mariel held a hat, a sixties print with a floppy brim, the guidebook just visible behind it. Jen wore jeans and a belted mac. They looked exactly the same as when I had last seen them.

'Excuse me, hi again, we were just wondering . . . we're looking for a woman called Rachel Freeman. She lives in House Callidora . . .?' It was Jen's voice, friendly, earnest, a little unsure of the local pronunciation.

'Callidora, you say?' Eleni hesitated, then looked over Jenny's shoulder and through the arch towards me. Her glance drifted towards the open door: this was my opportunity to vanish and instinct told her this is what I should do. She'd never lost that protective urge and I loved her for it. But this was where I lived, where I owned a business. I was not the same person as that tearful, jittery creature she'd rushed to, to warn of Oliver's arrival.

I held my breath as though about to swim a length underwater, and spoke. 'Jenny! Mariel! I'm right here, I saw you arrive a moment ago and I—'

'Rachel!' They turned together, their stricken expressions perfectly synchronised. Now I saw the difference. Both looked far older than I remembered; the years I'd thought I'd obliterated now returned to life in the faces in front of me, years of shock, worry, guilt. Here it was again, what I hadn't been able to bear, what I'd run from in the first place: my own grief mirrored. I had a sudden picture of Jen's face on the day of the accident. Her pain had been so raw, so *elemental*, I'd had to turn away from it as though from my own reflection.

'This is, well, a bit overwhelming . . .' I gave myself properly to the hugs. These had been my best friends, constants in my world, in Emma's world.

'Goodness,' Mariel said, 'I can't believe you've really been here all this time! It just doesn't seem possible . . .'

Jen was already close to tears. 'We've wanted to come so many times, ever since she . . .' She stopped, her wet eyes widening as she feared she'd already blundered, 'ever since you left.'

I nodded. 'You flew via Athens?'

'Yes, there don't seem to be direct flights from Britain, it's not the season yet, I suppose.'

'You haven't brought them with you, then? The kids, I mean.' I felt myself looking around, as if to set about the headcount required of all those times together with the girls.

'No,' Jenny said, awkwardly, 'we thought . . .

270

well, with school and everything.' But she was not good at hiding her thoughts. All this time and they still thought the same as they did before, then: that I'd unravel at the sight of my dead daughter's playmates, that I'd cling to them and frighten them, drag them with me to the brink.

'Good,' I said, lightly, 'because there's not much here to entertain children, I have to say, is there, Eleni?'

Eleni nodded uncertainly.

'And it's very steep, as I'm sure you've noticed, not at all suitable . . .'

I noticed the doubt in their eyes at this, as though I'd confirmed their worst suspicions: I was sounding far too breezy, officious even, like a representative of the tourist office. Whatever they'd been expecting, this was not it.

'Rachel?' Eleni said, obviously recognising the falseness of my tone and again offering to facilitate an escape. 'You must go back to work, no?'

Mariel and Jenny looked at her and then back at me. 'Oh yes, your shop,' Jenny said. 'How's that going?'

'Fine,' I said, nodding my thanks to Eleni. 'You'll see it while you're here. But my partner Ingrid is there at the moment, so I don't need to rush back. Do you want to come and see where I live?'

There was no mistaking the sharp exchange of glances at that, either. I sensed what they were thinking: it's real then, she *does* live here. She has been flesh and blood all this time.

As we said goodbye to Eleni, she reached out and squeezed my hand, whispering 'Goodbye' as though about to see me go to the gallows.

'It's OK,' I whispered back, 'honestly.'

I led them through the hotel and back out into the sunlight. The narrow passages and tricky steps made it easy for us to avoid conversation for the moment, and they expressed surprise when we arrived, only minutes later, at my terrace.

'This is you?' Mariel asked, with some delight. 'You're right in the middle of things.' She moved towards the terrace wall and leaned towards the cliff face. 'How lovely to have this view every day. So much outside space!' And it did look idyllic, my new domain, with its blue-painted gate and deckchairs, the woven rugs on the tiled ground, flecked the traditional way to break the sun's dazzle. Yes, impossibly charming in the afternoon sunlight—just the sort of image I would once have selected for a travel guide or a book about garden design.

'We're sheltered from the north wind on this side of the village,' I said, 'so the sunshine is lovely and warm, even in winter.'

'Mmm, it's so good to feel the sun,' Jen said, holding her face up to the rays. It was dull in London, no doubt, and I couldn't recall from Palmer's reports any holidays for her and Daisy since the one we'd arranged for them. A sudden look of concern on Mariel's face caught my attention. 'I'm surprised it doesn't make you a bit nervous being up here, Rachel, right by the edge like this. You know, what with your thing about heights.'

I pulled a face. 'Cured, apparently.'

'Really? How come?'

'I don't know, but it was gone from the moment I got here.'

She narrowed her eyes doubtfully. 'I don't understand.'

'I know, I was surprised at first, but now I'm used to it. I can lean right over the edge and not feel a thing.' To demonstrate I hopped over the terrace wall and stretched my arm out towards the sea below. 'Weird, isn't it?'

She paused, about to make some technical diagnosis, perhaps, post-traumatic something or other, but thought better of it and looked about for something new to comment on. 'There are lots of churches around here, aren't there?'

'Yes,' I said. 'That's why this area is called Monastiri. Oia is famous for its churches. This is where they take all those photographs you see, the typical Greek island ones, with the blue domes.'

'Are people here very religious, then?' Jenny asked, stepping forward hopefully. I thought of those visits to church she'd been making. Palmer continued to mention them regularly. It had lasted, then, her commitment to a new faith.

'Most of the churches are privately owned and permanently closed,' I said, 'except for their own saint's day, when they open up and have a party.'

'Oh.' That wasn't what she had in mind at all.

As I unlocked the door and ushered them into my cave I saw that they were uneasy once more, stranded amid the sparseness, murmuring politely as they looked about them. After the sunny, colourful terrace, this felt cold and lonely. Except for the one framed Panomeréa photograph of Kamari there was no decoration to speak of, none of the touches of the kind that had distinguished my home in London, no pretty pieces picked up in Paris antiques shops or tall crystal vases with long-

273

stemmed roses. No little girl's shoes and schoolbags . . .

'It's nice and simple,' Mariel said, and Jen nodded her agreement. I felt for them, I really did; what could they say, after all? 'Gosh, Rachel, what a perfect place to grieve!' I thought of their own homes: Mariel's orderly terrace, with its labelled drawers and the carpet pile striped like turf from the press of the Hoover; Jen's crammed flat, where everything was within tripping distance and armies of soft toys did battle with Bob's computer equipment.

'Do you use this as your office?' Mariel asked, reaching to touch the stacks of manila envelopes in the alcove by my bed. I jolted in alarm: Palmer's reports! And the one at the top was open, the corners of a stack of prints just visible between the white A4 pages.

'Yes, a bit of overspill,' I said quickly, and drew the little shutters that closed off the space. She stepped back, unsuspecting. 'Right, let me show you the kitchen . . .' I couldn't allow myself to think about the information those letters contained or to imagine Mariel and Jen's faces if they were to glance even at a single one. My instinct had been right, they'd never understand.

In the doorway, Jen was struggling with hiccups, forceful, chest-heaving ones, which gave the impression that she was about to burst into tears or, possibly, vomit. I watched her glance rest on the shelves of produce in the kitchenette: a two-litre can of olive oil, large jars of dried herbs, packets of coffee.

'So have you been living here all along, then?'

I found I couldn't look her in the eye as easily as

274

I could Mariel. 'Yes, after the first few weeks, anyway. I'm lucky to still have it. The landlord has said I can stay indefinitely. I'm like some sort of sitting tenant. Have you seen the view from the window? It's the volcano. And everything underwater between here and there is volcano as well.'

She glanced dutifully at the square of shimmering blue. I wasn't surprised that she responded less willingly than Mariel to my tourist guide's patter: she had not lost that trademark candour. '*Indefinitely?* You mean you're never coming back? But what about . . . everyone back home?'

An audible intake of breath from where Mariel stood beyond the doorway told me they hadn't planned to cut to the chase quite so early in proceedings. Don't rush her, her eyes reminded her friend, remember she'll be shocked to see us. Jen hiccuped again.

'There's no one,' I said, quietly, looking from one face to the other. 'I'm sorry, I don't mean that how it sounds. What I mean is . . . well, there's no one who can't get along without me.'

'That's not—' began Jen, but Mariel cut smoothly in.

'We understand, of course we do.'

'How *are* Cat and Daisy?' I asked, abruptly, as though it were understood that they were who I'd had in mind. 'Growing up, I imagine?'

Mariel, recognising no doubt that she was now aboard a runaway train, opted to stick to the matter-of-fact. 'Cat's had one cold after another. We had to see the doctor for her cough, in case it was tonsilitis. Toby had his out at her age.'

I wanted to mention her broken wrist, the schools situation, all of the events of the past few years that I'd followed from afar, but of course I couldn't. 'Do you still see Dr Williams?'

'Yes, he's still there, doing his flu jabs.'

The surgery on Broadhurst Gardens, the waiting room with the rocking horse. Ride a Cock Horse to Banbury Cross . . . 'to see a white lady,' Emma would sing when she was a toddler, 'upon a fine horse'. Some of the older patients would smile at the mistake.

'You can't move for pensioners at this time of year,' Mariel added. 'It's the same at work, I don't know where they all come from.'

She was doing well, subtly getting us back on course, but Jen just went right on veering off it. 'They still mention Emma, you know, the girls. Sometimes when we're looking at photos or we go somewhere we haven't been since . . .'

Since . . .? I managed a tight smile, willing her to say the words.

'We all do, we all miss her, she's still . . .' Again, she couldn't finish her sentence. What cliché escaped her this time, I wondered? I felt my throat fill with sudden anger.

'What, Jen? What were you going to say? Since she went to sleep for ever in Heaven? She'll never *really* be gone? She's still *with us in spirit*?'

Jen looked thoroughly menaced at this unexpected baring of teeth and took a step backwards out of the door and into the arch of sunlight. The rug had curled in the breeze, tripped her a little, and she looked down with an exaggerated start, as though she'd just saved herself from stumbling over the cliff edge. She

276

looked back at me with injured eyes. Now I was irritated that she thought she had the right to be hurt by my anger, that she considered herself of any consequence in all of this. What *were* they doing here after all this time? Surely they weren't here simply to tell me how sad *they* still were that my daughter had been thrown through a windscreen and smashed on to hot tarmac? That they knew how *I* felt? It was clear to me now that Eleni had had good reason to be cautious of this reunion, for I was thoroughly disturbed by this visit of theirs. Somehow, in transplanting themselves into my new private universe they had achieved the effect of pulling me back home. It might have been weeks, days, since Emma's death.

Mariel moved coolly into the space between Jen and me, looking from one stricken face to the other. 'Why don't we go and get a drink somewhere? We're pretty knackered from travelling and it would be nice to sit outside in the sun.'

'Of course,' I said, all at once ashamed of myself. Why was I finding it so hard to accept their presence here? Wasn't I lucky that they cared enough to have sought me out, to still care? I tried to think straight, to think what was expected of me here. 'Would you like dinner, or is it too early? A late lunch, some fish, maybe? I sometimes walk down to the harbour at Ammoudi at this time. There are restaurants there by the water.'

'That sounds great,' Mariel said firmly, 'Doesn't it, Jen?'

Jen blinked, eyes still offended. 'Yes, of course.'

Chapter 27

I led the way back down Marmara, past the Ilias to Panoméréa, where I left the two of them on the marble to dip down the stairs and let Ingrid know my plans (now I was pleased we had such steep steps down to the entrance, for neither attempted to follow). Luckily Manfred had just stopped by, so Ingrid couldn't delay me with too many questions, and I had set off again within moments. I could see Mariel and Jenny noticing the open taverna on the way, and a café too, the table in the window set with a glass of ouzo and a tall fluffy coffee, designed specifically to lure us in, but I didn't falter. Clearly I wanted to punish them, then, with an arduous trek—was that it? Or was it to give myself time to collect myself before the inevitable interrogation?

'Wow,' they exclaimed when we reached the castle ruins, more ruined somehow when empty of its revellers. 'This is amazing! Look at all this sky!'

'It's where everyone comes for sunset. The Venetians built it as a watchtower, but it was damaged in the earthquake and they pulled it down.'

They nodded, wary perhaps to talk of disaster, even the natural kind.

'We're going down this way, to the water.'

'This zigzag path here?'

'Yep, there's a road behind the village, but the footpath is more . . .' I trailed off. 'Fun' was hardly the word.

We descended in silence. I couldn't imagine

what conversation lay ahead, tried desperately to connect with the world inside their heads and not my own. How many conversations must they have had together since that day, conversations that began, 'What if . . .'? 'What if Cat had been the one to suffer from travel sickness that day . . .?' 'What if the impact had been at the rear of the bus where Daisy was sitting . . .?' There but for the grace of God went their beautiful little girls. But it seemed to me that the more they tried to conceal their relief the more they radiated it.

'It's still so warm,' Mariel said, as we settled into seats by the waterside, 'even at this time of year. They must still do decent business, then.' She was determined to persevere with the small talk, at least for now.

'Yes, we've been lucky so far this winter,' I said, obligingly. 'It's hardly rained at all. Not like last year.' I opened the menu. 'Right, not much point looking too hard, they'll just give us what they caught this morning. But how about some salad? Or *fava*, the local speciality? It's really delicious.'

'Fine, anything is fine,' Jen murmured.

'You order,' Mariel said to me, agreeing.

After the waiter had reappeared with water and bread, I turned sharply back to the two of them. 'So, how's Oliver? I assume you still see him?' I tried to suppress my own knowledge that most, if not every encounter had been noted in Palmer's surveillance.

Mariel's eyes softened as she considered. 'He *says* he's fine, but, well . . . To be honest, Rachel, that's partly why we came. We've been worried about him. He's drinking an awful lot. I think he's still hoping you'll come home, you know.'

I felt my brow crease. 'Surely not? Not after all this time . . .' Looking at their anxious faces I felt guilty. They deserved better than this from me. 'He writes to me,' I said. 'Every month or so. We've been in touch the whole time.'

'That's good,' Jen nodded. She paused, glanced at Mariel, and said, 'He's been coming to church with me, you know. I think it's been a good thing.'

'Oh?'

'Yes, that's why I asked about the churches here. You might find—'

'I doubt it,' I said, interrupting. 'You forget, Jen, that I grew up with the church. There's no need to convert *me*.'

'That's not what I—' Intimidated, she gulped back the rest of the words.

I looked back at Mariel. 'I thought he might have moved by now, it's such a big house for just one person. It was too big even for three.'

She nodded sadly.

'Have you been there much?' Been into Emma's room, seen if there's anything left of her.

Jen must have been making the mental connection herself for she said, 'He asked us to come over, when it first happened . . .'—that bothered me more than it should have too, when it 'first' happened, as though the death of my child had been a recurring event—'he wondered if the girls wanted to choose something of Emma's.'

I swallowed, remembering the picture of Cat with Emma's doll. 'That was a good idea. Though I guess they must have outgrown those toys long ago.'

'Here we are, ladies!' We all started at the sound of the cheerful male vowels of the waiter.

He had arrived with the fish, huge and blackened on its oval plate, and it was only as he positioned it between us that I remembered that Jen was a vegetarian. 'Shall we order you something else?'

'No, no, I'm fine with salad and potatoes.' She was struggling not to feel the martyr, I could tell, reminding herself that she was not the one whose life had been devastated beyond repair; what on earth did *food* matter? Again, I couldn't help focusing my anger on her. See, I wanted to snap, all those years we respected your principles to the letter, but the body of a fish isn't as valuable as the body of a child, is it? The catch of the day will be forgotten by tomorrow, won't it?

I turned back to Mariel, offered her first go.

'It looks delicious,' she said.

'You can't possibly finish all that between you,' Jenny said, a little sulky now.

I caught Mariel's eye and was pleased to see a little sparkle of amusement there, for I knew that she was remembering too how Cat and Emma would eat together, each clearing their plates and asking for more. 'We're *still* hungry!' Daisy, on the other hand, had always been the fussy eater.

'So what do you think about this legal case, then?' Mariel asked, passing me the plate and tending to her bones. 'Is Oliver keeping you up to date?'

'The man's dead,' I said, flatly, 'that's what I think. It should be enough.' I sensed I'd confounded them; Jen in particular looked bewildered. Doubtless the pursuit of revenge was considered quite natural in situations such as Oliver's and mine, cathartic even. I thought of Jen and her scalpels were Bob ever to stray; what would she be prepared to do, then, for Daisy's life? Or had that all changed now she'd found the Lord?

'I took the insurance money,' I added, annoyed with myself for feeling the need to explain. 'You probably know that. Oliver wanted me to have it. I used some of it for the shop.'

Mariel's frown cleared. 'Oh, not the lawsuit against Morris. That was just a claim for damages, wasn't it? I mean the new one, the civil case against the Lockley boy. Well, I say new, but it's been dragging on for ages now.'

I stared. *'Lockley?'*

'The kid in the passenger seat,' Jen added. 'Andrew Lockley.'

'I know who he is,' I said impatiently, 'I got a letter from him, actually.'

'Did you? When?'

'Years ago now.'

'What did it say?'

'Just that he was sorry.' I didn't feel inclined to give Jen the details; she was acting like she was part of some legal team herself.

'Hmm. Well, they'll no doubt bring that up in his defence.'

'His *defence*? Defence against what? The police never brought any charges.' I tried to recall what, if anything, had been said about Lockley's future in the weeks following the accident. He'd simply walked free, as I remembered. 'I'm sure there wasn't enough evidence to prove he'd been an accessory, or whatever it was.'

'That's right,' Mariel said, 'the police did say that. But this is a private prosecution, not a criminal trial. Oliver's funding it himself.'

282

'I don't understand . . .'

'The investigation by the insurance company brought up all sorts of stuff the police hadn't told you, or maybe didn't know. Like Lockley knew Morris was driving that day and still encouraged him to smoke dope and take the cocaine.'

'He won't go to jail or anything,' Jen chipped in, 'but it would be great, wouldn't it, to see justice done?'

Great? 'Not really,' I said, coldly, holding Jen's gaze until she looked down at her plate. 'What's "great" about whether it was Morris or Lockley who took drugs or encouraged the other or whatever it is you're saying? Neither of them meant to kill anyone, and Morris hardly meant to kill himself, did he? It was an accident.'

'Yes, but . . .'

'Of course,' Mariel interrupted quickly, catching Jen's eye. 'Rachel's right, it makes no difference. I'm sorry, we thought you knew. Oliver's very caught up in it and we assumed he would have mentioned it.'

I'd underestimated Oliver, then. It wasn't about the money at all, it was about blame, blame dressed up as a bid for justice (with Jen's help, he even had God on his side too!). And work, of course. I should have guessed that that simple claim for damages against Morris was never going to be laborious enough, not for someone whose ability to withdraw from the world and focus on The Work was legendary. Even during the aftermath of Emma's death he'd kept up to date, retreating for hours on end to the study with its fax machine and computer. Well, what could be more labour intensive than legal action? Long hours, the

283

apportionment of blame, a pile of bank notes spent or won: better than any prescription drug. Perfect.

There was something else, though, something only I could know. As long as Oliver's legal struggles continued, the people around him would use her name. They would write it in statements, key it into documents, they would speak it in testimony; it was a way of keeping her with him. And that, at least, I understood.

*   *   *

On the way back Mariel barely broke sweat, still keeping herself in great condition, evidently, and Jen, though breathless, was damned if she was going to be the one to complain and risk another tongue lashing from me. With the shorter winter evenings it was already getting dark and they both turned to me in relief when we reached the steps of the Ilias.

'Can we see you again tomorrow?' Mariel asked. 'I mean, only if you can spare the time from work.'

Seeing her exhausted face, I smiled as warmly as I could. 'Of course I can. I'll come to the hotel in the morning, shall I? Show you around properly.'

'You don't have to . . .'

'No, I'd like to, really. You've come all this way.' *For nothing*: the words dangled, unspoken, between us. I knew they would cry when left on their own, Jenny furiously, full of hurt pride and bewilderment, Mariel, too, in her delicate, lip-biting way. They'd comfort each other and then take it in turns to use the phone to call home and check on the children. They'd lie on their beds for

284

a while and look at the photographs they'd brought with them in their handbags, imagine the blissful squeeze of the first hugs on their return.

And I curled up too, with thoughts of *my* child. Our heads on the pillow together, her soft skin, her soft hair, her soft breath. All softness.

Chapter 28

They *will* be friends, that's what Jen had said. They'll always have each other. Did I add that or was it Mariel? No matter, we all meant it, that was the point.

Three girls, three mothers, three fathers. Living in each other's pockets as we did, it was surprising, perhaps, that the nine of us had gone on holiday together just once. The Algarve, a villa with a pool and maid, sprinklers keeping the immaculate, wrap-around lawns lush. It took a few days to adjust to the differing family dynamics and some were never quite resolved. Oliver, accustomed to reading his book in peace and taking little part in domestic routine, irritated Jenny to the point of obsession. Didn't he know that it was rude to fetch himself a drink without asking anyone else if they wanted one too? And why pay no attention to the children when we were so plainly here for their benefit? Bob, inexhaustibly gung-ho for the most part, would confuse everyone with a sudden, unexplained slump in spirit. Toby, a known hypochondriac, had a tendency to ruin magical moments by grumbling about a stomach bug.

'You know what he's like,' one of us would say,

and it was quite true. By then the three of us knew exactly what the others' men were like, almost as well as we did our own. Without thinking, we often referred to them collectively, as a tribe, just as we did the girls.

It was not the greatest success, that holiday. Two weeks is a long time in the health of three infants. Cat got an ear infection, Daisy suffered dehydration and was hooked up for twenty-four hours to a drip in the local children's ward. There were problems with bones in the sardines, sore gums over the ice pyramid things they insisted on sucking, and in an attempt to get them eating with us we avoided children's menus and were instead forever waiting for cataplana to cool or gazpacho to be warmed ('Don't like cold soup. No!'). An adult-orientated trip to Monchique in the hills was a predictable step too far, for the girls were bored and slouched about in a way that seemed to prefigure teenage ennui. 'I'll need a holiday to recover from this one,' Bob said, and we nodded, as though it had never been said by a million parents before us.

There were times, though, when everyone was happy: ice-cold rosé for us, fizzy drinks for them; a blissful hour when a coach at the nearby timeshare complex took them to play tennis (or, rather, to dodge balls from his machine while hiding behind each other). We fell over each other to take photos, every activity made more photogenic in triplicate: eating their ice creams; sitting in a row on a step; chasing down cats; standing at the edge of the pool, armbands on, tummies sticking out; in the sea, riding on their fathers' shoulders. And the genius of Mariel producing three bottles of bubbles for them to blow when all else failed to amuse—she'd been holding back for when things got really desperate.

Oliver and I had the room at the top of the house, with views over the gardens on two sides. I remember putting Emma to bed one night and, as I closed the shutters, I saw the two other couples, one out of either window, Bob and Jen with hands held, Mariel and Toby with arms around each other. I wasn't even sure if Oliver was on the premises, for he'd taken to wandering into the local village for a beer without thinking to tell anyone. And so, as the two couples murmured their sweet nothings, or so I imagined from my viewpoint above, mine were exchanged with my daughter.

'I love you, darling.'

'I love you, Mummy.'

'Sleep well.'

'What if I'm scared?'

'I'll keep you safe, don't worry. Don't ever worry.'

*   *   *

I arranged to meet them the next day at Panoméréa. Ingrid had had just two customers the previous afternoon and was happy to be left a second time with paperwork and a novel she wanted to finish. Introducing Mariel and Jen to her briefly, she was discreet to the point of disinterest and I sent her a grateful look I hoped the others wouldn't catch.

'We'll come back and buy something later,' Mariel said to her, politely, as I tried to shepherd the two of them out.

'We're going down to Armeni,' I added, over my shoulder. Though I dreaded another day like yesterday, my manner was no different from that of any expat pleased to be playing host to visiting friends.

'Sooner down than up,' Ingrid said, gamely. 'It's heavy going, guys, I hope you've got a bottle of water with you?'

They were prepared this time—Mariel had even switched her shoes for trainers—and were, I sensed, braced for any other odd new behaviours I might spring on them besides these enforced scrambles down the cliffside. They imagined I was testing them, testing their patience and their trust, and their new strategy was to use the location to get a foothold on the old me. Mariel was particularly good; I got the feeling she might have read up on the island overnight.

'So this is an old port, but the ferries go to Athinios, right?'

'Yes,' I said. 'Just on the other side of Fira. Until recently they came in here. Apparently it was quite a scene with everyone jumping ashore and scrambling up the cliff.'

Resting in the shade just above the settlement, we gazed down at the tiny church and the vaulted roofs of the buildings that lined the dark pebble beach. Today the place was barely touched by human breath. I told the others that there had once been seven shipyards down here and that all but one boatshed had now closed, and even this last one—where Dymas worked—was used only sporadically. I pointed out the scrub that clung to the red rock; the jetty from which the summer visitors boarded their tourist boats; the lone figure working on one of the buildings, his paint roller extended high above his head as he whitewashed the upper exterior in long, slow strokes. Then, facing the water, I said, 'I'm sorry I didn't come and tell you before I left. I wish I had. But I thought a letter would be enough. I suppose I didn't want anyone to talk me out of going.'

That knocked them, of course. In fact, I surprised myself with my sudden confession.

'It just seemed so extreme,' Mariel said quietly.

'I'm sure it felt right,' Jen added, all conciliation today. Then they started speaking together, interrupting one another:

'We went to your house. Oliver just said you'd gone. He was totally shocked.'

'It was like he was in a trance or something.'

'We didn't know whether he meant you'd gone missing or what . . .'

'I called Alysa. I felt awful bothering her, but we were so worried . . .'

'Then your note came . . .'

'Mine didn't arrive till the day after . . .'

' . . . but at least by then we knew you were *some*where.'

Alive, they meant; they must have feared I'd been tempted to follow Emma while still too maddened to comprehend where it was that she had gone. A bottle of pills, a bridge over the Thames; they'd thought about how crazed with grief they'd be themselves in my position. They thought they knew.

'We would have come a lot sooner,' Mariel said, lips twitching a fraction with emotion. 'We've been getting your cards for the girls, of course. But

289

Oliver made us promise. He wouldn't even give us your address. We couldn't understand it . . .'

'We got Bob to search for you on the Web. He's obsessed with it, knows all these weird websites . . .'

'Toby thought we should come, but after he met you at the airport that time, he said no, we should wait . . .'

'We should have told you we were coming, but we didn't have a phone number. We weren't sure we'd even find you . . .'

It was important to them to be able to tell me this, to relate their individual traumas, to fill in the gaps. They missed the time when we'd been a team, had known each other's every move. I heard them out, patiently, and then asked, 'When's your flight back?'

They were thrown once more. 'First thing tomorrow,' Mariel said, again the first to recover, 'but we can change it if you want us to stay. Why don't you come with us, Rach? There's sure to be spare seats. You could just come for a few days, stay with us, see how you feel?'

I shook my head. 'I can't. I have the shop.'

'But your friend can cover, can't she? Ingrid, she said how quiet it's been, there can't be many customers at this time of year . . .'

I didn't answer and they knew what that meant.

It was too early for lunch, but we were able to get drinks at the taverna by the quay. The proprietor, Yorgos, a jolly man with a weather-beaten complexion and cracked lower lip, spotted the new faces and pounced.

'You like boat trip? Still running every day.'

'I'm afraid we're off tomorrow,' Mariel said

290

politely.

'Tickets no problem, my son captain.'

'He always says that,' I smiled, '"My son captain." It's kind of a catchphrase.'

And they slipped each other that look again, the look that said, She knows everyone, doesn't she? She really belongs.

When Yorgos had shuffled off to prepare our drinks, I asked after Jake and his recent birthday, picturing the sweet, curly-haired boy by the girls' side in the photographs. The new third. He was five years old now, already at school. Almost the age Emma had been when she died.

'He's lovely,' Mariel smiled, 'so good-natured. You know, it's true, boys *are* easier.'

'You must miss him?'

She looked down and stirred her coffee. 'Yes. But it's good for Toby to have some time with him.'

'Cat will help.'

'Yes, she's quite the bossyboots.' She paused. 'As you know.'

I looked up. *As you know.* That was where the message lay. I'd known Mariel since we were twenty years old, I could read between her lines as well as any simultaneous translator. However unsuccessful this mission she wasn't going to let me disappear, she wasn't going to allow the connection to break. That ability of hers to wait a situation out, it was still there. Four or five years was nothing to her, she'd wait fifty if she had to.

I turned to Jen. 'You never did have another baby, then?'

She looked down too, wishing she had something to stir, but her drink was lemonade, it had come without ice or a straw, and there was no fiddling to be done in that quarter. She looked flustered, as though she recognised I required a new explanation, a better one than those I'd heard in the past. Did Emma's death make a difference to her? That was what I was really asking, wasn't it?

'I just don't think we can afford it,' she said finally, and glugged at the lemonade. 'Bob's still not that keen, he's struggling to get work . . .'

'He started up on his own, you know,' Mariel said, coming to Jen's rescue. 'Ages ago. Oliver might have told you, actually. It was quite soon after you left.'

'I did hear,' I said casually. 'It hasn't taken off then?'

Jen shook her head. 'Not really. And we sank so much money into getting all the kit at the beginning.'

'I'm sorry.'

'Anyway, we'd need a bigger place if we had a baby and I can't see that happening.'

'You do need more space,' Mariel agreed.

'Daisy's getting older, there'd be too much of a gap . . .' Still Jen went on protesting and still Mariel went on rescuing her.

'They just started secondary school,' she said, subtly changing the subject. 'Applications were a right old rigmarole.'

'Oh yes?' I said, adrenalin starting to splash. I wasn't sure I trusted myself today. I felt unpredictable. 'They're at Greencroft, I suppose?'

She nodded. 'Cat only just got in. It was a bit of a nightmare, to be honest.'

'Oh?' As I let her tell me the ins and outs of a

292

crisis I'd already experienced, I couldn't stop myself picturing Emma in the grey and red of Greencroft's uniform, just like Cat and Daisy. How she had loved school, right from the start. An image came to mind of me collecting her from her nursery school once, running late and the last to arrive. The teacher cut short her customary update to say, 'I shouldn't say this, Mrs Freeman, but there's something about Emma, something extra special.'

'That's kind of you . . .'

'No, it's true, it really is. She has a sort of . . . *quality* about her.'

Did she say that to all the mothers? Was it part of parent management, Lord knew, an art worth mastering in her line of work? In any case, we all thought ours was extra special; presumably that was how the species survived.

*   *   *

Before we climbed back up to the village, I led them to the far side of the beach to show them the driftwood that had inspired our decor at the shop. 'It's so beautiful, don't you think? Look how many layers of blue there are here, there must be three or four. And orange too, right underneath. You could never achieve this effect if you were trying. Can you imagine how many hours that wood has spent in the ocean?'

Surprised by so long a speech, they bent eagerly to look. Jen handled her piece deftly, as though checking the sole of a foot for hard skin, and for the first time during their visit I felt my heart stumble towards her. How the girls had loved it when she trimmed their toenails and brushed on the varnish, glittery purple or baby pink, colours chosen from her carousel of pots. She'd been so wonderful with them; Emma had adored her. I smiled, remembering, but she wasn't looking my way.

On the way back up progress was slow as we stopped at each turn to look at the views. I pointed out Callidora across the bay. 'It's easier to find in the summer because of the bougainvillea. It's like a bright-pink flag, you can spot it from halfway to Fira.'

They had given up now, I knew. When we reached the main street, all three of us panting heavily, Jen pleaded exhaustion and went on ahead to the hotel. Mariel walked me back to my house and I poured us visanto. For the first time I felt guilty, properly guilty, both for my silence since I'd lived here and for my deception of them with Palmer. Because it was deception, wasn't it? And perhaps it was time I gave it its proper name.

'I have been back, you know, to London.' The confession was a way of alleviating my guilt, at least for the moment. 'Well, Toby told you, of course. I've been more than once, actually. I've had to. Mum won't come here.'

Mariel's eyes filled with compassion. 'She still feels the same?'

'Yes, I don't think she'll ever come around. She never replies to my postcards and letters. It's like her hatred of Santorini won't even let her write the word itself on an envelope. It's become a phobia.'

'That's a real shame. Poor Alysa. Maybe if you had some news of her family? Have you tracked any of them down since you've been here?'

I shook my head. 'They all left after the earthquake, to the mainland.'

'What about the sister who died? Isn't she buried here?'

'I'm trying to find out, but I can't find her grave. You're right, though, maybe if I can show her I'm interested enough to have done my own research she might open up a bit. It's crazy, though, because she's the one who has the answers to my questions.'

'It's difficult,' Mariel agreed. 'You don't want to upset her more than you have to.'

And suddenly I knew. After all this time I finally knew why I'd chosen to come here. Far from being sorry that my mother couldn't bring herself to visit me here, it was *because* I knew she wouldn't come that I had selected it in the first place. Being with her terrified me, and not just because her grief magnified mine. The truth was that every moment I spent watching her grow old was one that Emma would not be here to watch in me. Here, in Oia, where the women looked and sounded a little like her, I had been with Mum without having to actually be with her. Those Christmas visits, well, they were the least that she deserved, but they were also, for now, the most I could give her.

Once I wouldn't have thought twice about sharing this insight with Mariel, this intelligent, thoughtful, loyal friend of mine, but now I couldn't. It was glued inside my mouth. Instead I said, 'They still have rumbles occasionally, you know, though nothing serious since fifty-six.'

She looked out to the dark islands of the Caldera. Volcanoes *and* earthquakes, she was thinking, *Jesus*, what a place; no wonder Alysa won't come back. 'Imagine not knowing when the next one's going to strike,' she said, finally.

'At least here you know it might.' At least you understand the danger and you've prepared yourself for it. Here, when the figure approaches with the terrible news, it will never really be out of the blue.

Mariel, watching me and knowing she'd strayed into indelicate territory, did the opposite of Jen with her panicked retreats, and chose instead to advance. 'Oh, Rachel, are you sure you're better off here? You've suffered the worst possible tragedy, the absolute worst! We just think you should be back home now, back with family and friends.'

'I have friends here,' I said. 'It's been a long time, you know.' And it was awful to meet her eye and see the tears there.

'I can't bear it,' she said, simply. 'I can't bear what happened to Emma. Our precious, precious girl . . .'

I nodded, clenched my jaw to stop my face from spasming.

'I keep thinking of her the day she was born, we came to the hospital, do you remember? She was so tiny, just a little mouse . . .' She was sobbing openly now. 'Toby and I, and Jen too, we'll never change how we feel about you, you know. We'll never forget, *never*.'

'I know.'

I held her hand and we were quiet for a while.

'I've been a bit harsh with Jen, haven't I?' I said, sighing. 'She just gets to me, all that church stuff. And she's obviously made Oliver some kind of special project.' Even as I spoke I recognised the unfairness of the words. All Jen had done was think of him, be there for him, when his wife was not. And she'd done it as much for me as she had for him.

Eyes dried, Mariel said, 'She's not herself at the moment. She and Bob, well, it's a miracle they're still together. They almost split up, you know, about a year after you left.'

'What happened?'

'She was going to come and stay with us, just a trial thing, but he sprang this dream holiday on her. It seemed to work wonders, actually. We were all really relieved. But it's gradually gone back to how it was, worse probably. They shouldn't be together, but I think they think life would be even harder if they weren't. And of course there's Daisy.'

'What an awful situation.'

She nodded. 'It's been the right decision, you know, for her not to have more children.'

Again I thought to myself, What were you thinking? To have interfered in the natural course of a couple's relationship? All I'd done, it seemed, was to sentence Daisy to a life without a sibling.

I nodded. 'Tell her I'm sorry, will you?'

'Of course, but you needn't be, she understands.'

'Mariel?'

'Yes?'

'I've been thinking a lot recently about that vow we made . . .'

'Vow?'

'About the girls, years ago. The pact.'

'Oh, that.'

'I feel terrible I'm not there for them. I'm Cat's

godmother, as well, I should be in her life, guiding her, doing things for her!'

'Oh, Rachel, don't say that. You've kept in touch with her, that's the important thing. Birthday cards, Christmas, that's enough, until you're ready.' Patient Mariel. She spoke as though months had gone by, not years.

'I just want you to know, I haven't forgotten. If anything happened, well, I would still step in . . .'

'Of course you would!' She sighed. 'Oh God, I hope we haven't upset you, turning up like this?'

'No,' I said, firmly, 'it's been lovely to see you.'

'Has it?'

'Yes.' And I knew it was wrong, but I was tired and I felt I'd done enough, I'd met her halfway, and now I could give myself permission to disengage again. Though we spoke for another hour or so, the rest was like conversation conducted through the letterbox of a locked door.

The next morning they left.

Chapter 29

Though I'd been to Christos's house many times since we'd become friends and Ingrid and he partners, I still looked forward to each visit simply for the beauty of his house. This being Oia, it had been built with views of the ocean in mind, with unobstructed visibility on three sides. How easy it was to imagine the original occupants looking across the rooftops to the church of Irini at the tip of Thirasia—the first church seen by the sailors entering the Caldera—before casting north for an early glimpse of sails on the horizon.

Inside, the walls were built from red volcanic stone and the floors cut from the same wooden planks as those used to build the ships of the day. Furnishings were a mix of traditional Santorini—wooden settles, gilded mirrors and painted chests—and imported antiques. The local woven runners you saw in every Oian home lay alongside thick-piled richly pigmented carpets from the East.

Eleni had suggested I come. While I had been busy with my London guests, she had been in the Town Hall looking up death registry and burial records. My aunt, one of only half a dozen or so to be killed in the earthquake, had been struck in the chest by falling rocks and had remained alive for twenty-four hours before her lungs collapsed and she lost her fight.

'She was unlucky,' Eleni concluded.

'That's one way of putting it.' There was unexpected relief in simply hearing the facts confirmed from a third party, as though I'd never quite believed my mother's own version of her family history.

A further detail had emerged thanks to the death of old Gaitis; various family diaries had been donated to the museum in Fira and Eleni had been permitted to study a single reference to Miss Phoena Vlachos. She had, it transpired, been fleeing from the main part of the village down to the water's edge when she was struck down. Presumably she'd been hunting for my mother and grandparents, worried for their safety.

I frowned. 'Why would Phoena be mentioned in a Gaitis family diary?'

Eleni shrugged. 'The family must have known

your aunt. She may have worked for them, they were very wealthy. I found many other names too. There is no mystery here.'

The only oddity was that her remains were not listed in the village. She had no box, no bone bill.

'I have checked all the lists and nothing.'

'That's it then.' I wondered if this was remarkable enough to take to my mother and re-open discussions, though I suspected not.

'You have asked Christos about all of this?' Eleni said.

'Yes, but he doesn't remember Phoena.'

She shrugged. 'I think he will remember Gaitis, though.'

The sound of footsteps on polished wood brought me back to the present. Christos appeared, casually dressed, a little strained around the mouth. 'Rachel, you're not at the shop? Is anything wrong?'

'No, no, Ingrid's just taken over. She said you were here and I wondered if I could have a quick chat.'

'Of course. I was just about to make coffee anyway, come through to the courtyard.'

We sat out in the shade. There was no sea view, but it was one of my favourite spots in Oia, utterly private and always cool, even in the hottest months. 'Eleni said I should chat to you again because I'm trying to find out about my aunt, the one who died in the earthquake.'

He nodded solemnly.

'We've just found out she's not buried here and I'd like to find her, to pay my respects. I just keep thinking, You *must* have come across my family, Christos, my mother and aunt. My mother isn't so much older than you, Alysa Vlachos.'

He shook his head. 'I can't remember them. I am sorry. I was very young, not even five. I remember only the children my own age. After the earthquake, those of us who stayed, we played in the broken houses.' He rose to his feet. 'Let me show you a picture . . .'

He came back with a yellowing print, a full-length shot of soldiers supervising the dismantling of the Goulas. 'According to my father, not every building was damaged enough to be torn down. But when the mayor objected, he was struck in the face!' To illustrate this, Christos slapped his own cheek and recoiled dramatically.

'I don't believe it; there seems such camaraderie in the photo.'

'Well, photographs are just a single moment, aren't they? And this was a long time ago, it was hardly a secret snapshot. It was probably set up.'

'That's true.'

'Your mother has told you, I'm sure, about the man who lay across his door, across the . . . what's the word?'

'Threshold? No, what happened?'

'When the soldiers came to pull down his house, he threw himself down at his threshold and cried, "Over my dead body!"'

I couldn't help thinking of my mother's comment about how she would only return over her dead body. It was a sad symmetry. 'And they let him stay?'

He nodded. 'His house is still standing now. He is dead now, of course, like most people from that time.'

'Like Gaitis,' I said, remembering Eleni's tip.

Christos's face darkened. He rapped his fingers on the photograph. 'How did you meet this man?' he demanded.

I blinked, surprised. 'I didn't. At least I don't think so. He may have come into the shop, of course, most locals have. No, I just happened to see people arriving for his funeral and Eleni told me who he was. She said he was a bad man.' It sounded ridiculous when I said it and I laughed. 'Well, you know what she's like.'

Christos frowned at my flippancy. 'She was right. My father was against him. He made money out of Oia, he sold our village in pieces.'

'What do you mean?'

'That was how it worked, after the earthquake.' He looked again at the picture. 'When they pulled down the buildings they were paid by cubic metre, so they took down more than was needed. Gaitis was involved. And he was not the only one, oh no. Afterwards he bought up so much of the village because it was very cheap. The *skapha* for my hotel, he used to own them. He refused to develop them himself, but he would never sell, either.'

He was glowering now and I regretted coming here and stirring all this up. I'd only succeeded in ruining his mood and learning nothing of Phoena. 'Well, at least there are still some of you left in Oia who remember how it was before. People who know the truth.'

His face cleared. 'This is true, but every year, not so many of us.' He looked at me with the small brave smile of a boy. 'And when we are gone, who will remember?'

*　　　*　　　*

302

'Another of your mysterious packages?' Ingrid asked from the doorway behind me. I was sitting at the makeshift desk in our 'office' underground, the week's mail open in front of me. For once I'd picked up Palmer's report on my way to the shop and not on my way back. 'Yes, just his monthly update. Nothing special.'

'He must keep the Hellenic Post in business single-handed, I reckon.'

I ignored the sarcasm. 'I won't be a minute in here, I'm just trying to clear this pile of invoices.'

'No hurry. I'll use the desk when you're done.' But she continued lingering. 'Anything exciting?'

'Just the usual stuff. We need to pay Manfred soon. He's so sweet, he never reminds me and I'm always late.'

'No, I mean from your friend Palmer?'

'I don't think so.' I brought the pages of his letter to the top of the pile and pretended to scan the words; I was much too ashamed to admit the truth to Ingrid, that the reports still came but I no longer read them.

That visit from Mariel and Jen, specifically that last conversation with Mariel, it had been like turning a sunlamp on a frozen window. And I was horrified by what I now saw through the glass. The idea that I should have the right to 'intervene' in the girls' lives, to override their mothers! In our years of separation I'd somehow managed to forget the rather crucial detail of their being devoted to their own children. Even here, in Santorini, there had not been a single moment when Cat, Daisy and Jake had not been with them. Their children *were* who they were. I'd thought repeatedly of how they might feel if it were theirs who'd been taken from them, but I'd hardly considered how I might feel if someone I didn't know, man or woman, was following Emma about, reading copies of her school reports, taking covert photos of her, meddling in the natural course of events—it turned my stomach. What a ghastly invasion of privacy. There was no alternative but to bow out.

My only saving grace was that in the madness of it all I had also forgotten what it was like to be a child, to be on the cusp of adolescence. From about the age of nine I had concealed every last thing that mattered to me from the woman in the bedroom next to mine, drip-feeding information to her through my father as and when I deigned; what earthly chance would some stranger have stood, lurking in the street with a notebook? Far subtler mysteries had beset Cat and Daisy than any that Palmer or his operatives might have divined, and many more awaited them. Yes, we had managed to monitor the logistical comings and goings, but we'd never come close to getting inside the girls' heads, of that I was now quite sure.

'Did I tell you?' Ingrid said, still hovering. 'Someone wanted to buy Santa Irini! One of those old widows who lives up by the windmill.'

I looked around, jolted from my thoughts. 'Really?' I had to admit I was a little torn by the news. I was delighted that we'd made the sale, but sorry not to have Irini watching over us any longer, heavy browed and benign. 'Well, that's great news! Well done. Did you have to knock anything off the price?'

Ingrid pouted. 'Are you kidding? I told the woman she wasn't for sale.'

I opened my mouth in surprise. 'But why? She's been hanging around for years. Besides, we haven't sold anything big all month.'

'We're doing fine,' Ingrid said. 'And anyway, she's not even on display. The customer saw her in the storeroom.'

'She was only there because we forgot to put her back out after the last time you insisted on showing her to someone! Of course she's for sale.'

'But it's obviously your aunt, isn't it? We *can't* sell her. It would be like selling, well, your granny.' Her eyes widened, visited by new inspiration. 'Rachel, that could be it! It's not your aunt in the picture, it's your *grandmother*!'

I sighed. 'Ingrid, it's not my anyone! I think you can trust me to know what my grandmother looked like, at least. I did meet her a few hundred times.'

She pouted, disappointed.

'Look, I know it's been fun to have this kind of mystery on our hands, but I think we have to accept she is not my aunt or any other relative of mine, living or dead. There can't be anyone left in Santorini who hasn't been in the shop at some point, and not one has had a clue.'

'It's just a matter of time,' Ingrid said. 'Someone must know.'

Yes, I thought, my own mother. And I wouldn't have to wait long to renew my attempts to draw her on the subject; I was due to make my annual Christmas visit in a little over a month's time.

'She got quite cross about it, actually,' Ingrid said idly. 'It was weird, but I got the feeling she was looking especially for it. She didn't really look at anything else and she deliberately wandered into the storeroom, even though I had the rope up.' She shuddered. 'They give me the creeps, these old widows. You know, they stay in black *for ever.*'

'Well if she comes back, we should just let her have it,' I said, turning back to my papers. 'Did you at least ask *her* if she knew who it was?'

Ingrid began laughing. 'To be honest, she was so old I'm not sure she knew who *she* was.'

She was right by my shoulder. 'Can't I just have a quick look? I've never actually read one of these famous reports. I reckon they're secret love letters . . . My darling Rachel . . . no, that's not right, he'll have a nickname for you, I bet, Pippin or something.'

'*Pippin?*' I started to laugh, but a moment later stopped, my heart punching against my ribcage. 'Hang on a second . . .' With Ingrid chattering in the background my brain had somehow been tricked into absorbing the words on the page in front of me, into actually reading some of Palmer's notes. 'Oh my God.'

'What? What is it, Rach?'

'Nothing.'

'Stop looking so weird!' Ingrid cried. 'What is it?'

'I don't believe it.' Whatever my recent intentions, in front of me was a piece of news that couldn't easily be unlearned: the mother of Subject A had moved out of her home, taking Subject A with her. Jen had left Bob.

*   *   *

It had happened within days of her returning from Santorini. Mariel had been right: mine had not

306

been the only demons Jen had come to confront. Notice had been given on the rental flat in Fairhazel Gardens that the family had occupied ever since I had known them. They'd moved there a few months after Daisy's birth, having previously shared a studio flat on Camden Road. The last of the boxes were still being unpacked when Mariel and I had first visited. Now Bob was spending their notice period there alone, while Jenny and Daisy moved in with Mariel and Toby. Suddenly the girls were not just in the same school, they were in the same house.

Abandoning my new resolution in an instant, I picked up the phone and dialled Palmer's office.

He coughed. 'I had a feeling I might be hearing from you.'

'This looks pretty serious.'

'They've had problems before,' he pointed out.

'Nothing like this. This time it's really over.'

'OK, well, if you're sure it's too late for marriage guidance ...'

'I don't think that's going to happen. I just want to make sure Daisy's got a roof over her head.' It will be my last involvement, I thought to myself, I'll just see Daisy settled and then I'll tell Palmer.

'What do you want to do?' he asked.

'Well, I've got an idea. Tell me if you think it's crazy ...'

I considered the facts. Jen and Daisy couldn't live with Mariel and Toby indefinitely. I remembered the layout of the Challoners' house as well as I did my own: they had three bedrooms, one for them and one each for the kids, which meant Daisy must be in with Cat (did she still have her bunk-beds, I wondered, the beech-wood ones

307

stencilled with flowers?) and Jen on the sofa in the living room, unless she was in the bunk-beds with Daisy, and Cat required to share with her brother in the smaller third bedroom at the top. Either way, it wasn't an arrangement that could last for long. Where was Jen thinking of going next? Her parents and two brothers lived down in the West Country, but she wasn't especially close to them, as I remembered, and in any case I didn't think she would pull Daisy out of her new school; she would surely want to give her some continuity.

Money had to be the stumbling block in setting up home on her own. My mind sifted through years' worth of reports: there had been nothing to suggest any reversal of fortune over the years—in fact, hadn't Palmer recently found Bob to be in arrears with the rent? And he'd referred more than once to a 'big hole' in their joint account. Savings could be hidden, of course, but in all likelihood Jen had none.

My plan, therefore, was for Palmer to find a local flat, rent it in his company name and sublet it to Jen at below market price. Not so low that it seemed too good to be true, but low enough to be affordable to someone who worked part time. He'd say the landlady had left the country to work long-term overseas, that the right tenant was more important to her than profit—just as Christos had for me. Jen would fall for this, I hoped, she was one to believe in altruism. In any case, it was all perfectly true.

*   *   *

The flat Palmer found was in Canfield Gardens,

close to where Oliver and I had lived when we'd first moved to the area together. Though it was on the top floor—their old flat had had its own garden—its occupants had access to communal gardens as big as a park, and it was easy walking distance from both school and the Challoners. Part-furnished, newly painted, ready to move into: perfect. It was also expensive, but I estimated that, if necessary, the remainder of Morris's damages would be enough to cover the shortfall between the rent I paid the landlord and what Jen would pay me for at least until Daisy turned eighteen. Palmer offered the asking price, signed the agreement, and collected the keys. Then he put a notice in the local newsagents and an ad in the weekly paper: Two-bedroomed flat in Canfield Gardens, overseas landlord seeks suitable tenant for below market rate, long let. Of the forty or so enquiries he fielded on the first day, not one was from Jen; nor on the second; nor on the third. On the fourth day, he posted a flyer through the Challoners' letterbox. On the fifth, Jen phoned.

'She's signing contracts tomorrow,' Palmer reported. 'They should be in before Christmas.'

'And the landlord knows to make contact only with your office? Never directly with Jen? She must never know what the real rent is . . .'

'He does, she won't, don't worry.' He paused. 'You want to know something weird?'

'What?'

'I'm starting to see what this is all about, you know, your godmother project. It gives you a good feeling, doesn't it, doing something like this for someone?'

I took a deep breath. 'Palmer, I need to talk to

you. After this . . . well, listen, I'm coming to London for Christmas, to see my mother. Could we meet?'

'Of course, sure, what did you have in mind?'

'Is there a pub near your office where I could meet you one evening?'

I wrote down the directions he gave me and hung up. I felt unexpectedly emotional, and the Jen affair was not the only reason. It was no longer possible to avoid the fact that, by ending the reports, I would also be ending my contact with him.

Chapter 30

It was the morning I was due to leave for London that Oliver's letter brought his first—and only— reference to the civil case against Andrew Lockley. He had won, it transpired, and a newspaper cutting supplied the details:

> Yesterday Andrew Lockley was shown to be guilty 'on the balance of probabilities', the standard of proof in the civil court, and declared an accessory to the death of six-year-old Emma Freeman. The epic and costly struggle that has made Oliver Freeman a heroic figure in certain circles may well come to benefit a wider group: the families of all victims of crime.

I couldn't celebrate, I could only think for the thousandth time of that cemetery in north

London, with the bare black trees and traffic rushing by. She didn't belong there. She hadn't had time to show us where it was that she belonged. Perhaps, like me, she might have come to belong here. I wondered often how she would have responded to my new home, our old family home, what she might have noticed in particular about the place. Children had an eye all their own, their lower viewpoint was a part of it, but there was also that need for the unformed mind to identify images it already understood; it was the foreign twists on familiar habits that they noticed, the schoolbags hung in olive trees, the hillocks of gelati inside the chiller cabinet. Here? Not the domed churches or the Caldera views. More likely the way the cake was served with a tiny teaspoon, making dainty eaters even of grown men, or the dogs and cats and the way they competed for attention, snapping at one another when the restaurants were full and there were scraps to be had. She would have relished Christos's story about the dogs following the hikers along the clifftop. She would have asked for it to be repeated until she was sure of every detail.

Yes, Emma would have liked it here.

It was a long time now since we'd discovered places together ('Let's go exploring, Mum!'), but sometimes, still, down at sea level, I'd be possessed by a shiver of déjà vu, remembering with perfect clarity sunny days together, holidays with warm sea water and big skies, the two of us coming inside from the park or the beach, lips tasting of salt and cheeks stinging from the sun, dazzled and groggy from a world overexposed.

After the relative success of that first Christmas visit to my mother's, I had returned a second time and a third, until it had become accepted as an annual arrangement. Mum seemed pleased enough, as though she'd expected less and knew better than to look a gift horse in the mouth (even if those gifts did have to be bought in airport arrivals halls to avoid bringing Santorini goods into her home).

Inevitably, we talked this time about the Lockley case. Mum had her own collection of press cuttings and, I was pleased to detect, a new sense of acceptance that the matter was now closed. She asked me about Bob and Jen too; she had not lost touch with my old friends and was keen to discuss the separation.

'I was never sure about him,' she said. 'There was always something not quite right about those two.' She'd never said that about Oliver and me, not once.

'Some relationships just aren't meant to last,' I said. 'When there are outside pressures, it's too hard.'

She didn't say what I knew she was thinking, that the outside pressures—like the bringing of legal proceedings against accessories in your daughter's death—were supposed to be borne together; that that was the only way they *could* be borne.

I decided to bring up the subject of Phoena right away. 'Mum, please don't be annoyed with me, but I've brought something from Santorini to show you.'

'What is it?'

Trying not to give in to nerves, I took the photograph of Santa Irini from my handbag and undid the wrappings. Now the moment had come for her unveiling, the face in the picture looked less like my mother's than I'd imagined. I began to feel silly. 'We wondered if this might be Phoena? Or maybe another relative of ours?'

She looked up sharply. '*We?*'

'Ingrid and I. She's the friend I own the shop with.'

'I see.' I was curious to hear genuine relief in her voice.

It was several seconds before she agreed to take the photograph from me. Then, to my surprise, she just chuckled. 'There's certainly a resemblance, but I don't know who this is. And I don't suppose her father was a sailor like mine. This sort of thing was only for the captains, love, the wives and daughters.' Of course, I thought, it was basic common sense. Papu, like his father and grandfather before him, had been a seaman and in no position to pay for portraiture of this sort. This could never have been anything to do with our family.

'I just thought I'd try. It's been a bit of a mystery for us. No one in Oia recognises her, either.'

Mum looked at me as though I were particularly dim-witted. 'Because she's not *from* there, obviously.'

'You think it was sent from some other place?'

'Of course, from her parents, I imagine.'

'Oh.' So Santa Irini had been submitted by her family for consideration for marriage to an Oian, like the miniatures sent from afar to Tudor kings.

313

It followed, then, that she'd been rejected. For her wilful look, perhaps, or for the inadequacy of her dowry.

'She was lucky,' Mum added. 'If she had married into a family in Oia she might have been dead.'

I decided to take advantage of her uncharacteristic cooperation. 'Do you still remember it, Mum? The day of the earthquake?'

'I was already twelve years old,' she said, frowning heavily, 'of course I remember.'

'What happened? I mean, how did it start?'

She looked at me closely, as though weighing me up, just as she had when I was little. She would tell, but only if she thought I was grown up enough to hear what she had to say. I held her gaze. I'm grown up enough, I thought grimly, don't forget that I have suffered too. Sighing, she seemed to reach the same conclusion.

'It was early in the morning. Five o'clock or something like that. Yiayia woke me and we looked outside together. I couldn't see anything, only dust, thick red dust everywhere, and my mother held me so hard against her I could hardly breathe. The noise was very, very loud. Big blasts and rolls, like thunder from under the sea. It went on all day.'

'What happened to Phoena?'

'We didn't know about Phoena at first. She was not at home. In the beginning we thought only of our neighbour; his wife was screaming that he'd been injured and we rushed to help. He had broken his arm, from the rocks falling from higher up. I saw another woman with her leg broken, as well. We all went to the shore, but the water was

314

moving up and down, you know, rising and falling. Terrifying.' She gripped at the arm of the sofa as if to a life raft and closed her eyes. I wasn't sure if she was trying to erase the picture in her head or sharpen it.

'Whereabouts was your house?'

'Not far from the castle. But we left straight away, my mother and I. My father pushed us into his friend's boat, with his family, and we sailed around to Perissa.'

'What about Papu?'

'He stayed behind to look for Phoena. My mother wept for the whole journey, and when we got to the beach she was even more upset, seeing the tents and the naval ships coming with supplies. I think she realised then that this was really a big disaster.'

'I've seen photos,' I nodded. 'All those ships on the horizon. It looked like wartime or something.'

'Worse, that day, because we had no understanding of the enemy.'

I nodded. 'I've been looking for Phoena's grave, you know, in Oia. I was worried about the bone bill.'

Mum looked at me, confused. '*What* bill?'

'For the bones, for keeping her bones in the church. But she wasn't on the list.'

'What do you mean?' Her voice rose and I feared for a second that she might be becoming distraught, but instead she gave another grim little chuckle. 'But Phoena is buried in Athens, Rachel, we took her body with us. There is nothing for you to worry about in Oia. There is nothing of our family there now.'

Except me, I thought, unexpectedly frustrated. I

315

should have been satisfied with her story, I knew, and maybe it was my disappointment about the photograph, maybe it was my desire for this trip to be about ending *all* my mysteries, all my deceptions, but I heard myself saying, 'There's something else, isn't there, Mum? Something you're not telling me about Phoena. How did she die? Why wasn't she at home like everyone else?'

'There is nothing else.' But I was right. She looked agitated, glared at me as though I'd betrayed her with one question too many.

'Tell me, Mum. Whatever it is, I want to know.'

She threw up her hands. 'Rachel, it doesn't matter what you "want" to know! Please think about someone other than yourself for a change.'

'What?' I gasped. 'I *am* thinking about someone else! I'm thinking about Phoena. What is it you think we've been talking about?' And before I could stop myself I was fifteen again and flouncing out of the door and up the stairs to my bedroom.

At the sight of my open suitcase and the piles of envelopes arranged inside it, I calmed down, instantly distracted. I hadn't brought the photographs, I couldn't bear to part with those, but the reports I'd gathered up and transported here, every single one of them.

- Subject A stayed home from school; her mother phoned in to report a sore throat . . .
- Subjects A & B were dropped at Fairhazel Dance Centre by the mother of Subject B . . .
- Subject B was taken to the Fractures Department of the Royal Free Hospital to have her plaster cast removed . . .
- Subject A turned eight and had her party in

the church hall. A magic show was performed by her father . . .

- Subjects A & B attended after-school French Club and were walked home by an unknown subject . . .
- Subject A fell playing with stilts in the school playground but was unhurt . . .
- Subjects A & B and their families attended the All Saints carol service . . .

I wasn't sure how long I'd been reading when I heard knuckles brush my bedroom door. 'Rachel? Can I come in . . . ?'

Mum. She turned the handle and stepped in, face contrite, but stopped at once at the sight of me on the bed, propped against my pillows, surrounded by pages and pages of white paper.

'What is all this?'

I could have lied, passed them off as business documents and swept them out of sight, but instead I said simply, 'They're reports.'

'Reports?'

'Yes. Private detective's reports. An investigator in London has been sending them to me in Santorini every month.'

'Reports about what?' She picked one up, eyes narrow with confusion. 'Who is Subject A?'

'Daisy,' I said, 'and Subject B is Cat.'

I knew what she was going to say and I was prepared to go along with it all, everything save the suggestion that I confess to the two families. Admit to doing wrong, though, certainly. Own up, that phrase from childhood. You need to own up, Rachel, and my father adding, 'If you don't admit what you've done how can you be forgiven?'

317

'I'm stopping it,' I said, pre-emptively, 'that's partly why I'm back. I'm meeting the investigator and asking him to stop.'

She just kept picking them up, one after the other, reading a line or two and moving on to the next. Finally, she spoke. 'I'm glad you did this.'

'What?'

'I'm glad.' She nodded, evidently quite convinced. 'It makes more sense to me now.'

'What does?'

'I just couldn't understand, all this time, why you didn't seem to care.'

I lowered my eyes to one of the thousands of lines.

- Subject B was observed accompanying her mother to the park . . .

'But you did care, didn't you?' she said softly.
I looked at her. 'Of course I did. I still do.'

Chapter 31

Palmer and I met on my third night in London, the day before Christmas Eve. Our meeting place, a large corner pub with huge windows on to the street, was much more crowded than I had expected, but we were able to find two seats on the far side of the bar, behind a wooden screen. It was a smoky little nook quite unlike the rest of the place, book-lined with leather volumes in the style of a Victorian library; on closer inspection, however, I saw that the books had each been sliced vertically in two in order to fit into the shallow shelves.

'Is that art, d'you think, or just extremely bad planning?' Palmer grinned, raising an eyebrow. His hair was noticeably longer than when I'd last seen him and it made him look quite different—more casual, more attractive. I wondered what had happened for him to have relaxed the preciseness of his presentation to the world. A woman, perhaps. The thought left me oddly deflated.

'What can I get you to drink?'

I saw a sign for mulled wine and asked for that. Watching him wait at the bar, it occurred to me that I'd known him for several years now but had never noticed him age. Those changes that occurred in the girls' appearance every month, I had been able to pinpoint them in the photos almost with a single glance. But perhaps that was it: you noticed change only in pictures, with the evidence freeze-framed in front of you. I had no photographs of Palmer.

'You look very well,' I said, as he placed our drinks on the table and settled on the stool opposite.

'You too.' I felt unexpectedly shy as his glance passed over my upper body. I was wearing a dark-red knitted top, an indispensable lightweight in Oia in winter but much too flimsy for London, and the lace-up neckline had come undone. It felt wrong meeting him here, in London, out of hours, like coming across a school teacher in the street at the weekend, the established roles undermined and the potential existence of others exposed. I'd never felt that in Oia, even during long afternoons when the girls had been forgotten and we'd talked

319

about ourselves. In Oia we had seemed to fit.

I opened my mouth and hesitated. Though I had prepared what I was going to say, I realised I had no instinct whatsoever as to what his reaction would be. 'Palmer, the reason I wanted to meet is that I think it's time to stop Project Godmother.'

He stared at me for a couple of seconds before looking down and letting his chin drop into a nod. 'All right.'

I gulped my wine; it was horribly sweet and chunks of boiled orange bobbed against my top lip. 'I've been a bit crazy; well, I'm sure that's been obvious to you. All that stuff about getting the girls into the same school, it was none of my business.'

'I don't know if I agree, actually. You did a good thing with the schools.'

'Yes, but some other girl lost out, didn't she? Because of me.'

'You can't save everyone. It's natural to focus on your own.'

I nodded, savouring for a moment the thought of the girls as my own. 'Even so, it has to stop. I'd hate them ever to find out.'

He seemed to think the comment cast aspersions on his own trustworthiness and replied, unusually defensively, 'Everything that we've done for you has been a hundred per cent confidential, you must know that.'

'Of course,' I said, hastily, 'that's not what I meant. I just mean I feel guilty about it, and, oh, just *silly*, I suppose.'

'People do, sometimes. You're not the only one.' He put his glass to his mouth, a pint of bitter, and again it was a detail that was unfamiliar, almost jarring; in Oia we drank wine, or beer from the bottle. I felt suddenly bewildered, as though I was having trouble recognising him.

'What about Jenny's new flat?' he asked. 'Do you want to keep that going?'

'Oh yes, definitely. As long as she wants it. We can't have Daisy uprooted again. She's at a funny age. Will you take care of that still? Just let me know if anything comes up.'

'Yes, of course.'

'But from now on I think I should just stick to sending them cheques on their birthdays, like any normal godmother.'

He grinned. 'I think that's a sensible compromise.'

I'd only drunk half of my wine but what remained was a cooled sludge of sugar and sediment. I put it down. I couldn't face negotiating the scrum at the bar for something else. I wondered what to say next but an uproarious outburst on the other side of the screen made conversation impossible for the next half minute. It struck me for the first time that everyone else was part of a big group, work drinks, perhaps; it was probably the last working day before Christmas. I remembered the days before Emma, diary crammed with get-togethers, sometimes several in one evening. How had I found so much to say to so many people? It was as if all of that had happened to someone else.

'How is everything with you?' I asked.

He shrugged. 'Ticking along, much as usual. The New Year usually brings in fresh clients, as you can imagine. People hold on for the holiday period and then, bam, they come to their senses and act.'

'Really? The time of year makes such a difference?'

'Yes, it's all that extra expectation over the holidays. In the end, that's what most personal problems are about, I find, people not managing each other's expectations very well.'

I didn't like the idea that in this very bar the relationships of the people around us were simply counting down to inevitable fracture. It was starting to feel rather cheerless, this meeting of ours, not at all what I had anticipated.

'And your family,' I paused. 'How are they? The garden . . .'

He smiled. 'You're very concerned about my garden. The garden is fine. There's more to do in winter than you'd think.'

'Yes, that's true. I remember. And the kids?'

He blinked, and for the first time this evening I sensed I might have pierced that diffidence of his. 'Well, I had a bit of a scare there, actually . . .'

'A scare? What do you mean? Are they all right?'

'They're fine, nothing like that, it's just my ex-wife. She's been threatening to move up to Glasgow. She's got family there.'

'When would this happen?'

'In the New Year some time.'

Now I saw what was really different about him this evening; it was nothing to do with his physical appearance, but the air he had about him, albeit well hidden, was the air of a condemned man. He must have been worrying about this relocation, allowing it to poison his thoughts of the future. *People hold on for the holiday season and then, bam, they act.* I could only imagine how it must feel to

322

be so powerless about something so crucial, to be prevented from contributing to the decisions that determined your children's welfare. It was a different kind of anguish from my own, but painful still. How cruel life could be for all of us. If someone told me tomorrow this was all a mistake, that Emma was alive and Oliver had taken her somewhere (*Glasgow*—so close!), that we'd been separated by human desire rather than divine whim, that she was growing at the same rate as Cat and Daisy, after all, then I'd be elated. Even if I never saw her again, I'd be happy for ever. Yet, from where Palmer sat, in a considerably more optimistic position than that, there was no end to the despair, only the prospect of more and more of it.

'It's not so bad,' he said, clearly sensitive to the distinction too. 'Matt's at college now anyway, and Zoë will go as well in a couple of years. I keep telling myself it doesn't matter where their base is.'

'Exactly. They'll spend their holidays wherever they want to. You might even see more of them. And then they might want to come back to London to work. Maybe Matt will follow you into the family business?'

He shook his head. 'He's already said no way to that idea. He's seen what it's done to me, I suppose.'

'What do you mean?'

'Just, well, it's exciting at first, I suppose, something to tell your mates at school, your father's a detective, like something from TV. But it's not like I'm tracking down great train robbers or serial killers. In the end, they've both just seen that what I do has destroyed family life.'

323

'It takes two—' I began but he silenced me.

'It was mainly me. I was too young to realise that you can never get those years back.' His eyes softened as they held mine, seeming to turn opaque in front of me.

I thought of Oliver and all that guilt of his. 'But you have years ahead together, that's the main thing.' I wanted to touch his arm, take his hand, but I didn't dare.

'Not if the kids are so pissed off with me they don't want to know.'

'Don't be down about it,' I said, but he didn't hear me, for the group of drinkers on the other side of the screen had spilled around to our side, encircling us in a wayward tide of goodwill. One overbalanced and fell against Palmer, while another held up airline tickets and screamed, 'Val d'Isère, here we come!' At this, a great roar went up. I looked up at the faces, every one reddened and swollen with alcohol. It felt like being on the pitch of a football stadium.

I looked back at Palmer. He wanted to get out of here, I could tell. Now our business was done he didn't want to sit here having me pry into his personal life, extracting details about his family visitation rights, the state of his garden, for heaven's sake. The facts were these: I had paid him to do a job and the job was now complete. He'd grown fond of Santorini, fond of me—but it could go no further than fondness.

To my horror I realised I was close to tears. 'Well, I suppose we ought to—'

'Rachel,' he interrupted, leaning forward. 'Before you go, can I ask you something?'

'Of course.' And I was staggered by the coursing

324

of pleasure through my veins as I thought, He wants to keep in touch, and so do I. So do I! I couldn't stop myself smiling.

'I always wondered, you know, why you've never divorced him?'

My smile froze on my lips. 'You mean—'

'Freeman. Your husband. You've never really explained.'

I stared, shocked. Not only was it the last thing I had expected him to ask it was also the last thing I wanted to answer. In any case, I could see in his eyes that he didn't understand, he couldn't understand. Wherever his children lived, they *lived*, and as long as they did he could never know. Lord knew, I didn't *want* him to be able to know.

'It's hard to explain, Palmer. I'm not sure I can really.'

There was a silence, and it seemed to me that his eyes emptied then, just went utterly blank. In the next second my head was full of another voice, eclipsing his and mine, and it took a second or two for me to make the identification. *You'll never leave Oliver, will you?* Simon's voice, sweet Simon. Why was I suddenly thinking of that, when I'd left Oliver years ago?

'Will we . . . will we keep in touch?' I asked, half whispering.

He nodded. 'Of course. I'll need to send you annual statements from the flat rental.'

'Oh, yes.' Ask him to deliver them in person, I said to myself, rescue this, it's not too late.

But he wasn't even looking at me now. I'd failed him. Despair descended in horrible cold blasts. 'I'll get the office to send a final statement of account. And just let me know if there's anything else we can do for you. I'm sure we could squeeze you in.'

'All right.' I turned to pull my coat from the chair back. 'Well, I ought to get back to Mum.'

'Of course. Goodbye.'

'Goodbye.'

I kissed him on each cheek, as I'd come to do at his arrivals and departures in Oia. I told myself that this was no different.

*   *   *

I knew what I was going to do before I'd even pulled open the door and felt the cold air whoosh against my legs and lift my hair from my face. I was going to follow him home. I wanted to see him put a key in the lock and turn on a hallway lamp and be at home, somewhere he didn't have to shrink himself into this anonymous, inconspicuous character he presented to the outside world. I remembered what I'd thought when we first met, that he had the face of a character actor. I'd been struck then by the set of his features, but it had turned out to be more than that; it was the body language too: the silent tread, the sympathetic nod, the mannerisms that might have been studied and replicated to perfection in a live performance. I wanted to know there was somewhere he could be the original version if he wanted to, the true version.

I put on my hat and gloves, doubled up the scarf and tucked it tightly into the collar of my coat. Lights blinked and voices rose, urgent and shrill. In every direction people seemed to be squabbling over cabs. There was evidently a chronic shortage. How was I going to do this, then? If Palmer was driving, I'd never be able to pick up a taxi at precisely the time and place I'd need to in order to keep track of him. Perhaps I could flag down a private car and pay the driver to follow him? Stop this madness, I told myself, there is no emergency here. If it isn't possible to follow him, just leave it and go home.

At that moment he came out of the pub, buttoning his overcoat and pulling up the collar, and with a glance at his watch turned left and began walking. I waited a few seconds and followed. Inside my woollen hat the sound of my footsteps boomed, slurred and sinister, like sound effects added to the soundtrack of a film. My cheeks were flushed, as much with embarrassment as the cold (tailing a private investigator of all people, like presuming to diagnose the medical symptoms of a doctor!). Again, I worried about taxis, but to my surprise he crossed the road, heading across the concourse of Victoria station and down the steps into the tube. I scurried after him; already a hundred bodies separated ours. Inside, I was unfamiliar with the ticket machine, fumbled for the right money, and only just got to the top of the escalator in time to see which platform he was making for at the bottom: Victoria Line, northbound. The Victoria Line, hardly familiar now, though I'd used it daily for so many years. The platform was crammed and when the train arrived just as many passengers joined as disembarked. The carriage smelled of alcohol and burgers and there were sections of newspapers strewn everywhere. Someone had left behind torn strands of Christmas paper from a gift opened in haste and these were now being trudged into the grooves of the floor. I felt the beginnings of panic in the confined space and focused on the tube map at eye level.

Wanstead, that was where Palmer had said he lived; out in east London on the Central Line. He'd be changing lines at Oxford Circus. Two stops. But he got off after just one, strolling right by the window of my carriage, and I barely made it myself before the doors squeezed shut. I ignored the indignant faces of those I'd had to shove aside and hurried along the edge of the platform after him. Green Park; what was here? A social call? Another client with an attack of guilt? I glided up the escalator after him, hardly knowing how long I intended to allow before aborting this ridiculous mission. I couldn't possibly expect to follow him into another bar and spend the evening there without being spotted. Then, at the top of the escalator he confounded me again, heading not for the barriers but turning for an escalator back down: the Jubilee Line. He'd moved house, perhaps. He hadn't thought to mention it because that was how it was between us—we knew odd details about the other but big things went unspecified. Again, I slipped into the next carriage along from his. This one was emptier and I was able to get a seat, sinking back and laying my hot wrists on the plastic of the armrests. That felt better. With a lurch I realised that this was my old commute home from Pendant. Back to Emma, to pick her up from Mariel's or Jen's or, if it was my turn, to hurry straight to school to meet all three of them, making sure I had cartons of juice or apples for them. They always demanded snacks as soon as they appeared and would devour them before launching into the day's news. It was only right, then, that we should sit out the mass disembarkation at Baker Street and carry on past St John's Wood to Swiss Cottage. Now I thought I knew what was going on: he hadn't moved house at all, he just wanted a last look at the girls, at Daisy's new flat, to see them safe before signing off this case, just as I seemed to need that final satisfaction of seeing *him* safe. A formal close to our business, a neat little symmetry. I thought it unlikely that he'd get to see them, however, for it was well past bed time, or at least bed time as I remembered it, eight o'clock. I looked at my watch. It wasn't even nine; they probably stayed up much later now that they were older, with hot drinks and TV. They'd be watching a Christmas movie, perhaps, struggling not to fall asleep.

He didn't cross the road by the tube station, as I would have done myself, or at College Crescent to walk the slightly longer way around towards the Finchley Road, but turned into College Crescent, past Buckland Crescent and into the curve of . . . of Belsize Park. I followed, appalled. Now I understood. This was not about Daisy's new flat, or about the girls at all. This was about me. The last look he wanted was of *my* house, Oliver's house.

The house was in darkness, but for a glow of light in the hallway visible through the stained glass of the front door, and another at the window of the upstairs landing—that lamp came on on a timer, I remembered, and stayed on all night, in case Emma woke up for the loo and got confused. So many times I'd thought of Oliver alone in our large house, leaving it empty for all daylight hours as he worked, returning in the dark when the streets were quiet and his the only curtains not yet drawn. So many times I'd wondered if Andy still came to do the garden every Thursday, or Jacinta twice a week to clean? Much of her time had been spent tidying Emma's toys and books, ironing her school shirts. What was there to do now? A wine glass to wash up, a couple of old newspapers to throw away? Whole rooms probably remained untouched from one week to the next.

Palmer came to a halt in the shadows a couple of houses beyond the one directly opposite mine. I stopped too, eyes hardly moving from my old front door. Visions of her in that house swam across one another: dancing in the kitchen and eating a strawberry at the same time; climbing up my body and making monkey noises; appearing in the doorway of our bedroom and, without a word, pulling up the corner of the duvet to climb in; shivering on the bath mat before I passed the warmed towel . . . Out of nowhere I heard Christos's voice in my head: *When we are gone, who will remember?* For me, that had become the hardest of all, the idea that when my aching body, and Oliver's, left the world there'd be no one in it to remember her. Daisy and Cat, asleep or awake in nearby streets, would they remember their first friend when they were grown up, when they had families of their own? Did they even now?

For a moment I couldn't bear to go on. The idea of submitting to another year, even another month without her . . . For a moment I was as broken, as extinguished as I ever had been. I felt my legs stagger slightly beneath me, but the sound of a groan made me pull up straight and look. Palmer

330

had slumped against the wall, head in his hands, as though somehow reacting physically to the pain of my thoughts.

Then yellow lights beamed on the tarmac ahead and a taxi braked right by me, delivering a woman to the house nearby. She didn't glance at me as she made for her gate and I wondered for a bizarre moment if I were actually there.

'Need a taxi?'

The cabbie was calling to me. Edging towards the kerb I leaned towards the open window and whispered, 'Yes, please.'

'Where're you going, love?'

'Ealing.'

'Hop in. Freezing tonight, isn't it?'

As we pulled away I didn't dare look behind me through the rear window. I couldn't bear to see my daughter's house, alight but empty. I couldn't bear to see Palmer standing there, head in hands, or imagine how long he was prepared to wait.

PART FOUR

I don't have plans and schemes
And I don't have hopes and dreams
I don't have anything
Since I don't have you
            THE SKYLINERS, 1959

Chapter 32

Oia, 2004

The morning Christos dropped by Callidora I had never seen Oia look so beautiful. It was early and the Caldera seemed to sleep, silver and still, its surface skimmed with puddles. There was even a soft mist hovering over Perivolos, as though summoned by the gods to complete the picture, and the *skapha* there, wedged into the rockface and half-hidden by design, were, for a moment, quite invisible.

Christos knew I'd already be up, I had my rituals—coffee and yogurt at my terrace table before I left for the shop for seven-thirty—but so did he have his, and touring his old Monastiri holiday units was not one of them.

'Everything all right with Ingrid?' I asked. This tended to be the first thought if either of us appeared unexpectedly without her.

'Yes, fine, just a little thing.'

I went inside to pour him some coffee. Handing him the cup, I saw he was reluctant to tell me this 'little thing'. 'How's business at the Swallow Suites?'

He brightened. 'Business is excellent, thank you. Ingrid did not tell you? We are fully booked from June until the second week of October.'

'Wow, Christos, that's fantastic. Well done.'

The new villas were beautiful, without prejudice my favourite of the honeymooners' complexes here. Christos's builders had worked the rock like sculptors, creating a complex that appeared to cling to the cliff by the grace of God (which, I supposed, it did). There was a pool-terrace restaurant, a wine-tasting cellar and a maze of shaded pathways and hidden nooks designed to make the guests' progress about the site more intimate with every step. I'd seen inside the guest rooms, of course, where Panoméréa photographs had been mixed with nautical paraphernalia and island knick-knacks, and where a pathway of rugs led your feet across the white marble floors in stepping stones of green and blue. A honeymoon suite named The Nest had a hot tub on the terrace and an outdoor fridge with champagne replenished daily. The staff had been trained never to say no, the sunset rarely disappointed and the visitors' book brimmed with superlatives. A PR agency in Athens had produced a brochure on high-grade paper, each page lined with tissue paper like a wedding album. 'Oia is a shared secret', that was their slogan. Ingrid had supplied the line and, like everything else about the place, it was pitch perfect.

But Christos had not come to boast of his business triumphs. He gulped his coffee and glanced at his watch. 'There was an Englishman looking for you last night in the Epik bar.'

I put my cup down. 'Oh. A tourist?'

'I think so.'

'But obviously not anyone you recognise?'

'No. A blast in the past, yes?'

I nodded. 'I wonder. From London, did he say?'

'Perhaps, yes.'

Of course, yes. This Englishman *had* to have come from London, it *had* to be someone from my old life. It had to be Oliver. Finally, years after he'd made his vow to wait for me, he'd decided he'd waited long enough. And so he had. Almost ten years! It was madness. And yet the thought of him coming here now, to make this separation official, was hardly less disquieting than when I had first settled here and it had been Eleni who'd come to my terrace to warn me. She'd gesticulated wildly, I remembered, she'd thought him some sort of wife beater.

Christos watched me, silently, and again I sensed his reluctance, sadness even. He of all people knew how it was to have an ex-spouse in the background of one's life, but there remained that huge, unspeakable difference between us: he was bound to his by the shared pleasures of their grown children, me to mine by the sorrow of a life cut short.

I shivered. The light may have been perfect but the early spring air was sharp. I considered going inside to fetch a cardigan. 'What did he look like, this guy? My sort of age?'

'Perhaps younger. Thirty or so. Not so tall. Black hair.'

'Really?' Well, that couldn't be Oliver, and Christos must surely have judged as much. Who, then? Simon? Toby? Bob? Like Oliver, none could possibly hope to pass for thirty these days. A thirty-year-old from my old life would have had to have been a teenager when I'd lived in London, but I'd known no students that I could remember. Then, with a start, I remembered the only other Londoner who had made contact with me here: Andrew Lockley. *If I could change what happened* . . . Surely remorse had not brought him here in person? Or, worse, revenge? Had Oliver's legal action destroyed his life? Don't think about it, I told myself, it can't be him. Years have passed since the letter, since the court case. He's forgotten all about us now, and so he should.

'Rachel?' Christos took a step towards me.

'Well, I'm not hard to find,' I said at last. 'Whoever it is can always get me at the shop.' I gave what I hoped was a dismissive shrug and Christos nodded, half relieved to play along. He'd done his job, delivered the message, and in person too, not through Ingrid. But that was partly my worry: he would have known I was due to meet her in the shop in under an hour's time, but he had sensed some sort of danger in this stranger and had come to warn me in person without a moment to lose.

'You are going with Ingrid later,' he asked, 'to look at the chapel?'

'Yes, I'm looking forward to it. I've always been curious about those private chapels.' The tiny family chapel attached to Christos's house, usually open only on its saint's day in March, was to be unlocked a second time in June for the Kafieris-Sullivan wedding. In spite of his status and the local fascination with his romance with 'the Australian', theirs was to be a quiet union, for Christos had been married in Oia before. Though his wife lived permanently in Thessaloniki with the children, it would not do to make too public a replacement of her in her home town.

He nodded. 'Well, I must go. But let me know about this man. If you need my help, I am here.'

'Thank you, I will. I'm sure it's nothing.'

As he withdrew up the steps, spry as ever, I

338

considered how our relationship had changed over the years. First there was that instinct to co-parent Ingrid, which still lingered to a degree, next I'd played gooseberry to the two of them, other times we'd been three friends undivided by any internal romance. But recently, since their engagement, I had begun to feel more like *their* daughter—the way they praised any faintly eligible male and sought to include him with pointed formality, like parents trying to manoeuvre their child into a suitable match; the way they brought me little souvenirs of places they'd been together. Occasionally, with a twinge of recognition that recalled the early years of Toby and Mariel, I thought about when it had just been Ingrid and me, before Christos came along. Mostly, though, I looked forward, as all the bereaved learn to do in the end.

*   *   *

The marriage proposal made by Christos to Ingrid was already part of Oian folklore, or so it seemed to me, having lived every moment of the campaign that preceded it and been called upon afterwards to recreate it repeatedly for the myriad well-wishers avid for eye-witness detail. Ingrid herself had not been the activist in the offensive—in fact, I didn't think I could remember her ever expressing a desire for marriage. No, that role had been seized by Eleni. There had come a time when it was impossible to see Christos and Eleni together without experiencing her lobbying first hand, sometimes long harangues in Greek that I (mercifully) could not follow; other times brief

339

exchanges when a group of us were having dinner and Ingrid had merely left the table for the loo. There was one time in particular that made me smile to remember. We'd been at Christos's house for drinks and Eleni had brought the subject up even before finishing her first glass. Christos heard her out for a while, making Anatole and me laugh by comparing her to his ex-wife, when she suddenly grabbed a bowl of sweets from the dresser and tossed them into the air like confetti. 'Look!' she cried. 'This is cruel! You even have the *koufetta*!'

Christos guffawed. 'Ingrid bought those in Fira—she doesn't have any idea what they are.' What they were, I learned from Anatole, were sugar-coated almonds, traditionally consumed at weddings.

As Christos and I chased the sweets around the floor, the long-suffering Anatole tried to silence his wife, adding in English for my benefit, 'I have told you before, Eleni, Christos waits for the snow.'

'*Snow?*' I repeated, confused. 'Here in Oia? Christos, I think you might be in for a long wait.'

'No, we have had it once, you know, many years ago. Less often than the earthquakes, it is true, but we have had it.' He then explained that Ingrid had seen snow when she'd been in England and had loved it so much she still talked about it now, years later. He felt, therefore, that the perfect marriage proposal must include this 'magical element'. He would wait one more winter, and if the gods failed him once more, he'd have to settle for a ski holiday. As he spoke I felt my eyes fill with tears. He'd been waiting whole seasons for the perfect moment! This, for me, typified the islanders' nature: the optimism, the love of drama, combined with the forebearance of the sailor.

And then, perversely, it *had* snowed. Not for very long, admittedly, but long enough for Christos to get from his site office at Perivolos up to Panomeréa, where Ingrid and I had abandoned our pre-Easter spring clean to stand at the window and gape.

'Ingrid, come out to the street a minute.'

I watched from the doorway as she joined him up on the marble, catching flakes in her palms until he snatched her hands in his and asked, 'Miss Ingrid Sullivan, please will you be the new Mrs Kafieris?'

Ingrid squealed. 'Sure I will.'

It was Valentine's Day the day it snowed. The locals regarded this as entirely fitting. Of *course* a coincidence so cinematic, so romantic, should occur here. Where else? For whom if not for the Oians?

'Thanks God,' Eleni cried when I rushed to tell the news. 'At last, at last, at last.'

*   *   *

'Bloody hell,' said Ingrid, 'is it me or is it a bit gloomy in here?'

'You mean you've never been in here before?'

'Well, I'm not exactly the spiritual type, am I?'

We peered about us in the half light of the chapel. 'Even so, it's ages since you got engaged and moved in. And to think you used to be such a fast worker.'

She laughed at that. It was true that the length

341

of her engagement to Christos had almost matched Eleni's wait for his proposal. Every time anyone asked her outright if they'd named a date, she would reply, briskly, 'Nah, too busy.' For me there was an echo of Jenny there, those dismissals of her desire to have more children—'Nah, can't afford it'—and no one was more relieved than I when the date was finally announced. A Friday in June, just as Cat and Daisy would be sitting their GCSE exams.

There were complications, of course. Trips had to be made to Athens regarding her passport and other administrative hoops jumped through in order for the marriage to take place. She had even been required to be baptised in the Greek Church, a ceremony that included an actual dunking in a barrel of water. She had gone to some lengths to stop Eleni and me attending the event and rumours of an illicit photograph had yet to be substantiated.

I smiled thinking of it. 'I must admit, I thought Eleni was going to divorce Anatole and get *him* to marry you if it went on much longer!'

'I know, but with the shop, and the Swallow Suites, it's been non-stop, hasn't it? Anyway, it's really not that important to me, actually getting married. Just being together is enough.'

I nodded, full of admiration for her, for nothing had been more important to me once than falling in love and fixing myself to someone else's star, getting the matter settled. I'd had none of Ingrid's self-sufficiency. The first time I'd lived alone was here in Oia.

'So what do you think?' she asked. 'Let's pull the door right open and get some light in.'

It blew in in warm yellow clouds and I looked about me. Ingrid was right, the chapel was austere, but it was also still and peaceful and had the most beautiful carved-wood altar screen. I was drawn to an icon of a saint on horseback. 'This must be the one Christos said was painted in Russia, in the eighteenth century or something. It's amazing that these places have such treasures locked away and no one allowed to see them.'

'Well, don't get any ideas about liberating them,' Ingrid laughed. 'If we tried to sell them in Panomeréa we'd only end up getting arrested. We'll leave the religious stuff for our museum.'

'Ah, yes.' There'd been talk, over the last couple of years, of our opening an art museum in Oia, a pipe dream, as far as I was concerned, but a pleasant one. It reminded me of the excitement of our first plans for the shop, when every conversation between us began, 'Wouldn't it be great if . . .' For Ingrid, though, it was a serious proposition. It was she, now, who led and defined Panomeréa. It was she who had found the miniatures we now stocked alongside our photographs, exquisite paintings on glass using traditional Theran techniques, the work of a British artist she'd discovered in Akrotiri. And it was she who had begun acquiring photographs taken during the aftermath of the earthquake, a period we had originally avoided, considering it a little ghoulish. But, again, she had made the right call, for in the context of our complete collection the images became positive, celebratory: the camaraderie of military personnel as they assessed the damage; priests playing music amid the rubble of a collapsed dome; and, one that proved to sell particularly well, nuns gathered in Fira to survey the damage to their convent. The roof had fallen in, but their headdresses remained pristinely in place.

We were skilled saleswomen now, Ingrid and I, we could spot at fifty paces the first-night couples, their eyes wide with all that glowing pink horizon, browsing the shops with minds too full of the sky to focus on any one object. Weaving expertly between them were the last-nighters, who had learned their tastes just as they were leaving and that was excellent news for the shops—faked paintings and all. The last stroll to the Goulas for sunset, the last dinner . . . only one thing could cap their beautiful experience: a memento of it, the perfect souvenir (the Australians used the word as a verb, said Ingrid, which seemed wrong, somehow). Yes, last nights, after sunset, that was the time when the shops did their best business and we were no exception. They'd come to us pleased with the world, free-spending from the wine, and leave with packages under their arms.

'I've just thought,' Ingrid said, half to me and half to the painted figure on the chapel wall in front of her. 'During the service, there'll be no one on my side.'

I slipped my arm around her waist. 'They probably don't do it like that here, it's probably not so formal, especially in a tiny place like this. We'll all just cram in. Anyway, there is someone, there's me.'

She gave me a grateful sideways smile. 'I know, but you're the only one. Eleni knew Christos before we did, long before.'

'Yes. Anatole and he were at high school in Fira

together, weren't they? What about Alexandros?'

'Still in Athens. He won't be able to come back mid-season.'

'Nikos?'

'Huh! He'd never be allowed to come, not even on a leash.' Nikos was married now, the father of twin daughters, and his wife, unsurprisingly, had forbidden him any further contact with Ingrid. 'It's been years, for God's sake.'

'What about Manfred? He's more your friend, isn't he? We were the ones who introduced him to Christos, as I remember, when he made that first big order.'

'Yes, but Christos has nicked him from right under our noses! He's commandeered him for that trip to Crete, hasn't he?' Manfred had recently been dispatched on an expedition to photograph Knossos and other sites for Christos's properties on the mainland. Ingrid and I were hoping to get some material out of it ourselves for a new section of the shop called 'Beyond Santorini'. 'He is going to take the wedding photos, though, Christos asked him especially.'

'OK,' I said, 'I give up. Everyone loves Christos. He's salt of the ground, as he would say. And you of all people must be able to appreciate that.'

She smiled, but the matter wasn't settled, I could tell. 'By the way, Rach, there was something I wanted to ask you.'

'Oh, yes?' I wasn't fooled by that casual tone, especially when I saw the forensic scrutiny in her eyes.

'Now don't get annoyed . . .'

'Why would I?'

'We just wondered, do you want to invite Palmer

345

to the wedding?'

'Palmer?' I tried not to show how startled I was. It had taken a long time for my friends to give up asking me about Palmer, but I had thought we'd finally got there. 'I don't think so, Ingrid, I don't hear from him now.'

'Why not?'

I felt a lurch of disappointment in my stomach, as I always did when I considered the night of our parting. 'I don't get those reports any more. Well, only one last bit of business we've got going, and he has an office assistant who deals with that.' I'd hoped differently, it was true. I'd hoped he'd see to that routine paperwork himself, make it an excuse to keep lines open between us. But he never had.

Ingrid nodded. 'I didn't like to say, but it was a bit freaky, you know, that spying business?'

'Yes, I can imagine how it looked.'

'That doesn't mean we can't invite him to the wedding, though. He's still one of your closest friends.'

'I haven't seen him for years, Ingrid. How can you describe him as one of my closest friends?'

She looked at me for a moment with real frustration but, perhaps sensing my hidden anguish, changed her mind and said, very gently, 'I think that's a shame, Rachel. You obviously got on really well. Everyone saw it. When I think of that whole period, starting the business, meeting Christos, I think of him too.'

'Me too,' I gulped.

'We *should* invite him.'

I could feel my distress seeping to the surface. 'Oh, please don't. He's sure to be busy.'

346

'I don't see why. It's plenty of notice.' As she stood waiting, hands not quite on hips, I realised I was going to have to do something I'd never done before, not out loud: define my relationship with Palmer, the relationship beyond our godmother project. *Acknowledge* it.

'I know it sounds silly,' I said, carefully, 'but our friendship, well, when he used to come here, he always invited himself, you know, when his work schedule allowed. I never invited him.'

'That's kind of old-fashioned,' Ingrid said, smirking. 'Making him make all the moves.'

'You make it sound like we were dating.'

'God, no. Courting, that's the word, isn't it? Dating's a bit too risqué for you two, might be a bit too likely to involve—'

'Ingrid!' I interrupted as sternly as I could. 'We weren't dating *or* courting or anything. That's all over for me, I've told you. I'm happy for you and Christos, honestly I am, but I don't want a relationship for myself again.'

'But you're far too young,' Ingrid protested, her patience spent. 'That's ridiculous! How can you give up sex at your age?'

'I'm in my forties now.'

She sighed. 'So? That's hardly decrepit, is it?'

'You sound like me talking to my mother! Well, not about the sex, obviously. Anyway, this is hardly the place—look at all the disapproving looks we're getting from the walls!'

Laughing, we came outside into the sunlight and began the short stroll through the passageways back to the shop. Though we now hired staff to help at Easter and in the summer season, it was still relatively rare for us to be out together during

347

the day. Other shop staff called out and waved. An assistant from the Swallow Suites came by, ushering a man with a cartload of potted trees, and stopped to chat about the Easter preparations that were keeping him busy. Another friend called out to invite us to the opening of a new bar. I soon realised, however, that I was the only one responding to the pleasantries. Ingrid had gone quiet, which could only lead me to expect more difficult questions about Palmer.

'I was wondering,' she said slowly, 'do you think I should contact my mother?'

'What?' The Palmer issue had always been bubbling under the surface, threatening to erupt, but this, this was so unexpected I just stopped in my tracks and stared at her. I didn't have the first idea what to say. 'Your *mother*?'

She nodded, squinting into the sun. 'Yes. Tell her about the wedding, invite her to come, maybe. Christos says we'll pay for her flight, put her up at the house and all that.'

Still I just stood in front of her, speechless. They'd already discussed this, then; it was half-decided.

'Rachel?'

'Sorry, my love. I don't know what to say. You've never suggested anything like it before.'

'I've never planned a wedding before. It makes me think . . . I don't know, just that everyone starts out expecting good things, don't they? She must have too, way back, before I was born. Maybe I should give her a break. I mean, do I really want to live the whole of my life and not see her again?'

'But it's just been so long—'

'Eleven years,' Ingrid said, interrupting. 'I

348

haven't seen her in eleven years. Imagine! Over a decade of your child's life—' She broke off, almost with a gasp, pulling the horrified expression she always did when inadvertently making reference to any parent-child separation.

'It's been a long time,' I agreed quickly. 'Have you considered that she may have a new family, though, a new life?' The same could be said for Palmer, of course, a thought that had tortured me repeatedly over time, and I blinked it away, as I always did. 'Would you even know how to get hold of her now?'

'I could find her. There's always the Internet I guess. You can track anyone down these days, can't you? And there's still three months till the wedding.'

If she still remembered she *had* a daughter. If she was still alive. I hoped she *was* still alive, that this was going to be all right.

'But what if she hasn't changed,' Ingrid said, grimly, 'what if she's still some old lush in the street? She must be, I suppose, if she hasn't bothered to look for me all this time. You know, if you put my name—or yours—into the search engine online, the Swallow Suites site comes up straight away, top of the list, with the link to our page. And there's our email address on there too. Anyone could get in touch.'

Her eyes clouded with disappointment and my heart ached for her. What a success she'd made of her life; she was as fine an adult as any mother could hope her daughter to become, and yet her mother had just let her go, lost touch even before she'd left for the other side of the world, and had never tried to find her. I couldn't understand her neglect, not on any level.

'I would think about it some more,' I said gently. 'This is going to be *your* day. And it may seem like it's Christos's show, but they're all your friends too now. If you don't belong here then nobody does.'

'Yeah, you're right.' She wrapped her arms around herself as if to warm her upper body, though it was mild for March and we stood in direct sunlight. Her gaze fell on the folded rugs stacked high in the window of the weaver's shop, every colour under the sun, riveted suddenly as though she'd never noticed them before. I thought unexpectedly of Emma drawing rainbows with felt-tip pens.

'Even if I ask her to come, it's not down to me, is it? It's down to her.' Ingrid stepped towards the window and reached her hand out, as though expecting to be able to touch the woven folds through the glass. 'It's always been down to her.'

All of a sudden the colours blurred and I turned my eyes away.

Chapter 33

Though Easter approached, Oia was still relatively empty and I didn't have to wait long to meet the mystery man Christos had spoken of. I was in the café opposite the shop, drinking coffee and checking the books in preparation for a visit from the tax inspector later in the afternoon, when I grew aware of someone watching me. I looked his way, careful not to meet his eye. Male, thirtyish, he was good looking, with a prominent forehead and green eyes. Was there at least a touch of resemblance to those pictures I remembered from the local press, that sullen-eyed nineteen-year-old who found himself, one sunny July afternoon, recast as a child-killer's accomplice? My heart rate told me no, this wasn't Lockley. Yet this was certainly the man Christos had met. Though he was dressed in standard tourist clothing, the details were wrong: no partner beside him or beer in front of him, no guidebook or camera, only some hand-held device that beeped every few seconds, causing him to frown and start dabbing at the keys with his thumbs. The rest of the time he kept his eyes on me. I had chosen a seat with my back to the street, while his faced it, and when I turned I saw that a portion of Ingrid's body was visible in our open doorway across the way as she stretched to dust a frame. I wondered how long this had been his stake-out and thought, for a second, of Palmer and his rear-view.

Finally I allowed our eyes to meet. 'Do I know you?' I asked, pleasantly.

'Are you Rachel Freeman by any chance?'

'Yes.'

'The same Rachel Freeman who's married to Oliver Freeman?'

'Why do you ask?'

'Well . . .' Without seeking permission, he pulled up his chair opposite mine and leaned chummily towards me. 'Cards on the table, Mrs Freeman. I'm Jason Cheatle, a freelance journalist based in London.'

'A journalist?'

'That's right. I've been asked to contribute to a special supplement at the *Telegraph*, about the government reshuffle, the new order and all that. Profiles of all the key players, the *real* players, I mean, not the ministers.'

'OK.' Though quite at a loss as to why he was telling me this, I tried to maintain a friendly expression. He was conversational in a way I recognised of London people: charming enough but unable to mask his intensity, work-intensity. He would get to what he wanted soon enough, there'd be none of the drawn-out sagas of the locals, the incident-filled preambles to everyday requests.

'Your husband will be in there, obviously. In fact we were thinking of making his profile our cover feature . . .'

I stared back brightly. Still I didn't know what he was talking about. 'Mr Cheatle, I'm not sure how I—'

'Please, call me Jason.' He scratched his face at the point where the cheekbone met the ear. 'I just wanted to talk a bit about his background, that's all. What might have led to this new public-spirited role, you know, after so long in the City. Perhaps something to do with the death of your daughter . . .'

'What?' We stared at each other, neither blinking. 'You can't have come all the way from London just to ask me about my husband?'

'Actually I'm on holiday with my wife, but when the paper discovered that this is where you were based, they asked me to come to Oia to look you up, see if we could have a chat. I hope we can.'

'I have nothing to say, I'm afraid.' Hastily, I gathered up my things and searched my pockets for coins. Damn, I thought, I only had a ten-euro note on me, I'd have to wait for change. Should have gone to the Ilias, after all, but I'd been worried I'd end up gossiping with Eleni and distract both of us from our work.

Dismay crossed Cheatle's brow, quickly replaced by exasperation. 'Mrs Freeman, Rachel, a couple of quick questions wouldn't hurt, would it? You're still married, aren't you? You've never actually divorced him, why is that?'

'I'm sorry, I really have to go.' I gestured to Naida, the waitress, and mouthed, 'Can I pay you later?'

'No matter.' She waved me off and turned back to the counter where a couple in hiking gear were dithering over their pastry choices.

'Mrs Freeman, please . . . !'

He was out of his seat and I half expected him to follow me, to pull at my clothes and detain me forcibly. But next time I looked, from the safety of my shop window, he had returned to his own table and picked up his mobile phone.

*   *   *

Our office, formerly the storeroom, was located directly under the footsteps of Marmara and therefore just metres below the spot where this Cheatle man sat. I went straight to the laptop and dialled up. It seemed to take an age to connect to the Internet and get me to the point at which I could tap 'Oliver Freeman' into the search engine. I stared in bewilderment at the lists of results. It had brought up hundreds of sites, most with the 'co.uk' suffix: the BBC, *The Times*, Channel 4 . . .

I started reading, clicking back and forth

353

between the pages. Well, his career certainly had changed direction. He was now a policy adviser to Number 11 and getting a lot of attention for some controversy over children's trust funds. It was a scandal, that much was agreed. Oliver was not the culprit, though, he was the trouble shooter, the hero. The word 'crusader' was used again and again.

Much as I respected Oliver's professional abilities, it was unlikely enough a change of circumstances for me to suspect for a second a simple case of mistaken identity: some other Oliver Freeman, perhaps? But, no, the next page I scrolled down included a photograph, a full-length snap of him leaving a Westminster office building. He was a little stouter than I recalled and rather greyer, but it was unmistakably him. The text alongside it reported a press conference he'd given and spoke of his uncanny reading of the Chancellor's instincts. I clicked again: a profile that had run in one of the Sunday papers. This one mentioned a long-estranged wife 'currently living a hermetic existence on the Greek island of Santorini'. Well, Jason from the *Telegraph* wasn't going to be able to add much to that, I was afraid.

I selected a new site, eyes stumbling as the words rolled into focus:

Though Freeman's career trajectory has been enviable, his personal life is believed to be rather less blessed. He married Rachel Headon in 1986, but the couple have lived apart since the tragic death of their daughter in a road accident in 1994. (He later won a private prosecution against one of the motorists involved, Andrew Lockley, a landmark case of its day.) Freeman's most recent romantic interest is said to be a former close friend of his wife.

I stopped short. A 'former close friend', what the hell did that mean? I scrolled down, but the text ended there; below it flashed a boxed advertisement for an estate car.

'Rachel?' Ingrid called from the front desk. 'Mr Frangidis has just arrived from the tax office.'

'Coming!'

Flustered, I closed the browser and gathered up my papers. Only then did it strike me that I couldn't remember the last time Oliver had written to me.

*   *   *

I remembered one thing, though, or to be precise I re-evaluated it. The Christmas before last while I opened Christmas presents at my mother's house, she had handed me a card that had arrived in the post. Standard Christmas greetings, a snow-dusted village scene, the kind of card that comes in big variety boxes. It was from Bob. Scrawled under his signature, he had added a P.S.: *I assume you know what's going on. Call me?*, followed by a mobile phone number. Looking for allies after his break-up with Jen, I'd supposed, and rather late in the day at that, for they had been apart for years by then. He thought I was completely out of touch, maybe, had remembered Jen's unsuccessful quest to bring me back, complaints perhaps about my unfriendliness and, finding my name in an old address book, had wondered if my vote were still up for grabs.

I was sorry for Bob then, sorry that he felt so friendless that he needed to look up old acquaintances like me, friends of Jen's with whom he'd never quite clicked in the first place; but I was hardly likely to take his side in affairs after all this time. No, the card was odd, but forgettable, and I stood it alongside the others on the mantelpiece, later slipping it into the bin when it was time to take them down again. Next I heard—in a note that came from Mariel with a thank you for Cat's birthday present—he had started seeing a new girlfriend and had moved into her flat in south London. Again, I didn't dwell on it for long, focusing instead on the second piece of news in that particular bulletin, that of Mariel having bumped into Simon and been told that he was about to get married to someone from the Pendant office. (I'd thought suddenly of that young girl I'd shown around a few weeks before the end of my time there, Helen or Harriet or someone.)

Now I wondered if Bob had not meant something else. Could it be that what he 'assumed' I knew was 'going on' was not the end of Jen's relationship with him but the beginning of one with Oliver? But no, it didn't make sense, there'd never been any attraction between Oliver and Jen, their names didn't even sound right together on the tongue. Out of the question. No doubt that I would have forgotten all about it, disregarded Cheatle, Bob and the whole matter, had it not been for other news. Just days after my encounter with Cheatle, in place of the usual annual statement for Jen's flat in Canfield Gardens, Palmer's office sent word that the tenant had given notice.

*　　　*　　　*

I was alone in the shop when I decided I would phone him. And once I'd made the decision I was impatient to get on with it, impatient enough to sigh loudly at the stooped back of a customer who lingered too long after closing time. All day the shop had been empty and he had to choose now to come and dither, forehead creased as though fathoming ancient codes, over the box of loose prints. A last-minute gift for his wife, I suspected, something they'd admired together earlier in their trip and later regretted not buying on the spot. A classic sequence of events; I'd seen it a thousand times. Usually I'd be understanding and helpful, oblivious of the clock; tonight I wished he'd just make his mind up and get out of here. Finally he approached the desk with his chosen prints and a half dozen questions that needed answering. I wrapped, stamped and bagged, then followed him to the door and turned the ANOIKTO/OPEN sign inward.

I had to look up the number before dialling, it had been so long since I'd last phoned him. 'It's Rachel here, Rachel Freeman.'

'*Rachel?*'

'A man came from London last month,' I said, unable to stop myself from blurting it straight out, filling the space that his silence left. 'A journalist.'

There was an audible intake of breath. 'Oh.'

'Palmer . . .' I blinked back tears. 'Oliver seems

to be rather famous these days. And dating the mother of Subject A, I understand.'

'You "understand"?'

'Oh, come on,' I burst out, agitated, 'if *I*'ve read about this in the papers, then *you* must have? Why didn't you let me know? One phone call! One letter! You could at least have put a note in with Jen's statement.' I sounded close to hysteria. I couldn't have come up with a less appropriate way to renew contact with him if I'd tried.

'Rachel, please calm down.'

I crushed the phone painfully against my ear. I was having trouble just hearing his voice, low, grainy, full of concern. It was a lifetime ago that I had interviewed him in that run-down B&B in west London, expecting never to lay eyes on the man again. I'd simply been grateful, I remembered, that he wasn't as bad as the other guy, the one with the oily voice, the one who thought I was a suspicious wife looking for revenge. It was a lifetime, too, since I'd left him on the street in north London, almost as sure that he shouldn't have been there as I was sure that I must never let him know that I'd seen him there. Was that the reason for this long silence? Not daring to risk it, risk humiliating him, challenging him about his feelings, challenging myself about mine?

'I've seen his name in the papers,' Palmer said, finally. 'Some government select committee or other, is it?'

'I don't care about that,' I cried. 'I'm talking about Jenny and him!'

'Ah. Did you get our note about her moving out of the flat? Is that what this is about?'

'Of course it is, Palmer! I've seen the newspaper

articles online as well—and Bob seems to have known for over a year! He sent me a note two Christmases ago, but I didn't realise what he meant. God only knows how long this has been going on.'

There was a long pause. 'What is it you want from me, Rachel?'

'I just . . .' And I didn't know what to say, didn't know what it was I wanted from him.

'Rachel?'

The line had become faint, as though diverted a hundred times over, and I gave a huff of frustration.

'Look, I don't mean to sound rude, but it's no longer my job to keep you up to date on your old friends.' It seemed to me there was an edge to his voice that I didn't recognise. 'And, I might add, it never *was* my job to keep you up to date on the adults.'

'Oh, come on,' I cried. 'After everything you knew about me, my situation, didn't you think I deserved a bit of a tip-off? To hear it from a reporter . . .' To my horror I began sobbing, water gushing out of my eyes and nose, and I snatched up a tissue from the desk and blew my nose.

'Hey,' he said, voice compassionate now. 'Don't get upset. Maybe I should have been in touch. I guess I assumed someone else would. But Freeman's not as well known as you seem to think, he's sprung up out of nowhere. I only saw a thing in the papers myself by chance.'

The newspaper profile will change that, I thought. Then everyone will know. 'And when Jen told you she was moving out of the flat, did she give you a forwarding address?'

There was a pause before he admitted that she had. 'Belsize Park. Your old house.'

In my mind thoughts surged: Palmer across the street, head in hands; Emma in her bedroom, dancing in her sequinned pumps; Oliver and Jen at the bedroom window, pulling the blind . . . 'How could he have time, with this new job?' I almost laughed out loud at my own question, for how had he had time with Charlotte? How had I had time with Simon? And without children one had all the time in the world, as I was reminded every morning when I opened my eyes to the glowing fanlight, challenged by the sun to fill its hours of light. The truth was that it would be harder for Jen to make time for *him*.

'I wonder how Bob knew?' I said, thinking aloud.

'Ex-partners tend to be a bit more eagle-eyed, don't they?' He left the remark hanging for a moment, then added, 'Of course, she may have told him herself if they're on good terms.'

That would mean it was serious, I thought, Oliver and her, something they were properly committed to. 'When do she and Daisy move out of the flat?'

'It's two months' notice, so they're still there for a good few weeks. I got the office to drop you a line as soon as I heard myself. We've notified the landlord as well, obviously.'

'And then to Oliver's house?'

'Yes.'

Oliver and Jen. I still couldn't believe it. It was as unthinkable as my falling in love with Bob, a categorical mismatch even before one considered any question of personal betrayal. But, I supposed,

360

it could hardly be considered betrayal, could it? I had left Oliver almost a decade ago; he owed me nothing, least of all fidelity. And Jen? Well, I was not on her mind the way she was on mine. She had not dedicated several years to having me watched; she'd never received updates on my day-to-day schedule. After that single, unproductive visit with Mariel when I'd treated her so unfairly, she probably hadn't thought of me from one month to the next. And those subsequent notes from Mariel, well, I couldn't be sure Jen was even aware of them, much less contributing her own updates.

And now she was to take possession of my old home. Would Oliver at least acknowledge the awkwardness of the succession? Would he remove all remaining items of mine from the premises before signalling for hers to be carried through the door? Or perhaps he'd rid himself of them long ago, another van, another windfall for the local charity shop.

I felt suddenly utterly alone. I heard Palmer pull on his cigarette, imagined the smoke slowly escape from his mouth and nostrils. 'The timing is terrible for Daisy,' I said, desperate now just to extend the conversation, keep him on the line, kid myself that he was here with me and not there in London.

'How d'you mean?'

'With her exams coming up in the summer. Too much upheaval, moving house and everything. I think it's very selfish of Jenny not to wait until afterwards.' I was aware of sounding like a petulant child.

'Maybe she thinks she's waited long enough.' Again he paused, took a drag or two on the cigarette. You should think about giving up, I thought, irrationally, before it kills you.

'Maybe.' My voice cracked again. It was wrong, I knew, to call out of the blue like this, to burden him with this. I hadn't even asked him how he was, how *his* life was working out. A part of me dreaded the answers he might give.

'Look, is there anything you want me to do?' Palmer asked, after another silence, and though his tone was gentle it had about it the ring of winding this up, of seeing me off. 'I'm sure I could make some time.'

'No, it's OK. I shouldn't have called you. There's nothing you can do. I was a bit thrown, that's all, and didn't know who else to call. I'll just have to wait.'

'Wait for what?'

'For Oliver to get back in touch.'

Chapter 34

Dear Rachel

It's been a while since I've written. Where does the time go? I hope you and the shop are flourishing. I think sometimes, on grey days, of the beautiful sunshine you have there.

Toby and I are well. Overworked, of course. The girls are preparing for GCSEs, at least Daisy is, I wouldn't presume to know what Cat gets up to, even though we share a home! She's a law unto herself.

Rachel, I'm writing because there's something you ought to know. I won't explain in a letter, but if you haven't heard from Oliver in the next few

weeks, please phone me. I'm on the same number.
  Love, Mariel X

Oliver's letter came less than a week later.

Dear Rachel,
I think the time has come for us to make our separation official . . .

I hardly needed to read the rest. Work came first for Oliver and if press rumblings about a messy private life were about to jeopardise his new career then he would be keen to execute a clean-up forthwith.

But perhaps that was unjust. Certainly, that was unjust. The truth was that he had accommodated this indefinite state of suspension of mine with extraordinary patience. I had been the one to leave and, despite regular visits to our home town and a decade's worth of written correspondence, I had not once sought him out to give him explanation or apology. In any other circumstances our marriage would have been dismissed as ancient history. But I couldn't allow Emma to feel like ancient history and therefore I could not allow Oliver to either. This was the answer I had withheld from Palmer that night in London—and, over the years, from Ingrid and Eleni—when asked why I'd never initiated divorce proceedings myself. Oliver and I shared a surname, the same name on that headstone in north London. *We* had created her, and as long as I was married to her father, a tiny piece of my girl remained alive, remained in the present day. And, for the same reason, I knew that

I would never revert to my maiden name, no matter how many Mrs Freemans succeeded me.

Grounds for divorce was separation of five years, and since we'd fulfilled that criterion almost twice over no consent was required, no face-to-face negotiations. We both knew, however, that we needed to meet, just once, before I registered my agreement to his petition. We owed that to each other, and to Emma.

*　　　*　　　*

It was a Saturday. The ring tone might have been a cat purring on my shoulder, it was so loud, and I almost hung up before he answered. But he wouldn't be in, would he? This wasn't real, there was no Oliver sitting on the sofa by the fireplace or plucking a dripping mug from the dishwasher and shaking out instant coffee straight from the jar, no Oliver reading the weekend papers while using his free hand to comb his hair, wet from his morning shower.

'Yes, hello?'

My heart pumped viciously. 'Oliver, it's me.'

Silence, appalled silence.

'It's Rachel.' My tongue was dry, fat in my mouth, causing me to lisp slightly.

I heard him clear his throat. 'I know. How are you?'

'Fine, thank you. And you?'

'Good, yes.'

'I got your letter, about the divorce, and I thought I ought to call and say of course, that's fine, whatever you need.'

'Ah, good, good.' Now he was older, there was

more of Donald in his voice.

There was a pause and I could hear muffled activity in the background; two voices, maybe three, and a short exchange of shouts. I tensed. One of those voices had been female—Jenny, possibly, or Daisy? Surely I hadn't chosen to call the very day that they were moving into my old home, into Emma's home? I wondered which bedroom Daisy would choose, pictured the piles of schoolwork, the mugs of coffee, a young blonde head bent over her notes.

'But please don't worry about coming here,' I hurried on, 'I mean, you needn't go to that trouble.' I sounded so stiff and mannered. Did he hear Alysa in *my* voice? 'Flights are packed at this time of year, anyway, with Easter coming up. I'll come back and see you.'

That was illogical; if he'd have a struggle to find a seat then so, certainly, would I. He didn't point this out but said, pleasantly, 'Fine. That would suit me better, actually. When did you have in mind?'

'Next week. But not at the house, if that's OK. Could you meet me in St James's Park, maybe? On Friday? Three o'clock?'

'Yes, all right. You mean by the lake? On the bridge?'

'Yes, perfect.'

Where we used to walk together, where we were walking when the contractions started, a week early, and we raced to the hospital in a taxi, even though we knew it might be hours before anything happened. It was just her early warning. I was sent home, not even a centimetre dilated. She didn't arrive until the next day.

She looked like her father, of course, for the first month or so, as they tend to. Corresponding photographs were duly exhibited and all agreed that the likeness was indisputable. Peas in a pod. Except for the eyes: hers were darker than his from the start, big glowing irises that dominated her face, and when she retracted the lids it was as if light poured out, dark blue light. Then the mouth would open, wide, wider still, taking over the whole face, and out would come the hot cries for milk.

The atmosphere of the house changed entirely with this tiny new presence. Her Moses basket had a magical pull; wherever I was in the house I'd be drawn towards it, as though my brain was confused that our bodies had been separated in the first place.

I'd thought I'd known what to expect, at least a little, for I'd been practising with Cat under Mariel's tutelage, scooping her up from her cot, changing her nappy, burping her after feeding. Cat had been feisty from the get-go, a fretter who stayed awake into the night for months, determined to see herself on a drip before she'd agree to a sip of formula from a bottle. I was anxious about how I'd cope with such demands myself, given that Mariel was not only the fittest woman I knew but also aided heroically by Toby. Would Oliver, a heavy sleeper, wake up in the night and take a turn when I was exhausted? Did my mother mean it when she said she would help, when her knee was giving her more and more trouble? Would Simon and my other single friends at Pendant even remember I existed?

It felt like the luckiest of dips when Emma turned out to be quiet and sleepy, content to be cuddled and carried around the house and garden, listening to the commentary she couldn't understand.

'You do put her down sometimes?' the health visitor asked me, only half joking.

'Oh, yes, she sleeps so much. And she lies on the rug too, just looking around. She likes watching the leaves.'

'Well, she seems very happy, I have to say. And putting on weight nicely.'

Cat had ear infections, chicken pox, gastric problems that took an age to diagnose and drove Mariel to despair; Emma, nothing worse than a stuffed-up nose and a little cradle cap.

'You'll pay later,' Mariel joked. By then she was juggling work, an unreliable childminder, and a baby who still wouldn't sleep through the night, just as Toby found himself required to travel for work far more than he'd initially hoped. 'You watch, she'll be the horrible tearaway and Cat will be good as gold.'

'I wouldn't be surprised,' I said. 'It does seem too good to be true.'

*   *   *

It was unseasonably hot in London the day we met, almost eighty degrees. Though the birds proceeded with caution, human life had decided to take its chances and all around me scoops of naked flesh were pressed into the regatta green-and-white stripes of the park deckchairs. The lake was

367

dazzling, a radiant Renoir canvas in the sun. It was almost a surprise to find women in jeans and sunglasses, not gloves and parasols, hurrying, not promenading. I felt very stiff and out of practice among the park goers, who moved with such trained haste around one another. In Oia, in the crowds, one merely shuffled.

He was waiting on the bridge as I approached from the Mall. There he stood, in suit trousers and shirt, round-bellied now. The blond in his hair had gone entirely (there was a moment of vanity when I wondered if the grey in my own hair showed in the sharp London light), the skin on his nose and cheekbones reddened, and Rosemary's fine bone structure all but lost behind the loosening skin. He was forty-two, the older brother of the boy I'd first met.

I would have liked to have observed for longer, just watched him breathe, but he saw me almost at once and put up an arm in greeting. We seemed equally sheepish as we made our way towards one another; I'd wondered if we'd pull up short, stand apart and shirk any greeting too demonstrative, but it happened quite naturally that we continued moving until we had collided in a hug. My breasts pressed softly against his chest. He kissed my ear through the barrier of hair and stepped away again, eyes averted.

'You got here OK?'

'Yes. I came in last night.'

'Staying at Alysa's?'

'Yes,' I said, also nervous of eye contact. 'Oh, look at the willows, they're all perfect and green. I haven't seen willow trees for a while.'

He nodded. 'Look over here, have you seen the

London Eye before?'

I looked across the water, beyond Westminster, at the slice of silver wheel against the cobalt glaze of the sky. 'It's pretty. Have you ever been on it?'

'Once. Some corporate thing.'

We walked. The park signs told us we could choose between the Royal Parks Constabulary, the Cabinet War Rooms or the Guards Museum. I felt protected here, protected by London, and by Oliver too.

He asked about Santorini and the shop. He said he'd looked on the Internet and come across our website. Ours sounded like a very interesting collection. I asked about his own change of career. He'd been sitting on a committee, he said, and had been approached by one of the Chancellor's aides. He'd had to decide very quickly about getting on board and his managing director had been so supportive. Well, how could he not? It was such a crucial cause. The newspapers were a menace though. He was surprised by how keenly the government strove to please them. It had reached the point where columnists were practically dictating policy.

I decided not to mention the journalist who'd turned up in Oia. 'I'm a little out of touch with British politics, I must admit, but this all sounds very glamorous.'

'Not remotely.' His voice was more clipped than I remembered, the final syllable swallowed before it was aired. He was frowning. 'I just think it's important that parents with no experience in finance get as good a deal for their kids as those who do. There won't be any state-funded university by the time this generation grows up, you know.'

This didn't sound like the same person who'd followed an unashamedly elitist path through independent schools and university and into the City, who had insisted on a private consultant for the birth of his daughter and had objected to her receiving a state education. But that was the point: this wasn't the same person.

'Of course,' I said. 'All children deserve the best. An equal playing field.'

'Precisely.' He had a different aura now, one of a man too pressed—or too wary—to offer any but the chief facts of the matter. He'd lost that professorial distractedness that used to set in when anything but business claimed his attention, itself a variation of the dreaminess I'd first loved in him.

'How are the girls?' I asked. 'Daisy and Cat? Do you still see them?'

He sent me a quick sidelong look. 'Yes, they're great. Cat's in a spot of bother at the moment, mind you. Well, more than bother, potential disaster.'

'What do you mean?' Anxiously, I thought of that last note of Mariel's, that comment about her daughter—she's a law unto herself. Typical Mariel to downplay her own crisis in deference to mine.

Oliver pulled an impatient face. 'Nothing that actually merits the fuss, if you ask me. Smoking, maybe a bit of dope, but she's done it before and schools feel they have to do things by the book.'

I frowned. 'Drugs? She's only fifteen, Oliver!'

'Sixteen,' he corrected me. 'Come on, Rachel, they're all at it at that age. What we did at college, they're doing at school nowadays. Our teenage pregnancy figures are the highest in Europe, you know.'

'She's *pregnant*?'

'No, I'm just saying that the world has moved on, there's no point being unrealistic about it.'

I reeled at that. We might have been discussing an errant teen of our own; we might have still been together and arguing about Emma. But I was the one who was out of touch, not Oliver.

He gave a dry laugh. 'I would try to sort it out myself again, but my hands are tied. I have to be above suspicion these days.'

Again? 'You've helped out before?' I asked, surprised.

'Here and there. I've spoken to her head a few times, vouched for her good character. And her character *is* good, that's the main thing.'

I nodded. I'd missed all of this and yet I knew, without needing to hear the details, that I wouldn't have been able to help, not as Oliver had.

'Will it be OK? She won't be expelled?'

'They call it "excluded" now, and no, she won't. It will blow over, it usually does with Cat.'

I digested this, less sure than ever of my machinations of old, hopelessly naïve by anyone's standards, and certainly compared with anything Oliver might have chosen to do. He seemed now to be such a . . . such a *player*.

'How about Daisy? Is she all right?'

'Couldn't be better. She's doing very well at school, actually. On course for straight As.'

'She always was clever.'

'Yes.'

'I was sorry to hear about Bob and Jen, by the way.'

'A long time ago now.' Another sideways look. I

gathered he was unsure as to whether or not I knew.

'Bob's still in the picture, I assume?'

'Yep, of course. He lives down in Forest Hill now, but he sees Daze every other weekend. She stays with him on the Saturday night. It's all fairly amicable between Jen and him.' He sounded like a stepfather already, his tone buoyed with natural pride—*Daze*, he called her—and that made me feel confused and sad and jealous.

I took a deep breath. 'Oliver, I know about you and Jen.'

His mouth opened in shock. Now I knew for certain he hadn't expected this, he genuinely hadn't, he wasn't prepared. 'Mariel?' he muttered.

'Actually, no, but that doesn't matter.'

'I waited, Rachel,' he said, 'I waited a long time.'

It seemed to me that he had quickened his pace a little and I needed to skip to catch up. 'It's not about that, Oliver, I never wanted you to wait, it's just, oh God, of all people . . . my own friend?'

He gave a disbelieving huff of laughter. Some friend, that's what he was thinking, some friend I'd been. 'Rachel, of "all people" she was the one who was there for me, right from the start.'

I gaped at the term, 'from the start'. Emma's death was not the start, I wanted to cry, it was the end. I was close to tears now. 'That's not fair. I was in no fit state to be there for anyone. I was close to . . .' I trailed off.

'We all were, Rachel. We all were.'

I hesitated. I had no right, I knew, but still my mouth opened and the words came out uncensored: 'Do you still think about her? About Emma?'

The question seemed to hover in the warm air and I'd walked on several steps before I realised he had stopped some way back and I was moving alone. Turning, I saw him raise himself up from the stomach and lean forwards as though straining to contain a terrible rage. It was frightening, like watching a bomb detonate underwater. 'Of course I fucking think of her,' he cried, and heads turned from the deckchairs and the picnic rugs, surprised to hear fury in so calm and civilised a space. 'What d'you take me for? Some kind of monster?'

I blinked, reached out and tried to touch his forearm, but he swiped my fingers away. 'I didn't mean that . . .' I stammered, 'I just meant that it's better to look to the future, isn't it?'

He carried on glaring at me with loathing, but still I couldn't stop myself blundering on. 'Even now. Days are easier when you don't keep reminding yourself.'

'I don't have to *remind* myself, Rachel. She's there, always there!' And the flesh of his face and neck trembled with his anger.

'I know,' I whispered, 'I know. Please don't be angry, look, let's sit down, over here . . .' Reluctantly he followed me to the nearest wooden bench. I took his arm and pulled him next to me, our bodies touching. My face was inches from his. The skin behind his ear was dry, pulling in tiny folds towards his neck. I wanted to stroke his head, now slumped into his chest, but didn't dare and took his hand instead. 'I'm sorry, Oliver, I'm really sorry. I'm sorry I ran away and gave you no say in things. I'm sorry you had to go through all that legal stuff alone, that horrible case against Lockley, everything.' Sorry for my pride, pride in

373

my own grief, contempt for his. Sorry for the weakness that still made it impossible for me to say all of this aloud.

For a moment the world around me groaned and strained, the traffic and the construction machinery and the planes overhead on their descent into Heathrow, and Oliver too, less angry now than distraught. I cast wretchedly about for someone else to blame. His mother! Where had Rosemary been when Jen was 'the one' who'd been there for him? Wasn't this man who groaned by my side as much a motherless son as he was a childless father or a wifeless husband? And what of his sister Gwen? His colleagues? Anyone but *Jen*.

'I should have come to you sooner.' How absurd it sounded, as though I was a week or two late with my condolences.

He stared at the ground in front of him. 'Why didn't you?'

'I don't know . . .' Without thinking, without asking, I moved my hand to the back of his neck and touched the bumps of the upper spine. 'I suppose I thought you could never have been happy again with me there to remind you.'

'I could never have been happy again.'

'I know. I feel the same. But you still have to live, don't you, to find some joy, or whatever the nearest thing is. It's hard, but there are moments sometimes, aren't there?' When you laugh with your friend and see the tears appear at the corner of her eyes; when you stand hundreds of feet above the earth and see how miraculously it seals itself against the water, and how it will continue to do so long after you've gone. When you meet

374

someone who seems to need no explanation of who you are. And it was only then, seeing Oliver's profile and sensing his bodily yearning for the one who could comfort him, not me, but Jen, that I realised quite how much I had missed Palmer. Why *had* I let him go? Had it been for the same complicated reason that I had not let Oliver go? For, just as Oliver represented Emma, Palmer would be linked always for me with Cat and Daisy, my accomplice in an undertaking I now regretted and hoped to forget. Or perhaps it was simpler than that; perhaps it was because I'd got into the habit of letting friends go.

My hand moved across Oliver's shoulder and I leant towards him to hold him. 'You have a new life, Oliver, you've survived, and you deserve every second of happiness you can get now.' I thought about how I had felt towards him all these years as I went about my parallel life. I had never been able to accept that his loss was as great as mine, never. I had allowed myself to believe that he didn't have the right to hurt as I did, or even the capacity. Our cardboard cut-out, our Tin Man, we had laughed at him, my friends and I, and my mother had known it wasn't the way it should be.

I had been mistaken. His loss had not only been as horrific as mine, it had been worse: he had lost Emma and me at the same time. I couldn't have made it worse for him if I'd died with her that day.

'I think she was happy,' I said, squeezing him, 'you know, that last day. I think she had fun on her trip.'

'I didn't see her in the morning,' he said in a whisper, 'or the night before. I didn't kiss her goodbye.'

375

'I didn't either,' I whispered. Not Emma, but him. That last day, in the study, I didn't walk across the room to him and kiss him goodbye. And I now knew something I had not allowed myself to think, or even to fear until this point: all my actions, all this time, had been born of my certainty that Emma had kept our marriage alive beyond its natural life-span and that her death had delivered us a release from one another that would surely have happened earlier had we always been childless. But now, I thought, wildly, how might we have been without her arrival in the first place? My own closeness with her, in particular, had annexed so much of what had once been reserved for him. He'd been happy for it to happen too, it had suited him to leave her care to me and surrender to an obsession of his own. But without her arrival I wouldn't have allowed that surrender, I would have insisted on conditions, to keep a part of him closest to me. Without her we would still be together, I saw that now.

I felt his distress ease and we sat in silence, bodies quite still, upper arms pressed together, until I became aware of him shifting, rolling his shoulders. He was pulling himself together, looking at his watch. 'I'd better get back to the car, my meter's about to run out.'

'OK.'

'I mean, I could put some more money in . . .?'

I shook my head. 'No, you need to go. It's fine.'

He straightened. 'Do you have a lawyer? Here in London?'

'I'll sort one out first thing on Monday and phone you with the details before I leave.'

'All right. Thank you.'

'Oliver?'

'Yes?'

For a second I was possessed with such yearning to take his hand and walk out of the park gates with him, to go back to being with him, being devoted to him, I wanted it so much I could hardly breathe.

He was waiting, trying not to show his anxiety to get back to where he needed to be.

'I just . . . I mean . . . I don't want any money from you. In the divorce. You gave me that cheque, at the beginning, the damages from Morris . . .'

He frowned. 'Your lawyer isn't going to allow that, and nor am I.'

I paused, not interested in this, wanting to say something else, even though it was too late, let him know that I loved him and always would, but I heard myself tripping on about the money, about the only thing that *didn't* count. 'Well, maybe something little then, the money we saved for her, I could take that.'

He nodded. 'I'll make sure we work something out.'

We turned to face one another. We said goodbye and kissed. Then he checked his watch once more and walked away.

Chapter 35

The road to Ammoudi had been closed all winter in order for repairs to be made to the parts that had begun to crumble away at the cliff edge.

Though the *karavolades* trail remained open, the restaurants on the water had shut too, bringing to an end my waterside ritual of over a decade. Even when the season was at its busiest and Ingrid and I worked flat-out in the shop, I had typically managed at least one trip down there each week for a solitary glass of wine or a meal—my last connection, in a way, with the person I'd been when I'd first come to Oia. Back then, I couldn't manage a day without one of those hellish climbs; every extra step up or down those cliff paths had helped delay the moment when the blade of Emma's absence would next slice away at my insides. Now, though, as the road reopened and the grills were fired once more, I found I was out of the habit.

I still went down to Armeni when I could. I would sit at a table at the taverna, watching the families of skinny cats surround the diners and mew for scraps until Yorgos ran out to shoo them away with a flap of his sandal. Often the diners would flinch from his cries more violently than the cats, only to be tempted next with tickets for the boat trip (his son was still captain).

In summer Armeni was a popular place for yachts to anchor, and the odd one or two appeared early, even before Easter. The sailors would surface for noisy lunches, the clatter of cutlery and popping of corks carrying across the water to us. It was still a little cold for swimming, but there were usually a couple on board willing to brave it, shrieking at first, but soon comfortable in their warm skins, heads bobbing together in the glitter.

The last boatshed was closed for good, had been for years. Last I heard, Dymas had taken work in construction on some new villas down at Baxedes. He still made frames for us, occasionally, first using offcuts of softwood from Christos's site and later timber imported by a merchant in Fira. Mostly, though, we bought our frames ready-made and in bulk, then stained or painted them ourselves. It was more cost-effective that way.

It was sad to see the workshop doors bolted shut. I thought of all the sailing ships built here in the nineteenth century, when those seven yards were thriving and when, in the spring time, the harbour was deep with schooners. Then, Oians lived in strict accordance with that cycle of repair and voyage, departure and return, over and over, regular as the tide; then, it had been known as Captains' Village. But its pre-eminence had been eroded with every new year of the twentieth century. The place had just been coming to terms with its reduced status when the earthquake struck the death blow. Only now did I see what a miracle it was that Oia had risen again, how people like Anatole and Eleni had literally brought the place back from the dead. No wonder Eleni's relationship with the tourists was bittersweet; to her the place was as precious as an eldest son—no one was ever going to be good enough for it.

*   *   *

At Panomeréa, as at most of Oia's tourist shops, twelve-hour-a-day opening resumed in good time for Easter. Hard labour, Ingrid called it, and there *was* something almost penal about those early weeks, more exhausting even than the end of the season when most shop staff really were half dead on their feet. At least by September we were used to it, inured to it, the standing, the smiling, the small talk. Which was why, alone in the shop one evening in the middle of April, my lower back was sore and I was conscious of craving a drink more than I should have. It was all I could do to resist the temptation to curl up under the desk and take a nap. I'd be quite safe to do so too, if I synchronised my slumber exactly with the setting of the sun. At that time of day, for an hour every day without fail, the Marmara was a ghost town, everyone gathered at the Goulas or on the west-facing café terraces. That was one thing that never changed.

Today, however, an anomaly occurred. Just as the sky was deepening to its most photogenic hue, a pair of slender legs in patterned tights picked their way down the steps of the shop and a young woman appeared at the door. She wore a striped dress that looked oddly familiar, teamed with a torn tour T-shirt and a long, skinny black scarf wrapped once around her throat and left to trail to her hip. She had thick dark hair and wide-set eyes that blinked repeatedly as they adjusted to the spot-lit interior. That done, she put up the palm of her hand in greeting.

'Hi there. Are you my Aunt Rachel?'

There was a violent clench in my chest as though a fist had knocked the breath out of me. 'I beg your pardon?'

'I'm Catherine. Catherine Challoner.'

'Cat?' For a moment I just stared, frightened and bedazzled all at once. She was like a figure in a portrait who'd stepped suddenly into three dimensions. She *was* a figure in a portrait who'd stepped suddenly into three dimensions, for I'd last seen her in the flesh when she was six years old, the morning of the day of Emma's death. I closed my eyes and looked again: there she was, staring straight at me, fiddling with her handbag strap, undeniably flesh and blood.

'You all right?' she asked, evidently amused.

'Is it *really* you?' I whispered.

' 'Course it is. Don't look at me like that, you're freaking me out!' Her voice was a well-spoken drawl, not at all the polished sound of her mother's, but something new, unexpectedly cynical, as though nothing in the world could surprise her.

'What are you doing here?' Under the counter my legs were trembling and for the moment I didn't dare risk getting to my feet.

'I came to see you, of course.' She smiled, Toby's smile, wicked and well-meant in one.

'Do you . . . do you actually remember me, then?'

She nodded. 'A bit. I've seen your picture, of course. Every day. You're on our wall. Mum and Dad's wedding photos.'

'Yes, of course. I was matron of honour.'

'And all those kiddie pics as well. Mum's got albums full.' She looked a little hesitant, before going on. 'I remember Emma better. We painted Easter eggs together. I was thinking about it just now, with all the Easter decorations outside. Oh, is it OK to mention Emma?'

'Of course it is,' I said. 'I remember the Easter eggs as well, now you come to mention it. They were very pretty. One of you won the prize in the competition at the café down the road.' Emma

381

won, I remembered—for Easter 1994, a lifetime ago for Cat, was still fresh to me.

'Well, it wouldn't have been me,' Cat said. 'I'm rubbish at art. Rubbish at most things, actually.'

'I'm sure that's not true.' Still I stared. She was tall and graceful, or almost graceful, because there was still something a little self-conscious about the way she moved, as though she were experimenting with being a grown-up, the concept still new enough for her to have wondered who else might have noticed. That jaded tone, I realised, was simply the faux ennui of the sophisticated infant, the adult child. This was how Emma would be too, wasn't it? Exactly like this. Don't think about it, I warned myself fiercely, don't start crying and upset Cat. But she was so very beautiful, so very vivid! Her vitality was almost hyper-real, her body so close I could feel its warmth and see the sheen of perspiration on her forehead. It seemed to me I could sense the pull within her between safety and adventure. Adventure, apparently, was pulling harder.

'What are you doing in Santorini?' I asked. 'Are you here on holiday with your parents?'

'Nah, it's just me.'

For a moment I feared she'd absconded without anyone knowing, then I remembered that she was sixteen, had been since January. I'd sent a card. Hers was the first birthday, then Daisy four months later, then Emma last, the June baby. Sixteen. She could probably travel without her parents' permission, she could do many things without her parents' permission.

She advanced a step or two and noticed the display of photographs nearest to her. 'This is a cool shop. Is it yours?'

'Yes, mine and a friend's.' I followed her gaze to a shot of two children sitting on a wall in Pyrgos, legs dangling, faces screwed up in the sunlight. How many times had I imagined who those little ones were, how their lives had been when the picture was taken and how they'd turned out later; how many times had I imagined that the photograph represented a real connection between me and this unknown past? But now, in front of me, was the evidence that a photograph is not the same, can never be the same. All those shots of Cat from Palmer, month after month after month, and not one had inspired a thousandth of the emotional force her presence had in just two minutes. For a second the Panomeréa venture lost all meaning for me. It was nothing more than two women's fantasy of what 'art' might be, it was empty, vainglorious. I thought suddenly of that awful phrase people used for an idea or a work project that fills the personal gap: 'It's my baby'.

I tried to pull myself together, for she was clearly expecting me to take the lead in this encounter. She'd done her bit; she'd got herself here. 'Cat, does Mariel . . . does your mother know you're here?'

This was met with a defensive look, followed by the wide eyes of the coquette. 'Erm, it's *possible* she thinks I'm staying with my friend Lara at her parents' place in Sussex. A nice quiet place to revise. Oops!'

'What about classes?'

'It's Easter holidays, of course. And before you ask, yes, I *have* brought my revision notes with me. So where's this, then?'

She was looking at a Nikos, one of only two that remained of our original Panomeréa stock. 'It's a place called Perissa on the other side of the island, completely changed now, you wouldn't recognise it. Tell me, how is Jake?'

As her eyes kept moving over the images, her fingers reached out to touch. 'Am I allowed to pick it up? It's not like a museum, is it? Sorry, Jake? Oh, a pain in the arse. Hang on a minute, I've got a picture from my birthday party! I can show you how butt-ugly he is now!' It was on the screen of her mobile phone and the model she brandished was silver and considerably more costly looking than those Ingrid and I owned. When the images were presented I could hardly make Jake's out from the huddle of shadowed faces. They were mostly boys though, interesting considering she was a girls' school pupil.

'He's the one with his tongue out. See what I mean?'

I smiled. 'Listen, Cat, I can't really close up here for another hour or so, not until after sunset. But why don't I make us some coffee here and you can tell me what's going on?'

'Cool.'

My hands shook slightly as I poured the water, but Cat didn't seem to notice. When we were settled on the old stools with our mugs, she took a theatrically deep breath and announced, 'The reason I'm here is because Uncle Ollie and Auntie Jen are having an affair.'

I let my mouth form a concerned 'Oh?', though I'd already been in possession of the information for some time, of course. I was again struck most by the exquisite paradox of her words, the childlike

384

'Uncle/Auntie' against the drawled 'having an affair' of some veteran of sexual politics.

'Everything's changed,' she said, mouth remaining petulant as her eyes beseeched. 'They *live* with him now. Daze *hates* it, it's just *grotesque*! But we thought, well, you're still married to Uncle Ollie . . .'

'But it's been almost ten years, my darling.' My darling, I'd called Emma that, how naturally it came to my lips.

Cat gave me an odd look, but let it go. She'd prepared herself, perhaps, for spinsterly eccentricities of this sort. 'Anyway, Mum said you were the only person who could sort this out. If you wanted to.' Mum hadn't said that, I could tell, not to her directly at least. Perhaps, though, there'd been a private remark to Toby, overheard and seized upon, shoehorned into the campaign of some larger rebellion.

I put my hand on her forearm, lightly, as though fearing an electric shock. 'We're divorcing, Cat. I'm sorry, I really am. I met Oliver a few weeks ago to talk about it. The decree nisi should come through next month.'

Her face fell. 'What? Uncle Ollie kept that pretty damn quiet. I *knew* I should have come at half term, I *told* Daze. God, why do they have to be so fucking secretive about everything!'

'He may not have felt like shouting about it,' I said, 'I know I haven't. But it's happening, and he and Jenny are free to see who they like.'

'Well, they shouldn't be. It's *sick*.'

'You girls don't get on with him?'

'Sure, he's OK. But he's not Daisy's dad, is he? He's her *uncle*.'

'Well, not technically. Not by blood.'

'Hmm, whatever.'

I tried again. 'Lots of your friends must have divorced parents, new families—'

She interrupted, 'This is different.'

I paused. It *was* different. 'How is Daisy handling everything?'

'Oh, she's not speaking to her mum. She hasn't been for ages. Not since they moved in. She spends more time at her dad's now. *She* can't be *bought.*'

I was surprised by the savagery of the tone. Two thoughts occurred: one, the girls' disgruntlement was directed squarely at Jenny; two, Cat and Daisy were close enough for Cat to feel her friend's indignation as if it were her own. However misguided I thought the first, I couldn't help feeling pleased about the second.

'Daze says her mum's spent so much of her life worrying about money, she's *loving* having whatever she wants now—'

'Look,' I said, interrupting, a little less patient now, 'Daisy's mother is not like that. If you think she's been "bought", you're wrong. She's known Oliver a long time, since you were all babies—'

'That's what I mean! That's what makes it so disgusting! It's like incest!'

I was tempted to smile. The illogical argument, the spitting passion, here were the very teenage melodramatics Mariel, Jenny and I had both hoped for and feared. We'd talked often of how we'd 'lose' the girls to adolescence, each, of course, secretly hoping to have in her charge the exception to the rule. 'They'll be monsters,' Mariel used to say. 'Girls are worse, as well, everyone says so. But we'll get them back. We'll get them back

386

when they're sensible adults.' 'All the more reason to have the shadow mothers standing by,' Jen had replied. 'When one of us loses it, the others can step in.'

I blinked, guilt rising. 'Daisy will make up with her mum, I'm sure. And her father will be all right. He has a new relationship himself, doesn't he?'

Cat looked at me with eyes like searchlights. 'You're not bothered, then?' She scowled. 'Silly question. If you were bothered you'd have come back ages ago.'

'Oh, Cat, I am, I promise you I am. I just know these things will sort themselves out.' No one died, it is all resolvable. What was it Mariel used to call the men's huffing and puffing? Mini rebellions. That was all this was too; everyone would be happy enough in the end.

I let her finish her drink in huge swallows as though she couldn't wait to stalk off (if it was possible to flounce while holding a mug of hot coffee, she had mastered the art), before asking, 'Where are you staying, sweetie?'

'Dunno.' She indicated a backpack left against the wall at the top of the steps.

'You're welcome to stay with me, but my house is very small. I don't even have a separate bedroom. Why don't I find a hotel for you, somewhere nice? Just give me a minute to make a few phone calls.'

The Ilias was full, with a large group of Germans four nights into a five-night stay, but the Swallow Suites were quieter. Closing up for half an hour, I walked her up to Perivolos and checked her in, reassuring her that she wouldn't have to pay, and left her to bathe and rest. In such luxurious surroundings, dressed as she was in those mismatching layers, her pack of Marlboro Lights clutched to her body like treasure, she had the air of a fashion model resting between takes. I decided not to mention the cigarettes.

'It's lovely that you've come,' I said at the door. 'Really lovely. You've grown into such a beautiful girl, Cat.'

'Aw, thanks, Auntie Rachel.' In one stroke she seemed both more self-conscious and more aware of my feelings. 'Sorry I was a bit rude earlier. Like you want to hear all this stuff! I'm just, y'know, a bit disappointed.'

'I understand, don't worry. We'll talk properly later.'

As I left, I had to stop for a moment at one of Christos's shaded loveseats to wipe away the tears and pull myself together.

*   *   *

I took her for a late dinner at the Black Pearl. I couldn't help but fantasise that she was mine, this extraordinary girl. She had put on great quantities of make-up for the occasion, her eyes enormous with charcoal eye shadow, but you could still see clearly how luminous her skin was, how young and clear the whites of her eyes. There was such purity about her, whatever the words that came from her mouth, whatever those antics hinted at by Oliver. And it took my breath away to know that the pride I felt in being with her couldn't be the smallest part of what Mariel must feel. What was it she'd said that time, about knowing how you feel about someone when you look at them and they don't

388

even know you're there? When she looked at Cat, her almost grown-up girl, how did it feel? If I felt Emma's absence like a roar of hunger, did she feel Cat's presence like a full belly, warm and safe and sustaining?

Cat agreed to my suggestions of both aperitif and a bottle of wine, drinking in a swift and practised style and smoking during every break in the meal. She might have been thirty-five.

'So,' she said, lifting her chin to exhale, 'I must have really shocked you, turning up like this?'

I paused. 'You certainly did. I'm interested that it's you who's come to find me and not Daisy herself.'

'I'm sixteen, she's not. Easier to pull off. Plus, she's studying.'

'Shouldn't you be too?'

'I am, I told you. But we've been talking about this, God, *all* the time, for ever, and it was ridiculous not to do something about it.'

'Oh?'

'We were sure you'd be able to help, but Daisy said it wasn't right for us to bother you. She said that would be "monstrous" for you. She can be quite pompous sometimes.'

'She doesn't know you're here either, then?'

Cat ignored the 'either', and said, ' 'Course she does. And Lara. You can't skip bail without accomplices, you know.'

I laughed. She had such charm. I saw exactly what they'd been up to, conjuring up ideas of my storming back and catching Oliver and Jen in flagrante, putting an end to this liaison that just happened to offend their sensibilities, regardless of the feelings of any of the subjects involved. I remembered very well the intrigues and scenarios of my own adolescence—they had been as real as any that had followed in adulthood. All that was missing at this age was the awareness that other people were not actors, they could not be scripted and directed, but, sadly, tended to want to react in their own ways.

'You know I'm going to have to insist you call your mum, don't you?'

'Already have.' She indicated the mobile phone on the table by her bread plate.

'I mean to tell her where you really are.'

She rolled her eyes. 'I suppose.'

She would do it, I could tell. What had Oliver said? Her character *is* good. 'You know, I think it's pretty brave of you to come all this way on your own, and on behalf of someone else. You must be very good friends.'

'Sure. Like sisters, I suppose.'

'That's how it was when I knew you before. You fought like sisters, but you were so loyal to each other as well. It was hard for other kids to get a look in. You'd say, "Sorry, there's only space for three."'

She went quiet, knowing that I was talking about Emma too, cautious for the moment about what to say next.

'Mum and Dad said we'd come on holiday and see you, but it hasn't happened. They *always* say stuff and then don't do it.'

I smiled. 'I meant to see them too, when I've been back visiting my mother. But I never got around to it, I suppose.' I paused. 'I'm sorry I haven't been around for you, Cat, while you've been growing up. I haven't been a very good godmother, have I?'

'I don't believe in God,' she said at once. 'So it doesn't bother me.'

I laughed at that.

'Do *you* have a new partner?' she asked suddenly. 'Someone here?'

I looked up, startled. 'No.'

'No one? Not ever? Mum said . . .' she broke off, pulled an awkward face.

'Your mum said I did?'

'No, well, not exactly. I guess she just said that might be the reason you've never come back. And you're so cool about Uncle Ollie, I thought that was maybe why.'

'No, sorry. There was someone, someone I liked, but . . .' I paused. 'But it didn't come to anything.'

Cat blinked. 'Why not?'

'No one reason, just circumstances, I suppose. Timing.'

'Oh.' Her face fell. Circumstances and timing were poor excuses to a sixteen-year-old. I tried to think of alternatives, truthful ones, but I didn't think fear and pessimism would fare any better.

'Will you *ever* come back?' she asked, grabbing for her cigarettes and tapping one expertly against the pack. 'To London, to live, I mean.'

' "Ever" is a long time,' I smiled.

'Yeah, like will school *ever* end? And then what? They get us all messed up about what? *More* school.'

'University? It's still better than working for a living. You're really on your own then.'

'Bring it on,' she drawled, lighting the cigarette. And seeing her that night, grown up and confident, I knew I had nothing to fear for her and never had. The young woman in front of me was so well prepared for the world that she'd already set out into it.

*   *   *

The next morning I had a meeting at the bank that I couldn't reschedule, and by the time I arrived at the shop Cat was already there. Fragments of her conversation with Ingrid carried up the steps towards me:

'I *love* that skirt, Cat. God, how tiny is your waist? It must be twenty inches or something. Can I borrow your waist for my wedding day?'

'I'm not that thin. You should see some of the girls in my class.'

'Seriously, though, have you ever thought about modelling?'

'Oh, yeah, I was spotted in TopShop—that's this shop in London, really cool—and this woman who said she was a scout took my picture and made me promise to go into the agency, but Mum wasn't keen, she says I'm too young and that models are vacuous and suffer from arrested development. Anyway, when I went with my friend Daisy they were a bit funny about my scar, so I thought, Fuck this, and walked out.'

Ingrid must have looked quizzical for Cat went on, 'Look, on my leg, here. It's all weird and silver . . . I was in an accident when I was little. I was all ripped up.'

'Oh, that must have been with Rachel's daughter Emma?'

'Yeah, that's right. She died. I had counselling

for ages. It was awful.'

'What was she like?'

'I don't remember her too well. I wish I did. Mum says we were gigglers together. Once I wet myself on the gym mat because she was making me laugh. We turned over the mat so you wouldn't notice it but Miss Morrissey had seen the whole thing. I had to wear a rancid old pair of pants from the sports cupboard. I remember that.'

Now I could hear Ingrid laughing, Cat joining in, Toby's laugh. 'I always wanted a sister. Jake drives me nuts, he's such a geek.'

'Borrows your CDs, does he?'

'Borrows my *weed*, more like.'

Ingrid made a conspiratorial sound but I could tell from the silence that followed that she was shocked. There was a time when she'd vomited into flowerpots, but it was she who was the grown-up now, planning a wedding, thinking about a family of her own some time in the future.

I couldn't bear to eavesdrop any longer and launched myself down the steps with an exaggerated clatter. 'So, young lady, did you phone your mum and ask her to meet you at Gatwick?'

She beamed at me. 'Yes.'

'Good. She's not too cross?'

' 'Course not. Well, a bit. Don't worry, she's not pissed off with you.'

'That's good.' I hadn't imagined she would be. I thought I knew exactly how Mariel would feel in such a scenario. Furious, for five seconds, then pragmatic. Yes, Cat should be at her friend's house revising, but she was not in danger, she was in safe hands.

'Listen, Cat, I wondered if you wanted to pick

something from the shop? A souvenir, a present from me. For your sixteenth birthday. And one for Daisy too. She can have hers early.'

'Cool, thanks! I'd love to.' She went straight up to the last two Nikos shots. 'I like these best.'

She must have seen Ingrid and me looking at each other for she said, quickly, 'Oh shit, are these, like, really expensive or something? There aren't any prices on them.'

I bustled forward, unhooking them from the wall. 'No, no, they're just our favourites. You have perfect taste. And I can't think of anyone I'd rather have them.'

She was pleased by that. I could sense her excitement rising as she watched us wrap the pictures and ease them into the stiff paper bags with the blue lettering and rope handles. 'Wow, thank you soooo much!'

'I hope we'll see you again,' Ingrid said. 'Now that you've seen the fleshpots of Santorini.'

'They don't seem very fleshy,' Cat said, giggling.

'That'll be right,' Ingrid laughed. 'We like it quiet here.'

Over coffee, waiting for the taxi by the bus terminal, I made a last-ditch effort at moral guidance. 'I couldn't help overhearing that you smoke, you know, not just cigarettes . . .'

She looked at me with an expression of pure disdain and I felt like her great-grandmother. 'Weed, you mean?' she said. 'What does Mum call it, again? Dope. No, pot. Pot, kettle, black, that's what I said to her. Dad told me all about what you lot did at uni. Didn't Uncle Ollie, like, shoot up or something?'

'He did not,' I corrected her. 'Everyone

394

experimented a little bit, I suppose. That's what I mean, I would maybe wait for college for that kind of thing. That's the time to try new things.'

'Sixth form, anyway.'

I smiled at the speed of her negotiation. 'I'll keep my fingers crossed for your exams, I promise. What subjects will you do at A level do you think?'

'French, I suppose. At least that's one I'm good at, after Mum's little incarceration *française*.'

'What was that?'

She told me the story with considerable relish, how a year ago she'd started seeing the 'wrong' sort of boyfriend. He was nineteen and she fifteen, and she'd quickly adopted his habit of hanging out in pubs and student-union bars, drinking, smoking and 'whatever' (her words). Mariel had acted promptly, however, taking a leave of absence from her job and whisking both Cat and Jake off to France for the whole summer. It had worked, too, for there'd been no sneaking off back to London in the name of love ('I couldn't be bothered, and anyway, Mum put me on a pittance of an allowance'), nor any defiant new liaisons with the local delinquents. Back at school for autumn term, her older lover was found to have moved on to someone new ('Bastard!') and Cat's French had improved enough for her teachers to suggest she take an A level in it. 'All's well that ends well, as they say.'

I raised my eyebrows. 'It sounds as though you might give your mum and dad quite a bit to worry about.'

She grinned. 'Dad says that's my God-given right. What can I say?'

I couldn't help myself smiling back. 'And what

about Daisy? What subjects is she hoping to do?'

Cat laughed. 'Oh, everything, most probably. She's so nauseatingly clever.'

And Emma, where might her interests have lain, I wondered. In the arts, like me, or in finance, like her father? Or might she have dropped out, living with some boy in a beach hut in Koh Samui, serving coffee in Cornwall, picking grapes in Santorini . . . How I wished I could send a message to every parent hovering at their teenager's shoulder. It doesn't matter what they do at A level or where they end up going to university, or even if they go at all, just so long as you get to stand in their sunshine a little longer.

'Good for her,' I said. 'Good for both of you. I'm proud of you.'

She smiled, pleased, and I saw again, just in the moment before she remembered to hide her pleasure, a little bit of the six-year-old girl I knew so well. 'Things will work out, I expect. Mum says I lead a charmed life.'

'Oh?' I smiled, tried not to hold my breath.

'No, it's true, you know. I'm not being funny, but I've just noticed that when it's all going wrong, something works out. I usually get another chance. Daisy too. It's actually a bit weird . . .' She trailed off, her attention caught by the arrival of the new waiter, a pretty, long-lashed young thing, the type that Ingrid would once have had for breakfast. As he noticed her watching she looked away with conspicuous disinterest, and I allowed myself to breathe.

Might any of that luck of hers have been down to me, to Palmer and me?

If so, they'd never guessed. They didn't know.

Chapter 36

A British couple were talking in hot tones on the terrace below mine. 'I *knew* we shouldn't have come here. It's totally unsuitable for Benjamin.'

'How was I supposed to know? The guy on the phone said there were swings.'

'Well, where are they?'

'They must be here somewhere . . .'

This went on for a minute or two in that frantic, fruitless way of couples under strain. Peeking, I saw by their paleness and their dazzled, squinting eyes that they had just arrived. The child, about six months old, writhed in its sleep, presumably unused to the heat.

I leaned over and caught the woman's eye. 'I couldn't help overhearing what you were saying and I just wanted to say that the Ilias has a lovely shallow pool and I'm sure the owner would let you use it if you just mention my name: Rachel Freeman. And there are little swings and a see-saw at the kindergarten, just walk up the main path towards Perivolos. You know, it's actually much easier while he's tiny and not walking. Imagine a toddler!'

Both peered up at me, the husband half scowling. I could see that he considered all of this none of my bloody business.

'Thanks,' the woman called up, managing a smile, 'that sounds great.'

I withdrew. I feared that my old fairy-godmother antics had made me a little too apt to interfere. *I couldn't help overhearing*—the rallying

397

cry of the village busybody if ever there was one.

I felt for them, getting their bearings in a village built on a cliff. They would have red lights flashing all over the place. I still did it myself now and again, responded to some primal pulse by holding out a hand to keep my darling safe from the edge. Each time I did, I remembered to pull my hand back to my side, of course, but I sometimes let myself see Emma skip to my side and hold out hers.

The next time I saw the family they were walking down Marmara, the child facing forwards in a sling on his father's torso, pulling at the sunhat that shaded his eyes. When they saw me they asked me to take a photograph of the three of them, and I did so with pleasure.

*   *   *

Having disgraced myself badly in our last phone conversation, I decided this time to play safe and send an email.

> Dear Palmer,
> Thank you for forwarding all the paperwork from the Canfield Gardens flat, I'm glad that's all tied up now. I wanted to apologise for my phone call, when I'd just found out about Oliver and Jenny. I'm sorry, I shouldn't have involved you, I wasn't thinking straight.

I stopped, fingers moving from the keyboard to the surface of the desk. Was I thinking straight now? A butterfly had hatched in my stomach and I heard Cat's voice in my ear: *Why not?* Circumstances, I had said, timing. Inadequate excuses, best left out of this particular missive. I would keep it simple:

> Do you happen to have plans for the weekend of June 5th? Ingrid and Christos are getting married and we wondered if you would like to come . . .

Eleni had devised an unlikely adventure for Ingrid's hen celebrations: a sunset trip to Skaros, the medieval capital that jutted from the cliff at Imerovigli in a great craggy pyramid visible from Oia—from our own roof terrace, in fact. Closer to Fira than to Oia and the highest coastal point of the island, Imerovigli was a favourite spot with tourists and the site of numerous luxury hotels. As we followed Eleni through the narrow clifftop lanes, Ingrid exclaimed how pretty it was and peered beyond the GUESTS ONLY signs with professional interest. It all felt a little claustrophobic to me: the passages were too narrow to accommodate any but single file, and in every conceivable spot holiday units were piled one on top of the other.

'When the shaking comes, all gone,' said Eleni, making no effort to lower her voice in consideration of the people we passed. Unnerved by her words, I actually gasped out loud when we reached the cliff edge. There stood Skaros like some gargantuan cylindrical storage jar, the volcano beyond dwarfed and discoloured by this dizzying new perspective. On either side of us, all along the clifftop as far as the eye could see, was frame after frame of identical tableaux: a terrace table, a holidaying couple, a wine bottle and two glasses. Rows of closed parasols pointed like lines of spears to the sky.

Eleni shook her head. 'You know, I would not let my guests sleep one night here.'

'Just as well your hotel is in Oia, then,' Ingrid pointed out, 'or you'd have a very poor turnover, wouldn't you?' She looked to me to share the joke, but I couldn't laugh along. My eyes were fixed on the sea below: a cruise liner had anchored near the port at Fira, a vast wedged white monster afloat in the Caldera. It felt as though we were in a hot air balloon directly overhead and I had a sudden vision of myself tipping forward and flying, landing perfectly in the deck-top pool.

'Look, that must be the path down,' Ingrid said, indicating the upper turns of a *karavolades* trail, which continued towards Skaros as a thin dusty track. You could see exactly where it levelled out before climbing once more, sheer drops on either side. The cliffside was stubbled with shrub— nothing much to hang on to in the event of a fall!—and the handrail, where it existed, was nothing but a rusting length of cable.

Laughing, the two of them pranced ahead, as sure-footed as cats on the steep path down. I did not follow. It was the cable that did it, liquefying within me what had for so long been congealed. Nausea came first, followed by a whirling about my head, working through my body until my fingertips felt as though they'd been dipped in fizzy water. It wasn't that I could imagine myself falling, as in some simulated sensation of terror, more that I could actually feel it, I knew *exactly* how it would feel when the water rushed forward to claim me. Then came the worst bit of all, a feeling of emergency so intense it was like wanting to tear leeches from my body: panic.

'Come on, Rach, let's go!' Ingrid called from below. 'It'll be sunset in a minute and we want to get around the other side for that. It's further than it looks, I reckon.'

'You know what,' I stammered, barely able to edge another step forward, 'you two go on without me . . .'

'What?'

'I don't think I can do this.'

Salvation came, appropriately, in the form of a church, one of the island's hundreds of one-room chapels, no larger than the chapel in which Christos and Ingrid were to be married. It sat stark and white in the sun, ready for the moment when its walls would be tinted pink and a hundred camera lenses would swivel its way. Somehow, hardly looking, I managed to reach its tiny forecourt, lower myself on to the wall and take a few deep breaths of air.

The others rushed back up to meet me. 'It is what I said?' Eleni cried. 'About the earthquake? We are fine here, only the houses will fall.'

'That's reassuring, Eleni,' Ingrid said, rolling her eyes. 'What's up, Rach? You look terrible!'

'No, really, I'm just feeling very strange, sick. Whenever I look down.'

Eleni grew serious. 'You are afraid of heights? I didn't know this.'

'You can't be!' Ingrid exclaimed. 'Not after all this time.'

'I used to be, years ago, but not while I've been

here. It seems to have come back.' I prayed they would go before they could fuss over the physical symptoms, for I was shaking now and on the brink of tears.

Ingrid looked worried. 'Why don't we all just forget it and go back to Oia?'

I looked at her, appalled. 'No, no, I'm absolutely fine. You just go. I'll take your picture when I see you over there.'

'Well, if you're sure . . .'

To my immense relief they agreed to set off without me. Sitting with my back to the terrace wall, I breathed slowly and concentrated on the small details of the world that directly surrounded me: the little church with its matching blue door and cross; the way the flaked plaster and paint made a map on the exterior wall; the blanched purple thistles and the fine, pale ash of the ground.

Every so often Eleni and Ingrid turned back to wave to me—Eleni in khaki, camouflaged against the dried earth, Ingrid, hands on hips, hair a stream of gold in the breeze—and I made sure to wave back cheerily. They stopped to examine fragments of the walls, once part of an intricate secret city, and pointed across to Oia, which looked from here like a layer of ice melting into brown mud.

Slowly, braver again, I moved to the edge of the wall and glanced down. Immediately I felt as one might on being dangled by the ankle from a helicopter over open water. The sea seemed to be lurching in time with my fear. I thought about my mother's description of the water rising and falling on the day of the earthquake, a detail that had stayed with me through the years. I had the

402

sensation that the island was moving. I closed my eyes.

They were out of sight when I next looked, they must have disappeared behind the great rock to explore the sea-facing side. I remembered something I'd not thought of since coming here. The Lake District, a mountain walk with Oliver and Emma, visibility getting poorer the higher we climbed, the path much steeper than we'd expected.

'You stay here,' Oliver said to me in an undertone, 'we'll go on to the top.'

'But shouldn't Emma—'

'She's fine,' he interrupted, 'she wants to come with me.'

'Yes, Mum, *we'll* go to the top, you wait here because you're scared.' She aped her father's long-suffering expression, wanting to impress him.

'OK, sweetie, but *be* careful. Promise.'

I waited forty-five minutes before beginning my wild scramble after them, terrified of both the drop below me and the thought of where the climb might have taken them. I couldn't escape images of her falling, of Oliver slipping and taking her with him, their bodies lying crumpled and inert in the dampness.

I hardly recognised his voice when it came. 'Rachel, what are you doing? Look at your hands! They're bleeding!'

I glared at him, maniacal, ready to attack him with my nails, and my voice came out in a horrible shriek. 'Where were you? I thought something had happened!'

'Calm down, you're frightening Emma. We were fine.'

'I was worried.'

'Mum . . . ?' Emma had never seen me in a full-blown panic before, she was shocked and upset, came over to hug me, but in that moment before she moved I glimpsed something new in her face, a sense of betrayal. She'd thought I was strong, always strong, but now she'd seen I could be weak.

The sound of clapping brought me back to the present day, the familiar and faintly absurd spectacle of humans applauding the sky. Sunset. Well, I'd been wrong that time, I told myself, my loved ones had reappeared quite safely, the crisis mine and mine alone, and I'll be wrong again here. But hikers who'd passed by the church after Ingrid and Eleni had left me were returning already. One couple who'd followed a good twenty minutes behind them were now back at the top ordering drinks in a bar. Soon I would have to go, follow the dusty line despite my fears, check that they were safe. I closed my eyes again and counted: one minute more, two, three . . .

When I next looked, there they were, perfectly safe, of course. Eleni arrived first, flushed and breathing heavily. 'Feeling better?'

'A bit. Sorry to be so cowardly, I don't know what happened.'

'It is very steep as you go across, you would not have liked this. Even I . . .' She put her hand on her stomach and opened her mouth wide in a soundless scream to show her sympathy for me.

'The view is amazing,' Ingrid said, joining us, bright-eyed and inspired. 'We found another little church down on the other side. Oh, and you can see the tourists watching the sunset in the Goulas through the binoculars.'

'The sky is a lovely colour,' I agreed, gamely.

She narrowed her eyes at me. 'You need a drink, a big one. Come on.' She approached me as one might a patient recovering from a hip replacement operation.

'I'm fine, no problem. You go first.'

'You go in the middle, then. We'll be on either side, just in case.'

At the top again, behind the toughened glass of a café window, I could look more sensibly at the shapes arranged in the sea below. So this was the region in all its brutality, places like this very village just a hair's breadth from vanishing, literally crumbling with every hiker's footfall, and yet time and again people made the decision to come here, to live here. What an extraordinary island this was; would I *ever* stop noticing?

'Well, that definitely put things into perspective for me,' Ingrid said, 'going right to the edge of the world before taking the plunge.'

'Are you getting married or committing suicide?' Eleni laughed.

'You tell me, old married woman!'

I felt myself relax, my strange attack already receding into the past, a feeling that deepened when the waiter brought us the best wine he could find. It tasted of blueberries and honey.

'Nervous?' I asked Ingrid. I felt suddenly mortified that my behaviour might have ruined the mood of what was supposed to be a celebration.

She grinned. 'About the wedding or about seeing my mother?'

'Well, either.'

'Not really to the first, yes, heaps, to the second.' She took a large gulp of wine. I

405

remembered the look on her face when the email had arrived, some livid combination of terror and delight. My mother *is* alive, she *is* sane, she *is* interested in reuniting with me! 'I don't believe it,' she had said, over and over, 'it can't be a practical joke, can it?'

'We will bring her here, yes?' Eleni said. 'To Skaros? Or does she fear heights, also?'

'I don't think I ever saw her above ground level,' Ingrid said, thoughtfully. 'Or maybe I did in the mall. How weird is that?'

Eleni and I exchanged a look. We had avoided discussing the Rachael situation on our own, terrified, perhaps, of glimpsing the other's worst fears.

'How about you?' Ingrid asked me, playfully. 'Are *you* nervous?'

'About . . . ?'

She rolled her eyes. 'You *know* what. Or *who*, I should say.'

Palmer. Our second unexpected 'Yes'. He was coming back and the prospect made me nervous; nervous and embarrassed, nervous and happy.

'I have never known what it is between you two,' said Eleni to me, watchfully. 'He is not married by now?'

Ingrid snorted. 'It's only you who's so keen to marry everyone off, Eleni. Anyway, take it from me, if he had a wife he wouldn't be *allowed* to come. Look at poor Nikos, he's totally under the thumb!'

'Perhaps we should keep things in Oia,' I said, changing the subject. 'I mean, it's going to be busy enough without sending people on excursions all over the place. Though Skaros is certainly worth visiting,' I added, tactfully.

'Skaros is very good,' Eleni agreed, 'very interesting. But Imerovigli, no.'

'Yes, Eleni, we get the message,' Ingrid laughed. 'You wouldn't let your guests spend a night here . . .'

Eleni clinked glasses with her. 'I would not let my *dog* spend a night here.'

*   *   *

Two days before the wedding, while Ingrid oversaw final arrangements at the house, I went to pick up her mother from the airport. Waiting with my cardboard sign for Rachael Sullivan, I watched the arrivals come, two by two, the occasional large group, through the doors from baggage reclaim. Even those not expecting to be met searched the faces and hand-penned signs—as though the god of transfer arrangements might have blessed them with a surprise limousine—before heading towards the concourse for a taxi or a bus.

No Rachael. I waited until my fellow sign holders had all been greeted and followed to their cars, and then I waited until a new set began to appear. Now the names on the signs were German and the passengers who appeared had different styles of hair and luggage. The board announced a charter from Frankfurt: again, no Rachael. I checked the monitors. Perhaps she'd missed the Olympic connection in Athens and was coming instead on the Aegean flight, next in. But when these arrivals had petered out too, and I'd been at the airport almost four hours, I gave up and joined the taxi queue myself.

Ingrid watched me from the window of Christos's house and even from a distance I could see her expression crumple at the sight of me returning alone. By the time she opened the door, however, she'd composed herself.

'I take it she didn't show up?'

I went to hug her—'I'm so sorry, darling'—but she resisted and turned away.

'It's OK. It's pretty much what I expected. I just had to know. Thanks for going.'

I followed her inside, trying to keep my voice light. 'Maybe she missed her connection and is coming in tonight instead? Or tomorrow morning? That will be it. Have you checked your emails?'

'Not yet. But there's no point, believe me.' She was in a mood I'd not seen before: beyond disappointed, it was maudlin, fatalistic, dangerous. As she turned her back to me I noticed that music was playing, a melancholy song that was faintly familiar:

I don't have anything
Since I don't have you

'Such a sad song,' I said, quietly.

'Isn't it? I found it on one of Christos's old albums. My mother used to play it all the time.' I saw that she had begun to cry softly, but when I moved towards her to comfort her she again motioned abruptly for me to stop. 'Not this version,' she went on, 'but some other one. She told me it made her think of my father. She was always in such a mood when she'd been playing this song.' She looked up at me, eyes fierce. 'Self-pitying old cow.'

408

'Maybe it's better this way,' I said gently. I wasn't sure where to put myself and hovered a while before settling on the edge of an armchair. 'It might have been a bit too emotional, her arriving just a few days before the wedding, when there's so much for you to think about. There wouldn't have been time to catch up properly. Perhaps if she visits later instead, when you're settled . . .'

'I've been here ten years, Rachel, I think I'm pretty settled!' Ingrid used her thumb and index finger to wipe her runny nose, pressing its tip upward into a child's snub. 'You know, even when I was little I was offended.'

'Offended?'

'By this song. How could she mean it? "I don't have anything"? When she had *me*?'

> *I don't have love to share*
> *And I don't have one who cares*
> *I don't have anything*
> *Since I don't have you*

'Oh, darling, I'm sure that's not what she meant. Whatever her—'

She interrupted again, flicking away my words with her hand. 'It's OK, Rachel, you don't need to console me. Go back to the shop.'

I hesitated. Perhaps that *was* the best thing to do, to leave her to her privacy, just as I preferred in times of my own upset. 'Paula is there, you know that. She's not expecting me back for another hour.' We'd planned on taking Rachael for lunch together, Ingrid and I, talked for ages about which would be the perfect venue. We'd booked Paula, our regular cover, especially.

'Whatever.'

At least this bloody song is finishing, I thought as it faded out, but to my horror it started up again, evidently playing on a loop.

And I don't have fond desires
And I don't have happy hours

'Shall we turn this off? I don't think it's helping.'

Ingrid ignored this. 'I've made a decision,' she said suddenly, and shot me an intense confrontational look. 'I've decided I'm going to go and see Christos and tell him the wedding's off. I don't think we should go through with it.'

'What?'

'Think about it, Rachel. History repeats itself, everyone knows that. I'll do the same thing my mother did. I'll have a child, Christos will leave me, I'll start drinking, I'll hurt it. How could I not? It's all I know.'

'Ingrid, no. It's not all you know, of course it's not. The fact that you've had that experience yourself will guard you against anything like it. Christos isn't going to leave you, he adores you . . .'

'He left his first wife, didn't he?'

'He married her when he was barely an adult. This is completely different. He's found someone he wants to end his days with, and so have you.'

'That's just a cliché,' she scoffed. 'I mean, how do *you* know? You left *your* husband, didn't you?'

'Yes, but the circumstances—' (That word again.)

'The circumstances were awful, yes, I know, but you still left. Who's to say I won't have the same

410

thing ahead of me?'

I tried to catch her gaze as it roamed across the surfaces of the room, the furniture, the pictures on the walls. When it finally came my way it was like the sudden flash from a magnifying glass and I almost recoiled.

'God, Rachel, you haven't got a monopoly on tragedy, you know! And those kids you're so precious about, Cat and the other one, don't you know that being there in person is the only thing that counts? Take it from me!' I gasped. Her cheeks glowed with anger. 'Why the hell do people get married in the first place, that's what I want to know? It's pathetic. Stupid and pathetic. Grown people acting like children, acting like happiness lasts for ever.'

'No one's saying that, Ingrid. No one has any idea what's going to happen. But you have to have faith in how you feel now.'

'Well, I have faith that something fucking bad is going to happen, that's what I have faith in.'

'No one has any idea . . .' I repeated. I was crying too by now, and, noticing, she seemed to start.

'Hey, God, don't be upset, Rach. I shouldn't have said any of that stuff.' She gave a long and painful sigh. 'Just ignore me.'

'I don't want to ignore you. And you're right, this isn't about me.' Standing, I took a step towards her and this time she allowed me to cup her elbow with my hand. 'Just think about it, please, before you talk to Christos.'

'I'm just scared. If it goes wrong.' She sniffed, using her sleeve now to wipe her nose. 'She's cast a spell on me. She's a bad person, Rachel.' She'd

411

caught that from Christos and Eleni, the notion that we were all good or bad, with nothing in between.

'And you most definitely are not. You and Christos love each other. You'll be a fantastic mother, if the time comes.'

'Maybe.'

'Definitely. That much I *can* guarantee you.'

> *I-I-I-I-I-uh don't have anything*
> *Since I don't have you-oo-oo . . .*

'*Please* can we turn this song off.'

'OK.'

I hit the off button and at once the atmosphere felt friendlier, salvageable. Voices, and the sound of hammering, carried through the open windows from the courtyard.

'I'm sorry she didn't come, I'm so sorry. But you've tried. You can never blame yourself now, never.'

Ingrid nodded. 'She would only have ruined it for me. I knew that, I guess. I just hoped there might have been a miracle. Look, I'd better go and see how the guys are getting on putting the canopies up . . .'

'OK. I'll go back and check on Paula. I'll let Eleni know what's happened too.'

'Thank you.'

She still hadn't moved by the time I reached the door to leave. Sitting there, fingers pulling at her lips, she looked for a moment younger than she had when I first met her, a decade ago.

*   *   *

By the time I reached the Ilias I was ready to explode.

'She didn't come,' Eleni said, quietly.

'No she fucking didn't! What kind of a mother *is* this woman . . . ?

Eleni reacted to my unusual fury by adopting my usual calm. 'I am thinking a different way. What kind of things are happening in a life to make a mother like this?'

'Nothing excuses it,' I raged. 'Children should come first, no matter what. If you're having trouble yourself you should try to hide it from them. They don't understand and they get upset.'

'Yes,' she agreed. 'That is true. That is how it *should* be. But when your children are grown up . . .' She paused, considering the sensitivity of what she was about to say. 'It feels different, you know, from when they are young.'

I nodded. 'I don't know about that, I suppose.'

She poured us both coffee and came to sit down with me. 'You don't think she has done this, perhaps, because she loves Ingrid?'

I stared. 'How could that possibly be the case?'

'She plans to come, I am sure of it, but she knows herself, maybe. She is trouble, she doesn't trust herself to come and not spoil this wedding . . . ?'

'I guess. I hadn't thought of that,' I said.

'Thanks God she is *not* here, on the plane today. That might be far worse.'

'Perhaps you're right.'

Later, Christos had his airline agent make a phone call or two. Rachael Sullivan had not checked in for her flight. Three weeks ago she had

413

gone into the airline office in Melbourne and exchanged the ticket for cash.

Chapter 37

Dear Rachel,
I wanted to let you know before anyone else that I am planning to remarry after our divorce is finalised. Jenny and I will do it quietly in London this summer.

I very much hope we have your blessing. Neither of us would like to think that we had caused you any distress.

Love, Oliver

I wasn't sure why, but the news made me drop everything and hunt for a photograph, one I'd brought with me from London but hadn't looked at for several years. Toby had taken it of the six of us, the three mothers and three girls standing at Mariel's kitchen counter stirring a big bowl of cake mixture. The girls were kneeling on stools, heads as close to the bowl as allowed. Cat, the only child with her face to the camera, had cake mixture smeared across her right cheek. 'You're like a coven,' Toby had laughed, 'look at you training up the next generation. It shouldn't be allowed.' Emma had asked what a coven was and Toby had explained, asking her if she was a good witch or a bad one. 'Good,' she'd said, face quite serious.

We had believed ourselves to be interchangeable, Mariel, Jenny and I, ready to protect one another's daughters in a heartbeat.

414

However long it had been since Jen and I were close, whatever tensions had been at play that last time we met, I had once believed with all my heart that she was the woman I wanted to mother my daughter if anything were to happen to me. Well, she had taken my place, after all, and I had neither the strength nor the desire to break our vow now.

Yes, they had my blessing.

*   *   *

Had Christos's 'secret' Oia ever existed, it certainly didn't any longer. It was Olympics year and the place had never felt quite so top heavy (and never would again, I suspected): there were so many visitors that the pathways couldn't contain them and they had to step into side-alleys to make way for each other. Scenes for a Hollywood movie had recently been shot here, on release in the US and inspiring fresh droves to descend (not that Ingrid or I regarded our customers as 'droves', of course). The Eastern Europeans had discovered us too, arriving on their cruise ships and coming in convoys of buses from the port, the name of the language spoken aboard displayed in the windscreen. Many made immediately for the churches, clustering around the doors in the hope that there might be something 'Greek' going on inside (a wedding, ideally). There was an established form to this: first try the door in hopes of gate-crashing the ceremony; second, withdraw, face chastened; third, wait outside with a video camera.

It was hardly news that the place was photogenic—I'd been making a living out of the fact for years—but it *was* new that the amateur photographers were getting almost as bold as the cats that jumped on to restaurant tables as the food was being served. They were quite willing nowadays to trespass on church roofs or private terraces to get their shot. Manfred blamed digital cameras. 'Everyone is a photographer now,' he said, 'and most wouldn't recognise a darkroom if they fell into one.' 'No, they'd think it was a flotation tank at their spa,' Ingrid joked. Eleni told us of one guest's recent complaint: settling down for breakfast on the rear terrace, he and his wife had looked up from their yogurt and honey to find a camera lens trained directly on them, two Chinese tourists murmuring together as they adjusted their tripod and set up their shot.

'They walked through the hotel to do this. Unbelievable to me! And they didn't speak a word! Do you know what it is that Anatole says is the least-used phrase in Oia?'

'What?'

'Boro na galo mia fotografia?'

'Please may I take a photo?' I translated.

'That'll be right,' Ingrid said, laughing.

*   *   *

To the tourists' delight, the weddings they so yearned to watch were held, more often than not, in the main church of Aghia Panaghia, spilling into the square afterwards in wild assemblies that drew villagers and holidaymakers in equal numbers and that at times resembled pandemonium ('This is a Greek word, of course,' said Eleni). As well as the sometimes eye-popping costumes of the wedding

416

party, the spectacle might include mules decorated with flowers, balloons released into the sky, fireworks, music and general clowning, scheduled or otherwise.

It was something of a feat, therefore, for Ingrid and Christos to keep their own wedding the discreet, fuss-free event they'd planned. They were helped by the fact that the walk from the house to the chapel, while bringing them into the public pathways, did not take them too close to the main drag. As the doors were closing for the ceremony to begin, only a smattering of interested faces remained outside, and the only camera was Manfred's.

My Greek had never much improved, but I told myself I could at least enjoy the occasion on a visual level. Christos wore a beautifully cut cream-coloured suit and Ingrid a long pale-yellow dress with shells sewn into the neckline. Her hair flowed loose and unadorned down her back, an effect as beautiful and simple as befitted the backdrop. The chapel was small enough to conjure up nerves out of nowhere, all ears alert to the faintest shuffle of the foot. A small child fidgeted and giggled. Manfred tried to restrain his clicking. In front of us, at our centre, the priest handed Christos and Ingrid white candles and placed the rings on their fingers. There followed the elaborate ritual of removal and exchange before their hands were joined for the rest of the ceremony. Throughout, their faces were as solemn as those of the icons on the walls around them, and as golden too in the yellow candlelight. Finally, the priest placed the *stefana*—the crowns of flowers—on their heads to signify their union. There was wine, a little walk around the table at the altar, and then they were married.

*   *   *

Oliver had had doubts about me, once. It had happened a few months before our wedding. He'd been out with colleagues, getting teased that he was too young to settle down, too good a catch, and they'd reignited suspicions of his own that he'd thought he'd extinguished. Had he proposed, and was he going through with marrying me, because of my father having recently died? Because I so plainly needed rescuing and he happened to be in the right place at the right time? The question he asked himself that evening was: Was it, for him, the wrong place and the wrong time?

With feet getting colder by the hour, he was in danger of losing one to frostbite. He made a deal with himself that if he stepped into the street and got a taxi within sixty seconds, he would go ahead with the wedding, go ahead with me. It would be a sign. But, if a minute ticked by and no taxi came, then he'd know it wasn't meant to be. He even counted down the seconds on his shiny new timepiece, a limited edition Swiss something or other he'd bought with his last bonus.

'I thought you knew,' his sister Gwen said, years later, a rare meeting between just the two of us, a little too much wine drunk.

'No,' I said.

'Wasn't it mentioned in the best man's speech at your wedding?'

'No.'

418

'He loved you, don't get me wrong. He was always committed. Just last-minute nerves, everyone has them.'

I hadn't.

The cab had come, obviously. As Oliver left the bar it was already pulling up, disgorging some drunken idiot and waiting to load the next. As his friends cheered him on from the pavement, he sat, on his own, satisfied that the regulation epiphany was now safely under his belt, and set off across the city to find me.

* * *

'Have I said congratulations yet?' I asked Ingrid.

'Only about a hundred times. But you know what? Not once in Greek!'

'Ah,' I said, 'but maybe "congratulations" is a Greek word?'

'No, I already asked Eleni. Latin.'

'Damn.'

There was something about the way Ingrid sat on the sofa, dress pooled beneath her folded legs, that made me think of the girls at Emma's last birthday party. She tucked her skirts under her to make space for me to sit next to her.

'Still no sign of Palmer?' she asked.

'No, he called again though. He's been able to get a seat on the last Olympic flight out.' Palmer had been stuck in Athens since nine this morning, a problem with one of the engines on his original plane and the rest of the day's flights booked solid. In a way it had been a relief, for a wedding and a reunion in one fell swoop might have been beyond my nervous resources. I didn't want another

419

incident like the one at Skaros; I pictured myself in a hysterical heap at his feet. No, this way I'd be able to greet him alone, and—it had to be said—fortified by a day's alcohol. 'If you miss him tonight, you can always see him tomorrow before you head off.'

'Good,' Ingrid said. 'I'm glad it was just a travel delay.' She had not mentioned her mother once today and, whether or not the pain remained, was unrecognisable from the broken creature of a few days ago. All evening long, in the courtyard of the house amid the palms and jasmine and honeysuckle and the gem-coloured clothes of the guests, she had blazed bright as the sun. I had never seen a happier bride.

'Listen, I didn't get the chance to tell you earlier,' she said, 'but Christos and I had a big chat last night, and guess what? He wants to help fund the museum! He thinks it's a fantastic idea. He said he'll help us attract other investors, maybe even get some government funding. We'd be able to bring down high-profile exhibits from Athens, really put Oia on the map.'

'I think it might be just a bit too complicated,' I said. 'Think how hard it's been just to renew licences for Panoméréa.'

'Oh, he'll take care of all the bribes and stuff.'

We laughed. She wasn't taking my protests seriously and now was not the time to demonstrate that I meant them. I wasn't sure when I had started detaching myself from her, perhaps the day I'd introduced her to Christos and seen the look that passed between them, but it had happened a strand at a time and today was the day for the last, most stubborn threads to come loose. Ingrid didn't need me, at least not as she once had, and I was pleased for her, pleased and proud. She would run her art museum independent of me. She might even take in some bright, ambitious young foreigner who'd come to Oia for bar work.

It was the natural order of things.

Knowing me well enough to not press the issue for now, she changed the subject. 'Can you believe all the presents we've been given? Everyone's been so generous.'

The gifts were arranged, still unopened, on a large polished table on the far side of the sitting room. There, in a smaller pile of letters and cards to the side, was my own. I was pleased when she said they would wait till after the honeymoon to open them; the last thing I wanted was to be present when she got to that little card and the documents folded within.

'It's a bit overwhelming actually. They've been arriving all week, even from people we didn't invite.'

'How lovely to come back after your honeymoon and have them here to open together. I remember that.'

She looked at me, eyes sad. 'Do you still have anything from *your* wedding day?'

'No, but I talked to Oliver and I might collect a few things, next time I'm home.'

'In London, you mean?'

'Yes,' I smiled. 'Funny to still call it home after all this time. Anyway, listen, Ingrid, don't worry about calling me while you're away, the shop will be fine. Enjoy it being just the two of you.' The couple were honeymooning in a private beachside villa attached to one of Christos's hotels on the coast near Athens. They would be away for over two weeks.

She snorted. 'Are you kidding? I know for sure that Christos has at least two business meetings scheduled while we're there.'

'Well, since I've had my own experience of being married to a workaholic, it might be better if I don't give any advice at this point, at least not on your *first* day of marriage.'

She laughed at that, glanced instinctively through the open doors in search of her husband. I thought about the moment, just an hour or two earlier, when the opening notes of a new Greek dance had raised a particularly excitable shriek among the guests and I'd looked up from my conversation to see the yellow swirl of her hair as she plunged right into the eye of the excitement. And I thought of something Palmer had said, the last time we met in London: *You never get these moments back.* Whatever had prevented Ingrid's mother from being here, I hoped it was worth it.

*   *   *

Taking the hidden short cut between my neighbours' terraces I arrived at Callidora at about the same time as Palmer did by the conventional route. As I slid heavily over the wall, I saw him standing by the gate in a light-coloured linen suit, grinning at my ungainly method of entry. For a moment I felt overwhelmed that he'd agreed to come to me, that he'd got that last flight from Athens. It seemed like some kind of miracle.

'Hi,' I said. 'You look a little rumpled.'

His grin grew wider. 'That's all you can say to

422

me? After four years?'

'Sorry. It's not a classic line, is it?'

'I'm afraid not.'

I stared stupidly at him. He looked exactly the same, sounded exactly the same, made me feel exactly the same. 'You made it then?'

'Well, by the skin of my teeth. I thought it might have to be a night at the airport, to be honest. I just checked in at the Ilias. Didn't recognise the girl—I guess Eleni and Anatole are both still at the wedding.'

'Yes, it was winding down a bit when I left. Come on in.'

As I unlocked the door he clambered over the wall on to the terrace the same way I had, coming to a halt a couple of feet from me. 'The party's not actually over then?'

'No, still going . . .' I waited for him to suggest we head up there; it was only two minutes' walk away and having come all this way he ought really to put in an appearance. I got the feeling he might have been waiting for me to do the same.

'I'm glad you're here.' I wobbled a little as I smiled. I had drunk an awful lot, I realised. Then I watched, almost as astounded as he was, as I reached out and took his hand, pulling him into the warmth of the house. As I closed the doors firmly behind us it was almost as though someone had sprung out from the shadows directly in front of me and started acting my part for me. I saw, puzzled, that I'd made the bed very precisely that morning and had left the lamps glowing in my absence.

'Rachel—' he began, his lips close to my ear, but I didn't allow him to speak, taking his face in my palms and leaning forward to kiss him. The sensation of his lips on mine was extremely strange. Even considering all the kisses that had gone before, eager and reluctant—kisses from Oliver and Simon and the others—this felt unfamiliar, unrecognisable, at least for the first few seconds. It was like tasting familiar treats blindfolded.

We took off our clothes and kicked them into a heap by the sofa as we moved towards each other at the edge of the bed. When I first felt his bare torso against me there was none of the unleashing of dormant desire I'd heard people speak of after long celibacy, only more of those sensations of blind-tasting. I realised I was frowning deeply, concentrating hard, and I didn't speak a word, terrified my thoughts would betray me as my body had. He was the one who spoke, repeatedly saying my name and paying compliments in the blurting rush of one who has kept his sentiments secret for too long. It embarrassed me and I was grateful for the dark.

'Are you sure about this?' he asked.

'Yes.'

We were on the bed, he was moving my legs apart and then he was inside me and there was a rhythm of pressing and clutching and I was aware of his quickened breathing, the smell and temperature of his breath. There was comfort in the heaviness of his body and the way it covered mine entirely. Then he kissed me and I felt desire, the fast, flooding feeling so hard to tell from fear.

He gasped, 'Oh, God.'

After he had rolled away, I felt his eyes watching my face in the lamplight, waiting for mine to meet his. Already I felt different. I was forty-two years old but had undergone some unseemly variation of schoolgirl deflowering. *Are you sure about this?*

'This is a bit unexpected,' he said, and the air between us was suddenly much too still.

I felt my face flame under his gaze. 'I don't know what . . . I guess I just went with an impulse.' An impulse I'd first acknowledged years ago, in that pub in Victoria, a farewell that had been supposed to be a new beginning.

He seemed to read my mind. 'I've wanted this for a long time.'

I nodded.

'Maybe since the moment we met.'

'Really?'

'I couldn't think of anything else.' At the sight of my disbelief, he stumbled, tried to correct himself, 'I don't mean this, sex. I just mean you, your face. I don't know, I wanted to see you as you might have been before I met you, when you were still happy.'

I felt tears rising, reached to touch him. 'I'm not sure that will ever happen, Palmer, not the way I was when Emma was alive . . . I'm sorry.'

'Don't be sorry, please don't . . .'

He clutched me for a long time, until I whispered, 'Will you stay?'

He didn't understand. 'My flight isn't until Monday morning . . .'

'No, I mean here, with me, not at the hotel? Until you have to go.' How quickly that instinct had returned, the female need to consolidate; once sprung, the male must be kept close.

He nodded. 'I'll do anything you want.'

It was only in the morning as we lay in bed talking that I noticed there was something worrying him, something causing a series of shifts and fidgets, malfunctions in that smoothly controlled body language of his. Coming back from the bathroom, I saw that he'd pulled on his shorts and was lighting a cigarette in the doorway, blowing smoke out on to the terrace. The sunshine behind him was like a fireball. It must have been at least noon.

Grabbing my gown, I tied it around me and stepped tentatively towards him. 'Palmer?'

'Yep?'

'It's OK, I know what it is.' My voice was admirably calm.

'What *what* is?' he asked, eyes wary.

'You're married, aren't you? You have a new . . .' I trailed off, thinking of the right word, 'a new life.'

Sighing, he reached out and touched my cheekbone with his thumb. 'You're so beautiful, you know.'

'Thank you.' There was something about the way he said it that my heart recognised as a farewell. I was right, then, he did belong to someone else.

He went back to the cigarette and took a deep drag. 'I'm not married, no.'

My heart lifted a degree. 'But you've changed your mind, there's some other reason why this isn't possible.' Not a question, a statement. 'I understand, you know. I never expected you to drop everything . . .'

'You "understand", do you? What, ready to give

me up so easily?' He smiled across at me. 'Believe me, I will do everything in my power to make this possible.'

'What is it then? Come on, Palmer, I know you. Something's up.'

He laughed at that too. 'Do you? We haven't seen each other for years.'

'But I still know you,' I said, simply.

He stubbed out the cigarette and looked away and when the gaze came back to me it was filled with distaste. I experienced another, much longer moment of unease.

'I gave up, you know, a couple of years ago. I gave up for about a year.'

I didn't know whether he was talking about the cigarettes or me. I moved closer to him hardly daring listen. The heat from outside was dizzyingly intense.

'There *is* something,' he said, finally. 'Funny you noticed, I didn't think you would. It's something I should have told you a long time ago.' His eyes hunted for his cigarettes, on the windowsill by my shoulder. I passed them to him and watched him light a second one. 'I just want you to know, before we do what we're going to do, that there won't be any more secrets. This is the last one.'

I frowned, puzzled. 'What secret, Palmer? Do you mean . . .?' I felt a sudden ache in my lungs. 'It's not something to do with the girls, is it?'

He shook his head. 'It's to do with Freeman.'

'*Oliver?*' Then the penny dropped, the ache was gone. 'Oh, you mean him marrying Jenny. It's all right, I already know. He wrote to me about it.'

One look at his face told me I'd guessed wrong. 'Are you OK about that?' he asked.

I nodded. 'Yes, I am. I really am. Now tell me what you were going to say. About Oliver.'

'OK.' He looked directly at me, eyes quite clear. 'It's about those damages he won from the lawsuit against Morris, years ago, do you remember?'

'Yes, of course,' I said, puzzled. 'Not long after I first came here. I told you that Oliver gave *me* the money, didn't I?'

'That's it,' he said. 'Well, I looked into it after you told me. I know you didn't ask me to, it was none of my business, but . . .'

'What was there to look into?'

He frowned. 'I know a little about this kind of thing and it didn't sound right.'

'How d'you mean? Are you saying he didn't sue Morris?'

'No, he did. Well, since Morris was dead he sued his estate—in effect, the insurance company, as you know. He sued under the Fatal Accidents Act, just as he said. But he didn't get much in the way of damages. It's a scandal really, how little you get in these situations. Anyway, he got a little under eight thousand pounds.'

My mouth opened. 'Eight thousand? But the cheque was for over three hundred thousand! That's what I used for setting up Panomeréa, for paying you . . .'

Palmer nodded, guiltily. 'It's a huge difference. I should have told you this before.'

My thoughts floundered. 'If he only got eight thousand, what was the money he sent me? Some kind of private thing with Morris's family?' But no, they had nothing, if I remembered, it had been Lockley's family who were wealthy.

'It was his own money,' Palmer said quietly. 'He

428

said it was damages, but it was his. He sold some investments to release the cash.'

I considered this for a moment, somehow less surprised than I might have been. It had a sense to it, in a way, for money was how Oliver communicated, and what had been missing in those letters of his had been present, after all, in the cash. It had been guilt money, love money, some kind of money too complicated to define now. 'Well,' I said briskly, not wanting to analyse this now, 'it was mine too, technically, wasn't it, since we were married? And there'll be more, I suppose, when the settlement is agreed.' I laughed. 'I must be the first wife in history who is saying the other side is offering too much.' I felt suddenly dumbstruck. *The other side.* I wanted to take the words back. I didn't want Emma's father to be the other side. Even now, so long after her death, I wanted her to know we were on the same side, on her side.

I saw that Palmer was still watching me, clearly not satisfied by my reaction. 'You're right, though, you know. I mean, why would Oliver be so secretive about it, why would he need to pretend it had come from somewhere else? I still had access to our joint account at that time. I remember he said I could take money whenever I needed it.'

He nodded. 'That's exactly the point. You *weren't* taking the money, were you?'

'Not after the first month or so, I had some of my own. But so what? It just doesn't make sense.'

'It makes perfect sense,' Palmer said. 'He was worried you didn't have enough. He wanted to look after you, but he knew you'd object if you thought that was what he was doing. He had to

429

help you without you realising that that's what he was doing.' He took my hand, laced his fingers through mine. 'Sound familiar?'

There was a silence. I looked with concern at his troubled face. 'I'm not sure why this is bothering you though. The fact that he did that for me or—'

'Or that I chose to keep it from you?' He grimaced. 'Both, I suppose. Especially when we spoke on the phone that time. I knew you'd be meeting him, I should have told you. It might have made a difference to the decision you made about him.'

I squeezed his hand in mine. 'Of course it wouldn't have made a difference, he was already with Jenny then. We met in London to discuss the divorce, not to get back together.'

'Are you sure?'

I thought about that day, that glorious afternoon in St James's Park, the resurfacing of desires I'd long given up for lost. 'I don't know. That's the truth. But the point is, nothing I could have said that day would have changed his mind because he'd fallen in love with someone else. And now—'

'And now?'

I paused. 'I realise *I* had too.'

He stared into my face, eyes searching. 'Really?'

I moved forward to kiss him. 'Yes,' I said, simply. 'Really.'

'Four years,' he whispered into my parted lips. 'We've wasted four years.'

I thought of four candles on a cake. A princess's castle-shaped cake, pink and white, with Jelly Tots and Smarties and marshmallows. I kissed him again. 'Four years is not so long.'

Chapter 38

A few weeks later

Souvenirs available in Oia: puppets; wooden Pinocchio dolls; bouzouki and drums; chess sets; herbs for gyros; herbs for tzatziki; herbs for Greek salad; pumices and sponges; books with Greek recipes in every language; boiled sweets; merchandise of every description for the Olympic Games 2004; jewellery made in Athens, in Milan, in Geneva; 'Minoan' jewellery made in China; 'objects of desire' in glass and silver; pistachio nuts imported from Turkey but labelled as local ('Come and see my trees,' the shop manager offered, and led tourists to a little courtyard nearby where four pistachio trees might yield half a kilo of the thousands he sold in high season). And the pictures, still the mass-produced prints of the smoking volcano, still the imported acrylics (poppies were popular this year). One woman did a roaring trade in pictures on wood panels, scenes of Oia that she painted by numbers behind a curtain in the back of her shop, brush in one hand, cigarette in the other.

Souvenir is not a Greek word but comes to us from the Latin, care of the French. I took my picture of Kamari, our first ever sale, still in Dymas's original frame with its layers of paint and tangy air. Manfred came by with contact sheets and let me choose a wedding shot of Ingrid and Christos. In black and white the contrast between their tanned skins and white hair and teeth was arresting. I saw the one I wanted straight away: she was attracted by something off camera, while his eyes were fixed on her. Manfred had captured in them such a sense of beginning, of inception. I wondered if it might be the light—though the picture had been taken in early evening, it somehow looked like dawn.

And then there was Santa Irini too, still in my possession, still not authenticated, the last oddity. She was meant to be with me, whoever she was. I wrapped the three pictures in the shop and put them in a Panoméréa bag.

These would be my only souvenirs.

At Callidora, Palmer helped me pack. A few books, gifts over the years from Eleni and Anatole; letters from Oliver and Christmas cards from Mariel and the girls; a stack of manila envelopes from when the Project Godmother reports had arrived by mail every month. There was surprisingly little, surprising to him at any rate.

'I thought we'd be at it for days, but this is just going to take a couple of hours.'

'You must have noticed I don't have much stuff?'

'I assumed it must be stored somewhere else.'

'People don't need much, when they really think about it. A few clothes, toothpaste, a coffee cup . . .'

'If you don't mind me saying, that's a very unusual view for a woman.'

I laughed.

'Is this lamp yours?' He was moving it from its place on the hatbox, blowing away a little dust as he did so.

'No, it came with the place. Everything did,

pretty much. I'm like Miss Havisham, aren't I? I haven't changed a thing.'

'Not to worry. I have lighting.'

'Oh good. Because obviously I don't come to you with much of a dowry. No ships and vineyards I'm afraid.'

'Those were the days.' He looked about him for the next item and his eye returned to the old hatbox. 'Have you ever opened this since you've been here?'

'You're very nosy.'

'My job, remember?'

'Yes, I always suspected I was Subject X.'

He grinned, still looking at the box. It had been moved several times over the years, according to the storage needs of Panomeréa. Now it sat by the chest of drawers, covered in a circle of lace, like those paper snowflakes children make at Christmas, with the lamp atop.

'The answer is no, I haven't opened it, not to take anything out, anyway. But I will.'

'What's in it? Sorry, tell me to get lost. None of my business.'

'It's OK. I am your business. Let's open it now.'

I got down on my knees and pulled at the lid. It was stiff, warped perhaps. Then I remembered it had always been a little tight. As I hooked a fingernail beneath it Palmer, sitting on the edge of the bed now, seemed to change his mind. 'You really don't have to . . .'

'You're worried about Pandora's box?'

He exhaled, half-smiling, watching.

A hatbox doesn't hold much. After all, it's designed for one lightweight object the approximate size of a human head. The first thing

I found was a photograph, the one of us on the train that I'd pushed out of my sight soon after coming here, posted inside without even looking, like late mail. There were other photographs of course, a handful for each year of her life: one of me cuddling her in the hospital, the smallest kitten in the crook of my arm; another of her in her Christmas ballet show, special red leotard and white gauze skirt; a pair of her first shoes, scuffed at the toe, untouched at the sole, the crawler's footwear; a daisy-patterned sunhat I couldn't bear to give up, remembering how she would pull the strap from under her chin and chew it.

Seeing what I'd kept reminded me why this was so long in the doing, for each object was a direct bolt of that true, material pain I'd felt when flight was all I could manage. I'd been insensible when I'd chosen these things, but now saw that there'd been a glimmer of method, of forethought. Schoolteachers' reports had been too much to bear, were always going to be, speaking as they did of promise and potential, but there was a birthday card from us to her, a birthday before she could read so the message had been for my own benefit—*To our beautiful darling, we love you more every minute, Mummy and Daddy*. The page was so filled with kisses that it looked sort of demented, and I remembered now making the crosses, not able to stop as though it meant a limit to our love, when there was no limit, and so I'd simply kept on going until I'd filled the space.

Emma's face had been unrecognisable after the accident, her hands torn apart too; she'd been wrapped in a blanket and the blood soaked blackly

434

through. I had identified her, officially, by the mole on her left ankle. Her feet were perfect, untouched, those tiny toes had been so much tinier once, still too tiny. I'd pressed those little soles against my face, held them there, the feel of them no cooler than on a winter day, and wished I could have her footprint on my skin for ever.

I showed Palmer the ring box with the bloodied lock of hair, rusted and powdery. 'I couldn't bring myself to wash it out. I wanted to keep, I don't know, her DNA, I suppose. Silly, because the DNA is in the hair itself.'

He handled the hair gently, like a giant picking a flower. Then he touched my hair too. And his thumb moved to stroke my right cheekbone. 'Her DNA is in *you*.'

I nodded, blinking.

He pressed my head against his chest, speaking over the top, and I could feel his breath stirring my hair. 'I know you expected to live on in her, but what you have to remember is that she is living on in you.'

I was crying now, burrowing my face into his shoulder in exactly the same way a child does a parent's. 'It's not the same. She would have had children of her own, she would have continued in them . . .'

He squeezed me hard and when he spoke again it was in a murmur. 'Why do people want a piece of the future? Think where we are. This could all end tomorrow, an earthquake, a volcano, but today you're alive.'

We held each other for a long time, until I'd soaked the shoulder of his shirt. Recovering, I pulled back, handling the objects again, even

435

managing a smile. 'My father would say I'll see her again in Heaven. That's where he expects to see me. Like we're going to have some sort of family reunion.'

'I thought you didn't believe in God?' Palmer said.

'I don't, not really.' The last time I'd spoken to Him in any seriousness, in all seriousness, had been in Jen's car, and I'd asked Him to spare her, to keep her alive, at the expense of anything; myself, her school friends, even Cat and Daisy.

'God can take a running jump,' I said.

Palmer's eyes strayed to the open doors, to the silk ribbon of blue where hundreds of feet below the sea met the sky. 'Well, He's come to the right place.'

*   *   *

I told Ingrid first, just as soon as she'd returned from her honeymoon and begun scaling that mountain of wedding gifts. She came into the shop brandishing the document I'd had drawn up by our lawyer in Fira, the one that signed over to the new Mrs Kafieris the Panomeréa business.

'This is too much, Rachel. I don't understand.'

'I'm leaving,' I said simply.

'What? Leaving Oia? Leaving the shop?'

'Yes. It's time. I won't be able to contribute properly any more, so it's much better that it's officially yours. And you're married to a Greek citizen now, it all makes sense.'

She looked from me to the documents and back again. 'Does this have anything to do with Palmer?'

I nodded, feeling pleasure at the thought of being with him again soon, being with him every day. 'He stayed for a while after your wedding. He helped confirm I'm doing the right thing.'

'So he's lured you back to London?' She looked glum for a moment, before making a conscious effort to brighten her expression. 'Well, I suppose if that's what you really think is right.'

I paused, face solemn, before breaking into a huge smile. 'Actually, no, it isn't. I've lured him here. I'm leaving Oia, not Santorini. We've found somewhere to rent by the beach in Baxedes and as soon as we're settled we'll be researching new business ideas.'

She stumbled into my arms, grinning wildly. 'Rachel, you cow! I thought you meant you were going back to London.'

'Well I am, but just for a few days, to visit Mum.'

'And he's moving here? What, selling up the private-eye operation?'

'Exactly. That's what he's doing now. And talking to his children, of course. Hopefully they'll come and visit us some time in the future. I need to get to know them if I'm going to be their stepmother.'

She looked at me with raised eyebrows. 'Stepmother? I would say slow down, but I suppose it has been almost ten years with you two.'

'Yes, what they call a slow burn.'

She fingered the documents, re-folding the pages. 'I'll keep the shop exactly as we agreed. Exactly.'

'No acrylic scenes from Taiwan?'

'No acrylic scenes from Taiwan.'

'I'll come and check. Now, as soon as you're

437

unpacked and back to normal, let me take you to see the new house. It's right by the beach.'

'I can't wait to see it.'

As I left House Callidora, I noticed a dragonfly high above the door, trapped by the mesh of the fanlight. A large bug had hovered in much the same place on my arrival, and Eleni had quoted a word in Greek I didn't quite catch. In English, she had explained that it was a sign of good luck. I'd never thought of it again until now.

*   *   *

Whenever I remembered walking home from school it was always warm, always summer, the sun snapping on like a bulb as I turned into my street. I would skip the home straight to my front door, wondering if Dad was back yet or if I'd be allowed to watch a favourite television programme beginning in ten minutes' time. On Mum's days off I'd hope to find a homemade cake cooling in the kitchen, maybe the chocolate one that rose so high in the oven its top was all cracked, which made the icing thicker in some places than others. Back then, I'd squinted into the sun, the hatless, unprotected child of a different time; now I kept my sunglasses on, glad of the sunblock I'd applied in the morning. It was horribly muggy, no cooling coastal breeze, *meltemi* the Greeks called it.

'Rachel!' Mum was expecting news, I could see. I'd never before visited in the summer months, after all, and had given no explanation when I'd phoned. What was odd was how optimistic she looked. I worried she thought I might have come back for good.

We sat at the kitchen table with our tea. 'I wanted to tell you I'm moving from my house in Oia.'

'Oh?'

'Just down to Baxedes, not far away.'

'It's windy down there,' she said, tone agreeable, matter of fact.

I waited for eye contact and took a deep breath. 'But I want you to know that I won't stop trying to get you to come and visit. Never.' There were echoes of Oliver in that proclamation, and of Mariel too.

She smiled, an amused, upturned smile she used to give Emma. 'It's all right, love, I've already decided I'm going to come.'

'What? Did you just say what I think you said?'

She nodded, sharing my disbelief. 'God knows how many years I've got left, I'll just have to hope I'm gone before the next earthquake comes.'

I stared, mouth open. 'And volcanoes?'

'More likely to die of the common cold—that's what Doctor Green says. Lord, my hands are sweating just thinking about it.' Placing her palms flat on the table, she rose from her seat and turned towards the doorway. 'Right. Now that's settled, there's someone I want you to meet.'

Still I stared, speechless. This was extraordinary. She couldn't mean a romance, surely, after all this time? But it might explain the miraculous change of mind.

'I'll just go and get her . . .'

'Her?' Listening to her footsteps as she climbed the stairs, I wondered who on earth she might be keeping secreted in another room. Whoever it was couldn't have moved a muscle in the fifteen

439

minutes or so I'd been here.

'Here.' She was back, holding a small, black-and-white snapshot. I took it, confused.

'Meet your Aunt Phoena.'

'*Phoena?*' The picture had been taken in Oia, unmistakably Oia, for it had that same lost sense of remoteness as the ones we sold in the shop. At its centre a group of villagers were processing together down the main street, on the day of a festival judging by the banners and decorations. Phoena was a strong-jawed and serious little figure in the middle, eyes fixed ahead, probably of a similar age to Cat and Daisy now.

'Mum, this is . . . amazing.'

'She was not clever or sophisticated or anything like that,' Mum said, 'but she was always in the middle of things, she always made things fun.'

I looked again at the picture. 'Mum? Will you . . .?' She nodded, even before I'd finished the sentence, 'tell me what happened?' I hurried on, unable to stop myself. 'I just don't understand about the earthquake, why she wasn't at home with you and Papu and Yiayia. It was so early in the morning, why wasn't she still in bed, like you?'

Mum looked down at her hands. 'She was at work. She had a job with a family in Sideras, you know this neighbourhood?'

I nodded. 'Yes, that's where my friends Ingrid and Christos live.' Odd to think of my aunt, the vibrant, dark figure of the photograph, striding through those quiet white passageways in the heart of the village. I thought of the houses on either side of Christos's, boarded up after the earthquake and hardly touched since, destined to remain half up and half down until the next one came. She

440

might have worked in either one of them, or even in Christos's itself.

'She worked as a maid. It was not easy work, but she was young, she had energy.'

And I would have been quite happy to have left it at that, with the thought of an early shift one cold morning in 1956 before sunrise, but Mum added, suddenly, 'The husband of the woman she worked for, he was a powerful man in Oia. He had begun an affair with my sister.'

'An affair?'

'It's true. The night before the earthquake she had not come home, had sent word that she was needed at the house. He had taken advantage of her once again, we heard about it later. When the dust came and the screams started, he sent her out of the house. He didn't want to be discovered with her.'

I considered this. 'But that would have made sense, anyway, wouldn't it? To send her home? Maybe he thought she'd be safer in a *skapho* than a *kapetanospito*?'

My mother shook her head. 'It would have been better to have stayed inside, I think. Gaitis survived, after all, and his wife and children. Phoena was knocked down outside, in the street, as she tried to reach the path down. Papu found her. She didn't even have her shoes on, she had been sent away in such a hurry.'

I blinked. 'Did you say *Gaitis*?'

'Yes. You met him in Oia?' Again, she shook her head. 'This is exactly what I feared would happen.'

I rushed to correct her. 'No, no, Mum, I didn't meet him. He's dead now, he died years ago. But I think I saw his wife, or someone who knew him,

441

anyway. And I think she tried to buy that picture, the one I showed you that time. I guess it looked enough like Phoena to have scared her.'

Mum nodded. 'She felt guilty, I suppose. Everyone feels guilty in the end. It's such a waste, though. It doesn't get you any closer to changing what has already happened.'

We looked at each other.

'I thought you didn't have any old photos?' I said, suddenly. 'Dad told me you got rid of them all.'

'That's what I told Dad.'

'Are there more, then? Where are they?'

She indicated with her eyes the room above, her bedroom. 'I wanted to destroy them once, it's true, but you need to have something to keep. Sometimes it's the only way you know for sure that someone was really there.'

She had a tin full, an old biscuit tin with a picture on the lid of two girls in frilled dresses, facing each other over a pot of tea. Ingrid and I would have paid a small fortune for a cache like this.

'You can take this back to Santorini if you like.'

'Really? I'd love to put some of them in the new house.'

'Then I will see them when I come and visit you.'

'Are you sure?'

'Yes, that is where they belong.'

We both looked up at the sound of a car braking further up the street and continuing towards us at a crawl, the driver evidently following the house numbers one by one. Then came the sound of parking, the engine being turned off.

We went to the window to look out. 'Mum?'

'Yes?'

'I hope you don't mind, but I've asked a friend to meet us here.'

'Who?'

'Someone I want you to get to know . . . someone important to me. I thought maybe we could have a cup of tea, go out for lunch together . . .'

I looked over her shoulder and watched Palmer get out of his car, a small blue thing in obvious need of the carwash. I remembered him telling me how, out on a job, he always parked with his back to the property, watching the comings and goings of the subject in his rear-view mirror. Today he'd parked facing it, with the sun in his eyes.

Epilogue

July 2006, two years later

The air around Greencroft School for Girls smelled of baked brick and scorched feathers. It was hot, Greek hot, and all doors of the main building had been opened to encourage a breeze inside. At the main entrance, a gowned figure and two others in smart suits shook hands with arriving guests, middle-aged couples in heatwave versions of Sunday best, proud parents all. Soon the constant stream had slowed and there were fewer lingering chats on the steps and more cries of 'I hope we're not too late?'. Finally, the gowned figure turned and went inside too.

I looked at my watch: 10.57 a.m. Out of the corner of my eye I noticed a pink balloon tied to the railing, barely pulling at its ribbon in the breezeless heat. We had arranged to meet at ten forty-five. I fumbled nervously in my pocket for the small invitation card and examined its text for the hundredth time:

Greencroft School for Girls Leavers' Ceremony 2006
Saturday 15th July at 11am in the Willis Hall
Please use main entrance on Greencroft Gardens,
NW6

I turned it over and read Mariel's note:

The girls wondered if you'd like to come? Mx

445

'Rachel! Rachel! We're late, sorry! You must have thought we weren't coming!'

It was Mariel's voice, and I relaxed at once at the sight of just her and Toby. I'd been expecting the whole group.

'Rachel, this is fantastic, we're so glad you've come.' Toby squeezed me hard. He was barely greying and still youthful, cool in a sky-blue floral shirt despite the last-minute dash.

'It wouldn't have been right without you,' Mariel said. She had highlighted her dark hair, I noticed, and wore a cream-coloured shirt dress over tanned sinewy limbs. I felt much older than the two of them, though we'd started out together.

'Where are Bob and Jen, and the girls?'

'The girls have been here since nine-thirty for a final run-through, and Bob and Jen had to be here by ten—they have to sit in special seats as the parents of the head girl.'

'And Jake?'

'Oh, he's at cricket practice. No sense of occasion. There's no love lost between the two of them at the moment, they're driving us nuts.'

There was a pause; this was when I would naturally enquire after Oliver. Would he be here too?

'We should go straight in,' Toby said, nodding to the only member of the welcoming committee to remain on the stone steps. She gestured for us to hurry. 'This way, please! I'm about to close the doors!'

'I couldn't get you a seat next to us,' Mariel said, once inside, 'you're upstairs in the gallery with some of the teachers and special guests. I hope that's OK. They're quite strict about it only being . . .'

'That's fine, of course.' I didn't add that it was actually something of a relief. It was never going to be easy, watching a class of girls that should have included my daughter having their achievements celebrated, but being separated from Mariel and Jen, sitting between strangers who had never known her would help a little.

'At the top of these stairs you'll come out at the back on the right, and you're on the second row. We'll come and find you as soon as it's over.' Before I could follow her instructions, Mariel took my arm and held me back. 'Rachel, there's something we ought to tell you . . .'

'It's all right,' I said quickly. 'I expected Oliver to be here, you don't have to warn me.'

She and Toby exchanged a glance. 'OK, well, see you in an hour or two.'

The hall was smaller and more intimate than I'd been expecting, the gallery giving a clear view of the stage, on which two semicircular rows were occupied by what I assumed were governors and VIPs. I couldn't see Jen and Bob, though my view of at least six faces was obstructed by a huge bowl of flowers on a table by the podium. Below, the audience was a matrix of hairstyles, the grey and the highlighted, the curled and the straightened, the crop circles of skin on the heads of the balding fathers. Were their owners to turn and look behind them, I would no doubt recognise a few faces, for there'd be Moss Hamlet parents among them for certain. Ahead of the parents, in the first four rows, sat their daughters, the apples of their eyes, the line-up of youth: long shining hair and snug cotton, ponytails and spaghetti straps, the occasional subversive with a peroxide crop or a tattooed shoulder on display. I couldn't see Cat and Daisy among them, not at first, though a shout of laughter soon gave the location of Toby and Mariel: four rows back from the pupils, right in the middle. There was no immediate sign of Oliver, however, either in the main audience or up in this gallery of extras. I imagined him slipping in late, seeing me in the row ahead and keeping himself out of view.

On my seat was a copy of the programme: speeches, music and a list of the girls' names in alphabetical order. There they were, close to the top: Daisy Barnes, Catherine Challoner, separated by just two other names. I followed the list down until I reached the Fs. Sarah Fanning, Kate Fryer. She'd have been between them. I allowed myself to see the name in the list: Emma Freeman, leaver. Harder to summon was her face, for every picture I conjured of her at this age was different from the last. It was impossible to settle on the precise detail of her features, her complexion, even her size and height. Only the spirit in her eyes held fast. That would never have left her, I was certain.

On stage, the gowned woman began making a welcoming speech. She, evidently, was Mrs Ratcliffe, the one who had been approached by Simon's father to tinker with the waiting list, the one who had been persuaded to take a liberal line with Cat's subsequent transgressions. She was speaking today of ideals, of integrity; but life was not so simple. I was grateful for her behind-the-scenes realism.

'This is the last time you will be together as a class,' she said, her voice amplified around the room, warm and maternal, 'and as much as it is a celebration of your achievements, it is an opportunity to reflect on what you mean to each other.'

She introduced the guest speaker, an old girl who'd done something in the City before running a successful organic-chocolate company. She talked about glass ceilings and giving back. Two girls sang, another played a violin solo. Then the girls were invited up, one by one, to receive their certificates and have their accomplishments read out and honoured.

'Makes you feel like such an underachiever, doesn't it?' whispered the woman next to me, a teacher possibly, whose breath smelled of cinnamon. I nodded politely, not taking my eyes from the stage. And it was true, the accomplishments of even the first few girls were impressive: lists of A levels and AS subjects, Duke of Edinburgh awards; help given at primary schools; crafts brought to the inner cities; European parliaments re-enacted; the aged and infirm fed and wheeled; books recycled.

Though the order was alphabetical, it jumped from Ahmed to Brigham and missed Barnes, for Daisy, as head girl, would go last. Cat, therefore, was the fifth to be called and I thought I detected a fresh stirring of interest as she bobbed into view. There she was, the same girl I'd met in Santorini, but restyled, updated. Gone were the rock-chick layers and heavy boots and in their place a dainty blue sundress worn with a broad belt and four-inch heels, which seemed to propel her forward into the space between her and her headmistress. She presented herself to the spotlight rather than

449

submitted to it, her stance both insolent and elegant. She was less the departing schoolgirl than the star witness at a trial. I felt the unmistakable thrill of pride.

'Catherine took A levels in English, French and Geography. She has represented Greencroft in the hockey team and performed as Elvira in *Blithe Spirit* . . .' Her achievements were rather briefer than those of the four who had preceded her, though there was a commendation for French. 'Cat has had a colourful time here at Greencroft and has inspired many younger girls with her flair for fashion . . .'

As Cat was dispatched back to her seat, wiggling her eyebrows at her classmates as she went, her position on the stage was filled by Alice Cross, demure in a spotted pink skirt and lacy white top. 'Alice wins our prize for History, and has a place to study Law at Durham. Well done, Alice.' And just then a woman sitting in the second row on stage stooped to her left to reach something in her handbag and I saw just enough of her face to recognise her: Jen.

She was older now, her hair short and smooth over her ears (what did she do in place of her habit of braiding lengths of her hair? I wondered). Even from this distance I could see that she was tired, perhaps a little overwhelmed, at the roll-call of successes to be applauded before her own daughter could make her appearance. She looked as if she might be about to rest her head on the shoulder of the figure to her right, Bob presumably, though he was still obscured by the flowers. The half-glimpse I managed suggested he'd lost a lot of hair and gained a fair bit of weight. My eyes returned to Jen. Seeing her face again, I felt a punch of remorse as I remembered our last meeting, how I'd wanted to be cruel to her. I loved her and envied her both together, loved her for all she had once been to me, envied her for what she had here now, in front of her, a daughter, *the* daughter, the dazzling star.

'As well as sharing the Hilda Buxton prize for Maths, Lucy wins a very special prize, new this year . . .'

At this, everyone in the hall drew breath together, which seemed to have an actual effect on the humidity levels, making the air even closer. I edged forward slightly.

'This is in honour of Gurinder, and is given to the school by her classmates. You will all remember Gurinder, of course, who died eleven months ago after a brave struggle with leukaemia. This prize has been given by her friends to honour the girl who has shown the most courage in her own adversities . . . I'm sorry . . .'

Mrs Ratcliffe broke off, unable to hide her distress. I watched, appalled, as the profiles around me trembled, eyeballs swelling with tears. Men and women dabbed at their faces with tissues and exchanged sorrowful glances with their neighbours. My neighbour had turned to the woman on her other side and they murmured together, one patting the other's arm. For the first time I regretted my presence here. I was the ghoul, the stranger at the service, waiting for the name that would never be called. Hardly daring breathe, I slipped away into the corridor, turned my back on the montage of sports day snapshots, the wall of lockers. Out of the window I watched the people in the street below, couples with pushchairs, flat hunters and estate agents, shoppers straining to manage too many carriers. So much life! And I thought of my own little ghost, my shadow daughter.

In my pocket, my phone vibrated with the arrival of a text message. I suspected Mariel first—she'd noticed I'd gone, perhaps—but then I remembered that she didn't have my number. I had phoned *her* to make this morning's arrangements. Checking, I saw it was from Palmer:

> Good luck, it will be tough today, so don't be hard on yourself. Let yourself be sad.
> I love you, P x

I pictured him in our little house by the ash-grey beach, where the breeze was constant and you could feel your own skin being weathered even as you stood in its flow. I felt instantly stronger.

By the time I returned to my seat they had reached the Rs. Scarlett Richardson was a theatrical triumph, she'd been Miranda and Cordelia and heaven knew who else, and was a whizz on the oboe. When she hurdled, fellow sportswomen could only trail in her wake. Off she headed to Bristol to study English and drama, if her grades matched up, which of course they would, Mrs Ratcliffe had every faith. If there was one girl we were going to see more of it was Scarlett.

Off they trooped, one by one, towards their futures. I saw from the list that I'd missed Lara, the friend Cat had spoken of in Santorini, the partner in crime, the third of the trio. Perhaps I'd meet her another time.

Mrs Ratcliffe paused for water just long enough for parents to start whispering to each other about what was next, what was last. The head girl and her two deputies. Deputies first, I hardly registered them beyond the modest smiles and hearty applause.

'And so we come to Daisy, Daisy Barnes,' said her head teacher, and smiled her first full smile of the morning as a slight blonde figure took the three or four steps up to the podium with the proud bounce of a child being called to blow out the candles on her birthday cake. At once I felt tears rise. She was tiny, shorter than Jen, and extremely pretty. Her hair had been pinned up to elongate the line of her neck and in her ruffled 1950s-style dress and kitten-heeled sandals she resembled a deb at her coming-out party. She stood, still and gracious, comfortable with praise, familiar with it.

'Daisy,' Mrs Ratcliffe began, 'has more than twenty-four hours in her day, so full is her schedule, both curricular and extracurricular. Known, of course, for her passion for modern art, she wins the History of Art prize. She will spend her gap year volunteering at Tate Modern, and has planned to travel too, destination unknown. Well, that must be the first time our beloved head girl *doesn't* know where she's going!' Laughter broke out, got caught in the fans and whipped up to us in the gallery. Figures in the front row shifted in their seats and I had a clear view of Jen wiping away tears with her fingers. Bob was quite motionless and, as Jen lowered her arm again, I sensed that the two of them might, for a moment at least, be holding hands. Whatever had broken down between them, they would always share Daisy. This was their girl. This was their best-case scenario.

There were a string of further commendations before Daisy was presented with her diploma and invited to speak.

'Ladies and gentlemen, parents and guests, I've been asked to say a few words on behalf of my class . . .'

It was the first time I'd heard her voice in twelve years and I couldn't have recognised it, of course. It was sweet and well modulated, and where Cat's was deliberately jaded, hers was eager and respectful.

'We're privileged here to receive such a fantastic education without our parents having to pay for it. Yes, we'd like to upgrade our chemistry labs, resurface the tennis courts, a new pool, maybe a spa . . .' As the audience chuntered accordingly, she startled me by saying, 'I'm sure many of you know that Oliver Freeman is my stepfather, but I won't go all political on you and start passing out pamphlets . . .' There were more chuckles now, and that change in the atmosphere that occurs when the celebrated and the powerful are invoked. 'Instead, I want to take the opportunity to thank all the parents and other people who have raised funds and made donations while our class has been here. I'm sure you're bored stiff by sponsored walks, but you've contributed to our futures and we are grateful. We really, really are. The government can't do it all, and thanks to you, we have the world at our feet. We are just as well prepared as the young men and women at the best independent schools.'

She held her hands together, fingertips touching her chin as though in prayer. 'As Mrs Ratcliffe says, this is the last time we'll be together as a class. It's really, really hard to say goodbye. So I won't even try. Thank you.'

Applause, cheering, a little stamping. Kisses for Daisy from the head teacher and the guest speaker who'd broken the glass ceiling. Flowers for all on stage. Then, as after all extended displays of emotion, the collective stretching of legs.

I considered for a moment just slipping away, as you read of people doing in books, as though they can move through doorways like breeze. I'd never quite lost that instinct to flee. But the entrance closest to me had now been closed in order to channel spectators down into the main hall where, it was assumed, we would naturally wish to join the rest of the gathering. At the bottom of the steps I collided with the girl in polka dots and a few heads turned as we apologised and rearranged ourselves. Looking up, I saw Cat waiting for me. 'Auntie Rachel!' She kissed me on both cheeks. 'It's so cool that you've come! Wasn't it just the most tedious thing in the world? I thought I was going to die of boredom, and I was part of it!'

'It was lovely, very moving.'

'Come on, everyone's over here.' She linked her arm through mine and led me through the throng towards Daisy, who stood with a trio of other girls by the stage. Jen and Bob, I saw, were in conversation with Mrs Ratcliffe above, while Mariel and Toby chatted with other parents just beyond Daisy. Mariel waved and mouthed that she'd be over as soon as she could.

'Daisy, look who I've got! Auntie Rachel, this is Daisy! Well, you saw her doing her thing, obviously. Daze, meet our long-lost godmother.'

Daisy excused herself from her group and turned to hold out her hand to me, every inch the well-mannered head girl. I couldn't stop myself from holding on to her hand for longer than necessary. 'Thank you for the beautiful photograph Cat brought back from Oia, and all those birthday cards. I loved the one you sent last year, for my seventeenth, the goldfish bowl with the volcano in the background.'

Now I had the opportunity to see her close up, it was hard not to openly scrutinise her face. Where Cat was her parents in both appearance and manner, Daisy seemed to have been redrawn and refined beyond recognition. Even her hair was sleek, held back with a patterned band and not a strand amiss. She had extraordinary poise and self-control for her age, but it seemed wrong, in a way, that there was so little evidence of Jen's fidgetiness or Bob's passion.

'You're interested in photography?' I asked.

'Painting more, but yes, absolutely.'

'Daisy's going to study History of Art at Cambridge,' Cat said. 'Well, you heard that. But I told you she was clever, didn't I, in Santorini?' She wanted to remind Daisy that she'd been the one to see me first, and so she had. The eldest of the three, she'd seen me before even Emma had.

'Yes you did,' I said, smiling at her. 'You've both done amazingly well. Congratulations.'

'You know what?' Cat giggled, looking at Daisy but including me in her confession, 'When I came off the stage I heard that old cow Menders going,

456

"That girl lacks humility", about me! Can you believe it?'

'Er, yes,' Daisy laughed.

'Plenty of time to learn humility,' I said, and as Cat beamed I realised mine had not been the remark of a mother or, for that matter, a godmother.

'Are you hoping to work in the art world eventually?' I asked Daisy.

'If I can. I may do an art administration course or something. It's so competitive though.'

'Well, perhaps when the time comes I might be able to arrange an internship for you. A friend of mine is planning to open a museum in Santorini. If your mother and father agree, of course.'

'That would be amazing! Do you mean it?' And for a moment she could have been five again. I remembered how she used to run forward to be pulled up in a hug, wrapping her legs around me and squeezing her arms around my neck.

'Thank you for coming today. Mum wasn't sure you would. Even this morning she was saying she wouldn't believe it until she saw you with her own eyes . . .'

I nodded. 'I'd like to say hello when she's free.'

'Definitely, though it looks like she's a bit stuck at the moment . . .' Over Cat's shoulder on stage I saw Jen turn from her huddle to glance discreetly at the mobile phone in her hand, and then towards the doors at the rear of the hall. Her body was only half turned, not quite in profile, but it was enough for me to see: Jenny with a bump, small, but unmistakable on her petite frame. I was forty-four, which made her forty-two. Not uncommon these days.

So, a sister or a brother for Daisy after all.

'Sorry, Rachel, we'll be back . . .' As the girls were pulled away from me into a nearby gaggle, I willed Jen to look down in my direction, but suddenly she was waving across the room and gesturing to someone else to join her. I watched as Oliver strode in, walked right by me as he made for Jenny, hastily stuffing his phone into his back pocket. Still late, still missing the kids' parties then. He pressed his hand first into Bob's, then the head teacher's, and then took hold of Jen's and didn't let go.

So, a sister or a brother for Emma.

*   *   *

I had dropped Emma off at school earlier than usual that last day. 'We should beat the traffic if we're lucky,' Miss Morrissey said, jolly as ever. The driver was already in his seat, busy consulting a roadmap.

Daisy had yet to arrive, but Cat was already on the bus and had saved seats for her friends. She called out to Emma and beckoned her aboard.

I smoothed my hand over Emma's hair as she reached for the handrail. 'Bye darling, have fun. Enjoy the smelly lily!'

And she'd brushed me off, as they did at that age, eager to slot herself into her place among her peers. Cat was right at the back in the middle, a seat free on either side of her, and I thought to myself, How funny, is that how they're going to be, then? The girls who sit on the back seat, the cheeky ones, the ones who sing rude words to the songs. And I felt admiration for Cat, for I'd never

458

been the cheeky one myself.

There was no reason to wait for latecomers, to hang around and wave the party off. Most of the parents simply saw their own safely on board and made a dash for wherever it was they needed to go. The kids might have their special day ahead, but we adults had nothing but the usual avalanche of jobs and chores.

I couldn't see her face properly through the window because it was tipped forward to look at something Cat was showing her. All I could see was the checked collar of her summer dress and the spun gold of her hair.

*   *   *

I found myself looking for Daisy's face in the crowd, seeing her already in a new light, linked forever now to Emma. It was too early to identify my feelings, but I knew they would be complicated, like every feeling I'd had in my life after Emma; there would be no sweet without the bitter. I was suddenly aware of my own abdomen, still remembered how it felt to have her growing inside me, curled around herself, our movements sometimes in harmony, sometimes in opposition. I looked around for refreshments: a table had been set up at the back of the hall with glasses and jugs of iced drinks.

I was helping myself to a second glass of water when I became aware of a woman a couple of feet away from me. She had stopped at a distance, as though having unexpectedly encountered a sheet of glass between us.

'Jenny!'

'I can't believe you're here!' To her credit, this was neither an accusation nor a question; rather, she made it sound like a miraculous discovery. 'I mean, it's great, I really hoped you would come.'

'We always talked about graduation, didn't we?' I swallowed, trying not to look down at her stomach. 'And when Mariel sent me the card, it just felt like the right thing to do. Daisy is wonderful, such a star! Well, I don't need to tell *you* that.'

Jen smiled and now I saw her daughter in her face very clearly. 'It doesn't seem possible sometimes, when I see the way the teachers look at her and talk about her . . .' I thought she meant she couldn't believe her luck that it was *her* little girl who'd emerged the most acclaimed, but then I realised she meant she didn't recognise this angel as the same person she encountered at home.

'They save the worst for their parents, I suppose,' I said, smiling.

'Don't they just.' She had that serenity all pregnant women do. It doesn't matter what you say or do to me, because I have all I need right inside me; the magnitude of my present purpose overrides all others. Oliver always said that all pregnant women behaved as though they were carrying baby Jesus. I'd done it myself, I supposed.

She must have noticed me lowering my eyes, because she said, 'You know, I guess. It shows now, I'm just getting used to it.'

I hesitated. 'Yes. Congratulations. And congratulations on the wedding too. Oliver wrote to tell me.'

As I smiled I saw the muscles in her face relax, the relief draining visibly, before her eyes met

460

mine again, full of gratitude.

'You're with someone now, aren't you? Out in Greece?'

'Yes. We're just setting up a new project, a children's arts centre.'

'Are you married?'

'No, we're not sure we're going to. We're happy as things are.'

She wanted to say something else, I could see, and I longed suddenly for those blurtings of old, when she'd had no secrets to guard. 'Listen,' she said, 'all those conversations we had about having another baby. You remember? We used to talk about it all the time, especially after Mariel had Jake.'

I nodded.

'I think I knew all along I didn't want more, not with Bob. The more he said no, the more determined I was not to put a child through that, the more I thought I must have made a mistake just by being with him in the first place.' Her voice was rising with emotion and she took a moment to steady herself. 'Oh God, this is going to sound awful because I know there's no comparison, of course there isn't, but a part of me envied you just picking up and disappearing the way you did. After Emma. And I hated myself for feeling that.'

She was getting breathless now and I took a step towards her, through the glass wall, until I was within touching distance. 'You didn't make a mistake with Bob. How could Daisy ever have been a mistake? She's amazing.'

'Thank you.' She smiled, perhaps expecting me to say more, but I didn't. I couldn't. Over her shoulder I saw Mariel approaching, eyes fearful.

'Anyway, the girls have been so excited about seeing you. I hope it will be the first of lots of meetings?'

'It's not the first,' I said, and she hurried to correct herself. 'I mean, I hope you'll get to know them again as well as you used to.'

I nodded. 'I hope so too.'

'Rachel,' Mariel cried, 'I'm so sorry, I got stuck with Cat's friend Lara's parents. They're not very pleased with her, it seems. I left Toby to deal with it. Oh God, I'm not being a very good host so far, am I? Are you all right?' She looked from me to Jen and back again.

'Fine,' I said. 'We were just catching up. It was a lovely ceremony.'

'I know. I can't believe they're grown up.'

'Mum! Mum!' Now Cat had joined us, face urgent. 'Uncle Ollie wants us all together in a photo, can you all come?'

'Yes, darling, there's no need to shout.'

'Well, come on then!'

'Come too,' Jen said to me. And she and Mariel each took a hand. I felt like their child.

In front of the stage they were all lined up, the girls in front, their fathers behind. Bob nodded hello to me, then seemed to change his mind and stepped out of position to give me a hug. 'It's been too long.'

'Too long,' I echoed.

Jen and Mariel slipped into place on either side of the men. 'You stand over here, Auntie Rachel,' Cat directed. 'At the front, right in the middle between Daisy and me.'

Oliver looked over the top of his camera and we locked eyes.

'Perfect,' he said. 'I've got you all in.'

And we faced him, Jen, Mariel, Toby, Bob, Cat, Daisy and I, and smiled. And for a second, maybe even two, I forgot that someone was missing.